BAD
BOY

Books by Edmund Schiddel

Scratch the Surface

The Other Side of the Night

Break-Up

The Girl with the Golden Yo-Yo

Safari to Dishonor

Love in a Hot Climate

A BUCKS COUNTY TRILOGY
The Devil in Bucks County
Scandal's Child
The Good and Bad Weather

Good Time Coming

The Swing

Bad Boy

BAD BOY

A NOVEL BY Edmund Schiddel

Macmillan Publishing Co., Inc.   NEW YORK

Macmillan Publishing Co., Inc.
866 Third Avenue, New York, N.Y. 10022
Collier Macmillan Canada, Inc.

Library of Congress Cataloging in Publication Data
Schiddel, Edmund.
Bad boy.
I. Title.
PS3569.C485B3   813'.54   81-17220
ISBN 0-02-607090-1   AACR2

10 9 8 7 6 5 4 3 2 1

Designed by Jack Meserole

Printed in the United States of America

Bad Boy is a work of fiction. Names, characters, places, and incidents are either the product of the author's imagination or are used fictitiously. Any resemblance to actual events or locales or persons, living or dead, is entirely coincidental.

BAD
BOY

KAY. Now it's agreed that I'm to write it down as well as talk it out. Having me put it on paper is Doc's idea, he's been nagging me to do it ever since they brought me here. He says he doesn't want me to bleep anything. It's so dead around here I'd almost write backwards in a mirror to give time a nudge and make it pass. Not that there is a mirror. Maybe he figures it'll keep me from cutting up. I admit I'm a cutup, and by now it's no wonder. What it comes down to is I've got my neck on this chopping block and Doc's asking me to move it a little this way and that before the ax falls. I'll start by getting on the record the kind of agreement it is. Here goes.

Doc's my shrink. Today as usual he brought his portable tapedeck, but something new has been added, a clutch of brand-new ballpoint pens and a stack of writing pads for me. I can't understand why, since everything's been taped from the start. There's tape that runs day and night, they can't fool me about that, any more than the sleep studies and closed-circuit TV they use to keep an eye on everything I do. And there are tapes they made when I'm under the talk drugs. One day it's something orangey in a paper cup, the next it's a big needle in the arm. They call it narcosynthesis—narc plus putting me together. Spacing me out on 3M .5 mil tensilized polyester. Each reel has a leader on which they note the date. When I'm under, I talk my fucking head off. The narc brings it back like you never can after a trip on acid, the mushroom, whatever. Cues to make me remember. Doc plays these tapes back to me. Of course there's an invisible tape going around

3

in my brain, loaded with secrets even I don't know. I figure they're trying to splice everything together, get a master tape that's got me on it from when I was a single cell right up to the sound the sharp edges made as I slid them into my old lady and old man. I like sharp edges.

Me—Phil Hanway. Philip Tenys Hanway, 6 ft. 2 in., 210 lbs., (I didn't pump iron with Renzo for nothing, but that comes later) white, Caucasian, WASP. And murderer. You could say Murder One multiplied by one making two. Matricide and patricide in that order. A few odds and ends, I'm left-handed, a southpaw. I'm the age I am plus those 9 months I kicked around inside my old lady waiting to be born. And the months since I did them as a pair—like 21.

Doc's not my first shrink, I've had a lot of head men, psychoanalysts, psychiatrists, lady alienists. At the Grover-hampton jail, where I was held the week after, I had three shrinks and the fuzz and the lawyers all badgering me at once. Like dogs going at an animal in one of those wire traps where the fourth side drops after the bait treadle springs it. The animal can't get out, the dogs can't get at it. There've been two judges on me too. No. 2 overruled No. 1 and ordered this new psychiatric interpretation so the hearings can proceed. It's called a fresh review. Fresh it is not. It's like life, all repetition. Since they moved me here from the jail, with a few stops in between, Doc's mostly been it. He's not the very top, Head Man's a dad in a tweed suit who comes in now and then and looks at me like I'm an insect they're taking to pieces, pulling off a wing here, a leg there. And there are three assholes in johnnycoats who monitor me in 8-hour shifts around the clock.

I don't dig Doc, though I guess he's no worse than the others. He comes Mondays through Fridays, usually the 50-minute hour, but occasionally stays longer, depending what we're picking up from the time before. Some sessions we're like old friends rapping, others it's the animal in the trap and I start cutting up. Then Doc calls in this karate gorilla and it's rough. You want me to put you in a jacket? You want another needle? You going to cool it? Doc says, Keep him

4

quiet. They do. After my cutup I go kind of dead anyway. It's not only the narc playbacks. Something's still trying to get out, Doc's right about that, he says my cutups only bury it deeper. But he's hung up on what he calls the beginning. Even when I'm shot, out of it, he never lets up. It's like picking at a scab till pus comes out. Today after the gorilla got through with me Doc shoved the pens and pads he'd brought across the table.

"I want you to try writing it, Phil. As you remember it. Just as it comes out."

That's the trouble, talking doesn't get all of it, narc either. I can't remember all of my life, my long teenage life. I have what he tells me is anterior and retrograde amnesia. I argue. I say, "Christ, let up, I'll never remember more than I have already."

He argues back. "Oh, yes, we'll get it, Phil. Writing is different. Think of it this way, it would be like coming upon a mountain a new way."

It is like a mountain. One day it seems we're at least getting into the foothills, the next the mountain shrinks down to an anthill.

"Try it. Take your time. You used to write things down."

I did. Along with all the other stuff they've impounded since the fuzz put Lilacs, my Home Sweet Home, under seal, there are all these bits of paper I used to scrawl things on and hide. Hundreds of them. Under floorboards, between roof-trees and slates in the attic. In boxes. Things I couldn't say. The secrets any kid has. They've even got my kindergarten drawings, my old lady with a big cock, my old man with tits. They use everything. For a minute I think Doc's trying to dump me. I see myself still more alone, pushing this ball-point, not even him to talk to, stuck with the johnnycoats who are not supposed to talk to me.

Doc reads me. "We'll still go on with our interviews," he says.

"And go on taping?"

"Yes, we'll continue taping too. You can begin writing anytime."

5

"I wouldn't know where to start."

"Well, start with today. Work back."

TODAY. That today was yesterday. Doc sits in the chair, I wander around, go to the window and stare up through the bars at the brick wall opposite. My view. It helps me answer questions, associate. Bars are nothing new to me. I thought we were getting nowhere. Suddenly he stopped me. "Say that again, Phil."

I know I've scored when he uses my name. I say it again— "If Camilla and Theron hadn't met, they might be living yet." I laugh. "It rhymes. I'm a poet and don't know it. Maybe that's the beginning."

Doc's dry, he doesn't laugh. "Phil, you do have a poetic way of putting things sometimes, but that's not even the beginning of the beginning."

This beginning is there, but deep, like a bomb that's sequence-coded. If we ever trigger it, BOOM, I'm really going to go up like a mushroom. Doc tries an old one—my first memory. "The cold rim of the pottie against my baby ass when I was being toilet trained?" I try making up stuff like that for him, but he knows when I'm shitting him. I have to admit this narc bit gets rid of time, squeezes it out of me no other way does. "The bars of my playpen." Farther back. "The bars of my baby bed that let down. And way back, kicking hell out of my mother, Camilla, waiting to pop out into the world. Listening to her talk. I always was a listener." Doc bites on that.

"Now," he says, "this feeling that you knew your parents before you were born."

That again. I have to watch it, I can't guess if he's trying to make me out crazy or prove I'm sane. I can see where he's coming from. What he wants from me is what the lawyers want from him. Motive. Is there remorse? Am I capable to stand trial? Will the defense plead diminished responsibility?

I stall—"Did I really say that?"

6

Doc puts the tapedeck on fast wind, finds a segment, plays it. One of the early sessions. One reason they're dragging this out is because of something that came out on that tape. They play this one back to me over and over, to cue me in to myself, I guess. It's really crazy, nut stuff about a little growing thing inside—always inside—inside Camilla—already hating the life it's going to have, sucking its thumb, dreaming of milk. Feeling my father Theron moving around outside while I'm hanging inside, upside down, counting time until I'll get out. I always could count time. And Nana, my grandmother's voice:

"Camilla, I know it's going to be a boy. You did do what I said—two days after your time? It never fails."

I could feel a shudder, then Camilla saying, "Yes, yes, I made sure of everything you said to do, Amy."

A cough, Nana's cough. Then, "Well, if it's not a boy, you'll have it to do over."

"Amy, please!"

Like that. On and on. I can't remember it all, nobody could. And there are other voices on that tape. Doc's—"Try again on that, Phil, you'll get it."

And Head Man's in the background—"This has got to be racial memory." Anyway, voices and conversations I couldn't have made up.

If it hadn't been for that particular tape, after the court hearings I might have gone straight from Groverhampton jail to whichever prison it's going to be, instead of here. What it comes down to I guess is that they think in some way I'm ahead of them, can cue them in instead of their cueing me. I understand that, the questions are really in me, but it's like trying to find a place on a map in the dark.

If you think of it that way, you might say I was aware of the map of my life with them early on. Say the map hung on a wall and I lived near a lighthouse, the beam would light up the map for a few seconds, and then everything would go dark again. I couldn't ever see all of it at once, it would light up and go dark before I could figure out where I was. It would have to be a beam that wasn't regular, the way a lighthouse beam is, only a flash now and then. At first there were only Camilla and Theron and Nana and me, but later everybody got on. I must have hated what I saw from the beginning, and that's what led to my doing what I did, when I finally saw the whole map. I think the disaster was in all of us from the time I was a single cell, growing along with me till I was grabbed and pulled out and slapped and cut away. To put it another way, it's as though Nana and Camilla and Theron were a threesome and I had them instead of their having me.

It's a great tape for making me remember. And it's my voice, no mistaking it, imitating everybody else. I learned to do this from TV, you know, those standups who face away from the camera and comb down their hair and turn around and become characters from the late-late movies. I'm not bad, I can be Camilla, Theron, just about anybody. Camilla was a great yakker, and she must have been on one of her big white martinis when she warmed up on another segment of that tape Doc likes to play back. Her voice is like acid burning through the polyester.

"Well, at least I never had to have that big thing of his stuck up me, Tilly."

Tilly's Mme. Orlando, almost as old as Nana would have been if she'd lived. She answers, "But Camilla, I don't understand—Theron's such a beautiful man, and sex is a part of any marriage—"

"That's what you think. Beauty is as beauty does, as Theron would be the first to say. In his way. Ways."

"Ah, yes, Theron's ways."

"I had my sex with my first husband and it was wonderful, but that, as again Theron might say, was that."

"Your first went fast, didn't he?"

"Yes, a rare kidney thing. Six months. Would you believe, Tilly, during my life with him I had three terminated pregnancies?"

"You didn't want—?"

"He didn't want."

"Oh."

"Theron and I got it over with first thing, as Amy wanted—"

"But you say he didn't—?"

"Never."

"You had a doctor do it?"

"No. Amy would have known."

"Then—how?"

"Tell you sometime. If we're ever on a desert island and have nothing to talk about—"

Something seemed to happen to the tape at this point, it's blank, so Doc turns it off. "Too bad," he says, "you almost had it."

"But isn't that just hallucination?" I ask him.

"There can be truth in hallucination," he says.

As I'm finding out. There has to be, because they narc me up so often. Funny? Well, most everybody there's been in my life up to now is either on or getting on, not only Camilla, Theron, Mme. Orlando, Nana, but my quote uncles unquote Frank and Bill—Camilla called them Bill and Coo—and the Old Wise Men, my grandfather Hanway's lawyers of the firm of Homer, Stanhope, Brockhurst and Browne. . . . Because the narc does dig it all out, right down to, for instance, the hard I got my first and only day at Groverhampton's Child's Garden—just a kindergarten run by a couple of old debs who didn't get husbands. My first chick was there, a little bandbox of a girl. I put my hand between her legs and rubbed up against her until I felt good. She scratched me, so I scratched back. But if I start with deep downunder stuff like that, I'll never get the rest under way. . . . The narc playbacks, me talking to me, wears me down. As I listen to my voice getting wilder, almost howling, that's when I begin to tense. Stuff like, "Yeah, I guess I did pick them, or maybe they reached up into the chromosome tree and missed a few or for all I know got an extra. . . . Blah, blah. I go on like that, and as the narc begins to wear off I have to listen to me putting myself down. . . . "All right, I know I'm a tearoom shit. But it's all sperm, man, and you know it. . . ."

Doc likes to stop the tape on words like that, tearoom,

sperm. He's such a fucking cube, I don't think he knew what a tearoom is until I explained it's a men's room where studs go to get sucked off when for some reason or other all cunts are closed to them. Doc learns from me, and sometimes I learn from him. He calls it the tearoom material now, says we've got to get to it. I block on it, can't think why he wants it. And sperm, he's always cueing that. The sperm sample. Because he hopes it'll get me onto that last night at Lilacs.

If only it had worked out. I'd planned to do mumsy and dadsy first, then self-destruct, and I almost succeeded. But Big and Little Smokey in their squad car spotted Theron's Ferrari and cut in front of me so that I landed in this stand of pines. I was stoned, and looking back I can see I must have overestimated my ability to keep one eye on the road and the other on the fuzz in the rearview mirror. I went off the shoulder and oversteered to get back and the Ferrari did a double flip. If it hadn't, I'd have crashed the abutment at the Groverhampton marina at 100 m.p.h. the way I'd planned. As it turned out, the Ferrari took it for me, even though I was knocked cold. When the Smokeys got to me, I was hanging over the wheel, and as I came to I could taste the gas running down my face. It seemed for a second I'd go out in blowup glory, like you see when cars roll over and over on TV, but they pried me out. So I practically delivered myself to them in perfect condition, not a scratch on me. That was when I had another blank, and then I was in the Groverhampton police station with the Smokeys and a big sarge slapping me to and talking me down.

It was all kind of one big room and a few feet from me was a guy they'd half stripped so his cock was hanging out, and they were dragging him across a paper shredder to make him talk —to give you an idea of the techniques to get confessions. But they had it easy with me, I answered their questions first time around. Like:

"Okay, junkie, give. What's your story?"

"I'm not a junkie."

"You're on something. What is it?"

I couldn't remember. "Shit," I said. "Dust, maybe. Shit, it's all dust, no matter how it's cut. I think I killed my mother and father."

"You think?"

"Well, they were dead when I left them."

"When was that?"

I looked at the clock. No clock has hands for me since Nam. I have this time thing, can't remember exactly. I made a guess. "A couple of hours."

"And where've you been since?"

"Riding around, till you sons of bitches ran me down."

"Save the compliments," the sarge said, not believing, but he played along. "So why did you kill them, sonny boy?"

"Because I loved them and they didn't love me"—I had no trouble saying that.

The sarge made a face, looked up the phone number for Lilacs, dialed, and waited for twelve rings.

"Dead people don't answer phones," I told him. "And it's Thursday. No Diego, no Schaafy."

"Who're they?"

"The butler and the cook."

This made the sarge hang up. "Boys," he said to the Smokeys, "get your asses over to this Lilacs place and check it out."

They checked, and when they came back, something they whispered to the sarge hit him. "Christ!" he said. "Twenty years in this business, and I've never had one of those. Get him in there quick, before the track cools. Get a sample, I don't care what you have to do to get it, but get it."

They rushed me into this place like an examining room in a hospital and stripped me and went to work. The first part I thought was going to be like shortarm in the army, pull back your foreskin, squeeze, turn around and bend over, spread your butt, but this was different. You'll see why I call the johnnycoats assholes—this one did the squeezing and spreading.

11

He said, "Man, you been laying up against a crack or beating hell out of it."

"I don't beat it," I said, which is a lie.

"You pissed since then?" he wanted to know.

I couldn't remember when then was. His rubber finger went up my ass, and I started yelling, and he was sort of giving me a hand job and moving this glass slide over the end of my cock and taking skin and hair samples. I felt like I'd had a triple-header and out front was a valve that had opened and emptied me. Not quite, they got the last drop, and this bastard yells, "Here's the ejaculate, sarge," like he'd discovered America. Just thinking about having my ass touched kills me, I started bitching about it to Doc today all over again. And the saliva tests, drawing blood, blowing into bags, shoe impressions. By the time I got to the scraping beneath my fingernails, I was bawling like a baby.

Doc hates this. I think maybe it's a way of punishing him, and he punishes back, explains once more that when it's a suicide case, even a suicide attempt like mine, sperm tests are routine. Because for some reason they don't understand a high percentage of people who self-destruct have orgasm before they do.

Doc waited, looked at his watch, and that's how I know it's Friday. He leaves on the dot weekends.

"So, Phil," he said, "the writing's under way, and if you keep at it I think we're going to get to it."

"You mean that beginning."

"Well, don't you want to know it?"

I tell him I don't give a four-way shit, all I want is it should be over.

"Well, some little detail might end it for you. Take your time and get it all in. Because, when you get right down to it, you're the only one who can really tell it."

"But what if I get mixed up, can't put it together?"

"You're putting it together whether you know it or not."

"What do you want now?" I asked him. "Like if they'd never met there wouldn't be me?"

He checks, then corrects me. "What you said was, 'If

they'd never met they might be living yet.' Don't hold back, Phil, let 'er rip."

I seem to be getting it out. Already I'm feeling like Ishmael in that movie, Moby Dick. Moby was supposed to be a white whale, but anybody could tell he was a symbol for cock. Ishmael floats away on a coffin made by this Indian, Queequeg. I got it from the book that they made out, since there are no chicks at sea, and Ish says nobody ever had a better wife. I remember his last words too—"I only am escaped, alone, to tell thee."

FROM the time Doc left me Friday to now is one hell of a long time. I've had (I counted) 9 meals, 3 jogs outside around the yard with the johnnycoats, 3 showers, and pulled off 4 times. The jackoff life. Man, do I need an easy sweet cunt to slide into instead of fucking my fist. You can't come more than so often. I might as well write. Masturbation, musturbation, same thing. You pull at your memory, and if you think back hard enough, you come with a real charge.

Let 'er rip, Doc said, and as I walk around in this crazy figure-8 way I've developed since being put here, don't think it hasn't occurred to me that ripping it all up isn't going to be a job. So far, I've only put down a few who were in my life, and there were so many others. I guess I'll just have to feel when to tell what, because it was all in its own order, in its time. I learned early how people go away, drop out, die, leaving holes in your life. Nana, gone so long in death. Renzo, the best friend a guy ever had, we had great bits together with chicks, but if we ever touched it was part of that, none of that Greek shit. Rudi Schaaf, a year older than I was, my first playmate after I did the scratch job on the chick at Child's Garden. He went, as in a way Renzo did too, after he found the cunt to go with the refrigerator and built-in dishwasher so there'd be no embarrassment about spots on the drinking glasses and the cunt could see her fucking face in the shine on the dishes.

13

And Hesper. Hes-per. My girl who was a whisper instead of a real girl. Her eyes were cornflower blue, and her hair like silk. A silken whisper I'd say to myself. Hes-per. Though I never saw her but once after the scratching, she'd have been the one I could have loved. I'd better stop working so far back and try to come closer to now.

There was this old guy at the Groverhampton jail in the cell next to mine, and he asked if it was my first time inside.

I answered him, just to be conversational. "Does anybody get to do in his old folks more than once?"

He looked at me. "This is my twenty-third time," he said. He was a cat burglar, and I guess like cats couldn't stop doing the same thing over and over. He said, "You'll get used to being inside, Sweetass. After the way I hear you did them, you're going to be way inside. I remember you—you made all the big TV channels. Made it real big in the papers too."

"You mean, they showed the way I did them?"

He looked at me harder, like he was glad there were bars between us. "Only parts of them, parts blacked out. Pictures of the house, the name of your folks beside the gates. A picture or two of you. It got through all right how you did it. Up brown. Shit, I can tell you right now, you're going to get maximum security or the nuthatch."

"Which would you take?"

"Oh, inside, any day," he said. "You'll get used to inside, and when they get you really there and all droplocks fall into place, you'll be inside so many insides you can't count them."

"Like in solitary?" I was in solitary in Nam.

"You'll think back on Nam with pleasure, Sweetass," he said.

I figure where I am now is already like a third inside. There was one other place between, with other guys, but when the shrinks heard me talking to others, they quick moved me here. Not that I had much idea of the place in between. When they move me now, down to narc, to court, it's handcuffs and hallways with no color and a van with no windows and more places with dead daylight. This is both a jail and hospital with top security. The minute they dumped me here, I heard Doc telling the johnnycoats, No TV or radio privileges, minimal conversation. Johnnycoats are all suckers, Yeah, Doc, Okay, Doc, which means it's almost all silence. Except there's this low hum, like a fluorescent tube about to short out. Maybe silence has a sound and that's it.

This security's because of my plan to self-destruct after I did the folks. No sheets on the bed, no pillow, a mattress you couldn't take apart with a bulldozer, 1 thin blanket. When I got here I was wearing my walkaway jeans and T-shirt and shitkickers, and since the shoes had laces, they took them first. Now I pad around in gym socks and these pants about 6 sizes too big, like those they gave us in Nam, except those had string instead of snaps. The head's in a corner under the barred window, no seat. During my first week I soaked myself with head water and with my right hand in it tried to stretch my left to an electric outlet in the baseboard. The johnny-coats and the gorilla rushed in and stopped that. The one way left now would be if I put my face in the head and sucked it dry, but the johnnys would probably give mouth-to-mouth, a diversion, maybe, if they were chicks. But no guy ever had my mouth, my ass either. When I was away during one of the narcs, they closed the outlet. There's just this graveyard daylight, 24 hrs. of it. When I'd finished with the writing yesterday and was asleep, they took out the pad and pen. They needn't have worried, I'm not going to be the first to destruct with a ballpoint. Maybe that's the way writing should be, written on water, or a message in sand to be blown away.

TIME's weird, hard to keep track of. I know I've been here awhile because the prosecution is getting impatient, pushing Doc to push me. Like we've got to move this one, we need the space, there are others waiting. Apparently nothing about Phil Hanway is going to come out easy, finding out why a dude like me with all this bread that could have been his should do such a fancy job on his old lady and old man and then try doing himself too.

The big event of the day before Doc comes is when one of the johnnies takes me for my jog around the yard. I work up a sweat, then he supervises my shower and shave. Doc insists on having me clean and all set up. His first look at me includes a manicure check. He likes them short because of the cutups. I hate the shave. You'd think in a setup like this they'd have electric razors, but no, just old-fashioned blades with a strop. They hold on to me, in case I might try it that way. What I hate even more is the way they keep working on my nails. They're still sensitive from the night they took the scrapings. The johnny who usually grooms me up is named Malc. He's gay, and black as telephones used to be. If I didn't make him hold the soap he'd practically take my shower for me. I play him along a little, let him get his kicks, because he's the only one who'll talk to me on the sly. The others make me feel I'm a number on a door. Malc wants to blow me, but so far all I've let him see is a semi before I rinse off and grab the towel. He says his sister out in Queens has saved a lot of news clippings about me, and if I'm nice to him he'll sneak in a few on the q. t. Malc's got to be S/M, the way he makes the manicure last.

Today he took so long, I finally told him I'd rather chew them. I did when I was in Nam.

"Maybe you chewed your fingers, but nobody chews his feet, man. Not unless he's a contortionist. Is you a contortionist? Show me."

He wants a crotch lookup, but I hung on to my towel. Farthest up he's gotten is the knees, one day when he pretended I had a jog strain. Today he was trying it higher.

"You must have brought my clippings," I said, guessing him.

"I brought you some. But you got to show some appreciation. Come on, show me the meat hard."

I let him see it hard. Just then another johnny came in with his jogger, and we had to stop talking. But before he locked me up, he slipped me the clippings. "Read quick," he

16

said, "I'll rattle loud if you have company so you can flush them down the head."

It was quite a wad. I had to flip, trying to memorize as I read, which wasn't hard because I knew the story better than anyone. Pictures of the house, file shots angled to show "Lilacs" worked into the iron of the gates, the lawns and hedges as they always were, one big stage set. "LONG IS-LAND MANOR SITE OF BRUTAL MURDERS." Long-ago pictures of Theron and Camilla at parties. "GIN LANE COUPLE IN HAPPIER DAYS." Which was shit, Vodka Alley was more like it and what happy days? But a great shot of me with a camp catchline—"HEIR REJECTS GOLDEN SPOON." Some nutshell stuff—KILLS PARENTS TRIES SUICIDE FAILS." The meat of the story was there, repeating like media does, sometimes telling a little more, sometimes less. . . . "Wealthy couple in their 50's found mutilated in bedroom of their showplace mansion in fashionable Grov-erhampton. . . . Their son, a Vietnam war veteran, was charged with the slayings. . . . Police retrieved a heavy mallet, a chisel and a razor-edged device for scraping paint in the murders of Theron T. Hanway, Jr., 52, and his wife, Ca-milla, at the couple's sprawling, 3-story mansion, Lilacs. . . . Police said the bedroom showed evidences of violent struggle. Mrs. Hanway had been strangled, and also stabbed 21 times in the chest and torso. Her husband had been beaten on the head with the mallet and stabbed repeatedly in the neck and throat with the chisel. . . . The couple's son, Philip, was appre-hended when he sped through a traffic light near the intersec-tion of Groverhampton Turnpike and the Marina Point Highway. The car he was driving, a Ferrari, registered in his father's name, was totally demolished. A check showed that his license to drive had been suspended because of numerous traffic violations and operating a vehicle while intoxicated. . . . The elder Hanway was the owner of Les Merveilleuses Inc., a Madison Ave. decorating shop dealing in rare antiques. Mrs. Hanway, professionally known as Camilla Carstairs Connolly, was editor-in-chief of Haute, the well-known fash-ion magazine. The son had recently been released from the army after 2 yrs. service in the Vietnam war, where he was a prisoner for the last 16 months. . . ."

Malc rattled the keys then, and I put the wad into the head. What I thought as I flushed was that all that print tells as much about Phil Hanway as what happens to an astronaut knocked out of his rocket and burned into the atmosphere. How it looked to the pigs and reporters when it was over and cold, not how it really was. And not enough about me. After all, I did it.

Of course it was Doc, bringing in the lawyers and old Tweed Suit. They kept looking at me and then at each other and not saying anything. Then they went out and I could hear them yakking down the hall. I couldn't hear what they said. Weird.

ANOTHER DAY and I'm still kind of shot from the shootup. Malc was on again, and while we were jogging couldn't wait to ask me how I'd liked reading all about myself. I told him the clips were okay, but wouldn't it be great if we could see the TV coverage.

He said, "Shuh, man you already love yourself enough without that. Hey, did you really do, you know, what they say?"

I bleeped him on that. He used his shower time to remind me that his sister has other clippings, but that I've got to give back.

He said, "Why don't you let me suck it for you instead of jacking off like you do? I sees you on the monitor. You be good to me. I can give you angles how maybe to protect yourself a little when they ship you out of here."

"Like what angles?" I asked.

"Like when a dozen guys gets you in a corner and you can't do nothing about it. Man, with that ass and that whang, you really going to be for it."

I thought, Okay, but Malc can give me more than clippings. He knows stuff. If the day comes when I get into a corner with Doc and the lawyers, I'll need Malc, and he can blow me then. If I do, I'll pass on something I heard a dude say in the booth next to mine in the tearoom—"Mister, out front's all yours. My ass is private. And what's above the waist belongs to my wife."

I'm going to cross that out and quit for today. I'd tear the fucking page up, except it would bring whichever johnny's on now and he might accuse me of trying to cut my throat with the edge of the paper.

MALC's on duty today, and when he brought my breakfast he said, "Well, Sidney tell me you writing your life story."

That tells me Sidney was the night johnny who took away what I wrote.

"Sidney say you scratch out something. He say you hand-writing like a half dead fly full of ink dragging its ass."

Malc talks like that, as though he's imitating spades in those series on TV. "Yes, sah, johnnys got orders to take it after you do it, so Doc can read it before he pump you, I guess. Sidney take it to Big Man, his secretary she stamp it, date and hour, put it in your Doc's box. Don't worry, johnnys not hired to read, just watch and track tape."

"Ever play the tapes back?" I ask, to see what I'll get.

I get, "We got better things to do than rerun tapes. I hear you turn over in bed, fart, crap, grunt when you pull your pud. Eat up, now, then we do your jog and shower."

He watches me eat. So I won't swallow the spoon, I guess. He's dishy today. "Man, think what a gas if they got the tapes mixed up." He laughs. "Like that one down the hall, he do his whole family, wife, kids, even the granny. Cut them up with a chainsaw and put them in garbage pails. He easier to figure out than you. They move him out today. He got life. We needs the room. But you're gonna stay awhile."

He shuts up suddenly, goes to the grill in the door. Footsteps and a jangle of keys. I figure it's a replacement for the one who did the chainsaw job. Malc takes my tray, counts everything, hands me my toothbrush from his pocket. I brush, give it back to him. He leaves. I'm allowed to crap by myself. On tape.

I think it's Monday. If I had a watch. I'm not the type to make marks on walls. Doc was late, and I got to thinking. We've had discussions about time, what's real. Life. If it's on tape, is it life? Almost everything's on tape or a tape of a tape, or like it says on TV, live tape. Is it real because on the narc playbacks I listen to myself? If tape breaks, gets destroyed, is that present tense becoming past? Or mixed up with somebody else's tape. I guess it just rots, like everything else.

Doc was late but cheerful. I can tell he's read what I wrote. I look at him and wonder about him. Did he get laid over the weekend? Is he married? Has he got kids? Where does he live, and does he think about Philip Tenys Hanway when he's away from him? I tried asking things like that at first, but I soon learned it's no use trying to find out anything. All I get is silence. Not that I don't use silence on him too. I don't ask if he liked what I wrote. If they don't tell you around here, don't ask.

He started bitching right away that I didn't begin where he suggested, If Camilla and Theron hadn't met there wouldn't be me etc. He didn't bring his tapedeck, but the session was just as rough as though he had. Before it got rough he said, "What you've written so far is interesting because it suggests what you may write from now on. It shows a certain confusion in tenses, but that's perhaps only natural with your trouble about time."

"You told me to forget about order," I reminded him.

"Yes. Memory's like quicksilver, Phil. It will find its form. Keep at it."

I looked at him. I thought, I could have written the Bible and you wouldn't give me shit. If I'd asked if he liked what I've written he'd have asked me how I liked it. Technique. Answering questions with questions. I'm saving him work, but murderers don't have options, suicides either, especially if they fuck up.

That was when he said, "And we'll continue to hope for, ah, further access to the unconscious."

His way of saying narc. "Christ!" I said. "That stuff affects me just like a knife."

That must have been when we got onto sharp edges. Still chasing early memory. I told how Nana kept this kid book about me, you know, mouthing at 6 months, solving my first problem at 1 yr.—I pulled out a drawer and dropped it and put it back. There was a knife in the drawer, and I couldn't forget it. Because when we got to 2 1/2 yrs., I would start screaming and by then was able to form a word to get through to her about that knife. Nana's explanation about it was that it couldn't hurt me because it was put away in the drawer. Up high, maybe a table. But I was sure the knife somehow would get out, follow me, find me. When I looked again it was gone, and I felt sick and angry. I couldn't help acting out the feeling I had then, until Doc closed the watch he puts down on the table to time himself, the only timepiece I ever see. It goes ting at the end of the 50 minutes, and then he takes off. The gorilla hangs around until Doc has gone and then it's only Malc and me. Then only me.

I hope what I spilled about Malc isn't going to lose him his job. Of course, he could be just another cog in the technique, because except for jog and shower time he's on tape too. Though Doc must know Malc's trying to put the make on me, he probably couldn't care less. Shrinks are used to the damndest things, somebody's blowjob could hardly interest them when you think of the other stuff that comes through on the grapevine. Like the girl who put a live cat up her snatch and they brought her here to find out why she did it. Wouldn't any fool know that? Why drag in Daddy Freud? My reaction, when Malc passed this on to me during a jog was, "That's the first cat I ever envied, because no guy ever really gets up there into all that mystery."

I kept wondering about the girl, wondering what happened to the cat. Pulled off. Gone with the sperm. That word. The ejaculate. Zip up and fill up. Tomorrow I'll start where Doc said to, If Theron and Camilla hadn't met, they might be living yet. Hope I got it right that time.

IF it comes out with confused tenses, that's the way it'll have to be. One minute it seems like now, the next minute like then. At night sometimes I hear Nana's cough. That couldn't be tape, unless it's the secret tape in my head. Cough. Cough. Hack. I can almost smell the cigarette she would light afterward. I think now that Nana was always in there, pitching, making sure the deal worked out. She must have had plenty of doubts and worries. As for Mr. and Mrs. Theron Tenys Hanway, Jr., late of Lilacs, Groverhampton, they knocked themselves out trying to make the deal work. Ten million bucks, invested and reinvested and the greater part of the principal untouched will make anybody knock themselves out. Multiplying for all the years since my grandfather Hanway's been dead. But while I remember yesterday's knife cutup, let me get something else off my chest. No R. I. P. for Camilla and Theron from me, let them fester in their bronze coffins, wherever it is they repose. All that came through, about the big memorial service and the bronze. I can tell you, if ever there's a resurrection, it's going to be tough tit for Mr. and Mrs. Hanway to push up those coffin lids. And they're going to look like a couple of monsters. The fuzz made me go to the morgue and look. A hard job of sewing, all right. But I'd been in Nam, where when it came time to decide who'd been who, they just shoveled them into the plastic and quick the Twistems and hung on the ID. The fuzz couldn't get over it that I didn't break up.

Obviously Camilla and Theron met. They never talked much in front of me, it took years to even begin to get a design on that jigsaw puzzle. It was like that, pieces. A look here, a silence there, bits of sentences from other rooms and places. Until I was old enough to figure out that, at certain specified periods, I was to be exhibited to the Old Wise Men,

Homer, Stanhope, Brockhurst and Browne, who would examine the manufactured goods, decide what part of me they'd approve, and what part they wouldn't. Forget Brockhurst, he went off somewhere and died. But he was the one who'd drawn up that Will for my grandfather Hanway.

The visits had a pattern. Camilla and Theron would talk with Mr. Homer a while. Then Mr. Homer would say, "Just let me call in Mr. Stanhope," and they'd talk more.

Mr. Stanhope would look at me and then say, "I think we should consult with Mr. Browne, he's more familiar with the file, and of course, what we want here, I think you will agree, is seeing that Mr. Hanway Senior's wishes are carried out."

Mr. Browne almost invariably said, "Yes, yes, yes. Quite, quite."

Often I'd be parked outside in the waiting room, until whatever it was they were deciding about me was settled. There was this old secretary who'd say, "Why, it's Mr. Hanway Senior's little grandson, isn't it! My my, how you've grown! Your grandfather was a wonderful man, wonderful." When I got older and could tell one Old Wise Man from another, I'd ask questions.

"Why do we have to go there?" This would be driving back to Groverhampton. Nana would be along, usually, and Camilla and Theron would wait, to see if she'd answer. When I asked a question there was this little time lag, Camilla or Theron waiting for the other to answer, and when neither did, Nana answered.

"Because your grandfather Hanway remembered you, Tenys. And very handsomely, too."

"Amy, I wish you'd please call him Philip."

"I'll call him Tenys if I like, Camilla."

"But how could Grandpa remember me if he's dead?" I'd ask.

"In his Will, Tenys."

"Are Mr. Homer and Mr. Stanhope and Mr. Browne doctors, Nana?"

"No, dear, they're lawyers."

Once, when it was only Camilla who'd taken me for inspection, I asked her, "Mom, what is it I'm supposed to be?"

"What you're going to be, dearest."

"But I'm what I am now. What am I supposed to be that I'm not?"

She'd duck it. "Philip, we're in traffic. When you're older you'll understand."

"I want to understand now."

"Wait until we get home."

When we did, she said to Theron, "He's asking those questions again. You answer him."

Theron ducked my questions too. What they both made me feel was that when they made me an I they forgot to dot it.

Nana never made me feel this way. Maybe she's an early memory. Her hands reaching down past those bars of the playpen, one with a big diamond, not shaped like other people's diamonds, but square, and her wedding ring. With a cigarette dropping ash in her other hand but still managing to lift me up. She'd squeeze me—"Wuzza, wuzza wuzza, how's my darling grandchild, how's my little Tenys?"

Any kid remembers people saying he resembles one side of the family more than the other, but there were always arguments about this, as there had been about what my name should be. Nana had wanted Tenys, and Camilla had wanted Philip, because it had been her father's name. "After all," she said, "any child has two grandfathers." She won. Nana said I was a Tenys, was going to grow up to look exactly like Theron. "Except he has my eyes," Camilla would say.

"Stop sparring, you two," Theron would cut in. And a door would close.

Sometimes I'd hear what was said after the door closed, other times there were too many doors, too much baffle between. But from the time I can begin to remember I've always listened. And remembered—except for now and then a baffle. It was the only way I could find out anything, where I was, what was happening. I watched, too, but mostly I listened, as though I was blind, which I'm not, having 20/20. That's where this talk from long ago comes from. Talk from doors open a crack. The dumbwaiter shaft. An old hot air register in the kitchen ceiling they forgot to take out when oil heat was put in. Phone extensions. And, while I'm on this, the wind talks too. So do pipes and radiators and water running from one place to another. And dogs drinking and just plain taking a whiz.

THERE was a photo of my grandfather Hanway in a square silver frame that stood on the table behind the living room sofa. Hair parted in the middle and combed flat, tab collar, necktie knotted tight, part of a pinstripe lapel showing with a little black rosette in the buttonhole. He had eyes that looked past you. As I listened to things said about him I grew to believe the eyes. Theron Senior. A gambler. A man with confidence that the next bet would be it, that if he went on believing that he would finally win. And finally he did. Nana knew more about him than anyone. Her eyes told the story of his gambling, how hard it had been keeping up a front in the world of embassies they moved in, Hong Kong, Luxembourg, Helsinki, and Paris and London at the end. The story as I found out about it by hearing it told over and over, now just jerky flashes from the memory lighthouse.

You'd think I knew what the matter was then, but I didn't. I did know a lot of odd things, though, things that had happened on dates long before I was born, or when I was too little to remember. Nana's dates in time, and Theron's and my grandfather's. And there was Mme. Orlando for Nana to talk to, Mme. O who'd become Ummie to me because I'd found an envelope in her purse on which was written Mme., and I figured the way to pronounce that was Ummie.

Nana and Ummie would sit in the high, glassed-in room on the south side of the house that had been done over from a conservatory. It was inside, but they always wore hats, big cartwheel ones, picture hats Camilla called them. The room had pink canvas curtains that drew across the top to cut out the sun. They'd begin talking in French about otrafwa, how it all used to be, then. There was always one story that was part of other stories, and each time I heard it, something was added or taken away. The story would drift like the spokes of sun coming through the curtains. I'd be listening, and after a while they'd break into English. It was like a French film with no titles at first and then needing no titles.

Nana had a special way of talking, ways of puttings things, beginning sentences in the middle and going back to pick up parts she had forgotten. Then she'd start over with, "However, Howsomever, However that might have been." A pause for a sip of her bourbon and branch water, a cough and a lightup, and then would come the dates.

"1938. That's when it was, Tilly, 1938."

"Wee. Povra Amy!"

"Duff had just resigned over Munich."

"Wee wee. And Halifax was in Washington. Amy, poorkwa—"

I write it the way it sounded. To the kid I was then. French. Wee wee. Poorkwa. I knew what Daypesh twa was, when Theron scolded me, and I got so I could figure out Connay, Connay pah and a lot of other words, but was glad when Nana came back to English.

"You remember how it was. I was at the fate of Vairsye when I got the Paris news, so to call it. Worse was to come in London."

Nana would tell the story, sifting it, going forward and back, getting rid of it once more. It seemed to ease her.

"The scandal at the Jockey was nothing compared to what happened in London. Senior promised me once again not to gamble, but of course it started all over."

"Poor Amy! How terrible!"

"It was terrible. What hadn't gone in Paris went then. I'd said if he broke his promise I'd take Son and leave him, and I did. I had one trunk in which I'd hidden the Tenys silver and my engagement diamond. There was barely money for our Clipper fares to New York. It was the diamond that saved us, Tilly, in and out of pawn, month in and month out."

26

"Until the money came. . . ."

"The money. Because of his Embassy connections Senior had powerful friends. Rothschilds. Baruch. Cassel. And Winston counted on him for certain things. Cassel once told him if he'd forget the red and the black long enough to play the gold market he could be rich. It was my leaving him and taking Son with me that changed Senior. . . ."

"He forgot the red and the black. But that would have been—'40?"

"Before Lend-Lease. The year of the transfer of the Cape Town gold to London. I've never understood. I only knew Senior was killed in an air crash over Lisbon. His plane had been mistaken for Churchill's. . . . You know the State Department, there's the sans origine cable for the widow and no explanations. I thought, That's the way it ends, they'll send me his effects and decorations—he was premier rosette, you know—and there won't be five cents for Son and me. . . ."

"How did you survive, Amy?"

"It was root little pig or die. I got the job at Les Merveilleuses. Sixty dollars a week, sitting shop. In those days it was just possible to manage on that. And the hock shop. When the lawyers told me there was money, I imagined it must be some nest egg Senior had forgotten. . . ."

"That turned out to be quite an egg."

"Yes, and the accumulation. Ah, well. Money like that always has strings, Tilly. . . ."

When I remembered Nana telling this, what would stick in my mind was a kiddie picture of a nest with a big, golden egg in it, growing, getting bigger, and a string drawn taut stretching to nowhere. The story always ended the same way.

"Senior was a man of strong family pride, Tilly—he wanted a grandson."

"Well, he couldn't ask for a more beautiful child than Philip," Ummie would say.

"If only I could have found a nice southern girl—"

"But I thought—"

"I'm fond of Camilla, Tilly," Nana would interrupt.

"Camilla is Camilla. Believe me, I did it the only way there was to do it—and that's God's truth."

Doc sits beside me on the bed. He grips my right hand, giving me the old friendship squeeze, checking reflexes after the narc.

"What's your name?"

"Phil—?" It comes hard.

"Phil what?"

"Phil Hanway."

"All of it."

"Philip Tenys Hanway."

"Where do you live?"

"Did live—at Lilacs. Groverhampton. Long Island. You want the county too, Doc?"

"Easy, Phil. No hostility, please. How old are you?"

"I'm 21. Plus the time since I came here."

"That'll do."

He lets go my hand, by which I know I'm back, as far back as I ever am after a narc day. They take me quick, writing or no writing. It goes fast after the needle. "Count backward in quarters from 100, Phil. That's it. Keep counting. . . ." If ever I've gotten past 91 3/4 I've forgotten. Then it's a zing of planets and then nothing. It's a big bandage this time. It was a big needle.

No playback, I guess. Doc waits. "Very good, Phil. Now, I want you to go on with the writing. Go on from the part in the conservatory, that you said was like an old French film. Where your grandmother says it was God's truth."

I'VE peeled off yesterday's narc bandage. The needle left a spot like an ink stain. Maybe memory bleeds once you've plugged into it. So I'll pick up on Doc's cue.

". . . the only way, Tilly. Senior's Will was ironclad, there was no breaking it. Son was to find himself a wife and ensure that the line of Hanways would go on. If he didn't marry before my death, the trust would pass to Senior's half-sisters, Edie and Lydia, living down in the Tidewater. I went along with all of it, clause by clause, in spite of Son's ways."

Sooner or later it always came down to my father's ways.

"But you knew about young Theron, didn't you?" Ummie would ask.

"I hadn't lived in the embassy world without knowing there are men who don't care for women. Yes, I knew. And no money was going to change that. I prayed—Lord, send me a sign. He did. I knew from the moment Camilla walked into the shop that she was the one. She was doing a sort of shopper's guide for Haute, which was just one more struggling little fashion magazine then. The shop was small too in those days, before Son took over, glad for any publicity. She came back several times. I'd make tea, as I did afternoons. She was beautiful. A little bitter, too. She'd been widowed long enough to know that second husbands don't grow on trees. Drifting—you know how it is, Tilly, needing someone to talk to. So did I. Sitting shop is a lonely business. We confided in each other, as strangers sometimes will. And then, suddenly, we were friends. She was still young enough to have dreams, and she had them. Haute was her life, but she wanted everything else, too, houses, position, the right people. She hadn't had a good marriage, though she'd been pregnant several times and hadn't gone through with it. You know, Tilly, when the Good Lord puts it in your way—"

"You take it. And believe in the miracle."

"Miracles have strings too, like the kind of money Senior left. However that might be. I knew the Will by heart, there was no time to waste. You might say I did the courting—I put it to Son and Camilla cold as fish on a plate. No bones. If there was a miracle involved, it was that that was the winter I had pneumonia. It was touch and go. Just before the crisis they came to tell me they'd been married that morning. I recovered. By spring, Camilla was pregnant. Little Philip was born the following January."

29

"Aquarius, isn't he?"

"On the cusp. I worry about him. I won't always be here. . . ."

That story came back again and again in Nana's talks with Ummie, sometimes long, other times short. Printed on my memory. . . .

I hear the johnnys in the hall, banging the supper trays, so I'll knock off for today.

MALC was off last night, and Woody was the johnnycoat. He's an old guy the others call Whitey. He's the color of a corpse. If you saw him falling out of a coffin in a Jap monster movie on TV, you wouldn't have any doubts. I tried a little conversation.

"How's the weather outside?"

Shrug.

"I heard it rain."

"Yeah."

Great, like talk at the dinner table at Lilacs during the week, when Ummie and Bill and Coo weren't there. Woody drummed his fingers on my clipboard, not even bothering to make marks, then left me to my night, which includes sunset, darkness, and dawn. I used to be a late sleeper because I crashed late, but not here. After my figure-8 walk in this 16-by-12-foot box I get under the blanket and try to pretend the 24-hour daylight's not on. The night started off quiet. I was beginning to fade when the guy they put in the room where the one was who did his family with the chainsaw got noisy. He started with a crying jag and banging on his door, then screaming that he was going to kill himself.

"I'll do it for him," I heard Woody say as he walked down the hall. Woody likes it quiet. One last howl from the new guy as he gets his injection. Woody always manages to hit the bone. Then quiet.

"That ought to do it for tonight," he said, speaking to a

woman who sits at a desk near the elevators. I can just see the corner of the desk, but not the woman.

"Leave us hope so, Woody," she answered.

I figure from her dark sexy voice maybe she's black.

TODAY DOC said, "Don't worry about which day it is." I'd asked him to tell me, but he wouldn't. I don't worry, but I'd like to know. For awhile I tried to dope out weekdays by whether it was Malc on duty or Sidney or old Woody. But that didn't work because the three are always switching schedules. I got one thing settled, though. I told Doc it seemed crazy for me to write down stuff with references to him in it. He answered it wasn't crazy at all, that was the way he wanted it. Anything about anybody, including him. Any order, just get it onto the pad. One thing will lead to another.

"Now, Phil, I want to ask you about two words you scratched out."

"How could you read them if I scratched them?"

No explanation as usual. He threw them at me, one at a time. "Wife."

"I never had a wife."

"Didn't you ever think one day you'd marry? How about Hesper? You wrote it divided, like two words. Hes-per. Who was she?"

I gave him brick wall on that. "What was the other word?"

"Tearoom. We've got to get to that tearoom material, Phil."

Brick wall again, though he tried, but finally he let up on it. Too late in the hour for a cutup, I guess. Just time enough to ask about Ummie.

"Camilla always said what a good friend Ummie was, but that she'd tell everything she knew."

When he was shuffling his papers and getting ready to go, he said Nana seemed to be talking a lot.

"She never stopped," I said.

"But you loved her."

"I loved her."

A good place to leave it for today. But it left me feeling alone, out of it. There are all kinds of being out of it. Hours here when the halls are quiet and nothing's going on. A little like solitary in Nam, when I lived my whole life over every day, talking it out to myself without any Doc, figuring out who, why, when. The horse already ashes in the barn that's burned down.

There was the New York apartment I remember, on 73rd Street off the park, where we lived the first years after I was born. Where the bars were. And the knife. The lawyers had bought Les Merveilleuses for Theron, and he was out of town on decorating jobs most of the time. Camilla went to Paris and London for Haute twice a year, which left mostly Nana and me and sermpts—she pronounced it that way. There were strings of nursemaids and nannies for me, all colors of brown. Nana called them darkies.

"And when I think what we pay them up here," she'd say to Ummie. "Down in the Tidewater our darkies got five dollars a week and glad to get it. . . . You know, Tilly, my father used to say darkies can wear any size shoe, anybody's old eyeglasses, didn't matter. His father before him had an outside kitchen and made them whistle as they carried in the food, to make sure they weren't chewing. Why, do you know, last time I was South I had to stand in line for a cab? And had to share it with two of them?"

When I heard Nana talk like this, at the bridge table, when Ummie and other ladies came in afternoons, I thought it must be a joke. But nobody laughed. It was just as serious as Things have changed since your day and mine, and None of them want to live in and Trouble keeping anybody these days. . . .

Others came and went and lived out or lived in, which meant they occupied one of the row of rooms off a hallway beyond the kitchen that led to the service elevator. Butlers—Ah Chun, Taylor, Mr. Varney, and finally Diego, who stayed, and had his own apartment over the garage at Groverhampton, which was later. He got along with the brown girls and Schaafy, always called Mrs. Schaaf to her face and with respect, because in Germany, where she had lived before some war, she had been a lady. She was a widow and had children and lived out and had more time off than the others, Sundays as well as Thursdays. It was a Thursday when Diego and everybody else was off and the house was empty that I did what I did, what I had to do.

But that was all long before that Thursday. I'm getting ahead too fast. To go back—as Doc says—it was Nana who decided we should move from town to the country. It was because of something that happened one afternoon when the black girl who was nursemaid then took me to play in the park. Nana usually took me, but that day she had something else she had to do. Almost always we crossed Fifth Avenue and walked down to the zoo, then over to a playground where other kids were brought by their mothers or nurses to play in the sandboxes and climb up and down the bars. Somehow the girl got mixed up about where we were and asked somebody, and when she came back to find me, I was gone. I wandered around and followed the paths and looked at the people, but I had this scary feeling that I would never find my way out. I started to cry, I remember, and I think maybe got hysterical, but then I found Fifth Avenue again and started to cross. There was this terrible noise of brakes and I was almost hit by a taxi. Then cops asking who I was and where I lived, but I couldn't remember. "Poor little boy," people said, "where is your mother?" I must have been lost for hours because it was almost dark when the police brought me back to the apartment. An alarm had been sent out and the Old Wise Men alerted, and Mr. Browne was there and there were people from newspapers and TV. They asked if I'd been kidnapped. Mr. Browne told them all to go away, I was perfectly all right, the family wanted no publicity.

Nana was out of her mind with worry and fired the black girl on the spot, and when Camilla and Theron came home, there was a big conference about what had happened. "Just think," they said, "if he had been run over. Or killed. Then

33

what? Yes, then what?" The upshot was that Nana said the city was no place to bring up children and that it was time to look for a place in the country. A house with a garden, where there would be room to play.

I suddenly realized that I was important, an asset to be protected, and I liked the feeling that gave me. It was all of it a new kind of attention, a new world. From then on there was always a string on me, I was watched to make sure I was where I was supposed to be, and when we moved out to Groverhampton, the string went with me, you might say, along with the bars and the knife.

NANA had an inside track on the house deal. Through her embassy connections she knew a woman whose mother was in her nineties and still living in the house her husband, a tycoon they called him, had built when they were married. The house was in Groverhampton and was called an art nouveau cottage and had thirty rooms. The old lady was hard to budge, but it was finally agreed, when they got her out, that Theron and Camilla would buy and move right in and renovate afterward. They were both crazy about the house. Nana said it wasn't Southampton, but it had a lot of land and a view of the ocean.

It was a big white elephant of a place, the kind you see in late-late movies on TV where people come down to breakfast in riding clothes and choose what they will eat from a hunting board loaded with covered silver dishes.

The house had a name, Lilacs, which would never be changed because it was hammered into the iron gates leading from the road, and there were lilac hedges. There was a fish pond beyond the slope below the gate lodge and a carriage house with servants' rooms above it—the apartment Diego lived in—and greenhouses at the back. There was everything, even a mushroom cellar. It all had a wonderful smell, I knew even then it was the past. Camilla said it was something she could work with, it would be perfect for the entertaining she had to do for Haute. And Theron answered that it wouldn't be a cottage when he got through with it, he saw it as a pavilion. He touched a stained glass window showing girls with long hair floating in a stream and surrounded by waterlilies. "All this will have to go," he said, and it did. Everything was rebuilt and painted in light colors and in came the big blackamoors standing on gondolas in the front hall. Two of them. Two of almost everything. White Chinese jars, screens, chairs. Uncle Bill said Theron was queer for pairs, and Uncle Coo said why mention the pairs.

Camilla picked for herself the rooms on the second floor front, which were sunny, and went out and bought everything she needed in one afternoon. Modern things. "Something around here is going to be me," she said, "no broken-down deez-weetyem, just creature comforts." Theron's rooms were in the back, and I was down the hall. They moved me all the time, farther and farther away from them, I didn't know why. But as long as Nana was there, it was all right.

I think that before the Old Wise Men started prodding Camilla and Theron to send me to Groverhampton's Child's Garden, I was an okay kid. I guess the memory of it keeps coming back because I haven't told everything about what happened there and how it seemed to influence everything afterward. On Child's Garden afternoons the kids were all given little cardboard shapes and were supposed to put them back into different colored boards they'd been cut from. It was a breeze. I finished before the others and looked around and thought Now what? That was when I got the hard and touched the little girl sitting next to me and the scratching happened. The teacher made a big scene of it and sent me home. Nana saw the scratches on my face and phoned the teachers. The girl's mother phoned Nana and a little while later swooped up the drive in a big Rolls. She was wearing a big mink coat that dragged and a nightgown and had come in a hurry, and the little girl was with her. They were both crying, really wild. Nana went to the door, and there was a discussion about which had scratched first. The girl admitted she had.

35

"And did you scratch back, Tenys?" Nana asked me.

I said I had, and Nana made me apologize.

"But Hesper was only protecting herself," the mother said. "That monster of a boy touched her first. There. She was bleeding."

"My grandson was bleeding too, Madame," Nana answered her.

"I can see you are not a lady," the mother said. "There should be a law preventing people like you from moving into neighborhoods where they don't belong. Why, I am told the boy's father is nothing but a—"

Nana didn't let her finish, just closed the door and sent me upstairs. Camilla and Theron came in and got in on the end of it. I listened as Nana told them and they went over and over it. Nana came upstairs.

She said, "Let this be a lesson, Tenys. Little boys don't touch little girls for any reason. Don't ever forget that."

I didn't. But I could still hear Camilla and Theron talking.

"I hope you know who that was," Camilla said.

"Yes, I recognized her. So what? Just a bag in thirty thousand bucks' worth of mink."

"And from the most important family in Southampton. We're doing a piece on her next month in Haute. Think of me."

"Or you could think of the kid for a change."

"I think you should punish him."

"I'm not going to punish him. I'd probably have scratched back myself. Let's not make a production of it. He did it, he apologized. That's that."

"Well, at least he seems to like girls," Camilla said.

I couldn't tell Nana about getting the hard. It happened sometimes when she or one of the black girls bathed me. Nana would slap me and say to stop working up my privates. The black girls just giggled.

WHEN I get back from my jog and shower, the pad and ball-point are waiting. So I sit down and write, letting it out of me the way I did as a kid, when I scratched it onto any scrap of paper handy and hid it from myself, hoping to forget. Narc has made me remember a lot of those things. It burns me that I'm making it easier for Doc and the lawyers, but at least when I write, they don't narc me up so much.

I think moving from one place to another can be a big thing for a kid, it was for me. I'd never waked up to birds singing or had so much space to play in that was empty of everybody else. It was a big move for Schaafy too, she had to find a house for her family in the village and start all over. Nana helped her. She said a cook housekeeper who took re-sponsibility and did the house accounts was a lifetime trea-sure, anything for her, anything. Schaafy had her own TV in the kitchen for watching her soap operas and a room where she could lie down. Camilla bought what was called a battery of all new copper cooking things that hung from the ceiling beams. By then there was Diego. He was from the West In-dies and a character, everybody said. He called Nana "Lady Hanway" and Camilla "Mistress" and Theron "Boss Sir." Bill and Coo were "Mr. Bill and Mr. Coo," Ummie was "Com-tesse." She'd been a countess once in one of her early mar-riages. They all loved it. And for a while longer there were more of the black girls to watch over me, before the shrink ladies came. Diego got along with all of them between Nana's hirings and firings. But he got along with everybody.

The house to me was locked doors with secrets behind them I couldn't know until they were unlocked and opened and then—all except one, the library—were disappointing. Camilla and Theron were locked doors too, all keys I tried to find to make them notice me and love me seemed the wrong ones. They had kept the apartment in town and were there a lot of the time, leaving me to Nana and the others. When they came out they fought a lot, did all kinds of front num-bers, so I wouldn't know what was going on. Sudden silences and looks and "Not before the child, please." Often Camilla would march up to her part of the house and slam the door and close herself off from everybody until she went back to town, leaving Nana and Theron and me. But I was beginning to figure some things, I was learning to stretch my ears.

The Old Wise Men must have given Theron a free hand, because the renovation began and went on steadily until everything was the way they wanted it. There were two kinds of decoration, the rooms for everyday living, where you could sit and lie down, and other rooms for what Camilla called important entertaining, those crammed with the deez-weetyem, kanz, and katorz. The Tenys silver was spread all over the dining room, which had a long oval table and chairs with oval backs. Camilla liked the green baize door that led from the kitchen, she had always dreamed of a house with a green baize door, she said, but Nana had Theron hide it with a Chinese screen, because it reminded her of a house she once had in Paris. When it was finished the O. W. M. came out to look it over. Mr. Browne did the talking as usual.

"Well, Theron," he said, "I think your father would approve. It's quite an investment."

"Good French furniture is like gold," Theron answered him, "it goes up all the time."

That impressed Mr. Browne, the way the land opposite the gate impressed him. "In the end it's land that lasts," he said.

There were mirrors everywhere. Dim and flaky, not like modern ones. I used to talk into them, hoping somebody would talk back. The beginning of my belief in magic. Nobody talked back, but I pretended they did. I had a lot of good friends who lived in those mirrors. The trouble was I couldn't see them and they couldn't see me. It's hard to remember it all, how it was, all bits and pieces, like a puzzle partly put together and the rest all jumble. Or maybe it's just hard to remember people if they were mirror people, not really there.

Nana was there. For a long time. Nana reading to me, teaching me to read, eating alone with me in the big dining room with Diego serving. Bathing me, putting me to bed, kissing me goodnight. Most of my days were spent in the house, wandering around. Sometimes, like an animal, Nana or Diego or Schaafy turned me out into the garden. I couldn't see beyond the hedges. Every now and then would come a voice, "Not too far, Philip." "Come back, Tenys darling." I had the usual secret cigar box with a dried waterdog I had found in the basement, some bird feathers and arrowheads. But Nana sometimes had to be away, in town, and I had to make do with Schaafy and Diego. The O. W. M. came out from time to time and kept track of what was going on. Once I heard them discussing my preference for my own company. This should be discouraged, they said, and to remedy it they found a day school for boys, Greenwood. It was between Groverhampton and Southampton, and I was driven over on weekdays by Nana, or by Diego, if she wasn't there. It was a small school, but there was plenty of control. I found that what teachers teach isn't necessarily what you learn. What I learned was trying to make them think I'd learned what they were teaching. But I failed. I was too intent on being myself and doing what I wanted to do. I didn't last long at Greenwood. I saw the report—"The result of Philip's Kohs and Binet-Simon indicate that basically he could be an achiever, but first his tendency to dawdle must be overcome. . . ."

I learned something else around that time, that the world was inhabited by grownups. And me. They would always try to stop me from doing what I wanted to do and try to make me do what I hated. Being dumped into a pile of other boys was supposed to build character. I began to have a life private to myself and secret. I wanted to dawdle. I wanted to be me.

Doc's been and gone today and reminded me I should be writing. I didn't write yesterday, and he asked why. He seemed disappointed. "You're doing all right," he said, "I want you to go on." So I told him the truth—I forgot where I'd left off. "Not that that matters," he said, "always write

39

down anything that comes into your head, whether it follows what you've told or not." But he reminded me about the dawdling, and my wanting to be me.

Actually, my decision to be really me came later, after all the dawdling and day schools they worried about. I was still trying to please them, in my way. Sooner or later in all the talking they did about me, the scratching bit would be gone over. I remembered it too, especially the girl's name. Though I'd only heard it one time, it was still with me, like a whisper I could make myself call back anytime I liked. Hesper. Hes. Per. And though I knew about the Greenwood report, I couldn't remember what I'd done or hadn't done that got me the ax there. I recall Nana saying other boys had to be considered too, and Theron answering her that all boys did certain things, it was part of childhood.

First I was taken to be examined by a doctor who took care of Nana. He said, "You know, Amy, all childhoods are mysterious. Children are as different from each other as adults. I'd not worry, he'll shape up. Physically, he's sound as a bell." There was another doctor—he had to be a shrink—who walked me around the lawn and kept asking me what I thought about myself. I told him I didn't know, I was just me. He told Theron and Nana—I remember Camilla wasn't around, she was in Paris for Haute—it would be a good idea to bring in someone psychoanalytically oriented, to live in the house and make an evaluation of what my problem was. It was Theron who called them shrink ladies, not me, he said it one weekend when he was talking to Ummie and Uncle Bill and Uncle Coo at the bridge table.

Mademoiselle Benna was the first one, someone Nana knew from the past who'd been a governess to children who'd turned out well. Mademoiselle was old and fat and wore big Mary Janes that made her feet look like baking potatoes. She winded easily and couldn't keep up with me as I played my games all over the house. But often she read aloud to me and spoke in French, with the result that I began to be able to understand things Nana and Theron talked about and wanted to keep from Camilla. Mademoiselle didn't last long.

40

I think the next one was Miss Rucker. She was young and wore a pants suit and looked exactly like those women on TV in scrubbing commercials, where they show the lady of the house that their brand of powder cleans spots out of the sink better than anyone else's. She seemed to know all about me and would ask why I had said or done something, and would then write it all down as a report. Camilla and Theron both wanted her to stay on, even Nana thought she was getting at what was called Philip's problem, but Miss Rucker wouldn't stay. There was a big session the night she left, I was sitting on the stairs between the big white Chinese jars, my ears pointing straight up. She said the problem was beyond her scope and she thought that an alienist was the only answer. I sort of liked Miss Rucker, though she never got out any spots, and I was fascinated by the way her pants buttoned and the way she undid them when she went to the john.

I know Miss Ellwood was the last one. I think she was some kind of nurse out of a job. Anyway, the whole Lilacs scene was beyond her. She was heavy on long walks and nature and explaining to me about animals, though I knew a lot more about them than she did. Schaafy didn't like her because she asked for tea at all hours. Schaafy always said she'd rather do a seven-course dinner than go through all the tea business the way Miss Ellwood liked it, so many saucers and heating cups and whether to bring the pot to the kettle or the kettle to the pot. I heard Diego tell whoever the black girl then was that Miss Ellwood was an English dyke, and that English dykes are the worst. Anyway, for once Nana and Camilla and Theron agreed about something. Miss Ellwood had to go, and go she did, but not before she'd told them I was a lonely child, that what would be best for me would be a playmate, a boy around my own age. "Children work out so much between themselves," she said. She was right.

I asked Diego what a dyke was.

"Where you hear that word?"

I wouldn't tell him, because that would have given away my listening post in the room over the kitchen where I learned so much. But I kept after him, and rather than have

41

me use the word, he lowered his voice and told me, "Dykes is ladies that loves each other, instead of men. You don't want no truck with them." He laughed. "I see how you love ladies yourself."

It comes back as I put it down, the way he talked, how he never pulled punches with me, though I tried with him.

"How do you mean?" I asked.

"I see you peeking at that Miss Rucker, when she go where everybody sometimes have to go. Find out what you wanted to know?"

I had to admit that all I'd found out was that she buttoned her pants differently from the way I buttoned mine.

"Ladies' pants not like ours," Diego said. "Everything different front and back, you soon find out. Meanwhile, you stop shaking your joy stick so much, so when it's time to start getting it off them, you got something left. I see you in the greenhouse. I don't snitch."

"But—you mean I won't be able to do—it?" I was worried.

"With that whang you got you going to have no trouble. Your pappy—Mr. Theron—" Diego stopped, didn't finish.

I was finding out what I needed to know anyway. Watching, listening, waiting for it to happen. The hardest part was finding out what it was.

As USUAL, Doc picks on something I wrote last time to hang questions from. The first thing he wanted to know today was did I ever find out what Diego was going to say about my father and didn't. I didn't feel like talking about Theron today, I doubt I could remember that anyway. So then Doc got onto masturbation, when did I begin? I told him when I was being bathed. Had I masturbated mutually with other boys? I didn't make a practice of it, but it happened a number of times. So what? Didn't mean I was gay. He told me Malc's reports show that I masturbate now, but I wasn't going to get into that and I said Doc must have remembered what I wrote about Malc earlier. He remembered. He says I do it exhibitionistically, and that it's clear I was aware of sex very early and was a highly autoerotic child.

We had an argument about that and left it that if I'm going to tell him certain things I'll write them. It's quicker. "Now don't hold back," he said, "I want everything on that." I couldn't promise. I thought for a minute he'd decide to narc me, but he's beginning to understand he gets stuff from my writing it down that he doesn't get from needles and yakking back and forth. He's such a nut for details.

Diego had called it that—it, and I guess if I called it anything in my secret mind it was that. It. I couldn't figure all of it, only bits at a time. I knew it was connected with men and women being different and doing something with each other that made babies. It was at the bottom of everything, and I suspected there were all kinds of it, between ladies, and guys too. Everything about it was fascinating. I can't remember when I wasn't aware of myself, my cock and balls, my asshole, even my nipples tingled when I was being bathed, and Nana scolded me, and the black girls giggled. By the time the shrink ladies had gone, I was bathing and dressing myself, and I started having fun with no interference. Whenever I was alone, it could happen. I stayed away from other kids after Hesper—look what happened about her. Not that there were many kids after my day schools. When they decided to take Miss Ellwood's advice and find me a playmate, there were only two possibilities—Renzo, who was the gardener's little boy, and Rudi Schaaf, Schaafy's youngest son. Renzo turned out to be a long chapter in my life, many chapters, really, but Camilla thought Rudi Schaaf would be safer.

Rudi turned out to be just as interested in it as I was, and knew more. We speculated a lot. We both knew it had something to do with making babies but were confused as to how it was done. Rudi was sure that what his mother and father had done every morning made babies, although he himself had been the last baby, and they had gone on doing it after he was born, and no other babies came. Rudi's father was dead now, but when he was alive the minute he woke up in the morning with a hard he put it into Rudi's mother. Rudi knew because his bed was in the same room. Well, we knew that when you wake up you have a hard and have to pee, right? So at first we thought that was what Mr. Schaaf did, put it into her and peed. Rudi said his mother hadn't liked it much, he'd once heard her talking to some other woman and telling her how hard his father used her but that it was a wife's duty. After his father died, he found a box of condoms in a drawer. It was clear these had been to prevent babies. Rudi brought them along one day and we put them on and peed into them, or tried to. Peeing with a real hard isn't easy, we decided it didn't make sense, it had to be something else that came out and made the babies. We pulled off a lot, but nothing came out of us.

Then one day it just happened that we found out. One of the black girls had just quit, Diego was in Groverhampton on an errand and so wasn't keeping track of us as he was supposed to do. Schaafy who said she couldn't be everywhere at once was in the kitchen, watching her soaps. So Rudi and I were able to get away into the woods at the end of our property, where you could see an old bridge where Groverhampton Road cut off the main highway. There was a man standing under the bridge, pissing. He made a sign to us to come over and we went. He didn't put his cock back into his pants, just stood there, shaking it. His cock was getting hard and there was a funny look in his eyes as he stared at us.

He said, "Hi chickens. Let me see yours. Show me your little teapots."

We were afraid, especially Rudi. He said No, his mother would think it was wrong, wouldn't like it if she found out.

"You don't have to tell her," the man said. "Haven't you learned never to tell anything?"

He dropped his pants and started pulling on himself. "I bet you chickens can't shoot yet, can you?" he said. "I'll show you, but you have to show me yours first."

We were dying to find out anything, anything at all, so we unzipped, just standing there with our dicks out. We both had hards and started pulling along with him.

44

"This is great," the man said, watching us, and after a lot of huffing walked toward us. "Here goes," he said, and shot all over the ground and we saw that what came out was thick and white and heavy as it dropped. Right after, the man looked scared and took off in a hurry. Rudi and I went on trying but couldn't get anything to come out.

"I think it's maybe that we've got to be older," Rudi said as we cut back to the house. But at least we'd learned that the pee part of his theory was wrong.

"My folks always did it in the morning," he said to me. "When do yours do it?"

I told him I didn't know. I didn't.

"Maybe that's because they're rich," Rudi said.

"What's rich got to do with it?"

"Well, separate beds. My mother says your folks have like their own apartments, bedrooms, sitting rooms, baths, everything. She says sometimes they don't see each other for weeks. She does the sheets. She thinks they don't do it."

"But they have to do it," I argued. "They're married. Don't married people have to do it to stay married?"

"I think you're kind of dumb," Rudi said.

I guess I was. But the two of us kept working on the problem, trying to get the heavy white stuff to come out. Rudi hadn't learned from the man under the bridge, and he must have told his mother something, because one day when Camilla was in the kitchen talking about food with Schaafy I heard them through the hot-air register.

"Mrs. Hanway," she said, "I'm going to have to have more help from Diego. I can't watch Philip all the time."

"Why, I thought everything was going well," Camilla said. "Rudi and Philip get along very well, don't they?"

Schaafy hedged. "Mrs. Hanway, boys do what they do. You can rap them over the kunckles until you're blue in the face, they'll still do it."

"Oh," Camilla said. "That. We've talked all that over with the doctors, they say it's perfectly normal, not to pay any attention."

"Yes, well. . . ." Schaafy often stopped there when she wanted to say more. This time she added, "Well, men. It's a filthy dirty thing, if you ask me."

Camilla didn't ask. But she talked something over with Nana and Theron. I guess anybody could guess Rudi and I were a team intent on finding out things we weren't supposed to know. Theron suggested that Renzo might be a good substitute for Rudi, but Camilla ruled that out. She said she didn't want me playing with Italian working-class children, besides, she knew that Renzo's father drank on the job. At least Rudi was, so to speak, in the home, and with him around, Schaafy was a good influence on us both. A good Lutheran, Nana added, and they were strict and the very best.

Doc says he wants everything, so I'll wind this up by telling something I never told anyone, not even the shrinks when they were trying so hard to get at what was wrong with me. First, though, let me say I don't think anybody takes into account how lonely and boring being a kid can be. Rudi Schaaf still came to play, but bringing it back now—not so many years ago but it seems like centuries—I realize it wasn't Renzo who first turned me on. My first turnon was with Rudi. I didn't know anything, as he always said, and because he was a little older and already in grade school, he did know a lot compared to me. We weren't getting many highs, just playing around in the house, beating off in the attic. Camilla and Theron were away, I remember, Nana too, and nobody noticed we'd sampled the liquor kept on the dining room sideboard and cadged some of Nana's cigarettes. So when Rudi told me about nutmeg it seemed a big thing. Schaafy, being the great cook she was, had lots of spices. We took some nutmegs out of a jar and went out to the greenhouse and grated them. When there was enough, we washed it down and waited. Nothing happened. Then we were sick and threw up. But suddenly it was wild. Rudi looked big as a house to me, I even looked big to myself, and we got these great hards, and they wouldn't go away, though we pulled off over and over. This must have gone on a long time, because when Schaafy and Diego found us it was dark. There we

46

were, floating, in a cold sweat and couldn't swallow right or talk and with our cocks showing through our pants. Schaafy thought we had taken poison and called the Groverhampton Rescue Squad, who asked right away if we'd been making model airplanes. Meaning had we been sniffing glue. I don't know about Rudi, because that was the last time he came to play, but I never did nutmeg again, and when I did glue it was nothing like it. I found out tripping makes or breaks friendships, and nutmeg is one hell of a bad trip.

I was beginning to make my own life, I had to, or I wouldn't have had any, except other people's. I've often wondered what life then would have been like if I'd been allowed to play with Renzo instead. Renzo, who came so much later and lasted and became a friend.

COUNT on Doc to start off with Renzo. I told him all I knew at that time. Renzo's father cared for the grounds. On days when grass was cut, Renzo would ride up on the seat of the mower. I was not allowed fun like that. I remember feeling how great it would be if Theron and I could do something together. Renzo's father drank on the job or sometimes didn't show up, and once Camilla sent Diego into Grover-hampton to find out why. Diego took me along. Renzo and his family lived in an old trailer by the railroad station, and his old man was inside drunk. While Diego was talking with Renzo's mother was when we first said anything to each other. I liked him better than Rudi Schaaf, but as things turned out, there had to be a new gardener, one who didn't drink, and for years that was all I saw of Renzo. But I never forgot him. Maybe it was like a crush kids of that age get on each other. When we met again, years later, we synched right away. But I'm getting ahead of myself, of those days when I was working to find out what it was and turning on to Camilla and Theron and trying to make them turn on to me. I soon found they weren't going to touch me, they'd let me stand and yell until one of the black nurses or Nana picked me up.

47

They were getting whatever love from me that Nana didn't get, getting my rage too. Loving was a one-way street.

I know it sounds crazy, but deep down I always had the feeling they were strangers to each other, the way I seemed to be a stranger to them. I was dying to know if they did all that stuff that went with love. Not everything I found out came through the old hot-air register. Another listening place was the serving pantry. It was L-shaped, so I could keep out of the way or hightail it through the green baize door if I had to. One day Schaafy had shooed me out of the kitchen. She was talking to Idene, one of the black girls hired to help Diego clean.

"This is one weird scene," Idene said. "What's with Mistress and the Boss?"

Idene was Diego's responsibility. I could tell Schaafy didn't like her. "What do you mean, what's with?"

"Well," Idene answered, "I know there's dirt between them."

"Stop right there," Schaafy said. "Mrs. Hanway is a fine woman, in business, very big in the fashion world. And Mr. Hanway is one of the most famous decorators in New York. Why, there are pictures and things about them in the papers all the time."

"Fashion shit, decorator shit. Something's funny."

"Funny how?"

"That pretty man ain't decorated her in a long time."

"That's none of your business," Schaafy said, trying to be patient. "All couples have their problems."

"I get it every night after I go home," Idene said. "Some mornings too."

"You stop this kind of talk. I'm going to report you—"

"Don't try to shush me. I hate places like this. And another thing, pretty man's old mama calls me a darky. I'm hauling ass out and you can shove it up yours."

Idene left before Camilla came home. When Schaafy told her she said, "Well, another one gone. If they'd stay in domestic service this country wouldn't have the unemployment it does."

"She said to mail her a check."

"I'll mail her check," Camilla said. "I just might sign it Franklin D. Roosevelt. He's the one started it, Mrs. Schaaf."

"Oh, I thought it was your president. Lincoln." Schaafy's knowledge of American history was poor. "Better that she should go then."

So Theron was a pretty man. He didn't decorate Camilla. I went on being detective, but I couldn't find why she didn't get it. Diego hired and fired the black girls, or they simply left. There was one named Rose who lived in and had her room near his apartment. They would talk up a storm as they went through the house, cleaning. He would explain how she must dust under surfaces as well as those that showed. Another day, listening, I learned a little more.

"Sometimes when I run my rag along all this gold shit I wish I had a bomb to blow it all up," Rose said.

"You just go back and run your rag again," Diego said. "Boss like to be able to eat off it and Mistress wears white gloves."

"I bet. Mr. Theron's a sex piece, all right. Is he her fancy man or what?"

"Hush your ass, girl. We don't talk about them, nor Lady Hanway either."

"I got a big brain," Rose said. "I see things."

"Well, don't stretch it. Just run that rag."

"But what about the kid? He adopted or something?"

"He's like Boss, spitting image, you hear that."

"Yes, and I hear he's got his mother's eyes too."

Diego slapped her. "Listen, nigger," he said, "just because I'm jumping your bones don't mean you should think."

But I started thinking, stretching my brain. What they talked about was sex, it had one more letter than it. Pretty man, fancy man, sex piece. The vocabulary kept growing. Cock, ass, asshole, tits, cunt. Cunt was hardest to find out about, impossible to really see. Even then I was nuts about it, getting it downwind, reading in a book about the odors of love. One shrink, the alienist, heard me out on this, and his conclusion seemed to be that kids who have no brothers or

49

sisters can be freaky. Maybe I was. One minute fooling with myself, the next being taken downstairs by Nana to be viewed and handed around by adults. "Isn't he beautiful? The spitting image. But Camilla's eyes. A perfectly darling child." Then I'd be taken back upstairs where I started from. If they'd known how darling I was they'd have fainted dead away.

Doc says what I wrote yesterday is probably a screen memory for something else. He explained that's like something erased that's beneath something written after. But I didn't erase, or write on top of anything. Too deep for me. To me a screen is put up to hide things. When I get further on, I'll remember this and kick over the screen and what will be there will shrink his balls.

I was an upstairs child, and I always associate being above them all and watching and listening with Nana's being with me, my being with her. After the shrink ladies went, she moved out from the city to stay. Her trunks were moved into the attic. Ummie spent a part of most weeks to keep her company. Theron fixed up rooms for her that were next to his own. It was nice being a kid when only Nana and Ummie and Schaafy and Diego and the black girls were there. It was when Camilla spent weekends—she usually stayed at the apartment—that it would be different. And when Theron finished an out-of-town job and was there too, it was even more different because they fought all the time. Uncle Bill and Uncle Coo, if they were there, helped a little, but not much. I was still giving them cues to love me, but it never did work. Picture a kiddie whore doing whatever it is old pervs want them to do, and you have me at this time.

Don't think I was being let off anything. I had a tutor, kind of a nice, slow guy named Benjamin, though he let me call him Benjy. He drilled me every day and saw to my exercise but didn't live in. It seems to me now that I was born knowing how to read, though it was Nana who first read to me and had me read back to her. Stuart Little, who was a mouse, Charlotte's Web, about a spider. I could never really buy Stuart or Charlotte, and I had my own mice, white ones, in the greenhouse, as well as a secret spider that was as big as my hand and lived above the furnace. I would snap my fingers when I moved near him and he would move a little, then move back. I was a pushover, always more interested in the alphabet letters on blocks than the blocks themselves. Anything I built always fell over. But I'd read anything, labels, road signs, any letters or papers I found in drawers. Every month I was taken in to be looked over by the Old Wise Men. And I got it—it was a waiting period for me, until I would be sent to my first boarding school. I waited.

There would be times when everything seemed to be going all right, or they all pretended that it was. By then there had been the big housewarming, after most of the house was done over, and all the people from Haute came and there were extra people to help and photographers and stories about it in the papers. Mrs. Theron Hanway this and Mr. and Mrs. Theron Hanway that, as Ummie said. And there were house parties and other parties to go with the houseguests and then smaller parties after the house guests had gone home. I would have loved to be in the middle of everything, but the shrink ladies and the alienist and the doctors had sort of dug a trench between me and everyone except Nana. I'd get a line here and there, as I watched and listened.

"I hear he's a difficult child."

"I heard a genius."

"No, no, just difficult."

Laughs.

"Wouldn't you be a difficult child if you had them for parents?"

"He looks old enough to be in school."

"Boarding school, Camilla says. . . ."

———

BEFORE I tell about my boarding schools, I must tell about the old man's library. Of course, Nana wasn't there all the time, and Benjy only came mornings, so I had time to burn. Nana would go into town with Ummie, just for the day, or sometimes they would take trips together, and it was a long time between seeing them go and waiting for them to come back. Once they went a long way somewhere, to a place called Mayo's, because Nana was having so many colds and bronchitis.

At that time there were still parts of the house the way the original old lady had left it. Sometimes I felt I was being done over like the house, doing the work myself. Working on it that had become the 3-letter word sex and the 4- and 5-letter ones too. The ones that never went completely away and that nobody would talk about except when I was overhearing them and then if I asked questions they would clam up.

You could see when the beams were opened up for rebuilding that the house had first really been a Long Island farmhouse and had then become the big cottage when the old lady and old man added onto it. There was this room on the first floor that had been the old man's library, and until Theron made an atrium of it the doors to it usually were kept locked. The old lady had kept the place just as it had been in her husband's lifetime, which was one hell of a long time ago. There were shelves covering the walls and a ladder for climbing up to reach books that were high up. Filing cabinets covered with dust. A long table where the old man had laid out his books to look at them, with an ancient phonograph at one end. Albums of old-timey, thick records that only played on one side. The place had a smell that didn't go away—I guessed it was what Nana and Ummie called otrafwa and talked about. When. The past. Schaafy or Diego would give me the keys and let me play there in the times between the lady shrinks and tutors, like Benjy, who came and went. Schaafy worried about the dust and my not being warm enough, but as long as I wore a sweater she let me play in the library and stay as long as I liked.

I had never seen books like the ones stacked in the lower shelves and on the long table. Big and heavy and bound in leather with pages the color of milk and brown stains at the edges. Some of the books were two feet wide and a yard long and hard to lift, but when I got them onto the table, turning the pages was easy. It was magic, there was always something new ahead. I had no idea what the things in the room meant, except I knew that since the time it had belonged to the old man the world had done a couple of double flips.

My favorite big book was one with anatomical plates by someone called Leonardo. There were scary ones, because he mostly drew parts of bodies, skulls with tops sliced off, hearts with blood spurting out, muscles and tendons and bones with no skin covering them. Babies inside before being born, heads bent forward, hands holding their knees, feet crossed, and a cord running into them from the mother's body. Guys in all positions. There were pages of cocks and balls. I felt myself as I looked, checking to make sure I had everything. Then I'd always come to one page that had smudges of fingerprints because it had been looked at more than others. It showed a guy and a chick naked and pressed close together, they were sliced down the middle to show the spinal cords and all the jive of veins and organs, half of him, half of her. The guy's cock was pushed up inside her and his hair was flying backward and he had an expression on his face showing he was really digging her. The chick was just sketched in, legs, butt and one tit hanging. It was such a great turnon I could forget about the veins and spinal cords and really get off on it. But there was another drawing even more exciting, a woman's legs spread wide and old Leonardo looking right up into her, showing the cunt, even the asshole. Though there were words written at the edge of the page, vulva, labium majus, minus, the kind of words you memorize right away, I had a sneaking suspicion that something wasn't right, all there. Even a kid could see that Leonardo dug guys more than chicks, and later I found out I was not wrong. But something else written in the margin clung to me—Tears come from the heart and not from the brain. I've always remembered that. I had great times with Leonardo.

But he wasn't all, though usually he came first, and after I'd made sure the door was locked and given myself a hand job, I'd dust off some of the old records and play them on the phonograph. They were scratchy and full of noise, but often I understood what was on them. One was called Love in May, a thin, screechy voice singing with a tinkling piano—"The green is on the gorse again, The wind is on the sea, The meadowlark is singing, is singing in ecstasy. . . ." I knew about sea and wind, meadowlarks, and looked up gorse in the old man's dictionary. But ecstasy—it seemed to be a word that was the sum total of the ones sung before it, I trembled with happiness when I heard it. I played other oldies, too, there were joke records, Uncle Josh, Collins and Somebody. One I'll never forget, The Rooster and the Hen. It had a nick and didn't play through, a real nut number, and when the needle came to the nick it jumped and repeated, "Down there by that air quittax. . . ." I knew from the song this couldn't be right, but there it was. That air quittax. Quittax. Crazy. A word that wasn't really there, but that I couldn't get out of my head. Later in life, when I was having a brush with TM, I had to have a mantra to meditate on, a secret word only I knew, and it was Quittax. Now I've written it down, maybe the gurus will be after me.

It's easy to remember that big, cold library, climbing up the ladder and taking down books, crouching by the phonograph, listening. I let myself get high reading everything I could, sneaking books past Schaafy and Diego to my own room, turning dusty pages at night with a flashlight under the covers.

There must have been a beginning of a kind there, locked in with the old man's secrets, wondering if someone would come along to tell me what it was all about, touch me and say, It goes like this, you begin here. Nobody did, though I began something. Some days I'd feel a tightening all over, as though someone else's clothes tugged at me and all those voices breathed, Live, Philip! Live!

54

WELL, Malc or Sidney or one of the other white coat monsters forgot to pick up what I wrote yesterday, and when I came in from my jog, there it still was. I looked through it before Malc came to whisk it out, and it taught me don't go back, only start over every day, let Doc connect it. Live, Philip! I did very little living for a while, because there was always some school or other they'd found to send me to and get rid of me.

Schools. My schools. I want to get through with them, the way they got through with me, one by one. Child's Garden. The day schools—Greenwood, the Tucker School, and a number of others there's no point in mentioning, and I'm just plain going to skip. Then the boarding places, beginning with Merry Hill and—again skipping a few—ending with St. Andrew's. St. Andrew's, which I hated most of all and was pretty much the end of their trying to mold me into what old Gramps had had in mind. They happened to me, I guess, or maybe I happened to them. What's the difference?

First, Merry Hill. There was one of the big conferences with the O. W. M. in their offices, an important one because they were all there. As usual Mr. Browne did most of the talking, though Mr. Stanhope butted in occasionally along with the other two. I sat outside in the waiting room with the old secretary and listened as usual. "Oh, it's a crucial point," they said. "This one simply has to be right." Mr. Homer thought entirely too much had been made of the scratching bit. Scratches healed, he said, and it was behind us, in any case. "Well," Mr. Stanhope said, "if we limit him to a male environment, there won't be any little girls. Boys his age need other boys, to build a firm framework for masculinity."

"I was drawn to little girls at Philip's age myself," Mr. Browne confessed. "Only natural. But we'd all like to recommend for him a most excellent transition. Merry Hill. I was a Hill boy myself before I moved on to St. Paul's. Now, Merry Hill is run on strict Christian principles. Just what his grandfather would have wanted. No spoiling of the boys. And, very important, Anglo-Saxon in tone. You won't find any boys there from wrong families. . . ."

Nana was present at that meeting, but I don't remember that she said anything. I figure now that at that point in time as they say, Nana carried the package my grandfather had stuck her with, Camilla had bought it, Theron was trying to please his old man after death the way I was trying to please him in life. Though I wasn't entirely sure what the package had in it. Anyway, a package.

There was nothing merry about Merry Hill. It wasn't even on a hill. It looked like an institution. Everything was as bare inside as outside. Boys were crowded together eight to a room. There was a footlocker at the end of each bed and a chair beside it to hang your towel on. The housemother worked with a flashlight after lights out. She worried about our bowels, it was called emptying your garbage. "Have you emptied your garbage today? No? Well, go in and sit until you do." The food was predictable, especially the shit on a shingle, which is what we all called the creamed dried beef on Thursdays, and we had little mince pies Sundays. Grades were everything, and you could cut the discipline with a knife. I didn't seem to be a grade type. Every month what was called the ranking list was put up on the bulletin board outside the dining hall. I wondered how it was done. Latin 58.3. Punctuality 74.9. I was the silt at the bottom of the lake because I was the first boy in Merry Hill history to get 0.00 in physics. I guess I helped that one along a little, since I'm hostile to heavy water and chem charts, not to mention atom bombs and napalm and agent orange. The teachers complained that I didn't pay attention and spent my time looking out of the windows, which I probably did. I was soon pitched out of Merry Hill—"We simply cannot keep him in the school as long as his behavior is as it is. . . ."

What behavior, I wondered. Camilla and the O. W. M. quick got me to a psychologist, a new one, for what was called an assessment. That was no answer. My tests showed me to be above average, IQ 140. Spatial dexterities excellent. But inclines to focus on design in the abstract, rather than structure. I liked that one. But they weren't getting any light on me. The report said there was a bloc—it was spelled that way—but whatever this bloc was remained to be determined. For a while old Benjy came back to tutor. The next year there was another kind of Merry Hill. Call it Grim Valley. Anyway, I'm going to draw the veil over it, as it did over me. The O. W. M. were getting plenty worried. And then came St. Andrew's.

NOBODY could ever forget St. Andrew's. It was old, expensive, hung with tradition, and hard to get into. A production. I'd never have been accepted if the headmaster hadn't been a connection of Mr. Stanhope's. Diego put on his chauffeur's uniform and drove us to Connecticut, where St. Andrew's was. Camilla was in one of her great suits. The headmaster seemed more interested in her than in me.

"My wife says she couldn't live without your magazine," he said. "Even I read Haute sometimes. How shall I address you, as Miss Connolly or as Mrs. Hanway?"

Camilla was being the mother part. "Mrs. Hanway," she answered.

"Mrs. Hanway it shall be."

As usual, I was discussed in the third person. "I see he has had a bit of trouble adjusting. . . . Tutors. Ah, yes. . . . Well, Mrs. Hanway, no problems, we have a staff psychologist here, of course, should any little problems arise. I'm pleased to note that his reading skills are so highly developed. To the good, certainly. Well, we'll see to it that his interests are channeled. . . ."

St. Andrew's was very English. Forms. Matrons. Masters instead of teachers. Washbasins and pitchers. A low-grade fag system. Everything was status. Other boys had fathers who were trustees of Yale, Princeton, Harvard, where they would go after St. Andrew's. Their families had camps in Maine. Their mothers were skiing in the Arlberg or in Reno getting divorces. I heard a lot about the Costa Brava and the south of France. It got through to me right away that Theron was only a decorator and Camilla just a lady editor. Not owners of corporations. Though there was all this bread to come, we were, by comparison, poor as snakes.

St. Andrew's really was WASP, and status was usually settled in the showers. Some of the boys had rags. There was horseplay and towel snapping, and this one guy named Sheehan who went around yanking foreskins. He wasn't big or macho, but he was lousy rich—like his old man had the New York Times delivered to him by special messenger at midnight. He staked out his territories the first week, and everybody had a place on his totem pole. I was somewhere in the middle. Though he made it clear I was nobody, I was big, he never yanked me. But one poor guy, Leake, who was puny and didn't have any balls, was low man. Sheehan went for him and forced him to wear a stone with a string tied to it, hung from his foreskin, to bring his balls down. If Leake didn't wear it, everybody yanked him. Leake made it even harder for himself by explaining that he had balls like everybody, but due to a condition, orchid-something, they hadn't come down yet. He was going to have an operation next year, to bring them down. Leake was miserable.

The masters and matrons never knew any of this. Everything was very smooth and settled. It was assumed that all of us, Hanway, P. T. included, was going to go on, as my grandfather's Will stipulated, to become Ivy League, with those powerful connections, skimming the cream off what life offered. I knew from the start I wasn't going to make it. So did everyone else.

It was all so fucking fake. The only way I could stand it was to go on writing down the things I felt and thought and stashing them where I hoped they wouldn't be found, in my footlocker, usually. But the matron went through everything, made notations about the state of the sheets, what was kept where, all that. One day she found something I'd written. She must have read it, because she began staring at me in a funny way and hurrying away whenever we happened to meet in the corridors. She had given my miserable me-to-me to the headmaster. I was called up on the rug and given a hard deal. "Are you aware, Hanway, that your acceptance by St. Andrew's was somewhat conditional?" I hadn't known that. "One would think," he said, and he had what I'd written on his desk and was going through it as we talked—"one would think you'd put the energy you spend on this drivel into your classwork. Hanway, did you know that your possible suspension was a subject at the last quarterly board meeting?" How could I? He didn't let up.

"This story about boys in showers. Where did you get that?"

I didn't say anything to that or anything else he asked me.

Finally he said, "I think I'd like you to have a talk with our Dr. Foulkes."

Dr. F. was the school shrink, just an old M.D. who'd read a book on psychology. I was way ahead of him.

"Hanway, how do you feel about yourself?"

"I don't know what you mean," I answered.

"This—this stuff you've written borders on pornography. Is it because you're not happy here, Hanway? Is it because many of the boys don't like you?"

"But I think they do like me," I said.

"Not nearly as much as you like yourself. Do you propose to occupy space and a bed and go to classes and do nothing? St. Andrew's has a long waiting list, you know, Hanway."

I was given what was called one last chance.

They kept what I had written, and I wanted it back so it could still be mine, but every time I asked for it I got the ice-cube treatment. I was getting it from all sides anyway. But it was poor Leake and what happened to him, or what Sheehan made happen, that decided me. Leake had the bed next to mine. He cried a lot in his sleep. In addition to the stone he had to wear, he had really crazy anxieties. He worried about what was circling above us in space. He knew a lot about what was up there and would get out of bed at night and hide in the basement because he'd figured it was time for something to fall. They found him there one morning, hanging from a heating pipe. A terrible stillness went through the school and classes were suspended. There was a memorial service for him in the chapel. I sat next to Sheehan. When it was over I simply walked off the school grounds and kept going. I had only a couple of dollars, I never had enough spending money, and I'll get to that, but I made it back to Groverhampton okay. Camilla and Theron were away, but Schaafy phoned to Nana in town and she came out and stayed with me. The Set Masters Report on me when it came was murder. I practically learned it by heart. I was 14th in the 2nd Set of 15 boys. Mathematics very elementary. "French— has some colloquial efficiency but will not learn verbs. Scripture—shows no interest. Writing: formless but very rapid. Spelling: Fair. General Conduct: Tends to fantasize. Does not adapt to School ways. See attached note."

It took me a long time to set eyes on the note. I was described as, "stubborn and intractable, resistive to all efforts. . . . Not the type for St. Andrew's. It is with regret. . . ."

I didn't have any regrets. All I could think of was Leake. If I looked forward to anything, it was getting back to the old man's library. And Nana. And me.

ALL I get from Doc for all the trouble I went to about my schools is another complaint that there's a screen memory. Not about Leake, I told him all of that. No, something else.

"How long did it take you to hitch from Connecticut to Groverhampton?" he wanted to know.

"Not long. A day, a day and a half."

"But overnight?"

"Yes."

"Where did you sleep, if you had so little money?"

"On a cement ledge under a bridge."

"Nothing else to tell me?"

"No."

"Well, screen memories do surface," Doc said, and he

made a tick on his chart. He left me early, I think that one down the hall who needs so many injections to keep him quiet is beginning to interest him more than I do.

I had a couple of dreams last night, maybe leftovers from old narcups or yakking with Doc. I was with Theron, the way I never was with him, and we were standing looking out over the ocean. There were seagulls flying all around us, and I felt him touch me, and I threw my arms around him and kissed him like a lover. Next to me and warm and someone I could talk to. I can still feel the rush of love, a little like the raging happiness that comes with a wet dream when you wake up. I woke up, but it wasn't a wet dream, I wasn't even hard, and I was crying real tears. I was remembering how he never touched me unless he had to, only maybe sometimes when I was helping him in his garden, like handing me the spade or brushing past. Then I went back to sleep and had another dream. Standing by the window of the old man's library and looking through the shutters. Camilla was below in the drive on a black horse. Its coat was made of mirrors. I felt safe because I was behind the shutters. Then suddenly the horse reared and she galloped toward the house and crashed through the shutters. I blacked out, the dream ended —I mean I knew I was dead as the horse trampled me down and that it was a dream and not real.

An easy day with the ballpoint. I deserved it.

In those school years I think Lilacs was my trap. I'd hardly be registered before I'd begin to think of escape, begin to scratch in any way I could to be let out. Sometimes I made it through Christmas or a little after, but never long after. By spring I was back and in the old man's library. After St. Andrew's, Nana was having weekly treatments in town because her sinuses and chest were giving her trouble. Days she left me, I'd shut myself into my favorite place and read and look at the books and play the old records. An excitement came over me as soon as I closed the library doors after me, as though a

secret mechanicsm in me was beginning to work. It had always been there, this mechanism, waiting to be triggered. It
was magic, it had to be, and finding it involved ways of doing
things that had nothing to do with the heavy cause and effect
the shrinks and tutors and all my schools tried to drill into
me. By lowering a steel needle onto an old record I could
listen to a piece of past time, hear a song over and over, and
the song was all for me, and when it had finished, I could
make it happen again. Scratchy time and all. I understood
that magic bypassed logic, but didn't know how. I thought
maybe it had something to do with what you did accidentally
and would be there and waiting to work for you if you could
find the right accident. Maybe touch a certain color over and
over. Or do one thing before or after another. Until there
would suddenly be magic. I did all kinds of crazy things,
trying to find out where magic was hidden. Jumping up two
steps and going back one and then jumping the next two.
The alienist got this out of me and said it was a way of
making time I didn't like go by quicker, and it showed I was
trying to find ways to make people like or love me. Well,
maybe. I played Love in May when it was May, and the
Rooster and the Hen while I looked at books about roosters
and hens—the Quittax record—but I couldn't make magic
appear. If that turns out to be what Doc calls screen memory,
okay. But that's the way it was.

AND there was so much of it, and so much of it is a blur. Nana
came and went. So did Ummie and Uncle Bill and Uncle
Coo. The family, Theron called them. There were the weekends Camilla gave for people on Haute, or someone she was
doing a big fashion piece about for the mag. The family were
always there, helping out, making things go. I had my own
funny life, writing down what I was thinking and hiding it,
making it with the house shrink of the moment, I think it
was Miss Kauffman, a girl who was doing her thesis at Co-
lumbia on dawdling in adolescent children. I was beginning

62

to keep my secret self to myself. I hated old Kauffman, she was ugly and was always pulling down her clothes to make them seem to fit. I had a kind of maze I'd follow every day— from my room to Theron's and Camilla's, seeing what I could find out, wandering through the downstairs rooms touching all things alike in color, changing the colors every week, until there weren't any more, then starting over—the old man's library, the greenhouses, the garage, sitting in Theron's cars and imagining I was driving—the mushroom cellar that had once had fat old toads living in it that Diego poisoned.

And there was Sebek. He was an alligator. There's hardly a day I don't think of him. He belonged to a period of my life when I needed to love. Anything. Anybody. Diego. The black girls.

It was during a bad winter. Nana had had one of her bronchitises, and her doctors sent her to Florida for the cold months. Sebek was a present from her. A funny little remembrance that would make the trip through the mail, maybe be a conversation piece for a few days and then conk out. "He'll die," everybody said. "Who ever heard of an alligator making it in this climate?" Well, if he died on me, I thought, I'd dry him the way Camilla and Theron dried out friendships and kept them, as souvenirs. But Sebek was wiggly and lively, fresh out of the egg. I was fascinated by him and Theron said I could keep him, even took me to a pet shop to buy a glass box for him. I always thought old Kauffman told him to do this, so he'd seem a good father and interested. The box had a landscape in it, sand, a pool, a fake palm tree, an electric bulb to keep Sebek warm.

I'd named him Sebek because he arrived the week I had found a book on Egypt in the old man's library, and it showed a god with an alligator's head. Sebek was well behaved, didn't move much, looked up at me with wonderful eyes like jewels. He grew, fast at first, then slower. I kept him in the window of my room. But Camilla couldn't stand him and every day said he had to go and finally made me move him out to the greenhouse. Sebek hated it there—and now I think this has got to be part of something that went haywire. That spring Camilla went to Paris for the mag and Theron was doing a house in Virginia. That left only Schaafy to fix my meals and Diego taking plenty of time off and one of his new black girls. And old Kauffman.

I was lonely. I saw no reason not to bring Sebek back into the house. It made him a lot happier, and he moved around more. He would raise himself up and put his little feet against the glass and look around. He had a funny wavy mouth. He smiled. You could see little teeth beginning. I think he wanted to get out, and I guess he did, because one day when I was down in the library I heard screaming upstairs. It was Miss Kauffman.

Diego was yelling at her. "Don't! Let him alone, he don't hurt nobody. Don't touch him. Wait, I put him back. . . ."

Miss Kauffman hadn't waited. By the time I got upstairs the toilet was flushing, and she was poking Sebek down with a brush. That was when I really let loose and went for her. I kicked her as far up her legs as I could and pulled at her tits, and it took Diego and his new black girl to get me off her. Old Kauffman was shaking and crying. I thought maybe she'd clear out, but she didn't. She stayed until Camilla and Theron came back, and there was a big hassle about me, as usual.

"I could sue you for this," Kauffman told them. "That child is a monster. I've only stayed on because it was my duty to warn you that something must be done. You see, in the light of the trouble he had at Child's Garden, this hostility must be evaluated. . . ."

Lots of that stuff. Then Camilla begged Kauffman to stay. "We think you've worked wonders already."

"No, no," Kauffman said, "not possible. You must get him into the hands of a medical analyst at once. Now, the Berger Clinic . . ."

Theron blew up. "Clinic? Philip's not crazy."

"Disturbed," old Kauffman answered him. And took off.

I had a hard time about Sebek. I cried about him almost all the time. Theron said that sooner or later Sebek would have died in captivity anyway, and to forget about him. Theron was a great believer in forgetting.

Not me. When I'd see an alligator on TV I'd think of Sebek and wonder if maybe he was underground in a Groverhampton sewer, still alive, growing, hungry. Diego said maybe he'd been flushed all the way to New York. He said hundreds of alligators lived in sewers there, just waiting to get out and eat people. I hoped he might get out and gobble up old Kauffman. I felt sometimes a little like an alligator myself, lying low and quiet, waiting for the split second when I'd raise up and snap. In the end I did just that.

Doc's always stopping me on some word and saying, "Shall we associate on that?" It works. For instance, take screen— anytime that word crosses my mind I remember the night when the Chinese screen between the kitchen and the dining room toppled because Nana stumbled and fell against it.

It was a loud crash, I heard it even through the thick doors of the library, where I was waiting for her to come home. I ran out and found Schaafy standing terrified in the kitchen doorway. Nana had stopped to get a drink to take up to her room and had somehow tripped and fallen headlong. Blood was coming from her mouth. She looked like a thin, old bird who had mistaken a pane of glass for sky. She was out cold. It was Diego who knew what to do, first phoning the Groverhampon Ambulance, then crushing ice and palming it into Nana's mouth to stop the blood. It didn't really stop it, and when the ambulance men carried her out there was a trail of it stretching to the front door.

I don't know where to begin on that. I know I wrote down what I felt about it at the time, the paper it's on is probably still stuck between the rooftrees and slates in the attic, all rotted away, probably, like memory itself is. Or time, that I have so much trouble keeping straight and in order. After a week in the hospital Nana came back, then went away again. The second time, they found she had cancer and operated. She was gone a long time that time, but then she came back to stay. There were the conversations in hallways—"We think we got it all, though of course we won't know until . . . She'll be uncomfortable while she's on the cobalt. . . . For the time being, the oral medication should do it. . . . When we go over to injections—well, we'll have to play it by ear. . . ."

So they hadn't got it all. Everything began to change then, for Camilla, for Theron, for me. All kinds of things were talked about that had never been mentioned before. Every day, when Nana had gotten herself together, she'd come downstairs in one of her big cartwheel hats and settle into her chair by the garden windows and begin on her bourbon and cigarettes. Theron had bought her a special kind of cigarette holder that had another cigarette inside as a filter and was supposed to help with her coughing. It didn't. And she talked all the time, to me, to Ummie, who came out and stayed with her days at a time, Diego, Schaafy, Camilla and Theron in the evenings, the nurses when they came on duty. At first there was pretending that she was going to get well, but then the coughing spells got so bad she couldn't make it downstairs and stayed in her room. The O. W. M. came to see her and brought papers to be signed. Their visits wore her out.

Nothing stopped her talking, about family, mostly about her side of the family. The Tenyses were better born than the Hanways. The Hanways had once had some money, but my grandfather had gambled it away. Winston had put him onto . . . Barney had helped. . . . The Hanways had lacked the number of quarterings they needed for Cincinnati. But less well born or not, they were family, and she'd always forgiven my grandfather in her heart. Senior, living and dying as she spoke of him. She wanted to go back into the past, as if by talking about it she could do it over. She began to worry about how things would be without her. The stories were long, old and worn, about how it had all been then and when. How Senior had wanted a grandson—"If only he could see me now." She asked for promises—Theron must promise to let Aunt Edie and Aunt Lydia know when she died. They were sisters of my grandfather, half sisters, younger than he'd have been if he had lived. Aunts. They weren't quality, but they were family, Senior would have wanted them to know. "Promise me, Theron." Theron promised. She asked me for promises too—wouldn't I please do what the O. W. M. wanted, go back to school, try again? for her sake. The estate's sake. Everybody's sake. I promised, but even then I knew you didn't have to keep deathbed promises, and I crossed my fingers behind my back.

I couldn't bear her suffering. I had heard that prayer helped. I prayed and it didn't. The needles went in and out. I even tried magic. It was November, winter, the eleventh month, so on the eleventh day I ran eleven times around the tree outside her window. That didn't work either.

I'd sensed for a long time that Nana had something to tell me she didn't want others to hear. Something she'd tell me when the time came, as they say. "Tenys, my little Tenys. You're the last one. But there's no real family and I worry." Whatever she tried to say went past me. One day when I came into her room I hardly recognized her. She hadn't put on makeup, and her head was bound up in a towel. A place on her neck was beginning to show blue—the cobalt, the nurse said. Nana had stopped eating, even her cigarettes and bourbon were forgotten. She slept most of the time. It would be like that, the nurses said, she'll just go to sleep. But when it seemed about to be over, she'd wake suddenly and start talking again. Beginning in the middle of some sentence said in the past, trying to get through to us, past time, past the pain. But she had trouble finishing what she started to say, broke off. A little at a time I could feel death creep into her as she went back, back.

"Tenys? Are there lilacs?"

"No, Nana, it's snowing."

"There should be lilacs."

"There will be, come spring."

"There should be now."

I learned to lie. "There are lilacs now."

Long silences, lengthening.

"Or is it snow? Are we alone?"

"Yes, Nana."

"I wish I could remember—"

The nurse came in, gave an injection, went out.

"It doesn't signify, Tenys. Close the door."

The door was already closed.

We were all wanting it to end. The day she died, Theron had stayed home, and he and I were together in the room. Camilla had gone to bed, she was worn out, she said, with waiting, and the doctors had said it was something that would go on and on. Theron was holding Nana's hand in his. Nana opened her eyes. Instead of speaking to Theron, she looked straight at me.

"Tenys," she said, gasping, "don't let them do it to you, Tenys. Oh God, forgive me, forgive me if I did wrong."

Then her eyes closed, and her breathing became uneven, there was a sound like little firecrackers going off in her lungs. The nurse came in. It would be soon, she said, the heart was decompensating. The firecrackers changed to a rattle, the rattle filled the room. It went on a long time then suddenly stopped, and there was no sound. The nurse looked at us, it was over. She started to cover Nana with the sheet, but Theron stopped her.

"Get out," he said.

"But Mr. Hanway, it's customary—"

"Get out," Theron said again, and the nurse left.

Then he turned to me. I was terrified. "And you," he said, "you get out too." Even before I left the room I saw him throw himself onto Nana and cry out, "You can't go. Don't leave me. No. No."

Camilla was waiting outside in the hall. I could see Schaafy and Diego and one of the black girls leaving. They had been there through it all, had heard everything through the door.

"You'd better call the doctor," Camilla said to the nurse. "Say it's for Mr. Hanway."

68

"Mrs. Hanway," the nurse said, "this sometimes happens. I wouldn't go in there if I were you."

"Don't tell me what to do, just do as I say," Camilla said.

The half hour or however long it was before the doctor arrived was one of the longest stretches of time in my life. Maybe it was then that I began to have my trouble about time, listening to the sounds coming from the room where Nana died. It took the doctor and two nurses to get Theron away from the bed. The doctor had to hold him while one nurse sneaked up with an injection. The three walked him to his bedroom and laid him out, as though he was the one who had died. The injection worked fast, like the ones the johnnycoats give here when the crazies down the hall get to be too much.

Doc came in today with a frown. He asked what had happened yesterday.

"Yesterday?" Sometimes I pick up on his last word and make a question out of it, the way he does with me.

"Yes. You seemed to be going fine. Why didn't you finish?"

I hated him for pushing me. Putting down what I did about Nana knocked me out, and I don't remember much of it. It wasn't enough, nothing ever is. He saw my expression, then said that things were beginning to come out about Theron and Nana that hadn't showed up on the tapes.

"I want to know what happened after they gave Theron the shot. There's a blocking there, Philip," he said. "Go back and try to get it."

I remember feeling numb inside. I couldn't stand Camilla's handling of the details, you'd have thought she dealt with undertakers every day. I knew one thing, I'd break up if I stayed around while they took Nana away, so I went to the box room over the kitchen and sat by my register. Schaafy and Diego and the black girl were already talking about it.

"Poor old blue lady, how she suffer," Diego said.

"Time she went," the black girl said.

"Yes, Diego," Schaafy said, "it was time. Mrs. Hanway was a nice woman, a lady."

"Lady or not, everybody goes the same," the black girl went on. "What I want to know is, now what happens to the money. Don't want to work no place the money ain't going to come down and stick."

"Hush up," Diego said. "Nothing for you to worry about. No money ever going to stick to you."

"Well, it's been a terrible strain"—Schaafy's voice.

"And it ain't over yet," Diego said to this. "You heard through the door. That last thing Lady Hanway say she not say to Boss, she say it to the kid. And that ain't good. I think that's why Boss he go to pieces and start yelling like he's doing."

They talked back and forth. I don't know how long I listened, but when I left the box room Theron was up and Camilla was pouring black coffee. They were phoning everybody, to tell them, arguing about the order the calls should be made. Finally Theron said he had to let Aunt Edie and Aunt Lydia know. He'd promised.

"Are you sure we want to do that?" Camilla asked.

"I said I would and I will. Get me mother's address book."

Camilla found the book, Theron phoned the telegram.

"Theron, really," Camilla said when he had hung up. "Why did you tell them the day of the funeral? They may come."

Theron was shaking a little. They were going to quarrel, no matter what was said.

"Let them come, they're my aunts. And don't forget, they're in the Will. Article seven."

"I'm not likely to forget. Old southern belles from some backwater—"

"Tidewater." Theron could turn nasty. "If they do come, they won't be those wagon train leftovers of yours out in Bad Breath, Montana, or wherever it was."

"You shit."

70

The O. W. M. had been phoned first, and Mr. Browne drove out next morning, to see if he could be of help. He was Nana's executor and the first thing he asked about was her big diamond. Ummie and Uncle Bill and Uncle Coo had been coming for the weekend anyway. It was like some terrible party with all the drinks and trying to go on as though nothing had happened. There was a notice in the Times— "Amy Tenys Hanway. Widow of the late Theron Hanway, Sr., once prominent in diplomatic circles." All about my grandfather instead of Nana. The day before the funeral, Aunt Edie and Aunt Lydia arrived in a taxi.

Camilla took one look at them. She said, "I don't want to hear ever again about wagon train leftovers. My aunts look like people, not a couple of old fringed lampshades dyed black."

"I can't help how they look," Theron said.

"How long are they going to stay?"

"I don't know."

"They brought enough luggage for a month. They're not going to be my responsibility after the funeral, let me tell you that."

There was more, but I've forgotten it.

I GUESS I gave out on what I wrote about yesterday. Whatever day. Not Doc. He wants the funeral. Okay, the funeral.

Everything was done as Nana had wanted it. A service in New York, followed by cremation. Though there had been a special notice asking that flowers be omitted, there were wreaths and sprays and baskets all around the coffin, which was covered with a pall of white orchids sent by Theron. There were dozens of old ladies. The O. W. M. in the front row. A curate in a white surplice who spoke of Nana as Our Daughter in Christ. Lots of stuff like, "In the midst of death we are in life. Tho he were dead, yet so shall he live." What I felt as I listened was that in the midst of death I was in life, alone. Afterward there was a long ride in limousines to the

71

crematorium, which was farther out on the Island even than Groverhampton. There were only family and Ummie and Bill and Coo. Nana's coffin was already there, still with Theron's pall on it, behind glass. The place was like a chapel and there was organ music as Nana was lowered into the flames. You could tell the music was a tape, it ticked when it turned off, and the flames looked fake too. We all drove back to the house. Uncle Bill and Uncle Coo made drinks for everybody, except Aunt Lydia and Aunt Edie, who asked for tea. They did most of the talking, with Ummie and Camilla listening, and Theron waiting for it all to be over. Talk like, "How beautiful the service was." And, "Poor Amy, she had it the hard way. But what a wonderful wife she was to Senior, through his adversity and all. Who could ever guess he'd beat the odds the way he did?" Theron couldn't take it and went upstairs. We all heard the slam of his door. And then came the pounding on the walls and the same crying out and sobs of the night Nana died. It was far down the hall, but it echoed and sounded even louder.

"Camilla, dear, don't you think you should go to him?" one of the aunts asked.

Camilla just stared at her and set down her glass.

Ummie said, "I think it's been a long day and we should all go to bed. Bill, you clear up."

We all went to bed. The sounds from Theron's bedroom went on most of the night. Ummie stayed with Camilla, and the uncles did what they could with Theron.

The aunts stayed on. To see what they could find out about the Will, Camilla said. Diego told Schaafy they were just two old birds looking for pickings. Ummie tried to find out when they planned to go.

"Why, we thought we just might visit awhile," they said. "Down Tidewater way nobody comes all this way without visiting, even if it was for a funeral. You all don't have to entertain us, we're used to entertaining ourselves."

It's all scrambled and out of order in my memory now, but I remember they were very interested in what was in the Will. It had crossed their minds that in this life you never know. "Anything can happen. Why, plane crashes—think of it, whole families wiped out at once." Camilla bore up, but she'd shut up like a clam. Until the last evening.

By then, I had found a new listening post, the big blue sofa by the far fireplace where no one ever sat. I listened to Aunt Edie say they were all right, her husband had left her six figures, but it was hard going these days on the income from that. It was Aunt Lydia, though, who got things off on the wrong foot that last night.

"Tell me, Camilla, what's your definition of a lady?"

"I haven't the faintest idea. What's yours?"

"Why, a lady's a lady. Amy was a lady, never the slightest doubt. Camilla, we've been wondering, what's going to happen to Amy's things?"

"What things?"

"Well, she had lovely clothes, all from the great houses and like that. We couldn't help seeing her trunks and boxes in the attic."

"What were you doing in the attic?"

"Oh, Diego showed us around—you said make ourselves at home."

"Meaning, you want what's in the trunks," Camilla said.

"We'd be glad to take them off your hands, wouldn't we, Edie?"

"Certainly we would," Aunt Edie said. "Why, Camilla, dear, have we said something wrong?"

The phone rang at that moment and broke the conversation, but I could tell Camilla had set her jaw. When it started up again, the aunts asked a few loaded questions.

"Camilla, we've been meaning to ask—where are you from originally?"

"Montana."

"Montana. Well."

"Camilla, is that all of the Tenys silver in the dining room, or is there some put away?"

"That's all of it."

"Amy certainly got the best pieces. What was your pattern, dear?"

Camilla waited, then said in a dry, harsh voice I'd never heard before, "Since you're asking me so many questions, let me ask you one. What's your definition of tacky?"

"Tacky? Why, tacky's tacky. Like being a lady. It is or isn't tacky, isn't that so, Lydia?"

"It certainly is, Edie," Lydia said.

"Thanks for telling me," Camilla said. "And now, you must excuse me. I've a hard day tomorrow. Some women work, you know."

The aunts left next morning.

IT's today. I guess time's moving, but it doesn't feel like it here, boxed in as I am, thinking back, writing back, sometimes even seeming to go back. I'm getting stir crazy, maybe. Malc's been off and I've had Woody and the gorilla for my jogs and showers, which makes it even more dead, they hardly say anything. But Malc came back this morning, and he's still being the comedian in the shower.

"Man, they are really taking you apart now," he said. "Between you and me, I think shrinks is funny. I knows about you. I could tell them if they'd ask me."

"Do they ever ask you?"

"No, I'm just a johnnycoat with a chart to keep. I keeps it. What you do, when you do it. Whitey has his chart and it's the same."

Last night I stayed awake thinking what I'd written about Nana. Her dying was for me like coming to the edge of the world and trying to hang on and not fall off. I wrote down those things she said just before she died, not in order, maybe, and not exact, but is memory ever exact? After she'd gone I had my first experience of feeling dead myself. The being alone and not being able to cry. I think the kid I was then died with her, leaving another Philip behind. I became somebody else, but what I had been before haunted me. I spent long afternoons in the attic with her trunks and boxes, going through the photographs and scrapbooks. The record

74

she had kept of me—the card sent out announcing my birth, a smaller one attached with a blue ribbon giving my name, date, and how much I weighed. Her big, old-fashioned handwriting, noting my first word, my weight as I grew, snapshots of me at 1 yr., a birthday party when I was 4. The way I wrote my name. Then it stopped.

But she had loved me.

And there were all the pictures of Theron, one a clipping, "IN THE EMBASSY CHILD WORLD," staring out at me—myself. Nana against silver backgrounds with flowers. Holding fans. Ummie, with feathers in her hair. The same faces done over and over, looking different but then the same. Crazy that I should remember the scrawls beneath the photographs, DeMeyer, Sacha, Lenare. Even then I was picking up my useless information. I don't know why it was these things that at last brought it home to me that Nana was gone, that nobody would ever care about me the way she did, that things that had happened with her would not happen again. She was dead, leaving me. I cried then, cried for days, but always by myself. I began to know what being lonely was. I think that was really when I began to be on my own. I knew I would have to make my own world. And keep it secret.

Up to about then, there had been the mumsy and dadsy bits, as well as all the times we didn't use names with each other. They were the ones who decided we'd use first names, and it was all right with me. I think now it was one more way of putting me down, so I couldn't get close to them. And what happened when I was with them was that I took off the mask of myself, so they couldn't know me. If they weren't going to love me, I wanted to be a stranger to them. To put it like that.

Doc says let it stand when stuff like that comes out. So there it is, for what it's worth.

That last night with the aunts I almost went nuts listening to Theron, to Bill and Coo, talking him down. Ummie said all things come to an end, and that Theron would come around. He seemed to, but even then I wondered. Now I think he never did.

I was still looking for answers, any I could get, still working on it, and them. I wondered when they did it, when he got it off her, to put it Diego's way, and was having doubts they did it or he got it. Camilla locked her door at night, but Theron often left his ajar for air. One morning when I woke I was sure I heard something. I'd learned when you can't figure something out, surprise can help. I crept out into the hall. Nobody. Nothing, just the morning air coming through Theron's door. There was a little square sitting room that led to his bedroom, and I went inside.

He slept with his head against the light and the curtains were blowing into the bedroom. He had pushed back the covers in his sleep and seeing him was like looking at one of the Leonardo drawings. He had a great body, like a barbell boy's who knows when to stop. He was me as I would be, and seeing him like that was a turning point of some kind for me. Maybe I saw then what Diego had stopped short of telling me. He was pulling off, making it last, giving himself a great time, his eyes closed, no expression on his face. It was a great turnon, and as I stood watching I got hard and pulled with him, in time, stopping when he stopped, waiting, beginning again when he began. I saw him make it and shoot into the air and then he let out his breath and was still. I didn't quite make it at the same time he did, but when I did it was magic, the first time the white stuff came out big, like his. Better than being just with myself. He had made it happen. And it was secret. He would never know. I crept back to my room. After that, I was hung up on him. I followed him down to breakfast—and nothing. Just his one look and word to me and his fast coffee and cigarettes and off to town in whichever car Diego had warmed up for him.

But I went on thinking. That morning he was doing what I did because I had nowhere to put it. Though he did. All he'd have had to do was go down the hall and put it into her. But he didn't.

There it is. "Let it come out," Doc keeps telling me, and I did. No screen memory. Or maybe I've knocked over the first screen.

WHAT was it I wrote yesterday that brought them all down on me this morning? Even my jog was put off, and Malc took a powder. The first I noticed something was off schedule was when I was standing looking up out of the window at the brick and the sky, wondering what kind of day it is, and suddenly I knew I was being watched. Not on the monitor, I'm used to that, but real eyes through the grate in the door. I turned and there was this broad, this nurse, and right away I knew she's the one who sits just beyond where I can see. Come to have a look at monster boy. But why now? And what a turnoff—like 40 years old and rimless glasses that caught the light and a mouth made for sour grapes. I'd had this fantasy that maybe some night when things quieted down and my monitor was asleep she'd come to the grate and give me a blowjob. No more fantasy about that, I'd sure have to have my eyes bandaged if I knew it was her. She? Forget it. Anyway, she was the first of what I've come to think of as my appointments, made at the convenience of others.

Tweed Suit was next. I can always tell when he's on his way, the gorilla walks ahead and jangles his keys. Today he had Baby Cube with him. I haven't put down anything about Baby, because I wish I'd never have to see him again. My defense lawyer. I'm his baby, I get it, but he's not mine. What would he know about what I know? I could strip my brain case raw for him, and he'd never catch on. From the minute I first saw him, at the Groverhampton jail, I tagged him as No. 1 Cube of all time. Cute Wall Street hair with a brushed down part, Brooksy suit, button-down collar, tie. Baby Cube of Cube, Square, Rectangle and Oblong. Like my O. W. M., these lawyers are fraidies, tangle you up in pairs or foursomes. Baby still has to have it off with himself, much less anybody else. I think he might be reading what I write for Doc, he looks a little shriveled at the edges. Let him shrivel. He never comes alone because I scare him shitless. He should

77

relax. I wouldn't knock him off if they threw me back and fucked me over and gave me a brand-new life.

Gorilla hung around while Tweed Suit did his act of staring at me as though I'm some animal about to become extinct. Picking up the papers they always bring with them, putting them down. All one more way of making me say and do things I don't want to. Baby Cube wanted to go back into Do I think it would have been the same if Theron had been home that Thursday night, instead of my coming in and finding Camilla alone in the house? Shit like that. For a good half hour. How should I know? Things can only happen one way, not two, and I said so. Baby Cube nodded. "Oh, yes, yes." He always plays it Me Deep. Finally he said, "Well, Phil, think about it—it could be very important. We can't do our best for you if you withhold. Not that we can ever know it all."

Fucking right he'll never know it, because even if I could get it back second by second and tell him, he couldn't get it. So he shut up. Doc came in then, and I noticed his squint. I get it mixed up with his smile. He talked loud as he always does to make it seem it's all Miller beer and we've got the time. Whatever it was I wrote, they all showed they'd read it. Since Doc never lets up on how I must put down everything just as it comes out, I can't get it. Shrinks. A guy I knew once—at St. Andrew's, I think—had had shrinks put on him by his folks, he said they were all innocents with dirty minds, when you hand it to them on the shit platter they get a little upset. It was weird, hearing them try to double guess me, when Baby Cube's question is something I'd never thought of. I think they were all trying to put me on the defensive.

All at once I said to them, "Why don't you all fuck off. Ship me out to anyplace you decide, but let up on that Thursday night and the old folks. And the order I did them."

Doc said, "Well, okay. Maybe it'll be best just to wait until he writes it out."—As though Phil's going to be a good boy.

So the gorilla filed them out, Baby Cube sweet and clean as when he came in, Doc and Tweed Suit talking as they walked toward the elevator. I listened, and what I got was, "You've got to remember, we can't have this if we have that. It won't wash in court. It's got to be one or the other, not both."

Whatever I can make of that.

I was glad to see Malc, even if he was late. We had what's beginning to be usual during the jog, an argument about whether to run silent or yak. He likes talking because he thinks it winds me and I'll cut my time. No way. He thinks too something may come out that he's missed.

He's the one who winds first. He says, "Okay, take it by yourself," and falls out and waits till I've finished.

When I'd sweated Tweed Suit and Baby Cube out and was soaping up in the shower, Malc started putting the make on me again. He knows I won't let him touch me, so now it's compliments.

"How you get yourself into that great shape, boy? You pump?"

"A little."

Then he spoils it, tells me I'm not going to have my own private jog time when they get me inside of where I'm going. This translates I should give thanks for him.

"You one big beautiful kid—and you knows it," he follows up with, and a lot more of the mental seduction crap.

Okay, I know it. I didn't argue it. I always sweated out the day before so I'd feel good. I was in great shape once. I mean, if I'd sold myself for one of those underarm torso commercials on TV I'd have been great. Sometimes I wish I'd done something like that. One thing that could never be said against Theron was that he didn't set a good physical example. I mean, that morning I found him beating it, it wasn't like looking at your old man, he was like the middle comeon spread in Playgirl. Tops.

THAT was when I tried to reach out to Theron. I think what I felt for him at that time was a mixture of love and hatred, love because he had turned me on to myself, hatred for myself because I was so desperate to love someone. Because he had gone to pieces about Nana, I took my own pain about her and poured it into love for him, trying to get him to love me, which for me was the same thing. I tried to love Camilla too, but she was too far away. Now and then when Schaafy touched me or hugged me a little, I'd look between her breasts and almost go crazy as I hugged back and would pretend she was Camilla. That didn't work. But there was Theron, so all by himself, like me, but in another way. If I couldn't make him love me, I could love him, which was better than nothing. I would wait for him to drive through the gates evenings he came home, hang around him, watch everything he did. He would change from his city clothes to jeans and a T-shirt and go out to work in his garden. He was really great looking with his rosy blond skin beginning to peel before his summer tan, his bright yellow hair all blown from his drive out in his 1933 Audi cabriolet, which he used on fine days.

It was still the time I hoped magic would work for me. I knew there was some connection between Theron's garden and the way he felt and behaved. When he worked in it and it grew well he was happier and paid more attention to me. That was magic. He'd let me come out and dig and rake with him. He had all kinds of roses, snapdragons, lilies, even Christmas roses, and the entire plot was laid out in designs of dwarf box, to set off the colors. When weather was good or there weren't people besides family on weekends, he worked in it, and it was practically perfect. He never showed it to anybody. All he ever said about it to Camilla was, "I don't want the gardeners to go near it, make sure you tell them it's out of bounds." She told them, she had no interest in it, all she cared about was having the lawns velvety and the garden paths and drive gravel-raked and white. Telling the gardeners was only one more housekeeping detail. On her pad.

The only thing wrong with Theron's garden was that, though he'd fenced it in against rabbits and groundhogs, there were cats getting at it, coming from somewhere. We knew it was cats because one day Diego had found two of them taking each other apart, and there was blood and cat fur all over the fence. And the godawful smell of cat. Diego said the cats belonged to a couple of old ladies who lived in a farmhouse up the road and who fed stray cats, any cat nobody else wanted. The fence didn't do any good, the cats jumped onto the top of it and down onto the dwarf box and crapped and hoisted their asses and sprayed and everything began to die. The box showed gray where the cats had been at them. As Diego said, everybody knows cats won't shit on their own property, they pick somebody else's. I must have still been a soft kid then, because it did things to me when one day Theron threw down his shovel and said to Diego, "Those fucking cats. They're killing everything. I'm about to give up."

He didn't give up easy. He tried the polite country ways, wrote notes to the old ladies asking them please to keep their cats away. He telephoned. I remember he said, "Cats have an affinity for boxwood, they're defecating on my property." At which whichever old lady it was hung up the phone. She came right over—Diego said it was to get a look at Mr. and Mrs. Theron Hanway, Jr.—and Theron showed her what the cats had done.

The old lady was embarrassed, she said, "Mr. Hanway, how can you use such a word with women?"

"What word?" Theron asked.

"Why—defecate," she said.

Theron was losing his temper. "Well, would you like shit better? That's what I find when I cultivate, cat shit. If you don't keep your cats away, I'm prepared to take legal action." The old lady almost fainted.

The cats kept coming. I couldn't see why Theron should be so unhappy or go to court when there was me. It came to me that if I got rid of the cats for him it might be the magic that would make him love me. Because there is magic doing something secret for someone you love. I went behind the scenes, to put it that way, and I tried it in nice ways first. I watched for the cats, chased them, used stones. But cats don't take hints, much less orders. They simply stared at me and went on doing their thing, crapping and backing up their asses and spraying and then went back where they came from. I'd heard Nana say, If a hint won't do it, a blow will. So I put a little backbone in my magic.

There was a wire box trap in the greenhouse, one of those with two ends that flip open and shut. You open one end and leave the other closed, and there's a treadle in the middle where you put the bait. So when the cat goes in to get the smoked Scotch salmon—that's what I used, Schaafy had plenty on the shelves—the open end drops, and you've got your cat. I got each and every one of them, one at a time. It was quite a project for a kid, and I had to keep it secret, so the magic would work. I had to wait for the trap to spring, usually in the early morning, and get up quick and get the cat out of the way. Man, did those cats hate it, for once they weren't making their own decisions, like on TV, Meow, I'll eat it, Meow, Meow, I won't eat it. They ate it. I never liked cats anyway, the way their bones squnch around inside their fur really turns me off. So what I had to do then wasn't as hard as it might have been for some.

Because let me tell you, it's one thing to trap them and something else to kill them. They all fought, I had to figure a way to do them without getting scratched. I'd get a can of Theron's rose spray and give them a couple of blasts, always remembering the roses they'd spoiled for him. That was a beginning, then came the wire. Cats are hard to wipe out, you have to keep at it. I used to pull the wire tight, then loosen it nine times, to see if that nine lives crap was true. It is. I'd let them come back a little, let them think they were going to go on shitting and spraying, then I'd tighten the wire and hold it until they got the idea. It was really kicky when the old lady came to the door and said she simply couldn't understand it, her cats were disappearing one by one, and she wondered if we were doing anything, if there was any connection. I just stood back and looked innocent, the way the cats looked. After all, you learn as you go, right? And something else—I found I was getting a charge from the magic, and when finally the cats were all gone, I was almost sorry there were no more. When I was wrapping them in plastic bags and laying them in the bottom of Diego's garbage cans, I'd feel great, sure the magic was working. I'd put the cats out of their miserable lives so Theron wouldn't be miserable and suffer. The magic worked, but only part of it. Theron nursed the garden back until the box and flowers looked great. The part that didn't work was the part that was supposed to make him love me.

I never believed in magic after that.

IT's getting to be just like home here. Wisecrack. Sort of like the O. W. M. discussing me in the third person. He. His. Him. As though I'm not here. Tweed Suit once more, tapping his finger on something typed up that Doc's showed him. A tweedy stare at me, then, "I thought we were going to get him off this."

"We're moving it as fast as we can," Doc says.

"Well, get him off or on. But we've got to get him out. Don't forget, we've got quotas like any other hospital. Others are waiting."

I'll bet. Guys who chop them up and leave them behind in motels. Sons who've been kept thirty years in attics by their loving mothers. I'm not allowed newspapers, but Malc reads them and tells me.

? days later. Later than when? Well, whenever I wrote my last day's stint. Time's hard to track when you're in a box being watched like an animal and taken out on a string and brought back to have the lid clamped back on. They took me somewhere, did things to me. My scalp is full of little scabs. Well, the body knows things.

If I've figured out anything about why there was no ballpoint for however long it's been, it's this—Okay, I knocked down a screen, burned through a screen memory. So I was turned on by my old man, got hung up on him. Not long. But trust shrinks to be crazy about anything like that. Like if you were discussing the great art of fucking and mentioned there are other ways beside the missionary position, right away they're interested. I scratched little Hesper and never heard the end of it. I yanked old Kauffman's tits and kicked her crotch and that was supposed to have some deep meanings. After all, who was disturbed enough to drown Sebek? Not P. T. H. I wandered around the mazes of the house, silenced a stack of shrinks, was taken to the O. W. M. at stated times and would even dream about 25 Wall Street and old black Trinity Church, but always came back to my hot air register, my dumbwaiter shaft, and all the baffles of staircases that gave me the family quarrels hot off the griddle. It goes without saying, I was a jackoff artist, but what guy isn't? And no matter what's said about it, I didn't grow hair on my palms. I didn't need Theron's Playgirl to know how I looked with a hard on, in a mirror. By the time I was beginning to have hair around the places you have it, I'd had quite a life as an eavesdropper on life at Lilacs.

The way it writes itself out you'd think it was all school time with me in and out of whichever one and back again. Fall when I went in, winter as I came back and dogged it out with the shrink-tutors, spring when the O. W. M. took stock and everybody got nervous about what to do with me during the summers.

There were as many summers as winters. Camp Mujeemooksin. Camp Silverlake. There were lots of lakes. Treats— candy and gum but have you used your Waterpik, your mother was very explicit on that. Keeping fit. Body duties. It's equally important to wash between your toes as behind your ears. Not thinking it sissy to keep your nails trimmed and shapely. There was usually an old teenager who cared for sunburns and gave you Absorbine Jr. for athlete's foot. And the ones who still wet their beds, or if they didn't, had their fingertips immersed in warm water while sleeping so they would wet them. Boy jokes. Joke boys. Worst of all, the counselors, old Boy Scout types in khaki shirts and shorts, tennis shoes, hair worn off the sides of their legs by the pants

84

they wore in winter. At a time in my life when passion was eating me alive, they put saltpeter in the beans and gave lectures on the evils of the solitary vice, saving yourself for the right girl about to come along. Women were holy vessels, except Mummie, who had to be missed. I didn't miss Camilla, but I had, long before my summer camps, begun my Camilla-watch, and this file grew every day. I made private inventories on my secret slips of paper of what Theron had piles of in his room and Camilla in hers. As editor of Haute she was sent all kinds of books and mags that she brought home. And there were others that Diego carried up from the mailbox. Camilla had her copies of Playgirl too, and some of the stories were great. Prose like My breasts were quivering and my thighs streaming with desire when he came through the dawn—I pressed my body deliciously against his, curve by curve, as his eager hands found my longing mound— Like that. He/she didn't matter, I changed it around to suit me, I could always get off on words as well as pictures. Did Camilla get off on all the beefcake and pricks? Theron did. And I did, on the words. But flesh works both ways. At least I didn't have to use mirrors.

THAT was around the time that the O. W. M. came up with this summer deal for me out in Wyoming. A summer camp, but with a difference, for boys with Oedipal troubles. The O. W. M. had talked with some of my shrinkies, and all kinds of words like that began to turn up in their sessions with me. I was still a little chickenish, part of my hair hadn't decided which way to grow, freckles, a zit or two. But I was beginning to look the way I do now, okay, sometimes great looking. The camp was called Six Walk. This was because long ago some Cheyenne braves got lost from their tribe and never got back. They started from scratch and stayed, and since there were six of them—Six Walk. The camp brochure really romanced it. Now it was run by an old guy who'd made a study of the

American Indian and was cashing in on what he knew. I saw right away when he met me at the airport in Wyoming that it was going to be a weird scene.

"I am White Hawk," he introduced himself, giving me a crusher handshake, letting me know he'd pumped iron in his time. He looked like his name, big schnoz, white hair to his shoulders, a band of beadwork around his forehead. "We use Indian names here," he said, looking me up and down. "I shall call you High Pockets."

We drove what seemed hundreds of miles into this forest where the six braves had got tired of walking. There were forty boys, all with names he'd given them. Yellow Cloud. Black Knife. We slept in pairs, three pairs to a tepee, on beds of pine needles. The nights were cold, and we froze our asses off trying to keep warm. I guess it was White Hawk's way of saving on blankets. My pine needle buddy was named Big Elk and was from London. His father was a peer. He'd had a lot of trouble accepting his parents, he said, and had been through the shrink mill like I had. But English version. He said White Hawk was really a cloth mother.

I didn't know what that meant.

Big Elk explained. His father was a scientist and into animal responses. Monkeys. To find out what a monkey would do if there was no mother, they made one out of cloth, and the monkeys had to make do with that. The monkeys clung to the cloth mother. We'd all been sent to Six Walk to unscrew us from family constellations that had gotten screwed up, and White Hawk was supposed to be an authority figure with both mumsy and dadsy sympathies.

"Your pater and mater still making it?" he asked me.

I said I didn't know, and I still didn't, really, and probably had a secret hope I could say yes.

Big Elk and I got along. He called the camp Six Pack, and soon everybody else called it that too. We did sleep six to a tepee and were packed in. And the Cloth Mother was an authority figure. Whenever he wanted attention he'd shout "Yoonkh, fellas!" A sound sort of like a wolf being tortured. We heard Yoonkh all day long. At night we sat around a big campfire and sang Green Grow the Rushes Ho! I'll give you one ho. One is one and all alone and ever more shall bee-hee-so-o-o. This song had twelve verses, and every time you added one, you had to go back and repeat all the others in order downwards to One ho. The top was, Twelve for the twelve apostles, Eleven for the eleven that went to heaven and Ten for the ten bright shiners. And down. We learned Indian songs too—Ay hay bay tahn in go tho ho, hay isha ga wagen ya in go tho ho wah hah!

The Cloth Mother was hung up on Indian drag. He had trunks of it, beadwork moccasins, deer-bone breastplates, eagle feather headdresses with bustles to match. We all had to put on Indian brown greasepaint and wear this cruddy stuff and dance around the fire while Mother beat the drum. Afterward, Mother would tell long stories. One was about an Indian called Strange Person who was different from the others in his tribe and wandered all over the world by himself. Both Big Elk and I identified like mad with Strange Person. "If only we could wander in the world," he said one cold night, when we were stretching the blanket. "We'll always be strange and will never wander." There was no wandering away from Six Walk, Mother was like a computer and knew where each of us was all the time.

It wasn't all like that. There was swimming in the buff in a lake that was colder than any Massachusetts lake. Indian games with balls that you kicked. Boxing. During workouts Mother was always there to wipe you off, the way he was when we were putting on the greasepaint. There were sort of group therapy sessions where you were supposed to get up and talk about yourself and your old man and old lady. I never did—how could I make anybody believe Theron or Camilla? Big Elk had the same trouble. Sometimes the Cloth Mother would really get going and explain to us that winning in the games we played wasn't the important thing. The game was. And fine bodies pitted one against another were beautiful. The companionship to be found with other boys could be meaningful, something to remember in later life. One day when he was spouting this stuff, Big Elk, who had been having a hard time holding it in, started laughing.

"Who was that?" Mother snapped. "I want the man who laughed to stand up."

Nobody stood up. But Mother wasn't called White Hawk for nothing. His eyes lighted on Big Elk and then me, because I was beginning to laugh too.

"Yoonkh! Big Elk, stand! High Pockets, stand!"

We stood. We couldn't stop laughing.

"I'm ashamed of you both," Mother scolded us. "Yoonkh! To your tepee. No powwow for either of you tonight!"

We didn't feel punished. We yoonkhed and laughed like wolves as we fought for the blanket. Later there were man to man sessions with Mother for both of us. Didn't we understand that friendship between a boy and an older man could be a fine thing? Like that.

"We do this kind of thing better in England," Big Elk said after his session.

I think he was homesick. So was I—it was that bad. But I stuck out the eight weeks.

That was one crazy summer, but I learned a few things. That your ass is divided into two parts. That you had to fight like the song says like a tiger for your honor. I fought. And won. Some of the pitches the Cloth Mother made were exactly what Renzo and I used to get from jam daddies— Whoa! I'm getting ahead of myself. That Six Pack summer I'd seen Renzo only those few times, as a kid. My real friendship with Renzo came later.

I HAVEN'T put this down because of Malc, but now I know that even if he talks it doesn't matter. I knew they'd taken me off somewhere, given me more tests. I said the body remembers, and it does. There's a feeling in my cells of being clamped down and maybe photographed or x-rayed, looked into secretly. I guess nothing's forbidden here. Don't move. Click. Now you can move. Click. Hold it. Click. The little scabs all over my head, even down into my cheeks, are beginning to come off. During my shower today I asked Malc what it was they did.

"They got a big machine that looks into your brain," he said, "I know they did that test on you."

I asked if he was there.

"No, it was Whitey's day, but I seen the paper on it. When the nurse put it in the box they keep your things in."

My box. This is new.

"Everybody got his box," Malc tells me.

I was all soaped up, and I could tell he was getting his usual kicks.

He said, "You want to see the paper?"

"Sure. Why not?"

"But you got to give."

Still the same old blowjob proposition. Long ago I learned that when somebody wants something off you, you don't give it easy. Or give half. So I let him feel me and told him to bring me the paper and then we'd see.

He brought it with my lunch. It was nothing, only an outline of a head with lots of little numbers all over it, where they put the needles in, I could see that.

"An electroencephalogram," Malc said, "an EEG."

I knew that. What interested me was what was written below. Within normal limits. So?

"You got nothing to worry about," Malc said. "There's lots more stuff about you."

I didn't bite. I'm glad I didn't, because when Doc came in he brought this tin box and put it down on the table.

"You don't have to go behind my back, Phil," he said. "You could have asked me."

I looked at the box, the kind used in banks, shiny black with a flip lid. On one end were strings of computer digits, followed by a dash and HANWAY, P. Me.

"You're not our run-of-the-mill patient," Doc said. "You have certain rights."

"Rights?" I gave it back to him and laughed. "What rights?"

Of course no answer on that. But he showed me a clutch of what was in the box, doctors' letters, my Alice Heim test, my Rorschach.

I remember those ink blots, even some of the things I said as they showed them to me, which is the idea. Like, I was always interested in anything about sex from the beginning. Anybody. Women, girls, even guys, I'd size them up and undress them in my mind, wonder what they were like underneath as they say. Mouths tell a lot, and eyebrows. Once a guy told me that you can guess a chick's bush by the thickness of the eyebrows, even if they pluck them. And he said the opening in a guy's cock is like the shape of his mouth. I checked that, I have a little mouth down there, and I can make it smile or look mean, whichever I like. I've always had these feelings, I mean, anybody I see, even just some guy sitting outside handcuffed to a guard, waiting to be shoved into his space here and locked up, I try to guess how he'd be with chicks. That gets me on to chicks he's had. And in no time I'm seeing their tits and the way they walk and think what it would be like if I'd had them in bed. Or on the beach. Stripped. Being together. Touching is so beautiful, almost any touching. What's hideous is this frozen way they handle me here—excuse me, the way they don't handle me. Or handle me while I'm out cold and can't feel it. Any touching here is dead and frozen, as if murder's a dust that will rub off onto them. Even Malc treats me like a cute corpse. Well, I can't help it if nailed down like I am, sex has gone to my head. The jog and shower doesn't get rid of a thing, just keeps me in shape.

And Malc talks. There are no secrets about Phil. Which doesn't mean I'm not supposed to go on writing my secrets out.

WHERE was I? Okay, Six Walk. I never saw Big Elk again, but some of the stuff we'd hash over lying on the pine needles under that scriny blanket have stuck. Like him, I was up to here with being on trial and probation, and when it came time for Camilla and Theron and me to haul ass down to 25 Wall, to Homer, Stanhope, Brockhurst and Browne and lick the boots, I'd begun to figure out the finer points relating to me and the checks that arrived quarterly. For Theron and Camilla, not for me. I was on short-leash allowance, never enough—the way my grandfather would have wanted. Mr. Brockhurst had conked out, remember, and the others looked dead to me too. Dead or not, they gave up hard on the private schools. I never knew what the Cloth Mother's report on me was, but there was something that I knew would eventually make the O. W. M. give up. It would be a little at a time, but I was beginning to win. Not that I had any idea what I'd do once I had won, or even what winning would be like. All I can get back from that historic meeting that sent me to Tucker is shreds.

"Oh, I'm afraid that's not at all what Senior wanted for him. . . ."

"What are we going to do with him?"

"Well, he shouldn't spend more time by himself—"

"Doing whatever it is he does."

"What does he do?"

"What kids his age do, I suppose."

"Diego says—"

"Mrs. Schaaf says—"

"Well, I'm for giving Tucker a try. I can get him in—there's always a long waiting list, you know. . . ."

Tucker was a remedial school in Massachusetts where problems of adolescence were a specialty. Outside, it was the same old red bricks and lawns you weren't supposed to cross and woods for walking in with your counsellor. And, no shit, Daddy Freud or not, the same compulsive chapel with alphabetical seating to make you feel guilty. And a principal we called Dr. X, because he came straight out of a monster movie, his wife ditto, and a cushy, comeon niece, on whom hangs my tale. But no tail.

It was around that time I gave up trying to find in me the self they all wanted me to be. Mr. Stanhope's "We must look ahead, here," Mr. Homer's "Yes, entrance into Princeton is considerably more difficult than in his grandfather's day," Mr. Browne's "He's very advanced physically for his age—" I picked up my cues. Girls were getting to be my problem. Not only the black girls Diego found, but any girl I saw. And it wasn't any one girl, or real girls. The girls I invented for myself were sometimes the worst problem. I saw girls everywhere and wanted them all. I couldn't think of anything else. They were my torment, and there was no getting rid of it. Tucker and its remedies didn't stop me from thinking of them night and day. The sight of their wonderful different-ness from guys, tits beneath blouses and sweaters, the tock of their asses as they walked—I was crazy all the time. I woke every morning thinking of them and it, and there was a dead-line to be made toward them every day, every week, a dead-line I couldn't meet. I wasn't having sex with anybody except myself, but beating off wasn't enough anymore, it was like a drug you take for a hangover, but the hangover never went away. There was no drug for forgetting girls, only girls them-selves.

I'd been hung up on it, sex, for a long time. Any woman I saw I undressed, beginning with the tits, but never getting down to cunt. In my mind. But mind was no good. I had always listened to my body, if it was hungry I ate, if it told me to take a whiz I did, and now it was telling me to reach out and touch. I had tried hard to find out what was really between a woman's legs, and it was steady work. I'd tried quick gropes on some of the black girls, even tried a few of the Haute girls who came for weekends, but I never made it. The statues and pictures weren't much help. Getting down to the nitty-gritty of what cunt is actually took me years. I was still on this while I was at Tucker, trying to find out, pre-tending I was settling in only because of Dr. X's niece, on whom, as Doc would put it, I was fixated. No fix.

Holidays came. The O. W. M. were babysitting me be-cause Theron and Camilla were away, and they decided I should dog it out at Tucker. Two other boys had nowhere to go either, an Egyptian who seemed not to have heard of girls, and a leftover from a Hollywood marriage who had spastic problems. Great company. Dr. X and his wife took pity, and we were asked to dinner. His niece was there, and she was still coming on for me. She was like sunlight in a forest, darting in and out of rooms, smiling, shaking her big mane of reddish hair. Now that I put it into words, it's so obvious she didn't know what she was doing for me. But I bought the whole thing. She suggested we go for a drive—did I have a car? No? We could use her uncle's if I could drive. I could drive a little, Diego as he washed and greased and polished the cars at Lilacs had let me practice on the white gravel drive, even let me try it up and down the lane. I was still a month away from the age when I could get my junior license to operate a car with parental approval during daylight hours. But I went ahead anyway. It wasn't daylight, and Long Island is different from Mass. I did something wrong at a crossing and had my first run in with a fuzz. He phoned Dr. X, who got it from his niece that we'd parked and I'd tried to get it on. I'd built it up to myself, I mean at first it was the fear I'd do something wrong with the car, and then I think that because I didn't know what to do, I came on too fast. It was awful. And I knew her uncle would do what he did, call the O. W. M.

He said, "I thought better of you, Hanway."

"But it was her idea," I said.

"Go to your room, Hanway."

The O. W. M. arranged for Diego to drive up to get me. I was never gladder to see anybody. He didn't have to ask me what I'd done, he knew.

"I been watching you sniffing a long time," he said. "This time did you get it?"

I admitted I hadn't.

"It'll come," he said, "hard or easy, and when it does it'll be like the first olive out of the bottle. The rest just happen."

And that, as Theron came back from wherever it was and Camilla from Paris, was that.

This time it was.

I HAD BEEN at Tucker for what seemed forever, and when Diego and I got back, I ran all over the house, maybe to make sure it was empty, so I could suffer. There had been changes. First I saw that Nana's rooms, closed since she died, had been reopened and freshly painted and made into extra guest rooms for weekends when Theron gave a bash or Camilla had some of the staff of Haute to stay while they worked on a project for some future issue. There was a smell of plaster. At first I couldn't believe it when I opened the doors to what had been the old man's library. But there it was—or was not. Gone. All different. Not a shelf or book or record remained. I broke into tears.

"Why?" I asked, "why did they do it?"

Diego answered. "Your old man, he do it so he have a place to keep his toys."

I had almost forgotten Theron's toys. Nut stuff that proved what a nut he was. Big mechanical dolls is what they were, which he'd collected for years and kept at the apartment in town or in the shop because they were so large. Now here they all stood. The life-sized monkey in a red braided suit and pillbox hat. When you turned the crank on the side of the box on which he sat, there was first a rattle, like a kazoo, and then the monkey raised his hat and put a cigarette in his mouth and from it came a puff of dust that was supposed to be smoke. There was the ballerina on toe turning this way and that, kicking one leg in the air, the swordsman circling his blade and lunging forward and back. And music boxes played inside each of them, slowing as the gears ran down. Fun the first time, almost like kid magic, then dead end. What the rattle made me think of was the sound Nana made before she died. It was another death.

Winter came early. Days began with Diego waking me and saying, "Yes, sir, Mr. Philip, rise and shine. Got a nice breakfast waiting for you downstairs." He had perfected his Gone With the Wind manner, waiting on me at the dining table, always with a winking in his eye that said it was all fake, a joke. The house was spooky, nobody to listen to. Sometimes I'd help Diego work on one of the cars, and as a reward he'd give me lessons so I could get my junior license to drive when spring came. Other times I sat with Schaafy in the kitchen, watching her soaps.

They were weird. Everybody seemed to have been married to everybody else at sometime. There were lots of children who didn't belong to their real mothers and fathers but had been adopted by other people. People would start to say something, and then when it became interesting, they'd fade it, and another set of people would begin talking about something else, and that faded too. Most of the characters had brain tumors or car accidents and were in hospitals. I watched because the girls had this great hair, usually blonde, and they tossed it around so much you could almost smell the hair spray. They had great tits in the long shots, but when the camera moved closer it was all these big faces asking, "Are you all right?" or "Do you want to talk about it?" There was always one scene with a guy and girl in bed, but though the guy had taken it off down to his jock, the girl was always covered. I'd managed to feel a few tits, but seeing them swinging was something else I was going to have to wait for. I got tired of that, and the rest of it that winter. I felt like one of Theron's toys waiting to be cranked. The hardest part was finding things to read, now that the old man's library was no more. The only books in the house were French memoirs prettily bound and jammed into the antique bookcases. Furniture. And the servant girl romances Camilla read. Which left the playgirls in Playboy and the playboys in Playgirl.

My mechanism wasn't working. What they all wanted was the dead me. Son but no son. The O. W. M. were getting desperate. One weekend Mr. Browne paid me a visit. He had a driver-nurse because he had had some kind of stroke. He'd brought his whole bag of tricks, and it was plenty heavy. Life's goals. . . . "Time, my boy, doesn't allow us to go back, only forward. . . ." He had no doubt I'd soon come to terms with myself. He sat with one hand stretched out on a table. The hand looked like a silk stocking full of nightcrawlers and twitched. I'll just put it down the way it comes back to me. No notes, no tape. A takeoff into memory.

"You are young, Philip. I was young once. But I was less fortunate than you. I had to save during my working life, so that at sixty-five I could retire with sufficient capital. Now, you were endowed by your grandfather and have the satisfaction of knowing that, ah, when the Will's stipulations have been met and the funds distributed, your mother and father will be compensated. Which is as it should be."

I kept my eyes on the nightcrawlers.

"You don't say anything, Philip."

"What do you want me to say?"

"That you will make the effort to do what your grandfather wished. It is, I'd say, just not too late. One must earn life, Philip."

"But if there's all this bread, why should I do anything but what I want?"

"What is it you want?"

"I guess to be me."

"I find your calling it bread distressing. Well, enough for now."

Shit like that. And there was lots more. When he left and his driver-nurse was tucking him into the car, he said, "Philip, do both of us a favor. Get yourself a haircut. Meet you halfway." Between his wormy fingers he stretched out to me two dollar bills. I took them to be polite. As he drove off I formed two words I didn't speak.

Fuck you. And then shouted, "Old man!"

IT must have been a holiday or a long weekend. I realized when Doc breezed in today that I've been putting it down faster than usual. Now he's back, and it's a new week. We went over Tucker and the long depression I had after the old man's library was thrown out, and Doc made a little private joke.

"And then what, Phil?"

One of my kiddie lines, And then what.

Then was when I first got it. As Diego said, off them.

I'll have to write it with my fly open, I can't write it like it was a sunset or roses in Theron's garden. I knew it was there, I couldn't guess what it would be like when I got it, but it was the greatest.

Her name was Marjorie, and part of any day then was following her around as she did the rooms, finding excuses to watch her. She was always ahead, I'd be trailing her up the front stairs, and she'd be going down the back ones to the kitchen. I worked at it. Talked to her as she worked, telling her how beautiful she was. Her skin had a dusty cinnamon sheen that made her different from the other girls Diego hired and fired. I learned from her never to give up, and you'll win. One day she was sitting on a chair in the hall where the linen closet was, holding a stack of sheets and pillowcases, resting from going up and down those stairs so often. I caught up with her. She smiled. I put my hand against her cheek and told her what a beautiful color she was, that I was crazy about her skin. That seemed to turn her on, I guess she was tired of Diego calling her nigger and Schaafy treating her as though she was underfoot. She'd had that.

"Boy, you really wantin' it," she said. "Boy your age supposed to be in school. Why you not in school?"

I didn't answer.

"Go long now," she said.

There wasn't anybody around, and I followed her into the linen closet. The light was on. I could see the back of her knees as she lifted the linens. I put my hand up her thigh and at last felt where I wanted to go. She stopped dead. She was leaning back against a pile of something, and when I closed the door she didn't say anything. It was then she touched me back, and I knew she'd play. I unbuttoned her uniform and found her tits, and that turned her on more. She was giggling, feeling me up, pulling at my zipper. I helped her with that and flashed.

She said, "My my, we real hotted up and ready. Well, go ahead, Boy, but don't take long."

I had what I'd waited for, the first parting of flesh and the slide all the way up. She helped me. It must have been a joke to her, because I shot my load right away and lay there against her, panting. I thought I was great, I had found it, got into that thing that was so secret, and I had known what to do without being told.

She hugged me. "You a big comeon," she said. "You don't know anything about girls. Get off now."

I got off and she moved away. "Boy, you got to promise me one thing, this is our secret. You don't tell Diego, not anybody. You promise me."

I promised. I could tell she'd let me at it again, and now that I knew I could find it without looking, I was set. She really was a nice one, she taught me how to wait and hold it for her and let go when she was ready. Until it was a real fuck. It didn't mean a thing to her, though I started getting dreamy about it, and when Camilla came back she fired Marjorie right away. The excuse was that she didn't like the way Marjorie used an iron. I was moony and sad and made a big point of saying goodby.

"You all right, Boy," she said, then laughed. "When you grow up you'll be better." Then she whispered, "But not so fast, you find out girls like it slow."

After she had gone, Diego told me he had rigged it for me. "And don't you forget it," he said. "Maybe sometime I want to go in somewhere and you fix it for me. Right, man?"

"Right, man," I said.

SLOW to get writing today. Doc's just left. He had an emergency and came late. He'd read the Fuck you old man bit and asked how old I thought Mr. Browne was.

"I don't know. Eighty?"

"And how old was Theron? Then."

"The year I was booted out of my last private school—I think he was forty-six."

"And Camilla?"

98

"They both lied about their ages. Camilla dreaded fifty."

"You've told me a good deal about Theron," Doc said. "How about Camilla?"

Actually, I've been remembering her a lot as I've been putting it all down. I think it was because she hated being touched that she never touched me. In my Nana-kiddie days, when I grabbed on to her she stiffened and waited and called out, "Amy?" And Nana pulled me away.

One of my first memories is of Diego knocking on her door and carrying in her breakfast after she'd unlocked. She never came down to breakfast. Many days she simply didn't come down but stayed in her rooms and worked on the next issue of Haute. Schaafy and Diego killed themselves getting things the way she wanted them, her trays, her messages transcribed from her pad listing things to be done. And when she came out dressed for the city, or just for Sunday brunch, she did look like those perfume ad beauties on TV with the great eyes and moony nails and everything floating and moving just right. I figured she had to, it was part of her job of being editor of Haute.

She hadn't always been like that. There was an old tin trunk in the attic, beyond Nana's, and I had gone through it. There were snapshots taken in Montana when she was a girl, standing between two people I knew were my other set of grandparents. Dead. Everything in the pictures looked like the part of Groverhampton that Renzo's family lived in. But though Camilla's hair was darker, her eyes were the same, glittering and sharp. Later pictures taken in New York with her first husband showed her wearing a hat, which she never did anymore. Her eyes looked out of the picture as though she knew what was going to happen to him, as though life had dealt her a hand without even a Jack or 10. But the eyes said, It's going to be a full house if it kills me. I get back a couple of things Nana and Ummie said about her too.

"I've got to hand it to her, Amy, Camilla really has worked on herself. But she had it from the beginning, don't you think?"

"If she hadn't had it, she wouldn't be Mrs. Theron Hanway, Junior" —the kind of line Nana couldn't get through without coughing.

"Or Camilla Carstairs Connolly."

"She's tough as catgut."

"Oh, I've always known that."

I was never sure what Diego really thought. Out front, Ummie was fond of saying she'd never seen the like, the way he watched Camilla's every mood, like a willing slave. I get back something else, a snatch I heard through the hot air register. One of the black girls—it may have been Rose—had brought Camilla's breakfast tray into the pantry, and Diego was checking it.

"This wrong," Diego said. "You got to get this white folks camp right. De silver vase go here wid de single rose. De cup here. De pot wid de hot water Mistress drink go here."

I was used to his funning talk, so was Rose. They had a patter that went on all the time. Rose played back. "And Mistress drink de hot water till she do."

"No, no," Diego said, "Mistress don't do in de morning, morning time too valuable."

"When she do?"

"At night."

"Hush yo ass, man," Rose said. "You not supposed to talk about Miss Dainty like dat and take her money too. I bet she shit in de morning like everybody else."

"Maybe she don't shit at all," Diego said, "or if she do, it like macaroons, she dat dainty like you say. . . ."

I remember Schaafy's voice breaking through. "Stop this, you two! I hear you, and what kind of talk is that? I won't have it in my kitchen! I've a mind to report you to Mrs. Hanway."

"Or you could report it to Hitler," Diego sassed back. He knew how to handle Schaafy.

To TELL the truth, I forget where I leave off one day and am supposed to begin the next. No wonder, so much time between, stretched like a rubber band, then snapping back. And no space for time to be in. But that's being what Doc doesn't want me to be, deep. "I'll do the interpreting, Phil, just you write."

He says I start writing about Camilla and then get onto something else, and it's a block. Bloc? It must be that I don't want to think about her. But to get it over with—Camilla.

I don't know why, but remembering her in those years she's always walking forward, like a candid shot in Haute, all fixed up, more highlight than shadow. She had a way of moving and sitting down and getting up that wasn't like anybody else. And you could tell if she was in a room, even if she wasn't saying anything. She had presence, Ummie said. Always on, Theron said.

Even weekends when there was nobody to be on for, when there were only Theron and Ummie and Uncle Bill and Uncle Coo, who were old shoes, family, she was on. Uncle Bill was her right-hand man at Haute, she said without him no issue of the mag would have gone to the printer on time. Uncle Coo worked for Theron, took over the responsibilities of the shop when he was away on the big decorating jobs. That made it a tight clutch.

I wasn't doing as much listening and checking as I once did, because, let's face it, I wasn't a kid anymore, and when you know the kind of stuff I knew, you grow up fast. But after my bootout from Tucker, I was usually hanging around weekends, playing it dead in the big sofa by the fireplace in the room where they played cards. I was grounded, and the way they were handling it then was to wait and see what I did next. It was my move, and I wasn't moving.

Camilla often brought her work home with her, and the makeready of the next issue of Haute would be lying around, and between hands they'd talk about it.

"Well, what's the theme this month, Camilla?" Ummie would ask.

"Everything's Brown."

"You've got to be careful with a color like that," Coo would crack, giggling. "There are so many shades of it."

Ummie, who could see it coming, interrupted—"Now, please don't start using that word—"

"Isn't that what it all is, Ummie?" Theron would tease.

Everybody knew the word. I'd probably looked at the makeready, which had pages of gorgeous brown chicks raunching around Paris, or standing against some landmark with their legs apart, looking insolent. A full back spread of the fag designer who'd invented The Brown Idea, stripped to his belt and wearing a brown diamond on a chain. Brown hats, dresses, handbags, shoes. Everything Brown.

Camilla was always the last to make it downstairs. She'd call out from the upstairs hall as she walked, apologizing for keeping everybody waiting. Working the staircase, Theron called it. And the others would make a big scene about what she was wearing.

"Darling, you look perfectly marvelous!"

"Whose is it?"

"Oscar did it just for me."

"Fab. Divine, dear."

"Shall we play?"—This would be Ummie.

"How's about a drink?" Bill would ask. He was usually bartender.

"All right," Camilla would answer, as though she didn't really want it, was doing him a favor. "A small one."

"But keep them coming, Bill," Theron would kid.

"Stop it, you two, and let's play." Ummie again.

It comes by the yard. Like Muzak. Camilla and others. Camilla and herself.

"After her, you come first," Uncle Coo said of her.

Once Camilla was on TV, giving an interview, it was a tape of course, and we all sat around, watching it together. Camilla did all her set lines—"There is no longer an age thing for women—A woman's best years are always ahead of her—The second part of a woman's life can be better than the first." She was asked how she managed always to look the way she did, and she admitted she worked on it, massage, exercise, rest.

"A little drink now and then, Miss Connolly?"

"Well . . . an occasional glass of champagne. . . ."

Theron broke up at this, because the first thing Camilla told Diego to do when she came home was to make her a pitcher of martinis. She didn't care about the chilled crystal glass or the zest of the lemon, she just drank what was in the pitcher. And, come to think of it, it took a regiment of those people who do hair and wax baths to keep her looking so great. I remember once there was an inch the masseuse couldn't get off, and Camilla set her jaw. She went off to work with a hard-boiled egg in her purse and made it on black coffee all day long. Her pitcher of martinis, natch—the joke on that was that gin unclogged the arteries. What she didn't eat that Schaafy went to so much trouble over would fill a book. Anyway, the inch came off.

Maybe Camilla comes off best in one-liners.

"Darling, not now."

"Ask me another time."

"Theron, please."

"Bill, take over. Please?"

And there was her pad. Pads. They were all over the house, with pencils attached. Everything I ever needed was scratched onto one of her pads. Her letters when I was away at schools were perfect, exactly what my grandfather would have wanted. "I have ordered six white oxford shirts for you from Brooks. . . . Theron says make do on the pants till you get back and can be measured, something about outside seams and the rise. . . ." And the miserable allowance checks enclosed. For a long time, I borrowed from other boys, but that was no good, there was always the paying back—

Doc is right, I get onto something else. I don't want to put down much about her. With other people, yes. Maybe.

I ASKED DOC if I'd unblocked enough about Camilla. He gave me one of his sideway looks, like I was making a bad joke. Shrinks can't stand for you to use one of their words. Right away he said it could be put more simply, to remind me that he gets stuff out of what I put down for him I don't know is there. Maybe so. I had a teacher in Eng Comp once who said always remember how much the reader of anything supplies for himself. Anyway, Doc said not to worry about anything except going on writing. So maybe I unblocked a little.

Something came back to me today I'd forgotten about. When I come back from my jog, Malc takes away my shoes because they have laces, and after the shower hands me clean socks and T-shirt. I'd noticed these always seem new but never thought about it, except that they were like in the army GI issue. They're so fucking hipped about everything being clean, my not having anything that's mine.

"What's it?" Malc asked. He notices everything.

"Why are the gym socks and T-shirt always new?"

"Man," he answered, "I told you over and over, you're special. Rich boy. You rates."

"Oh. I thought maybe you'd just washed them for me," I kidded.

"I got to do a lot of funny things on this job, but washing out your socks and shirt's not one of them. You mean you don't know who bring them?"

I shook my head, looking innocent. I learn more from him that way.

"Why, those old ladies you don't go down to see," he said. And went into it. "They're trying to help you, maybe get you off, or off easy. They talk to Doc, the lawyers too."

That's when it came back. It happened a few days after I was brought here. Before I'd learned the ropes. A guard came in and said he was going to take me down to the visitors' room. I hoped it was Renzo come to see me, so I went along.

Right away I saw through the thick glass they have to separate you from outside who it was. At first I thought they might be a hangover from narc, but there they were, Aunt Edie and Aunt Lydia, looking the same as I remembered them from when Nana died. All fringy and lacy, but not in black. Dressed fit to kill, Nana would have said, and Aunt Lydia was wearing a chinchilla stole that had been Camilla's.

They started talking at me through the grill. "Poor boy,

how terrible it had to happen. Nothing like it had ever happened in the Tenys or Hanway families, it must have to do with bad blood on Camilla's side." They'd come up to tell me that they loved me and that I could count on them for anything they could do. Not that they could do much. How did I like Doctor Worozinowski—some such name—who I figured is Doc. When I had paid my debt to society, I would come to them for rehabilitation—they had moved the family things down to the Tidewater farm, so I would have my heritage. Like that, for the whole visiting time, and they stayed every minute of it.

It was a real sweat. I looked at them and didn't say anything. After a while I could see they were nervous and glad for the thick glass and the grill. This made them talk louder, as though I'm deaf. On and on. I mustn't lose hope. All I wanted was for it to be over, and I made up my mind I'd never go through it again. I was dying to ask them if they'd packed the Tenys silver safely and if they'd at last gotten Nana's old dresses, but I didn't.

The funny thing was, they kept coming back to see me. But I'd found out that even if you are twice a murderer, you don't have to see old bats who come to see you in your cage. I never went down again. What I wanted was for Renzo to come. But he never has.

So that's where my fresh gym socks and T-shirts come from, my cigarettes too, I guess, and all the food. If only they'd send me in a few dime bags of Panama Red I'd like that better, because then I could get at lots of the stuff Doc is dying to know.

Well, Doc—how's about it?

WHEN I slip out of writing about me and make a crack at Doc it upsets the talking, writing, talking more. Today he asked if I really thought he'd give me maryjane. I know he could, because he has an office in the building, and once when I was down there bombed from narc, I saw on his wall a license to dispense coca leaves and marijuana. I told him I remembered this.

"I doubt cannabis would open any doors you can't open by yourself," he said in the stiff way he has whenever drugs are mentioned.

"You're wrong," I said. "You shoot me up with all other kinds of shit, maybe a nice joint or two would bring great dreams."

"Dreams are not what we are interested in," he said, getting rid of it.

But he picked it up as a cue. How much did I smoke? I've been expecting him to get onto that, on my being dusted out that night. Not so fast, I thought, that's yet to come, really. The shit I got together with Renzo was almost kid stuff, in the beginning. There'd been the nutmeg with Rudi Schaaf. Everybody chewed morning glory seeds at St. Andrew's. And there was so much jive about pot that by the time I'd been Tuckered out I'd had my share of joints. And I'd been known to help myself to Camilla's up-the-ass barbiturates she brought back from Paris, they could really dream you up to yourself if you put them up and then stayed awake.

Well, WOW, as they used to say that summer I lived on after Tucker. You do live on. I knew there were evil stars watching me. I had learned to listen in a new way, to what was between words, as well as the words themselves. I was picking up all kinds of stuff about the people Camilla and Theron had out for the weekends and party bashes. Pot's a smell hard to get rid of, in fact you can't get rid of it. More than one of the Beautiful People doped, and when the word coke was used it didn't mean Coca Cola. But I don't think Camilla and Theron did more than drink, they had to be too careful about what the Old Wise Men might think. The O. W. M. drank themselves. Old Mr. Browne on brandy was even more of a cube than when sober. Mr. Stanhope had a nose like a strawberry going bad. And Mr. Homer was hung on wine and used to bring his own along to lunch. When

Diego opened it everybody said they could smell violets, but it always seemed plain old vinegar to me.

Everybody drank. Camilla kept them small and kept them coming, as Theron said. He had a funny way of screwing up his face as though he hated the stuff, but came back for more. Uncle Bill and Uncle Coo were, as Ummie said, just plain American drunkards. She nursed her sherries-on-the-rocks. Even what Camilla was beginning to call staff drank—she was getting so upstage now she was upstaging herself—except for Schaafy. When Schaafy came back Mondays and saw the bottles Diego was putting out for garbage collection she threw up her hands and said, "Ach, du Lieber!" I don't think she'd have stayed with us if she hadn't had her Sundays off. But Camilla and Theron seemed happy with the arrangement. They had caterers from Southampton when it was a big show, and if it wasn't the batching of the family weekends—Camilla called it that—they all went out to a restaurant.

That was how I found out about Chez Florence in Groverhampton. One Sunday night it was late and everybody was smashed, and they decided to go out, but everything was closed except Florence's. I was just between being left behind and being taken along. By this time I was officially allowed beer. Big deal. You'd be surprised how smashed you can get on a six pack. But I was allowed to have wine that night along with them. Florence, when she saw how much money the table was spending, came over to the table. She only did this for people she thought were somebody, and I could tell she knew who Camilla was. And as she talked, she noticed me. Her eyes were like bright slits as she looked straight into mine. She got it, like that, and it was a synch. Later that summer, when at last I began to break away and had to have somewhere to go to keep from going nuts, it was to Chez Florence I went.

Quite a lot happened that summer. I got my junior license to drive, with parental approval, limited to daytime hours. It was the summer following my being alone in the house with only Schaafy and Diego and the black girl. When

I was beginning to figure it out in terms of myself, as they say. I was still dumb, just letting myself go, writing the stuff I wrote and stuffing it between rafters, roof slates, anywhere. A little romance of misery and desperation that could have been titled Hard Times, because its hero thought about sex all the time and was almost never far from a full hard. I had plenty of time to think about my whole lousy life. And Camilla's and Theron's. Because I had tumbled at last to the fact that I would always be a prisoner of myself and them. A prisoner too weak to leave, although the door was open, like here it's triple-bolted. But they were prisoners too. Of me. Of the O. W. M. and the Trust and just plain dogging it out, until the old boys decided that Philip Theron Hanway truly existed and my grandfather's kooky Will was fulfilled. And they were just as much prisoners of each other as I was of myself. I know Schaafy worried about me, that I wasn't eating enough of the great food she made, and Diego acted like I was some helpless nerd who had to be kept track of so I wouldn't do something crazy. Both couldn't help trying to be parents to me, but it was no good. I was still having fantasies about being maybe an adopted child and hoping that one day a big limousine would sweep up to the house with my true parents in it and that they would be the perfect escape. Into love. Because being without love is like missing a faculty. Like seeing with tunnel vision maybe, or hearing only sounds that are far away.

But I was seeing straight, and listening. I guess in my fumbling way I was trying to rip myself off from the history that accounted for my existence. I was, to take a word from the Will, the issue of a transaction to inherit money. I was a Ha Ha in the face of fate. I'd learned in my way not to monkey with fate. Nana and Camilla and Theron had monkeyed with it, and look what happened. Me.

All I ever wanted was to be me, and I was beginning to be. And another thing, I was always glad it's now. I think what I finally did was inevitable, regrettable as they all say, but not to me. I am the guy without regrets. I'd fought all my life for the right to be myself, to do nothing except what I wanted, not to give a fuck about what anyone thought. Most of the time I never wanted to do anything at all, and what I did I was either made to do or went along with because it was easier than going against people who wanted me to do it. They all had their plans for me, and I tried and did say shit to them, but there was really no way to get away and do nothing.

I think I'd have made a great jungle child, dropped in the woods somewhere, with wolves, maybe. I'd have been okay. I'd have made it the way I wanted to. I wonder whether wolves would have tried to tell me what to do and beat on me like Camilla and Theron, until at last I did what I did to be free from them. Even here it's no more a prison than Lilacs was, or my time as a P.O.W. in Nam. Maybe I am crazy, perverse, as one of the school letters said. But that crazy summer I began to like the way I was. Me.

And there's the secret me that kept me going through everything. And still does. And it's going to stay secret. I don't think they can get at it. If Doc's so great, let him guess at it, figure it out for himself. I wasn't always so secret—until the cats. I think that was when I began to close the door. It'll never open, not wide. Not under the needles and narc. It's happened that some nights I dream of that last cat, and I know that's the beginning of my secret life. Deciding I wouldn't put down anything I wanted to be or do. Okay, I was theirs, belonged to them. I was even hung up on them. But I learned how to get away and come back and did. Hundreds of times. From the schools to Nam. They had me right up to that last night when I put them on the bed and left for good. I'm free from them at last. It's freedom with a padlock, but still better than being theirs. Doing them as I did was the top of my life. In a way, when I think myself over, I'm an extraordinary guy. If, as Doc sometimes says, I'm a split personality, okay. The two ends met. Then.

BEFORE they take away the ballpoint at night, I now write a word on my wrist, to remind me where I stopped and where to pick up. It doesn't mean it will come out exactly in order, but it helps.

Me as I was finding myself. Then, the old otrafwa they all talked about. As it had been. When things were better. I'd learned to bleep out most of this stuff, but can't forget some-one named Elsie they went over and over. She had been the world's first interior decorator and had lived to be almost a hundred. Ummie had actually known her. And when Bill and Coo would get on to how old she had been, I'd go into my private TM until they changed the subject. To more now, as Ummie would have put it. Quittax. Quittax.

It was one of those great June days, and the fireplace opposite the sofa where I stretched out and listened was banked with ferns. I always made sure no one saw me come in. It was a very quiet day, too, without Schaafy of course, because it was a Sunday, and Diego had gone to see his sister who was sick. Schaafy had left a shepherd's pie to put in the oven and a salad ready to be tossed. This meant I would eat with them as they batched it at the dining table, part of their way of keeping track of me.

There were three kinds of conversation those bridge weekends. Talk when all five were together—gossip with Camilla and Bill about the mag, what Theron had bought at Parke Bernet for the shop, Ummie on the past and Coo camping it up and giving cues. If either Camilla or Theron went out of the room, the talk changed. If they both left, there was first a silence, to make sure they were out of earshot, and then what was said could be really wild.

That day Camilla had gone out to the kitchen to put the pie in the oven, and Theron said he had to call a client and went upstairs to use his private phone. The silence fell.

Then Ummie asked, "Where's the miracle child?"

"I don't know. Up in his own room, probably."

"He's very fond of his own company."

"Wouldn't you be?"—There was a bitchy edge to this.

"But have you noticed how he's grown up?"

"Yes, and exactly what the doctor ordered, spitting image of Theron."

"And with Camilla's eyes," Ummie added, and was I ever sick of hearing that. "Do make us another drink, Bill."

I could hear Bill pouring and stirring. "Maybe Philip's a spit baby," he said.

"Now, now," Coo put in, "Don't be dirty mans."

"You're both horrid," Ummie told them.

Another silence as they sipped.

"I suppose it was a doctor," Bill said. "It had to be insemination."

"He's a real tube rose," said Coo. "Another year and he'll be exactly my thing."

"Now who's dirty mans?" Bill asked. "Well, they've got a great act going. If they can keep it up. Camilla keeps it up, I know, because I'm with her day in and day out."

"Mmm—?" Ummie made sounds like that when she was going to tear somebody's story down.

"And I think Theron does pretty well too," Coo said. "Remember, I'm with him at the shop, times he's not away."

"Or at the Ever Hard Baths," Bill said.

"Yes, but the curtain's always down on what really goes on."

"Except when it sometimes flies up with a flap," said Ummie.

"But they really did pull it off," Coo said.

Bill laughed. "Ummie, darling, why don't you take out some of those hairpins. Let's bitch. I know you know things we don't."

I could tell Ummie was feeling her sherries. "Well, there was no doctor involved, I can tell you that much. That was out of the question, Amy would never have had it that way."

"How do you know?"

"Camilla once told me all about it."

"Tell us!"

"If I do, you'll both have to promise to keep it graveyard."

"Oh, we promise," Bill and Coo said.

Ummie made them wait for it. Then, "Camilla says they both really did try. Getting smashed. Acid. That mushroom thing that's supposed to turn you on. Not that Amy suspected, you know how she was, wife and husband, sex follows. Camilla wasn't getting any younger, and they had to have him so the checks would start coming. Amy practically turned down the sheets of the marriage bed and put Theron on top."

"Not that that would have worked," Bill said. "Theron simply never could get it up for girls. He's told me himself how his old man used to take him all primed with Spanish fly to this whorehouse in Paris—"

"The one opposite the Bibliothèque?"—Coo interrupting.

"Is this my story or yours?" Bill asked.

"Let Bill tell it, Coo."

This time it was Bill who made them wait. He said, "It simply wouldn't work. Every time Theron saw what he'd have to put it into he threw up."

"How disgusting!" said Ummie.

"Theron still says rather the world's ugliest man than the most beautiful woman," Coo added. "So go on, Ummie."

"I will if you fags will shut up. There's nothing to it. All it takes is a simple kitchen syringe, the kind you use to take fat off the gravy."

"Really?" Bill started to laugh. "Oh, my God!"

Coo was in stitches. "Help! Stop me, somebody, I'm going to have the vapors. Ummie, it's too marvelous."

"I've only told you what Camilla told me," Ummie said, adding that only that week she'd read an article under the dryer about women doing that very thing. "So you see, dears," she said, "we girls can make it without you. Camilla was ahead of her time."

"But that makes Theron a syringe daddy," Bill said, and Ummie started laughing with them. They couldn't stop, even when Camilla came back to the table.

"What on earth's so funny?" she asked them.

"Just one of Coo's awful jokes," Ummie said. "Your deal, Camilla."

Theron came back too. "Now where are we?" he asked.

"You and I are vul," said Ummie, cool. "Bid, Camilla."

Right through the sound of Quittax I can still remember

that bidding. "Two spades . . . Pass . . . Three no trump . . . Pass . . . Four no trump . . . Pass . . . Five hearts . . . Pass . . . Six no trump . . . Double . . . Redouble. Camilla made it hands down. That was the end of the rubber, and we all had lunch. I was hungry and ate all that was left of Schaafy's pie. Right afterward, I went outside and vomited it all up onto the lawn.

I DIDN'T need a word on my wrist to remember what I wrote yesterday. I got it pretty much right, I think, because some days in life don't cloud over but are filed as bright as they happened and can be taken out and remembered almost as if they were in a folder.

The vomit on the lawn. I can still see it, part of life that had been bolted and wouldn't stay down to be digested. I wasn't a fool, I knew it wasn't just food, it was all that stuff I'd been fed as a coverup. What I'd heard turned me inside out like a glove. But even so I was still trying not to believe what the truth was, and I was clenched in a battle with myself because that kind of truth hasn't any way of getting out.

I knew that what I'd heard would paralyze me. I'd never be able to be like others. I wouldn't give a shit about the past, their when, or the future, making it, adding to that big golden loaf. How could I? I'd heard jokes about some kids not being right because they had been strained through a silk handkerchief. I wasn't even that, not even a tube rose. Just a syringe baby with a syringe daddy.

I did whatever the next thing was—went out to the greenhouse to rinse my mouth under the tap there—and saw a devil's face staring up at me from the bottom of the sink. I knew it was petals of red peonies that had withered and the image only lasted a second, but as it came through to me it was all the magic I'd tried and failed to make work. There was a devil—he was that vomit on the lawn, too. And I was different from what I'd been up to then. The heart can be torn out of a kid if you have the right hook, and they had it.

Remember, it was the same heart I'd tried to love them with. I was ripped open, wide open, needing to melt into somebody, girl or guy, whichever came first didn't matter.

I don't know how their day ended, only mine. I remember darkness. I was still obeying the rule not to drive after sundown, and I gave them a wide berth as I walked down to the lane and through the gates toward Groverhampton. It's not far. There was a Sunday night dimness lying on both sides of the tracks and the expressway. I found my way to Chez Florence and went inside.

I happened to go in by the bar side, where Florence always sat, all 300 pounds of her, behind a glass screen built around her table to keep off drafts and where she could keep an eye on what went on, and I soon found out that plenty did. There was another entrance to the restaurant on the next street, but regulars usually came in through the bar.

She remembered me. "Are you alone?" she asked.

I said I was.

"How old are you?"

"Old enough."

She waited, stacking me up. "Okay, just make sure to act your age."

I went over to the bar and ordered a beer and I could see Florence giving the bartender the nod. I knew there'd be no hassles. There was never more than so much light at Florence's, and it took me a minute to see that I wasn't the only customer. The next thing I knew was the bartender setting down a shot glass next to my beer and pouring it full of whisky. Then a voice beside me.

"That's a boilermaker."

"I know," I said.

The man was wearing a white safari suit and had a great tan and was old, fifty anyway, and his hair was white and slicked back. He had kept up and had great muscles, like Theron. He started talking and at first I listened, only answering when I had to. How old was I. Where did I go to school. Did my people live around here. And all at once I knew what I needed was to talk myself and began spilling out my guts, letting my troubles loose and he was crazy about it. You'd have thought he was some kind of priest the way he listened. It doesn't take many boilermakers to make you lose track of exactly how it went, but he had this really great car, and he rode me around in it. At first I thought we were just riding, but then I got it he was taking me to his house, which was on the beach to hell and gone. You could hear the surf breaking outside, and he lit a fire. I knew what was going on, he wanted a son, and I wanted a father to talk to when there weren't any women anywhere around. He was a daddy, but I couldn't tell how jammed he was. A real jam daddy usually can't wait to lay hands on, but this one just kept talking. I finally got it that he knew who Camilla was and Theron too, and after that all I wanted to do was get the hell out. It wasn't easy, he'd put some dreamy waltz on the record player, he'd unbuttoned his jacket, but after a while he got the idea. And when he did, he made a production out of getting me home safely, waiting until I'd gotten inside and made a light before driving away.

That was how I met my first jam daddy, and that meeting was connected with finding Renzo again after all those years between. When I'd perfected my getaways to Florence's, that is, when I got over hewing to the junior license rule of not driving at night, at least the nights Camilla and Theron weren't home and wouldn't know about it, my life took a turn for the better. It wouldn't ever be right, I knew that, but I could stand it, and some of my times with Renzo were tops, even great.

Doc says I've been in a fugue state. One more shrink word, I couldn't care less what it means. Maybe it means I can't stand more of what they're doing, trying to get at me, ripping me apart and then putting me back together to suit themselves. You'd think I was writing The Great American Novel the way he gobbles up what I put down and wants more of. I know a novel is supposed to have a central character. A beginning, middle, and end. Not that Doc would know about that. I wonder sometimes if he's ever read anything but shrink books. Now and then something comes up about books, novels everybody knows or knows about, The Red and the Black, War and Peace. Actually one day we were on war— I told him it was too soon, I didn't go to Nam until after this time about Renzo I'm trying to put down now. Doc said he'd tried reading War and Peace but got bored. He said he thought maybe he'd seen the movie, and I told him that's not the same thing. I read it, all of it, to keep from being bored. I think he'd just heard of The Red and the Black. What I figure he reads, if anything, is junk like The Psychiatric Quarterly or MD, which he carries with him sometimes.

I know people in glass houses shouldn't throw stones. I couldn't read much before I left for Nam, and haven't read a thing since I got back. I'd love to read now, but how can I? There's nothing. Outside the grill, just beyond Nursie, I can see magazines on a table, but they're never picked up or read. There's nothing here. No life. Not even old magazines around the corner get read. Sometimes I start looking around for a book as though there might be one here. And remember Schaafy, trying to find something she'd misplaced. "Oh, I am despaired," she'd say, angry. "Now where did I put it?" I'm not even angry. I've made a nut inventory of every object in sight, from bed and chair to the thick plastic cup I've thrown and tried to break so I could get a cutting edge.

It's like that. There's my now, the situation as Doc calls it. I walk my figure-8 and lie down and get up and sit and lie down again and try to come back from the dead. The only sound I can hear is that silence that screams. And I've been like this all day. I want to start yelling and never stop. I need a cunt to put it into and fuck nonstop until I shoot my balls and fall down dead. The days have no time because nothing moves. If I had a box of tacks I'd swallow them. If the door had a knob on this side I'd beat my head against it until it was a bloody nub.

———

I GUESS I asked for it. A cutup. You don't get far with any activity in this place before you get what's called attention. I got plenty. Bandages on the insides of both arms. They tried hypnosis again. It doesn't work, never will. They want the next chapter quick. Renzo. I haven't been saving him, he just didn't come back into my life until I started going to Florence's.

There he was, standing at the other end of the bar, across from the door marked DAMES, where he could check the cute asses coming out. It was instantaneous—he started walking toward me as I walked toward him.

"Hi!" he said. "Remember me? My old man used to work for your old man."

"I remember as though it was yesterday"—people say that, but I meant it, he was just as I remembered, only grown up. We shook hands.

"I thought by now you'd be on your way to Hah-vud, someplace like that," he said.

I let that go. It turned out he'd seen me that Sunday night I'd walked from the house.

"How long you been working the daddies?" he asked.

I hadn't been working anything and said so.

"Come on," he said, "you can tell me. I've worked a few myself when I need a tank of gas or can't afford a nickel bag. But you don't have problems like that. Your old man's loaded."

"But I'm not," I said. I told him I was almost flat, I was down to nursing a beer until I'd have to take off.

He was taking in the Brooksy button-down, the J. Press imitation of whatever.

"Guy like you shouldn't have any problems," he said. "Work it while you've got it, I say, before Social Security gets you. Hey, you smoke dope?"

"Where is it?"

"Let's do it."

We did. It was as quick as that. He had a beatup Chevvy, and all I had at night was legs, so we cruised around, talking. Blasting was a bond, if we'd needed one, which we didn't. It was as though the time between that day Diego and I drove into Groverhampton was yesterday. Like I said. He told me about his old man, shot, his old lady, working to keep his sister pure and sweet until they could marry her off at Mama Chiesa. I filled him in on Camilla and Theron. I could see he knew a lot.

"Yeah," he said. "I know."

"But don't tell me," I said.

He got it. "Okay, we leave it there."

And we did. When he took me home, he drew up at the gate, didn't drive in.

"You got wheels?" he asked me.

I told him I'd just gotten my junior license and could drive daytimes, adding that Theron let me have the Mercedes.

That impressed him. "Mercedes! Man, we can scud any kind of chick with that. How's about we meet again tomorrow? Same time and place?"

It was okay with me.

"Hey—bring your wheels this time."

There was nothing to it once I'd made my mind up to forget about the night driving restriction. Diego said he'd cover for me. I parked in front of Florence's, so I could keep an eye on the Mercedes. That was before all the hassles about my driving with Big and Little Smokey, the traffic fuzz.

But before I get to Renzo and all those headaches, I must tell what Florence's was like. Her place was in an ordinary Groverhampton side street. The walls were covered with photos showing her with famous movie stars she'd played bits with in old films that sometimes turned up on the late-late shows. She'd been a knockout then, but she looked like a frog now, sitting behind her glass shield, watching everything, shouting orders. If she was on one of her prowling nights, it usually meant the fuzz inspector had been in to warn her again that her facilities didn't meet community standards and she'd better fix them. She never did, because all the Groverhampton fuzz were on the take and greasing a few palms was easier than ripping out all that old plumbing and partitions in the wrong places.

Weekends were a real gas. The head bartender dressed like Spiderman, except for his face, and his nephew, who helped out, was pretty enough to be Batman's Robin. Florence's was one of the first places in the area to have strobes, and with the jukebox blaring and all the yelling between tables and jive at the bar, the place really jumped. A whiff of pot hung over everything, hardly enough to notice, but it was there. It was always a tight squeeze in and out, and Florence kept it that way. All kinds of people came, Groverhampton blue collars, Southampton and Easthampton getaways, dads working it, along with girls in their leather and boots, hookers, gays, weirdos, name it, sooner or later they showed up at Florence's. All sweating it out together, because the air conditioning was terrible. By ten o'clock any night there was hardly anybody not turning on, peaking, from wilting flower children to old hips in Charlie Manson T-shirts.

The TV was at Spiderman's end of the bar, where the gays hung out. It was always on but with the sound turned off. Everybody grooved on what the tube was dishing out, say like it would be Casablanca, over the juke you could hear voices filling in the dialogue, telling Sam to play it again. And Florence would shout from her table that that was all wrong, old Bogie never asked Sam to play it again, and there would be a big argument about it. The place as they said then had great static, really was far out.

I FOUND OUT that first night Renzo and I made it as a pair how right he was about the Mercedes. Even in the Hamptons it's not a car you'll see lined up in rows. While I kept an eye on it from the bar window I could see people stopping to look at it. Renzo had lined up a couple of chicks, and we all stood together for the softening up, and I could see they were looking at it too. The blonde of the pair seemed to dig me.

She wasn't the greatest, but that particular night I was so hard up I'd have screwed my old lady, as they say. We passed around a couple of joints and got into the mood, and that was when I knew I'd found in Renzo what I needed. He knew all the ropes. Where the stuff was. When to close in. Where to park so it wouldn't be obvious. Careless parking with two guys and matching chicks can lead to trouble with the fuzz, but Renzo knew this place out by the marina that was safe and secret. I balled my chick, and he balled his, and I could see it wasn't any kind of special thing, just sort of a breakin for me. He was a stud with plenty of ideas, days ahead of everybody on having it sensual and easy and not such a 3D production as my times with Marjorie in the linen closet and what I'd been able to rake up in the dead afternoons since.

Diego had left the fourth garage door open, and as I eased the Mercedes into place, I heard his voice from his bedroom overhead.

"You all right, boy?"

"Okay," I told him.

"You dip your wick?"

"Yeah."

"They didn't notice you go out. Go in quietly, hear?"

I was quiet. It crossed my mind how weird it was that it was Diego who had waited up for me while Camilla and Theron slept. Not that I gave a shit. Maybe it was part of the plan to give me a little more rope, to see what I would do with it.

Because don't think it was a summer I was let off anything. The O. W. M. were playing it cool, but I could tell they were worried. Not as worried as Camilla and Theron. This slackening of the rope was a policy arrived at after many hassles and sessions at 25 Wall. After all, the O. W. M. weren't exactly losing money on the Trust. They wanted to win for their client any way they could, fulfill the specifications in the Will and like suddenly, mysteriously, unveil What Your Grandfather Would Have Wished You To Be. His Grandson. I got it. I'd gotten it long ago.

It was going to be a loose plan, until they saw how it

went. I guess like cause and effect, maybe. Or Thank God it hasn't been worse than it was. Is. They weren't all bad, I gave them that, and before Camilla went off to Paris for the fall shows and Theron flew out to do a house in Santa Fe, there were solemn talks. Talk. "There's no going back . . . We must learn from what we have to learn from . . . Take it from there. . . ." As I listened, it struck me suddenly that they were all, if you think of it a certain way, strangers. I mean, if I'd been brought up by those wolves, they were all people I'd never have met or known, much less been saddled with as my old lady and old man. They really were getting scared. It might soon be too late for me to become anything, and they'd lose all the money. I can't say I blamed them, in a way it was natural for them to be the way they were. As I've said, if they hadn't met, there wouldn't be me. But I've been over that.

Homer, Stanhope, Brockhurst and Browne thought what I should do now was orient—their word—to another way of fulfilling old Gramp's wishes. Private schools, Mr. Homer said, were not a cloth to fit everybody. Maybe a public high school. He'd gone into it thoroughly and found out that Long Island schools were of the best, Groverhampton Hi among them. I should have no trouble matriculating at a very advanced level, despite my depressing record. My IQ was this, my Alice Heim test was that. To them it figured. I knew they were bending to the wind. So was I. My wind was Renzo. What I'm saying is, after Renzo and I made the big synch and I enrolled at Grover Hi in the fall, it wasn't anything that shook anybody up. In a way, it had looked as though that would be the way things would go early in the summer.

Well, naturally the two things fitted together. You could say me, the glove they'd turned inside out, and Renzo the hand I was fitted onto. Renzo who'd never had any problems except squeaking through classes while he marked time for the life his old man and lady wanted for him to begin. To hitch himself to some housing contractor, maybe, or take up welding. Or masonry. He had good hands, not at all made for stone work. If he admitted to anything odd about himself, it was that one of his legs was a half inch shorter than the other.

He wore what he called a cookie in one shoe, to make up the difference. His mother was always after him to get married, find the nice Italian girl waiting for him on the steps of Mama Chiesa. Buy that icebox and microwave and knock her up and start in on the mortgage payments. He didn't really want that. He hated the idea of growing up already. He wanted to be at the peak of being teen-end with a perpetual hard and kicks and the wheels everybody must have to rev it up and get into living life and away from the American Death.

COUNT on Doc to hang onto yesterday's scraps.

"What was that, Phil, about American Death?"

I had to think a second. Maybe I got a little heavy, I sometimes do, for no reason. Then I got it—what I think of as my Vietnam flash. Like a couple of frames from one film spliced into another. I'll be thinking roses and violets, and before I know it there's this plastic bag with somebody in it I knew, only all blasted and burned with a splintered wrist hanging out. Like that. On for a split second, then off, and the roses and violets come back.

"Doc, were you in Nam?" I asked him.

Of course he wasn't. And all that's for later, as we've agreed, in some kind of order. Right now it's Renzo he wants.

How do I begin? Blank page. Doc says write the first word and the next, and then you've got two words, and add a few more and it's a sentence. Right. I've been doing it that way. But I said to him if he really wants it straight on, I mean no ladies mag shit like I looked into her eyes and knew she was the one for me—forget it. If I start on how it really was, cock and cunt and checking asses those screens are going to tip and fall over and it'll be what the movies call Restricted and X-ratings too.

"Perfectly all right, Phil. We want you to tell what you have to tell. We're not trying to restrict you. If anyone's restricting, it's yourself."

"Like how?"

"Let go a little more on your mother and father."

This slows me, I have to translate from Camilla and Theron to mumsy dadsy to old man and old lady—too much. I tell him I don't want to write about them, I hated them. "Nevertheless, try, Phil. It'll be imperfect, everything is. But something always comes through."—He gives me one of his Greek History looks. "Ever been to Pompeii, Phil?"

"No."

"But you must have seen pictures of plaster casts made of people caught in the Vesuvius eruption?"

"So?"

"They illustrate what I mean," he said patiently. "Those figures were hollows in the lava, and when the plaster was poured in, it became the images of victims as they died. Only fill in the spaces. Follow, Phil?"

I follow. But the best I'll be able to do will be to be the lava, fill in around where they were. Though there'll be plaster too. All this thinking back is like looking through a window at myself. The time outside is now and the time inside is then, and there are bound to be bubbles of nothing between.

One thing that pissed me off was that Doc at first thought that Renzo was the other side of the bed for me, that I was a fruit who'd hung on the vine too long and had finally fallen off the closet shelf. Nothing could be further from the truth. It wasn't like that. As I've put down before, we never really touched, not intentionally, unless we were both on a chick, in a sandwich or like that. I mean, none of that good buddy shit, like on beer commercials. He was always straight line for cunt and the chase, and when we met after all that time it was like time had saved us for each other. Brothers in the sex Mafia, but no kissing, not even a brush of cheeks like Mafioso guys do.

I mean, like once we were taking a whiz, and he showed me a little dark spot on his cock where some chick had been a little rough during a blowjob. He asked me if I thought it was anything to worry about. "Wait a minute," he said, and got on a semi so the spot would show bigger. "What do you think?" It had been blowjob week, and I showed him where a

123

chick had gotten a little too loving with me too. It was a laugh situation, and we both got hards on as we talked about it. But nothing happened, it was almost like a couple of docs checking symptoms in a clinic. I wouldn't have touched him for any reason, except as I said, sometimes with chicks it happened.

We were a pair, as old Florence said, and though she was an old sack now and through, she still had appreciation for young guys. As two guys working it together, we were better looking than most, the light and the dark, you could put it. Renzo was well built, with eyes that were black as his hair. A little moody, the kind of Italian who might have stepped down from a painting. Not all his old man's boozing or the family poverty seemed to have had any effect—he had it, and he'd always had it. He'd been a choir boy and now was on leave from Mama Chiesa and cleaning up as a stud, and even after he'd have to give up—and maybe be a welder—he'd pass on to his kids that thing that made chicks go for him. He was wild, always turned on a little and hard up for it. Sometimes when we hooked up, late afternoons, nights, whenever, he was already high. We had the same goal—we thought getting off was the greatest thing in life, and it was worth anything to get it and get it as often as we could. Now and then we'd be drained out from the strain of it. Days in Groverhampton are as long as anywhere else, and there'd be one of those extra hours, and we'd park and sit in the Mercedes or his Chevvy and let time catch up with us. He had the trick of falling asleep and waking up as though what had knocked him out had never happened, ready for the next thing, which invariably was chick or something leading to it.

"How's your hammer hanging?" he'd ask. He was always ready.

And I'd say "Hanging heavy"—which I usually was—or, now and then "Hanging a little light," which can happen if you ball as a way of life.

Whatever I said, he always knew what the order for the night or day should be. I'd seen him in action, and I knew he knew whether we'd make No. 1 choice or a No. 2 make do.

There were times we had to do something in reverse, as he said, a dog or a daddy, so that later we could skim the cream we wanted. Economics in the world of doing as you pleased could be hell, when you had to cut corners to make it come out right.

GROVERHAMPTON Hi was nothing I couldn't handle with my eyes closed. A breeze. And at Lilacs things were a little more relaxed, they weren't beating on me so much, and we were all getting along better. The big golden magic egg was still there, though, getting bigger the more was sliced off it. And I was getting as little of it as ever. Schaafy looked a lot happier with what she considered her people, the family reunited, there for most meals. You could tell that the O. W. M. had said something to Camilla and Theron, they were making an effort to understand what I did and dig it. I went out to school from the house just like a real little son and heir, came back, went out again. Diego seemed to like the new arrangement too. I think neither Schaafy nor he knew exactly what the deal about me was. They had their different ways of thinking. Schaafy's was, These are moneyed people, we all have a responsibility to that boy because someday it will all be his. Diego's was different. He knew I never had enough money, but he played it like a valet lending it to the king— and I always paid him back, so my credit would be good the next time. He knew a lot about me, I sometimes think more than I knew about myself, but he wasn't going to tell it. Maybe he liked keeping secrets from Boss Theron, because he was keeping so many of Theron's secrets too. Not that I didn't know, as well as Camilla, what Theron's action was. I think the only one who never got it straight was Schaafy, who had a way of behaving toward Camilla and Theron as though they were on the brink of making love and she scuttled out fast to give them their privacy.

And so that fall Renzo and I got into a routine. Grover Hi was great for me, I'd never had the experience of guys and chicks milling in halls together and rapping. Renzo understood a slowness I had in cottoning on, helped me every step of the way. One of the first things he taught me was let them come to you. There's a technique on that, but you have to have macho to use it. He made me believe I had it. You pick the chick, do your softening up work, and then when she's tumbling, give the chill. Turn your back, start talking to some dog you couldn't care less about, and Chick No. 1 really turns on and digs you. You turn back then, and she comes on and practically unzips you. I didn't believe this till I tried it, and I used it a lot.

Florence's was where deals were really made—and between the wheels, either of the Mercedes or Renzo's beatup Chevvy. Because if you haven't got wheels—haven't I said it yet? Well, you just have to forget it. But we were spinning then. Some weeks it would be all one-shots, other weeks one of us would cultivate a little romantic hangup and go it alone. At the start, I'd have the idea of finding someone I could maybe love and who would love me, but it was never like that, not until the very end—and I'm going to shoot around that for now. I never intended to get mixed up in some of the stuff I did, the dads, the tearoom. But that's for later too. And after we'd played it separate, when the chick cooled, we'd get back together and in business without noticing we'd been apart. Renzo picked up little things from classes, like the proper study of man is man, only he switched it to the study of studs is chicks, and fuck anything proper about it. Anyway, chicks were what we studied.

HE took a brotherly interest in me, did all he could to help me get out of the bind I was in without making me go into details about it.

"Look," he said to me one day, "do you have to wear that square Mad Ave shit? What's with those pants? Papa hand-me-downs?"

No, I told him, Camilla always bought them for me.

"They've got to go. I mean, we're not going to be airing it at one of your folks' swanky clubs. Turn on a little. You've got it. Flaunt it."

Remember Flaunt It? It came and went, like Making the Scene and Hanging In and Hanging Out and all the others, but that's when it was. I'd had uniforms at Merry Hill, and St. Andrew's there'd been a dress code, but now the great denim period was under way. To begin with, most dudes who weren't cubes were leaving off the underwear and letting it hang, the same way chicks were burning the bra. You could see in the gym that guys still wearing shorts or briefs were exceptions, like girls still in skirts. Chicks were beginning to dress in ways that could give you messages back and front a half block away. It was the side-zip for them then, so you could make out the box, and above it the 1 or 2 unbuttoned blouse or sweaters with the orbs swinging free. Guys had found out the way chicks had that if you wanted to project you had to give an idea of what was below the neck instead of just letting them gaze into your big blue eyes.

I bought myself a couple of pairs of working jeans and had my first lesson from Renzo. It was a Thursday, Schaafy's day off in the week, so we went down to the laundry. We bleached them out, letting them roll in the machine with plenty of softener, and when they were just dry and soft enough we pulled them on and did the necessary. His advice was to hunker a while, until they got used to you, then stand and walk around in them until they got to know you, until they were your last skin layer and you looked as though you'd been dipped in wax. Then you packed cock and balls hard toward a pocket, zipped up tight and began the work of making them really yours. First was to get on a semi and sandpaper over the meat so that parts that should catch the light were lighter and the parts that folded under were darker. A white highlight over the bulb. "You've got to give them the idea," Renzo said, "and you can tangle eyelashes later. Don't think chicks don't notice. For every box-check we do they do their own sizing up. And it wouldn't hurt either to sand your butt area a little, to show you sit down sometimes." But no cigarette holes, like accidentally burned in, that was for gays who wanted quick action. It didn't hurt to have gays show you a little appreciation, though.

Actually, what turned on one chick who hung on to me at Florence's was the attention I'd get from gay guys. She'd heard me get specific propositions, and when I turned them down—nicely, I was always nice about that—it seemed to make her feel I was more hers. Once some swinger came up to me and this particular chick and suggested we ball together, and that turned her off hard. Until she came on again for me. She wanted all of any guy she was having it with. In fact, I dumped her because like so many of them they practically want to put you in a box and nail the lid down and eat you later.

I know the part about chicks watching crotches is true because once I was standing around the corner from a clutch of them and one said, "I don't see how he manages to sit down."

And another one said, "Let me at him, when I'm through he won't be able to stand up." They laughed.

Another voice said, "My old lady was with my old man when he was buying a suit the other day, and she told him a gentleman always dresses left, and that's how you tell a gentleman." Lots of laughs on that. They went on talking, like a bunch of gay size queens. Five inches is parlor size. Six inches is average, but seven is better. And even eight if you take it in slow. I mean, there they were, using all the words, cock and balls, hammer, meat, dong. Some guys were like meat and mashed potatoes, big in the balls and almost no meat, or the other way round. Some dressed left, and some dressed right. I mean, it was like what I sometimes heard through Theron's door, when he and Bill and Coo were going over the same stuff.

But I got off.

To go back—chicks didn't worry so much about your ass, but gays did, and because of the constant problem Renzo and I had about enough bread to operate on, the hard cash he had none of and I had to squeeze out of Theron or Diego, how we presented our asses to the world was important. Just part of the whole thing. As for tops, usually it was shirts with sleeves rolled high, and since we were both picnic, opened in a V to the waist. No belts, no buckles, we could both hold up our jeans without help. Renzo had some great pairs, one I remember had wooden buttons instead of a zip on the fly. I used to worry a little about him, sometimes it looked like everything he had was going to pop. But Florence always checked him on that. None of the chicks complained, though.

That's pretty much what we wore when we were working Florence's. It showed we were in the market, and some of the outfits we had were great shortcuts, and chicks could make up their minds in a hurry. But sometimes we got tired of her place and would just hang out on any of the Groverhampton corners where the ugly stuff looked over the beautiful stuff, which we knew we were. Hanging light with a blast now and then, feeling no weight, feet just touching. Checking chickass and listening to their tick-tock walk and their heels and giving the whistle or not giving it. Whiffing the kwiff as it passed us by, Renzo called it. A word from his old man's generation, like scud.

I GET so wrapped up in putting it down and hashing it over with Doc afterward that I can go for days without noticing something here's a little different. Malc's been off, and it's been old Woody/Whitey or the gorilla. Now Malc's back.

"Did you miss me?" he asked as openers.

"Lay off that shit."

He handed me my new socks and T-shirt. He said, "Your old ladies been here, talking to Doc. I hear him say to them they're beginning to find out why you were such a freaked-out kid. Why you did it."

Did it. I did it. Yes, I did it—but time's all so run together it's almost as if somebody else did it for me. Malc keeps right on, the way he does when he's trying to get at me.

"I hear you asked Doc for pot."

"You must be reading it."

"I don't read. It's in the air. Did you think he would? That shit smells so if they gave it to you they'd have to give it to everybody. There's shit that don't smell, though. You should know. You had to be into dealing."

I got his message. He's offering me acid. It would be a gas, what might happen, but probably no farther out than some of the shit they've got on those tapes when I was under whatever narc it was.

Renzo did a little dealing. He had to. So did I. What happened to my allowance when I got it I didn't talk about. It's a long way from the first of any month to the first of the next, a little like the way there were sometimes too many hours in a day. I bought my first nickel bag at Florence's, all by myself, so don't think it was Renzo steering me. Then, when I was flush, I bought six nickels' worth for my miserable pocket money and got some guys to buy it at $8 a grain. Those days, those prices. And so I got into dealing in a small way. I wasn't addicted to hash, just smoked with the others when I felt like it. If I'd ever had to concentrate, which I never did at Grover Hi, I'd have been a mess. I knew more than the teachers anyway. Acid's different—like you believed in what it could do for you and it did it. I began to get a new glim on Lilacs and Camilla and Theron and the O. W. M. and the power trip they were on with me. I was a microdot, getting it all into myself. Freaked, as Malc said. If they'd been straight—but they were more freaked on getting that gold and going around in the squirrel cage than any nomads who took off for Afghanistan.

It all figured in its different ways, I knew that. Like putting your foot into a shoe, everything falls into place. Long before I'd gotten the idea how hard it was to make it without help. Ummie, who shuttled back and forth to Paris, when she came back often said, "I don't know how you stand it, that horrible man in the White House down in Washington, that American corruption." Though she always came back to stand it until she couldn't stand it again, Uncle Bill said. Groverhampton was supposed to be a straight town. It was a source of pride to its residents that it was free of drugs. It was known and understood that everybody drank, the liquor stores could hardly keep in it, as Ummie said, nursing her sherries. "What do you do in America but stay pissy-assed drunk?" They all did.

But the fuzz knew. That was the beginning of the time you couldn't go out in America without getting mugged, even in towns like Groverhampton. Maybe before Nam the potheads could be counted and kept track of, but now it was a hangout if you knew where to go. Same as in Easthampton and Southampton. The fuzz knew Florence's was a hangout and that there was dealing there. Not just pot but acid and mesc and peyote and most of all Lady—cocaine. Florence's was known to have the best shit anywhere around, except maybe for one place in Southampton.

I guess I was pretty desperate to get into life when I met Renzo again that time at Florence's. I'd gotten fed up with thinking about myself, books, playing records, beating off— the whole stinking make do of the life of loneliness. I had this hunger for skin, flesh, I needed to be the other half of someone. I wanted to see strange faces and talk to people I'd never seen and wouldn't see again. To try to dilute that creeping death at Lilacs, where Diego kept the cars spit-ready to go and there were new young black girls to mix up the polish used on the quinze and quatorze—1/3 finest beeswax, 1/3 turpentine, 1/3 attar of roses. The house smell. I was turned on by something else—broad beans that grew wild behind the old greenhouse and that smelled like come. My come, my sperm. Being wasted. Going nowhere. I'd heard there are only so many orgasms in a stud's life, and I wanted all of them. Renzo said if you missed one or let it go it would never come back. It was like being thirsty and dying in the desert and gulping down water, swallowing, swallowing, never enough. Nobody can imagine what it's like unless it's happening to them. There's nothing else. I think that was when clocks finally slowed down for me, when I wasn't being rushed into corners I'd only have to get out of and be dragged back. What I'm trying to get out is how great it was while it lasted, and that the end of it when it came you couldn't have guessed. It was like that Vesuvius lava. It buried me.

WHATEVER day it is. I stopped writing anything because I got so browned off with Doc. He has this way of picking some detail of what I wrote the day before—usually something at the end—and harping on it. I'd put in the kind of wax Diego used on the furniture, Theron's recipe, and Doc had the nerve to say I shouldn't bother with anything that unimportant but stick to things that matter.

So I decided it was going to cost him. He could have picked on the broad beans, it was their smell that gave me wild ideas. So I let him dig. This has its bad points because he lays on heavy with what my interpretation is, when it's his job to figure that. Here I am in this fucking noplace with no TV or radio, not a word to read, not even the darkness normal at night for sleep, pinned down like a frog in Biology being taken apart, and I'm supposed to do his work?

Like did I every try to imitate my father, do things the way he did. And of course the answer is no. How could I? Weeks he was home if he spent a half hour with me it was a lot. Except for that time in his garden. The cats. I've told that.

Not that I didn't have ideas about what fathers were supposed to do. I had TV as a babysitter, and I'd seen all these dads showing their kids how to shoot a basket or fly toy airplanes or go fishing together.

And did I ever try to imitate my mother? Why would I? I did the bit of going through her drawers and trying out her makeup, but that soon turned me off. She had a lot to do though with teaching me how to hate and hate more.

As for that peer group shit. I was never much interested in the kids at Merry Hill or St. Andrew's. And nobody could call Renzo a peer, this guy whose old man had never been able to keep a job and the whole family lived in this lean-to down by the Groverhampton railroad station.

I think I was influenced though by the way Camilla was always putting men down, beginning with Theron, as though she had him cold, and old Uncle Bill, her strong right arm at the mag, got the same treatment. She only paid attention to Theron when it was a trip to 25 Wall or something about my school.

I had to find mumsy and dadsy wherever I could. Schaafy. One of the lady shrinks. Diego. Once even old Mr. Browne. I think I invented myself as I went along.

And the O. W. M. were liking it better than they had. Since Mr. Browne was getting so old, Mr. Homer had taken over and would come out weekends to look me over and see how things were turning out.

"We're doing something right," he said to Camilla and Theron. "Whatever the discipline is, it seems to be working."

"His grades are good."

"Surprisingly so. If he goes on as he's going, well, who can say? We just may be able to undo some of the early mistakes."

"You think there were mistakes?"

"Well, I have found with my own children, childhood is mysterious. I think we've found some light at last."

My grades were okay. If there was light it was because of Renzo and the chicks and the freedom they were giving me. And Grover Hi was relaxed. It was one of those schools where most of the teachers had a beaten look, they knew they couldn't win, some were even afraid of the kids. The Principal had no expression on his face at all, it was a total blank. He played it a day at a time. He knew who was cooling six packs in the parking lot beyond the basketball courts, but he wasn't moving a muscle. Because if he did, too much would come down on him. He knew what pot smelled like—the halls stank of it—but he wasn't sniffing. Not him.

Doc can say this is an unimportant story, but I'm going to tell it anyway—how I came to get an 83 in this course. Romantic Literature. It was a real drag, with this old teach about to be retired and she just took it easy, reading out this great poetry and now and then looking up and asking for comments. One day she got onto Dido and Aeneas. You could tell she'd given up on getting a breath of life back from the class, but she was working from her notebook, and while we were all waiting for the bell, there came this question.

"Ah, yes, now. Sychaeus. Does anyone know who Sychaeus was?"

Well, before they threw out all the books in the library to make room for Theron's toys, I had read something about old Dido and a name stuck—Sychaeus. Like Quittax. So I raised my hand.

"Yes, Philip?"

"He was the husband of Dido."

You wouldn't believe what happened to Teach. She'd asked the question before, and nobody knew and now somebody answered, and it was me. I.

"Correct!" she cried out. I could see I was in her book right away. From then on she figured me for deep, and while she was reading out passages would look at me and smile as though I knew all the references. Though I hardly wrote anything on the exams I got the 83.

That happened on a day we went to class. An awful lot was thrown at us, and we didn't want it all. We were organized enough to know when we could skip. Nothing to do with Mr. Homer's favorite word, discipline. If there was discipline, it was simply doing what our bodies told us to do. We worked out in Gym a couple of days a week, we had to, what with hangovers from our Florence's life. We had days off from the chase when we just marked time.

Plenty of people like us, who've had it with the folks, were like that. Nobody talked about it. It was like a silent club with no handshake, members had no trouble recognizing each other and could be as different as Renzo and me. It had less to do with money than knowing it was no use. He crawled out of his shack into his Chevvy and I breezed out of Lilacs in the Mercedes, but we parked in the same lot. Nobody did much worrying about tomorrow. We used up any day as it used us. He knew he'd never have any money, and I didn't give a shit about old Gramp's gold. No motivation. The O. W. M. at 25 Wall could get themselves stuffed, and Camilla and Theron could have their trip while I was having mine.

TODAY was lawyer day, and Baby Cube brought somebody along I haven't seen before. Or if I have, I've forgotten. Maybe cubes who are lawyers look alike. They were on diminished responsibility again, and I just closed my ears and let them run on.

Listening to it all over again depressed me. These lawyer sessions make me restless, and I can't pick up where I left off yesterday. The thing that got me back onto it was a little dialogue I had with Doc afterward. Their word for it, dialogue.

"Why can't I have something to read?" I asked him. "I'm going nuts in here without TV, anything, not even a fucking radio."

"This hospital doesn't have a library," Doc says.

"But I can see magazines out in the hall. Why can't I see them?"

"The kind of things you're telling us in your writing are best done without media influence. It'll be to your advantage in the end."

"End of what?" I asked, because my life, if I still have one, stretches ahead like a sky with no horizon.

Then he turned on me. Using one of his techniques. Attack. "If you'd tell us a little more about—you call it a trip—very well, tell about the trip Theron and Camilla were having. Pick a day, a time. Their then, as you call it."

And he took off, leaving me with the pad and the ballpoint.

Okay, today's Pick It. I haven't written much about the big weekends and bashes Camilla and Theron gave. But I remember how I'd have to be there, to be shown around and do my act and hear all the crap about how much like Theron I was but I had Camilla's eyes and wasn't it unbelievable that anyone who looked as young as she did could have a son my age?

By what I think of as the first Renzo summer Camilla had become very big on Haute, everything was very grand and getting grander all the time. The mag got bigger every month, like the Times, you really had to lift it. At the top of what I learned to call the masthead in big type was Haute, published by Blah Publications A Division of Multiple Cities Media, and topping the long list of freaks who got it out was Camilla Carstairs Connolly, Senior Vice-President, Editor, and Assistant Publisher. Haute now had newspaper-size full-color ads for perfumes and all the shit of the rag trade. The front page was almost always a great almost life-size chick with nipples showing pink underneath whatever she had on. Haute had everything, book reviews, interviews with authors and the fags who made the rags, who ran whole pages of themselves, in case you hadn't gotten the idea. Harold of Paris standing in front of his chateau. Ass shots of jeans with some great name embroided on the right pocket. Haute was supposed to show you who you could never be, but take your breath away by running candids of the BP and the Ins and Outs who knew all about the Big Soft Life and how to live it. Haute never said a dress or a coat but the dress, the coat, like everybody better quick jump out of last month's dress or coat and jump into this one's. And everybody at the bashes wore either this month's thing or next month's to come.

I mean Haute really sucked, it was all so sick and phony.

The copy under the fashion shots sucked and spit it out in your face and you could like it or leave it. . . . Like—"With his feel for the importance of tweed knit and peau de soie Harold has married the button-down collar blouse to the inverted front pleated skirt. . . . Susie's swagger back dance dress in sexy black sequins. . . ." For pages. Months. Years. Front wrapped, back wrapped, you name it, like they used to say. Lots of otrafwa, too.

But the page called Haute Life was what everybody

turned to first, to find out who was In or Out or Coming Up—flash shots of people you knew already or would soon get used to. Names like Beppo Olivieri and Zuzu Janitell. . . . The Duchess of Loch and Lach rubbing noses with Tristan Shanks. . . . Spike Rothschild with Froggy von und zu Hosenhausen. . . . I'm making them up, but they were like that. Camilla and Theron appeared in the mag sometimes too. She had a rule, no oftener than four times a year, and they were never photographed together. "Mrs. Theron Hanway, our own Camilla Connolly, scampering in Orville's notched lapel evening suit." Camilla did scamper, or wing it, in public. ". . . Theron Hanway of Les Merveilleuses and Countess Tilly Orlando. The Countess wears her mother's 1914 Fortuny, Mr. Hanway the stacked layer evening shirt worn comfortably sans jacket." Theron did all right in Haute, often there were big spreads of houses and apartments he had done. They had it made. The long list under the masthead spent their time sucking up to Camilla, and the New Yokels could be pretty sure if Theron did them up of getting their mugs into Haute Life.

After I did the rounds to be polite I couldn't wait to get away to Florence's and Renzo, and since it was night and I couldn't take the Mercedes without their knowing, I got on the phone to Spiderman and had him tell Renzo to come and get me. As usual, he stopped at the gate. Lilacs had parking for 40 cars, but that night everything was full and cars were strung all along the lane. He couldn't get over what was there, the Rolls, the Audis, Porsches. He knew all about wheelbase dimensions and engine capacities, special equipment and hated his beatup Chevvy. But it got us there.

It was a dead night at Florence's, and when Renzo brought me back and dropped me, the bash was over and there were only lights in the downstairs sitting room. Camilla liked to do postmortems on parties. I heard her voice as I came in, Theron's answering. I'd heard so many of these hashings that I could tell without paying attention to the words if they were just starting or building up or about to end. Their voices echoing up the stairs were like another language. Then when it seemed to be over a door opened and it all came clear. Afterthoughts.

"Well, I thought tonight went all right. Didn't you?"

"I thought it was a crock of shit," Theron said.

"Is that all you can say? I killed myself."

"It showed."

"Bastard!"

They weren't through.

"Who was the Eyetye?" Theron asked.

"If you mean Oswald del Campo—"

"Not Oswald. Not del, Campo either. What was he, a cutter?"

Camilla threw something at him, and Theron laughed. "Okay," he said then, "you process your shit, and I'll process mine."

There was a silence. And suddenly they were through fighting. They were like that.

"Has Philip come in?"

"He's just gone upstairs."

"Get the lights, will you? Good night."

"Good night."

Doc came in hopping mad today. He's been mad at me before but never like this. When I've riled him his squint gets worse and he just sits in his chair and stares until he makes up his mind how to put it.

He said, "Level with me, Phil. Did Malcolm really offer you lysergic acid?"

"Of course not," I said.

"Then why did you write down that he did?"

"You told me to write anything. Maybe I fantasized it."

"Why?"

"Oh, I don't know," I said. "Maybe I figured a little trip would put a little jump into what I'm writing down. I used to write up a storm on my acid trips."

Disapproval. He doesn't know whether I'm tricking him

or not. Some of the narcups I've had have been pretty close to acid. I mean, in hallucination you never know which door will open next. He must have thought of that. To dislodge that loose stone that will let all the others come tumbling.

We talked about the way Theron and Camilla quarreled. I told him about a big battle they had when I was just beginning to remember. He'd beat her up and knocked her down the stairs, and she'd fallen against one of the big white Chinese jars on the landing. She hadn't been hurt, but the jar had crashed into smithereens.

"Do you remember what happened then?"

"He called her a filthy cunt. He often did. He said he was going to bill her for it at the end, when the estate was settled."

Doc wrote that down just as his watch went ping and he took off.

I lay awake a long time last night, trying to remember all the chicks there were. There weren't all that many. Maybe the great studs of history you read about lose track, notch their belts so they won't forget, but not me. I can remember them all, not always in order and there's a blank here and there, because as they say, all cats are gray at night. Most I can get back the way they were and the way it happened. You never forget your first. Marjorie. And then come the next times you can count and after you've stopped counting the real chase begins.

Time with Renzo just flowed. Everything went great as long as we worked within the system he worked out. Per se, he called it. Sex of and by itself, the dictionary would say. Drop of and by and leave itself and you've got the idea. Sex itself. It. Making it feel the greatest it can be, get it right, give it the most. We wanted to have it when we wanted it with chicks who wanted it the same way. If you wanted to go back, if she felt good, for a week, two maybe, but no more. Otherwise it got into emotions and hangups and that could destroy the whole idea. It becomes a game, too neat. They try to be toys. They figure how to turn you on if they want something. Bullshit and time to move on.

139

We were trying to get away from the cultural fuck, you know, the eyelash work, the too much talk wasting time and saying things you don't mean. Melting into each other while scores you could be having are coming in the back door and going out the front and you're still loning it with the same chick and losing out on everything else.

Per se was great. You're ready, the vibes are good and flowing toward her. She's on and flowing toward you. You should do it then. Not have to go through a lot of crud to do it on your back in a bed, though there are times when there's nothing greater than a bed. It depends.

I had a perfect per se almost right away at Florence's. This sort of tallish blonde in her side-button pants and blouse buttoned a little wrong was with me at the gay end of the bar. We were backed into the corner by the TV, and the place was jumping. There was no room to get in or out. She unzipped me and fondled my balls until I was hard, then guided me as she unbuttoned herself. I was in and it was perfect. Standups can be no fun, but she was a perfect fit. And there we stood, not saying a word, grooving, making it last while the gays pushed us together. She knew everything— we came together. Hard. We fell onto each other, letting the ones around us hold us up. It was a great thing, could never happen the same way twice. Being loose. Like hanging from a string in the middle of life. In it. With it. A truly secret thing.

But there are no real secrets. As I was leaving I had to pass Florence, sitting behind her glass screen. She didn't say anything, just looked at me. Then she winked and with her right forefinger made a sign. She didn't shake her finger in a scolding way, only moved it from side to side, not a warning exactly but a way of saying welcome to the club.

I WAS beginning to happen to life, instead of letting it happen to me. I wanted it that way, it was wonderful, I wasn't lonely. There was the time kind of life, hours and days you could spend like money that never ran out, and there was the life that had no time, when Renzo and I just did the next thing that took more money than we had. But I began to stick parts of both together, know where to cut it between the life at Lilacs and the life of letting me be me.

Camilla and Theron had upped my allowance, which was a joke they couldn't see because they didn't know how much bread it takes to get just from morning to afternoon. I took it cool as they gave it, I wasn't going to bust my ass in gratitude, and I knew it was the O. W. M.'s idea anyway. It wasn't much, what they probably dropped on a lunch in town during the week, but it was enough to deal with. They had their away time from me, which meant I had my time away from them. When we were together there were conversations, discussions, like everybody was talking to themselves. They were pretty cool, I mean they'd stopped doing those numbers on me, "Where were you last night? We hope you'll never smoke that horrible stuff." This with straight faces. "I wouldn't think of it," I said. And I didn't. I just did. There was pressure from 25 Wall sometimes, one of the O. W. M. dropping in to check.

"Well, how's it going, Philip my boy?"

"Okay."

"It seems to be more your bag, as I think you say."

"It's okay."

"Keep up the good work."

They were great at moving old Gramps's gold this way and that, it was weird what they couldn't see in broad daylight. One Saturday when it was Mr. Homer stopping by, I was climbing out of a real hash bash and Visine wasn't doing a thing. So I was wearing these shades, and when he asked about them I told him I had pink eye from studying too much. And he bought it. And he couldn't see Camilla playing it lady with old Oswald del Campo either, or all the young ass Theron was breaking into the business weekends. Both of them were hiding behind the skirt. That smashing man who's married to that beautiful woman who's the editor of Haute. They were processing it, keeping it together.

I needed lots of sleep, so I could never be an afternoon

guy, not and make it at night too. I never needed an alarm, as Theron and Camilla did. She never came to the breakfast table anyway, but by the time Theron was getting himself under way I was there waiting for him. I'd see him for this time, then maybe not for days. It was no great big thing, but I liked it. He had just waked up, and I wasn't going to make him listen to anything, I mean we kept it down, we didn't talk about Camilla or play it us against her. Mostly we talked about cars. After Theron had bought his Ferrari, Diego had put the Audi on jacks until it could be repainted. The Mercedes was mine daytimes. Diego had his hands full, because Camilla hated driving the expressway, and when she was in a heavy phase of working in town, he had to drive her in the Porsche and as often pick her up too, if she didn't stay at the apartment. This made a problem. Sometimes Schaafy had to use her own Ford for shopping at the supermarket in Groverhampton, and the week before Diego had had to pick up Bill and Coo in his Chrysler because they waited for Ummie and came by train.

"I've thought I might pick up a Volkswagen Beetle for you," Theron said to me one morning.

I guess I flashed distress. A Beetle. Right away I thought what would happen to the per se system. The Mercedes was perfect for nookie. So I waited a minute and then said, "But I thought that was part of the deal. I like the Mercedes."

Theron looked at me. "What deal?"

"The deal you put on me to graduate from Grover Hi," I said.

It pays to speak up. He got all the rest of what I was thinking without my having to say it. I mean, he finished his coffee and didn't answer right away. But then he said, "I get you. Break down along the Mile in a Beetle and stand on your feet a minute and you'll find out who you're not."

At least he was in my corner on that.

There weren't any hassles worse than that. I'd sometimes ask him for bread, and he'd always give me something, usually without saying anything. But once he said, "Don't overdo it." And he let it go at that.

We steered around a lot of other stuff, which maybe was a good thing. Because if I'd filled him in on my away life, and he'd told me about his—I mean, you could have sold it to Freud after he'd run out of ideas. After Grover Hi we'd see. What the O. W. M. thought. They might make settlement then, and everybody'd be off the hook.

And then what?

I DIDN'T think about then, or what was coming. After the communication with Theron the shrinkies think is so important, I'd walk out to the Mercedes and get off my feet and the day could begin. It began with Renzo. We'd meet in the parking lot behind the basketball courts, and I'd try to stash the Mercedes where I could see it from class. Not that we always made classes. It depended. Groverhampton had what was called the floater system, one class that floated through the others so you could fit five courses into what would ordinarily be a four course week. Five would be your first course Mondays, second on Tuesdays, it skipped Wednesdays because it fell during lunch hour, was your third class Thursdays and fourth and last on Fridays. We both had The Romantic Poets for our floater and could play with it a little. If it was a sure hangover morning, like Mondays, we'd sit in the car and begin on a six pack. Tuesdays we almost always made it. Thursdays could be a little sleepy because it was after lunch. It was a sleeper anyway, like I said, it had the teach who read out the beautiful stuff with comments from her notebook, and she could go days without waking anybody up with a question like the one about Sychaeus. We could drop the week's last floater on Fridays without her noticing.

Lunch was always kind of a headache, it broke the day in half without doing anything else for it. That's what I meant about not being an afternoon guy. Neither was Renzo. Florence, though she served lunch, was dead at the bar end, and nothing woke up there until the dinner crowd started coming. Schaafy would always make lunch for me, if I was alone, or Renzo too if I brought him with me. "No trouble, that's what I'm here for," she always said. Since I'd begun to drive she'd started treating me differently. More Young Master than just a kid to keep out of the way. Because she was German maybe. She was the same Schaafy but behaved more like a servant than the friend she had been when she came to us.

Diego never changed, except maybe to step up his act. "Yes, Boss. No, Boss. I do it straight away, Boss."

After lunch we'd decide how the afternoon would go. We could smoke a joint on our way back, or toke in the parking lot. It was unreal. What were classes you couldn't remember going to?

Renzo was more frightened of my home environment than I was of his, which was pretty frightened. The first time he came out to Lilacs he stood at the door. "Come on in," I said. And he answered something like "Wow." Everybody was saying Wow that year. I added that no one was home, meaning Theron and Camilla. "But they are," he said, pointing to Diego who was doing floors with his black girl, and when he saw Theron's mechanical toys, he almost took off.

"I know it's to freak," I said, and after a while he got used to it. But he was never comfortable, any more than I was when I saw where he lived. No room anywhere, a little black and white TV, a washer and dryer, his old lady boiling something on the stove.

His old man had wanted to see the Mercedes and came out. He was a wino, all broken veins in his cheeks, clots of blood in his eyes. I remembered him from the days he would ride on the mower, before Camilla fired him. He was polite.

"You look like your father," he said. "How is your father?"

"Fine," I said.

Then he looked at Renzo. There was love in his eyes. The look made me feel like the syringe had made me. A squirt. Till then, I'd never thought of that. To this day I think if anybody else ever thought or said it I'd drop dead. Or kill them.

We made it better at Florence's or on wheels than at Lilacs, though it was a good place to crash if we wanted to wipe out an afternoon, or a couple of those hours that hang heavy in the freedom life.

SOMETIMES I think Doc and I are like a couple of vines twined up together. He's the woodbine and I'm the bull ivy that's taking him over. He's never heard of half the stuff I tell him. It shows in his face. He'd never admit it because if he did I'd be the doctor.

My trip at first was to do at last what I wanted, get away from the folks and the whole thing of having to think about old Gramps and what he wanted. I didn't have any guilt about it, I only existed because of the syringe. They'd all ground on me so long, all the time I didn't have anything together and was too cut off from everything to have an act anyway. Underneath I'd been screaming Help me, somebody, I need help, without knowing what I needed help for. I had to cut myself loose in my own way.

I don't know why I didn't get into the drug scene before I did, it was such a solution. You smoked your joint and made your classes, and it was railroad time. You were there, but time wasn't. I mean it was a great way to escape and still be there. Two lives.

At the beginning drugs were not very big with us. We began with pot and for quite a while we stayed there. Panama Red. It just appeared. We could cop from almost anybody. There'd been a shipment of it the year before that the fuzz hadn't smoked out, and it lasted a long time. We copped from a couple of guys who had so much of it they set us up, and we dealt in it in a small way ourselves. Pushing's as easy as taking, anyone who's hooked learns how to do it. Theron had said not to overdo it, and I didn't. Nobody wanted a hassle, much less a bust. Quiet and no names and keep moving was it. Not keep the stuff on you, in case they were searching. We had a lot of stashing places.

I was handling it okay and didn't think of getting into anything else. It had never occurred to me I had options,

145

could arrange the universe to suit myself. But if you dope, you're going to meet people who are into all kinds of stuff, and situations do come up. One night when there were no chicks, this dad came up and gave us a couple of tabs of mescaline, and it was the perfect time, and we did it. You can take all the trips on mesc you like, it doesn't matter. It's great while it lasts. You love the world, and it loves you back. I mean, love just pours out of you.

I never did speed or smack, never used a needle. And I never really got into ups and downs either, though Renzo usually had them and counted on them for himself. There was a lot of trading of reds and yellows, downers, for pot. I don't think he ever fixed, but I'm not sure. He'd fix others up, though, and had guilt about it.

There were one-shots. We tried opium once and got really stoned. You know, dreams you can take into daylight and get rid of and then go back to life. Once on that was enough. What's fabulous is Lady, coke. It makes the panorama of life you've always been looking for. Highlights on everything. But it can cost you both arms and legs.

Hash and grass and acid were my trips. Dust came later.

The first time we did acid I thought it would be like getting stoned smoking a joint. Or maybe like grass and a little Lady. It wasn't. It was farther out than far. It's more like reality than reality itself. It shakes you up to find you've been there before. The truth about everything. You never really get all the doors open, there are always others. You can bliss on it or you can crack up.

We dropped some great trips together. I had one, though, that was scary. I found I had this third eye, I mean I couldn't get my head straight for days. And then I had a couple of lousy trips. One was a fear trip. The worst. I was afraid to move, to go through the door to where the acid was taking me. I was somewhere I can't remember. I came out of it, but I thought Man, forget it, and I did. Still, to go back and try to go through that door—if Malc pushed some A onto me, I'd try again. Doc please note.

I guess we did a little more dope than the rest of the

146

crowd at Florence's. The more we had, the wilder we got. I was playing doubles, it wasn't hard if you let the chemicals do your lying for you. But it could get to be too much, and we'd slow down. Drive out to the marina. It was always beautiful there. We'd just lie looking up at the sky. Great time. Quiet.

A YEAR is a long time in any life, I guess, and that's what it was, my time with Renzo, a year and part of the next summer. There wasn't anything steady or predictable about the way we scored. The sexual revolution may have taken place, but there are still all kinds of odds against getting it easy and uncomplicated. A fuck. You still had to have luck. It was either there or somewhere else. Sometimes the stuff showed up almost too fast to handle, and other times there'd be dead stretches when there was nothing you could parlay, and we'd just cruise around in whichever car it was that night. Everything went by so fast, I keep remembering Florence's—but it's like a blur. The static, the run-together conversations, whatever junk we were making it on, the comeon, and the getting out to get it on and getting off and rid of it and onto the next thing.

There was plenty of variety. It wasn't always teen, or stuff our own age. There were girls who'd been around, women who were older. You learn from women like that, there are lots of them. Florence's had them in pairs or singles, hanging around, buying their own drinks. It was easy to talk to them, set something up, and they were so glad to get it. They'd throw more at you than you wanted. They'd start putting on the Lib screws—Let me buy that for you—Why are you doing this, that. One who didn't look her age had a son older than I was, but it didn't bother her. She dug me, and after we'd been on a couple of times she asked me if I thought I could fall in love with her. Right away I asked myself how far it was to the door, I was getting out fast. Besides, she made me think of Camilla, how she'd have been if Theron had ever been on her. Who was the syringe baby?

What I liked was if it just happened without going after it too hard, and if I dug the chick and she dug me and we had it and let go of it and nobody got involved. I had one. She said, "Want to ball?"

I said, "Sure."

She said, "Let's do it."

When I wanted to do it again, she wasn't interested, she only liked it once.

Even if it went fast at the beginning, there was always, "My place or yours?" Then, "I haven't got a place." The older women had places, the teens never did. With them it was back or front seat, or a motel, which could lead to complications and could add up. The beach was best. It could be great at night, the ocean with its mystery and the sound of the surf. The blanket laydown and keeping the mosquitos away from your balls if it was warm weather, keeping your butt warm if it was cold. The laydown wasn't always worth the trouble—lots of chicks will go straight for a blowjob, if they've forgotten their pill and are afraid of the knockup. I was more afraid of the knock than they were. So there was a lot of head work, which can be great if the chick digs it. A different turnon from front and center. More personal. I mean, after you've both gone down, it's a whole different ball game. And there's sixty-nine, okay if you're a fit, but forget it if you're not.

But anyway. There was still this thing that bugged me. It was that no matter how it played out, it always seemed to be in the dark or shadows. I mean, you work out the physical arrangements and do your thing and you've done it, and when you come back from it, you wonder where you've been. There was something that had to happen to me, and it started in the days when I was hung up on the books in the old man's library. Leonardo's lookup. I'd never really seen the mystery, cunt. There were all the jokes to keep it secret—Boys have it all on the outside, girls on the inside—They're all alike in the dark. I was tired of playing it in the glooms, and one day when Renzo found this pair who wanted to go to the beach, I was ready.

We got into a kind of heavy thing with them, smoking a little and playing that vibes game you see on TV, you know, the one calorie scene with everybody feeling good about themselves, really making it, the tits jumping and the guys running in and out of the water and so excited about doing what they're doing and being where they are that they're busting through their jockstraps. We were both hot on getting laid, but somehow it was suddenly slowing up and going no place and there we were. Then Renzo got his girl away from the sand, and there I was with the other one, and the sun was going down, and I was primed and ready, and it either had to go forward or go back.

I'd noticed she'd been taking it easy on the blanket, staying away from the water, but she was turned on to me. There was a problem, she said, she'd had her appendix out and was worried that straight on would be bad for her scar. I told her it was no problem, there were other ways. Like sixty-nine? So we did that. The sandpaper feel where her bush was growing out made me wild. I was down there and the sun was right on it, if I'd had a flashlight I couldn't have done better. It was nothing. Two folds. A crack. What a guy burns himself out to put it into. I spread it wide. Old Leonardo hadn't put in everything. It blew my mind. I came, then came again. I couldn't seem to stop. It was more than a double header. I tried to say Sorry but couldn't say anything. I lay there breathing in and out, getting my fill of it so I would never forget, and I never did. What I had seen at last printed itself on my memory, and it's still there.

This chick was the greatest turnon I ever had, and though I balled her again, after her bush had grown back, it wasn't as great as that first time. That first memory was like a pill, all I'd have to do was remember that time I was down there and saw it all, and I'd feel myself getting hard, and that thing guys have with themselves would start. A lot of guys won't admit this, the kind of affair you can have with yourself, that goes on all the time in your mind, before and after you've balled your chick, chicks, no matter how many there are. Sometimes I'd be on my way out somewhere, maybe even with a date to ball, and this memory would hit me, and I'd have to stop and whack off and cool myself down. It can be a great turnon for what comes later, like taking a little piece of life that's only for yourself and nobody else involved. Even in this hollow cube it can still hit me. Writing about it's keyed me up and I'm hard as a rock so I'll stop for now and do the whack. Slow and easy and make it last because there's no date to ball later. So here goes and goodby for today.

P.S. It was a great charge. If Malc was on the monitor watching, he must have whacked off too.

Doc's going to be away for a few days, some doctor's convention. The way he told me, it was like he was going to miss me. I know there's this transference thing that takes place with shrinks, I'm supposed to get fond of him from telling all this stuff. That would be the day. His squint, that chinky black hair, and a body you can see even under the johnnycoat no chick would do a favor for. I think it's the other way around. Once or twice he's even touched me, patted my arm, put a hand on my shoulder. Maybe it's the pony tail I'm growing.

"You'll be okay, Phil," he said.

"What could happen?"

"You'll have no interruptions. You can put your mind to it. Write like hell, Phil. Whatever it is, write it out."

"Really unbutton."

"Well, let's say that sooner or later you're going to have to find that last door and open it. Try while I'm away."

And he took off—squeezing my arm first.

Made me think of that Jap thing, hara-kiri. It seems to me I've already made the big cut. My guts are all over the floor. Now he wants me to chop them up too. Before they chop off my head.

Okay, I'll try.

So Renzo and I went on mixing it at Florence's and drinking it up and turning on and balling. I liked it that it wasn't going anywhere, that it wasn't was the best part about it. You painted the picture and walked away from it. Like that.

We were two sides of the coin, all right. What he knew was different from what I'd learned, listening and watching. His old man and old lady were these plain Eyetye types. He could remember being in bed with them when they were screwing. Once he had wanted to ball his sister, but decided it wasn't a good idea. I mean, he'd never watched his old man pull off, which I had. Listened to Bill and Coo yak it up with Theron about sizes and types of guys they'd had, for instance. Renzo didn't really have hangups, only Mama Chiesa bothered him a little, and the economic bind.

That's where the trouble was for both of us. Never enough bread. He was supposed to be a box boy at the Groverhampton supermarket in the shopping mall. His old man knew the manager and had gotten him the job. Unpacking cans of food, stamping prices onto them, putting them onto the shelves for the moms to take down and load into their shopping carts along with the screaming kids. He was supposed to help them out to their station wagons and maybe sometimes they'd give him a little change, a quarter, maybe as much as six bits. It was a real bummer but he'd stuck it out until he couldn't stand it and quit. He never told his old man, who didn't ask any questions as long as Renzo brought home whatever miserable number of dollars it took to keep the family in pasta. And the old man's vino. He'd found other ways to make it, he'd had to. A little dealing. Dads.

Not all the supermarket customers were moms with kids, there were all kinds of weirdos who lived around Groverhampton, dykes and gay teams and loners like the dads. When they weren't working Florence's, they cruised around looking for jailbait. Renzo'd had a lot of trouble with this one dad who'd come in and stand and watch him. One day the market was unusually crowded and he was trying to stack these melons into a pyramid for display. It was tricky and some of the melons would slip and he'd have to pick them up and try again. The dad had been watching him and started to help with the melons, and Renzo could feel he was being groped. It was nothing new, it was always happening at Florence's when the bar was four deep, and he didn't pay any particular attention. But when he was through work, he reached into the pocket of his jeans for his Chevvy keys and found a century note. He couldn't believe it. He rode around for a long time, thinking about it, what it meant. It was a week in the month when the payment on the Chevvy fell due, and he'd already spent his salary at Florence's, putting it on tab. His family weren't starving, but they were expecting what he contributed every week.

When he paid his Florence bill, he cashed the hundred. Anything larger than a fifty was always brought to her to okay, and when she gave him his change, she treated him to one of her long looks.

"I hope this isn't what I think it is," she said.

Renzo told her it was the hand of God.

"Yeah, the left hand. Are you peddling it?"

He wasn't, or didn't really want to. But he had such problems. If it wasn't the left hand, it was anyway a hand. And century notes. Who sees them? You don't even get them from the big dealers in Southampton. The only ones I ever saw were in Camilla's purse.

The dad went on cruising him, trying to con him into a bit of action. A week went by and Renzo faced it. He made it a problem for the dad, but finally let him get him drunk. The next morning Renzo felt something grooving his ass— the dad had tucked another century where he probably wanted to go but never would, because Renzo was like me, private back there. No way. Well, he figured, a few blowjobs. He quit the bummer job and hung out at Florence's full time. When the dad came round, Renzo'd give him a little time, and for a while, like six weeks, he lived high and invested in a few dime bags and even paid off what was owing on his Chevvy. But the dad got tired of the deal. He told Renzo it had been great, but he liked variety. At that price he had his pick of the bait that hung around Florence's jukebox as well as the Groverhampton street corners.

Renzo made jokes when he told me about it. With a dad

at least you didn't have to be afraid of falling through a crack. If dads didn't do anything else, they turned you on for the real thing. Let them whitewash their fucking tonsils, but no KY glides into paradise. I told him about the night I'd let the dad in the white safari suit get his hopes up, and when Renzo had heard it all, he said I'd told the wrong story. What dads want is something with a few pimples, a poet, maybe, hitching out to Taos, New Mexico, or wherever it is pimply poets hitch to.

"And of course he knew about your old man."

"Get off that," I said.

"Okay," he said. "But there it is."

IT was there. This other world. I'd lived in the middle of it all my life, but until Renzo I tried not to think about it. When the TV was on at Lilacs and there was a gag about gays nobody laughed, they froze. There was the gay end of the bar at Florence's. Dads. It's hard to write about it. If I do, it'll look as though I'm something I'm not. I am not a fag, queer, gay, any of that. I mean, I could be shipwrecked on a desert island with Renzo and we'd never touch each other that way, no matter how heavy the heat. But no guy who moves from one place to the next doesn't know about it. It's the kind of information that's kept hidden, I'm not talking about the drag scene, which has always turned me off, because you'd think instead of the foam rubber tits and feathers and lace panties and garters and the other shit they pile on that they'd want to look like guys. It's guys the gay guys want, not women. It's weird. I understand the S/M leather and sweat comeon boys with their whips and chains and cock rings a lot better. Some straights play the other side of the bed once or twice and forget it, but others go on and off it all their lives. AC one week, DC the next, but they aren't really gay. They slip from one world to the other without thinking twice, because if you dig cunt it doesn't mean anything. But a chick can drive you to all kinds of stuff you didn't have in mind. Or your balls can. Sometimes if a chick isn't in the mood, or has the rag on and won't blow you just to be accommodating, guys can be talked into something else. And I'd be the last to say that when things are going that way it doesn't make a change. It makes you wonder, though, what really goes on under all the coverup.

The way it happened to me was one winter night. I was at Florence's by myself, because Renzo had found his trick and gone off and left me. I was just leaning against the bar, yakking with the others when this couple came up and started talking to me and buying me drinks. She was a smasher, but I could see he'd already set it up for himself, so I played it negative. We talked about this one and that one and how everything was running thin because it was winter and there was no beach life. They were after a 3-decker. He kept telling me how great she was in the sack. They were into poppers. I'd never done poppers, and they said I should try it, it was the best scene of all, pot and the pop. They could send me places I'd never been. I was a little pissed off with Renzo because he'd dumped me, and this couple had a place to go. So I went along with them, to this big white studio place with a high beamed ceiling. We did a few joints and got going. His action was watching another guy screw and get her wild. Up to then it wasn't too different from a few sandwiches I'd made with Renzo, and I got wild myself. I was giving them what they wanted, and they were trying to please me, as if just being me was enough. They got me crazy. She kept on saying, "Don't come, hold off. When you're going to make it, tell me, and I'll give you the pop." She seemed to be blowing me, a great job, I thought for once a chick with technique instead of teeth, doing it right. I held off as long as I could and she was kissing me and doing the pop at the same time. It was like I'd never had it. It blew my head off and I was so wasted I fell asleep. When I woke I did some back think like you do and knew she couldn't have been kissing and blowing me at the same time. It had been the guy who had the great technique.

I lay staring up at the beams high overhead, thinking I

should be angry, but I couldn't be. It was part of being an animal, real. Nothing would ever take it from me, it would be mine for life. To go on with.

IT had been great, but I'll never forget how the popper emptied me. I overslept and felt hollow all the next day. When I told Renzo about it, he said I should have my head examined, poppers were a bad scene, they could send you to the morgue. But he just laughed about the guy. "You can't make a guilt trip out of that," he told me, the war was over on that and I should get out of the trenches. I guess the dads had gotten him over the hump about that. He was trade for the bread that made it possible for him to deal and chick it up and keep his family going. The way he looked at it, he was so straight it might as well have happened to somebody else, except for the bread. Most times he had a lot more than I did, even with cadging from Theron and borrowing from Diego.

We had good days and bad days. Any two guys who spent as much time together as we did are bound to hassle now and then and we did. Some days we'd just pretend to be on the outs, to make the time pass. A good quarrel clears the air. And we found out that driving around the way we did, looking for the next thing, we'd become a combo and were noticed by the fuzz. Big and Little Smokey were a combo too and sometimes looked as bored as we were. I mean, they'd park in some lane like a couple of spiders to see what might come along and they could bust. Exactly the way we parked to get off the road for a little and do our own people watching.

One day we noticed the Smokeys were sort of following us, and we decided it was time to park for a while. We were near the shopping mall, and Renzo drew into the parking lot. We just sat there among the carts the moms had left behind. Then we noticed this old guy, one of the dads who hung out at Florence's, coming out of the stand of sumac and locusts at the end of the parking lot. He looked nervous and hurried to his car and drove away.

"How'll you have your oysters?" Renzo asked.

"Come again?"—I didn't get it.

"Daddy works the tearoom," Renzo said. "This is the big time, when the blue collar guys stop in on their way home from work."

I knew what a tearoom was, but I was still innocent about a lot of stuff, I didn't know there was one in Groverhampton, besides the Men's in the railroad station. I asked why it was the big time.

"Because," Renzo said, "these guys want to get their nuts off before they go home and their old lady tells them she's got a headache and the kids have driven her crazy. So he can just have his beer and go to bed, and it's over for that day."

Renzo'd known all about the place even before he'd worked at the supermarket and had the experience with the century note dad. Lots of guys worked it, like the blue collar straights, which meant there had to be gays to do the work. If you knew what to watch for, you could see there was a lot of action. Renzo knew all the types. He could tell a commercial boy looking for a little bread from some guy just tricking for kicks. The blue collar studs didn't fool him. There were oddies, too, waiting for a date or regular to show and go in first, or guys holding out for some particular type. These would draw up and park and slouch down until they'd sized up the situation. If they dug what went inside, they'd quick get out of the car and run into the stand of sumac and locusts and disappear. By the time it was dark there'd been at least twenty guys going in and out. Straights. Swishes. Leather stuff.

It was a funny place for a tearoom, and the reason it was there was sort of a real estate story. Groverhampton was different from the other Hamptons. It had been just a plain Long Island farming community that had grown up around a crossroads. When people began buying up the farms and turning them into showplaces, like Lilacs, there began to be a business section that after a lot of years turned into the shopping mall. The mall had been built at the same time the expressway was widened and the half cloverleaf put in, the cutoff for Groverhampton. Where the mall was now had once been a recreation ground with a picnic park with tables and benches and a comfort station. I could just remember it. Most of that had to go when they did the mall, and now all that was left of the park was a triangular-shaped piece of land with the trees and sumac. It was known as the Pork Chop because it was that shape. The tables and benches had been vandalized, but the comfort station was still there and had become a tearoom. There'd been some sort of hassle about the Pork Chop, it was land that belonged to people who couldn't be made to sell, or it couldn't be cleared. Something. The road people bypassed it and had forgotten it. There'd been letters in the Groverhampton News about what a blot it was on the town, and why hadn't it been landscaped and planted with the usual grass and crown vetch. But nothing was done about it, and the tearoom did a roaring trade. If the fuzz knew what went on there, they were too busy checking radar and what was going on somewhere else. Renzo said it was because they'd have to get out of the squad car to do anything, and they were too comfortable just riding around.

Renzo was in a funny mood that day. I remember his saying not to knock the tearoom scene. He said he sometimes got fed up with chicks trying to make such a production of letting you have it, as though they're doing you this great favor you're going to have to pay back. With tearoom guys it was nothing, they were even grateful for it if you let them have it. It was better sometimes than cruising around and not getting anything at all. It could simplify matters, at least get it over for that day. Or night.

He said, "Shit man, it doesn't always have to be chicks. There are times when I've had it off with a chick when I can't wait to get away and back to myself."

I asked him if he always took money.

"The payoff? No, not unless they want it that way. You'd make the scene big, you're a cupcake."

I was a cupcake, so what? It had been a long day with no prospects, and I wouldn't have been human if I hadn't been interested.

157

"Don't think about it," he said. "Do it."

I was chicken.

He got out and started walking, like he'd forgotten me, relaxed as he went into the sumac. Then he turned.

"Come on. Just remember, don't talk. Let them do the talking. Don't touch, let them do it. If it turns out to be for fun, give them one word. Thanks. If it's for bread, keep your mouth shut."

If there's one thing I can't stick, it's sitting in a car alone, so of course I followed him.

IF I live to be 100 years old, I'll never forget how I felt. It was sweet and evil, like when acid is about to take you over and does. Maybe what savages feel when they are being initiated into a tribe. No women. Magic, fear, terror too.

There it was, maybe a couple of hundred feet beyond the mall, sort of a little pavilion. You couldn't see it until you got close. The whole place was a shambles. The WOMEN side had been bashed in and was boarded up. There was a latticed fence around the MEN door and a heavy branch of woodbine hung over it like a curtain. Renzo lifted it and held it up as we went in.

The only light there was came from a broken window at the far end. It took a minute to see the three urinals and toilet stalls beyond. I saw right away that the first stall had a hole carved into the partition at cock height and an eye was watching through it. A guy was standing by the window, watching. Renzo went to the urinal nearest the first stall and unzipped. But he didn't stand close and look down, he stood far out so his cock showed. He started stroking the end of it and getting it hard.

When my eyes got used to the light, I saw what was scrawled on the wall over the urinals. SHOW IT HARD. GET SUCKED. WILL SUCK COCKS—and the day or date that had been there had been erased and another filled in. The kind of stuff you see in any public toilet, except this had been there for years and had been added to so it looked like wallpaper. There were drawings of crazy faces, cocks and cunts and messages. The biggest cock drawing had written on it JESUS SAVES, MOSES INVESTS.

The guy at the window coughed, some kind of signal. It was very quiet but you could tell there were guys in the stalls, waiting. The watcher was waiting until he was sure I wasn't fuzz or a hassle, and then he coughed again. Two fingers stuck out of the hole in the first stall, giving the comeon. Renzo went over to the hole and stuck his cock through and I could hear him being sucked. He was always a noisy screw, breathing hard and moaning until he came. Except for that, it was so still you could hear the sound of traffic on the expressway outside.

I was terrified. I stood there, frozen. I felt as if some kind of nerve gas had been pumped into me, tingling all over. I was watching Renzo and the guy at the window was watching me. He had his cock out and was pulling it. I'd had quick turnons, but never like this one, scary and exciting at the same time. It was like a game you didn't have to know how to play, it played out for you, you knew it already. The watcher was giving me signals with his head, but it wasn't until I heard foot tapping that I got it someone in the second booth was waiting.

Renzo was right about letting them do it. What I felt first was that I was really straight and had to protect myself by standing with my hands away from me, not touching even myself. I kept a tight ass. The guy must have been an old hand. He unzipped and undid me and folded back my jeans and let them slide down my legs. It was like velvet, smooth. His hands were soft. He stroked my balls and kissed me all over my stomach. I shut my eyes and when he took me it was a little like the time I'd had with the girl and guy in the popper combo. But it was better than that time, the risk and fear were the popper. I still had something to learn. The guy really know how to play me. The fear kept draining out of me. It was nonstop but slow, it was like hours, forever. I went somewhere then. Into myself. It had nothing to do with anything before. God taking hold of your soul. The ecstasy I'd tried to find out about in the old man's library. It. And it was over.

I felt sick, like you do after it's just happened, and couldn't wait to get away. He was a gent, wiping me, whispering, "You're great, kid, anytime." I wanted to kill him. I felt dirty and wanted to wash my hands, but though there was a basin, it didn't work. I ran out as fast as I could. Renzo had waited for me, and we walked to the car.

"Hey, how was it?" he asked when we'd left the parking lot and were on the way to Lilacs. It had been a Chevvy day, and he was dropping me.

I didn't say anything.

"You see, it doesn't always have to be chicks," he said.

I told him to shut up.

"Okay—but you're thinking something. What is it?"

"I'm thinking about my old man."

"Forget about your old man."

"If only I could," I said.

INSTANT SEX. If you're not gay, what's called trade, like me, you've got to learn a few rules about how a tearoom works. If you don't, it can be dangerous and the hustlers will work you. You can get rolled. There can be trouble, and you can land in court. Lots of it Renzo taught me, the rest I picked up myself.

The Pork Chop had a beat to it, a ritual. You kind of got the feel when you went in. Almost all the guys who went there came for sex and knew the rules, but now and then a square showed up just to take a leak. There weren't many of these, but they could break up the action sequence and make it go wrong. A real square peed and left in a few minutes. But if he hung around it could mean he was fuzz, playing games. The Groverhampton cops had decided to live and let live.

The main rules were speed and secrecy, getting in and getting your nuts off and getting out fast. And the silence. If action was under way, the lookout by the window kept an eye peeled and coughed and the guys who were doing anything zipped the fly and froze. Like if you've been smoking, you check the pad to make sure the shit is stashed and the evidence out of the way.

There were three kinds of players—the studs who stayed in their cars until they spotted their tricks going in and had dates maybe, the ones who stood around pulling and waiting to be propositioned, and the voyeurs. Which urinal you stood at was important. Center was coming on too strong, most stood at one of the end ones.

Before anything could happen, there had to be a sign that you'd come to play and the kind of player you were. You showed it hard and let them look you over and waited for a nod from the watchqueen or a foot tap in one of the stalls before you went in. Sometimes a guy to turn the place on would get right down on his knees and start blowing you, give a sample of how good he was at it. Other times there were real hustlers who'd make sure of the payoff before they'd let themselves be touched. The contract. You could tell when it was settled and money had changed hands because then they'd let the other guy pull down their pants so their stomach and balls and hair showed and the action began. It was almost always blowjobs. I only saw buggery twice, and since it hardly ever happened, everybody stopped to watch. It was such a production, all the hassle of getting into position and clothes getting in the way.

The rules about what could be done and not done were very strict. No kissing above the waist, and real trade like me stood with hands held away from the body. I never tricked for money, unless it was part of the charge they got out of it. It was kooky how they'd knock themselves out. Sucking cock can be hard work if a guy's a slow comer like me. I'd learned from chicks how to make it last to suit yourself. It was a shame to take their money.

Of course there were exceptions to the rules. It could get really wild sometimes. Guys who were making it separately could be drawn into mob action. I was kind of an exception myself. What I did when I came in was to look innocent and keep them guessing for a few minutes. Any teen can throw a tearoom, and I knew one who looked like me could do just nothing and not have to worry. I'd let them see my hard through my jeans and the rest just happened.

And there were the rules you make for yourself. I learned to pee right afterward, because as Renzo said, you don't known who's been there before you. And if some dad insisted on stuffing a wad of bills into my jeans pocket after I'd zipped —with a slip with a phone number—I tore up the slip and spent the bills on the next drinks. Renzo's advice just to do it and not think was okay, but I added some of my own to it—I forgot about it afterward. It was only like having a date with yourself, only No Hands. Better than Jack the Jerk. I could never have made that scene without Renzo. We didn't have any particular handicaps, except we'd agreed not to give in to Jack, to hold out for per se. It wasn't easy, you could ball all night and still wake up with a hard that wouldn't go away. That was what the Pork Chop was for.

Doc can't say I didn't unbutton about that.

You just think you forget. It's always there and comes out if you tap it. I'd said I wished I could forget Theron. How could I? Every time I looked at myself in the glass I saw him. It was a long winter. There were days that seemed different sometimes, but in the end they were more or less alike. Different from that day I listened too long and vomited and saw the Devil's face in the sink. The Devil is the biggest turnon there is. The Devil giveth and the Devil taketh away—didn't somebody say that? It was all beginning to be taken away, from Renzo in one way, and from me in another. And more ways than one, so small we didn't know they were happening.

Renzo was beginning to have trouble with his family. Not because he didn't come up with the dollars every week, but his old man had found out about his quitting at the supermarket. I heard all about it one morning when it was a Mercedes day and I'd come to pick him up. Like always, I gave shave and a haircut six bits that would bring him out so life could go on, but he didn't hear me. Nobody could have heard anything over the battle going on inside.

His mother was screaming that she worked her fingers to the bone to give him an education, and the thanks she got was that Renzo was cutting classes.

"He's getting to be too old for school anyway," his father said. "Why did you quit the job?"

"I hated it."

"So where are you getting the money?" His father was full of his morning vino. "What do you do?"

"What do I do?"—Renzo's voice, stalling.

His mother cut in. "And when have you been to mass? By now you should be thinking of getting married. If you don't hurry, all the nice girls your age will be gone. When I think that you're keeping some nice girl like Ellie Ruggiero from having a home!"

"Fuck Ellie Ruggiero," Renzo said. It was getting rough.

"A word like that before your mother?" I guess the old man took a swing at him. Something crashed. "I have ears," his father said. "I hear things. Get out. Don't come back."

"You mean, don't come back without the money you drink up."

The door opened, and the old man threw Renzo into the street. "Whoremaster!" he yelled. "That's what you are! I know about you and your fancy friend, always on the scud!"

The old man kept shaking his fist, telling us to go. I drove away fast. Renzo was all shaken up. His father's old-fashioned words. The scud. Scudding.

"You didn't hear the best part," Renzo told me. "They've found me a girl. She's dying for the icebox. Her old man's in the construction business and will give me a job."

"What are you going to do?"

"The next thing," he said.

I guess we did whatever the next thing was. Though his father let him come back to sleep—how else would he have gotten his vino?—you could tell Renzo hadn't been forgiven.

163

The fight bothered him. It took the rag off the bush, he said. After that it seemed it wasn't ever the hand of God, not even the left one.

We had freedom, though, because we both still had our wheels. We'd use the Mercedes every other day, Renzo's Chevvy on days between. That way it cut the kind of supervision I got from Diego, who had it handed down from Theron. Renzo never drove up to the house on days he picked me up, I walked it down to the lane and met him there. And I never went into his people's house, there'd have been no point. I'd let him drive the Mercedes sometimes, he got such a charge out of it. He had great reflexes, was a great driver. But I didn't often drive his Chevvy. When he took over the Mercedes, it was almost always if it was late in the day, we didn't want to risk the fuzz catching me at the wheel after dark, which was the big no-no about a junior license. Once it happened that Little Smokey stopped me when I was going home at the end of a day. He was nice about it. I asked how did they figure when day ended and night began, and he explained that if you had your heads on, even your glims, that made it night.

At first the fuzz didn't pay any more attention to me than any other guy driving his old man's car. A flick of the eyes as they noticed the make of car and the license plate of somebody rich. If there were no mistakes, parking tickets, violations, there'd be nothing. Then one day when I was meeting Renzo and was late, I slowed for a stop sign, my wheels didn't completely stop, and right away the Smokeys were on me. How was I to know they were parked in a drive, just waiting to pounce? They gave me a ticket and I had to go down to traffic court. The judge was an old vinegar face who beat the bench with his fist as he scolded. "S T O P means stop." Twenty-five and costs. I didn't have it, Renzo had to come up with it.

That could have been how it started to go downhill. I've often thought if I hadn't gone through that stop sign, none of the rest would have happened. Fuzz have a different kind of memory from other people. Like a computer. What Little

Smokey knew, Big Smokey knew too. They stored everything. If I turned left on red, I knew they knew about it, they'd add it in. I'd been picked.

I THINK it was some kind of fate that Renzo and I synched. If they'd let us play together when we were kids—but no use trying to figure out fate. It's a bitch and doesn't give a shit about what it does to people. We both had a desperate fear we might miss out on something, waste time we couldn't get back. That mushroom in the sky. I mean, in this country there's no one not turned on to the great blowup. No guy who's alive and breathing ever forgets there is a future, and that whatever is in it for him, there's going to be something the matter with it. Whatever is going to happen probably won't be anything he can control or guess at, and science can blow him up before he even knows it. There's so much science, and it's all weird. Take a little thing—did you ever think how crazy it is that though men have made it to the moon, when you see wheels on TV they're so often going the wrong way? They start up okay, but when they get to a certain speed they seem to stop for a second before they begin to go backward. Wagon wheels sometime turn all right, and usually tanks, though they have treads, not wheels. But wouldn't you think science could fix that?

Sorry, Doc, I didn't mean to get deep. Just a thought.

It was the worst of the Vietnam years, if you could say one was worse than another, and we were both full of real drive to get everything coming to us before fate began to monkey around. We both knew of guys who'd been scooped up and sent over, even some who'd gotten it and come back in pieces. It was possible to get Greetings. We knew the draft had loopholes—if your old man could afford it you didn't have to worry. If it happened to me, I figured the O. W. M. would fix it, but Renzo's old man had no clout. Underneath all the cool and the dealing, Renzo was a worrybird, and his worry got worse as he thought about the day the icebox would get him.

Neither of us had plans to lay down anything for Westmore-land & Co. The scud was one more way of trying to forget that the eye of the President was upon us.

And we couldn't spend more time at Florence's than we did. The scud simply means working chicks directly from the car. One chick. Getting her into the car and turning her on and tearing off a piece and then letting her down easy, I mean, either at the place you found her, or if she was co-operative, wherever she lived or wanted to be let out. It's like half balling or double balling, depending how it goes. Some-times the ball only rolls halfway, other times it's over and over. I always got a great charge out of these singles, even if we flipped a coin and I was sloppy seconds, or if we made a sandwich. You had to get a little stoned to do it right, fight the reality of it, forget the danger until you'd scored. The fear and excitement added an extra charge that made it worth all the trouble.

It was a game, like everything else. We didn't wear day-time clothes or the jive drag we put on for Florence's. We wore dark pants and top and a cap or hat. Either one will make you look like somebody else, hard to remember, in case there's trouble. Renzo had the perfect equipment, the Chevvy that was no color at night and had four doors, actu-ally better than the Mercedes for back-seat action. He always had a pint and a few joints in the glove compartment, in case the chick would take a drink or light up. And the ski masks, in case we needed them, though I can tell you screwing with a hot mask on begins to make it kink. We only put them on if we saw that it could be iffy, if the chick started having second thoughts or began memorizing faces.

You'd be surprised what just might be standing on a cor-ner, waiting for a bus, or for life to start happening to her. Or walking between two street lamps, ears tuned to the double toot. Chicks know right away when they're being cruised, but you can't always tell the ones you can get into the car easy from the ones who make it difficult. Some don't stop for the first toot and make you go around the block and toot again. It takes patience. When we'd pinpointed a score, we'd keep after her, even if she was a bus job and we had to tailgate the bus to her stop. If she lived in a lighted street or wouldn't play, you had to take off in a hurry and forget it. Chances were better if she lived near a dark corner and you could flash the curb, get it through her head you weren't doing jackrabbit starts and wasting your gas and brakes for nothing. She could be a cold chick, one you'd never seen before, or one you'd done work on already.

It was one of these we were sure we'd warmed up that killed our luck and did us in.

SHE sat in the middle of the front row in that Lit course with the old teach who read while we snoozed. I sat at the far left of the row and Renzo at the other end. She'd driven us crazy from the first day we saw her. We'd watch everything she did and try to get her to look at us, but she never would. We'd both tried to make it with her after class, but she played it stupid, as if she didn't know what we meant. Renzo was sure it was an act. We'd both grind in our jeans as we watched her staring straight ahead. Teach was on automatic, reading out about the light of common day and how the rainbow comes and goes and we were busting our balls. Renzo said he was going to cream right in class if we couldn't find a way of breaking her down.

He did research on her. She was a poor girl, she waited part-time at this burger stand out on Groverhampton Pike. He'd tried to talk to her there but couldn't get past the burger and milkshake. But he found out that she worked a late shift alternate weeks and when she was through took the late bus into Groverhampton, waiting for it by the side of the road opposite the stand. He took it as a good sign that this was one of her late weeks. If we got a little stoned it was almost an abstract problem. It had been an off week, and we were sick of the tearoom, so we lined it up. It would be a mask job, at least until we'd see how it went.

Suddenly there she was, standing on the Pike at the bus

stop, waiting. The bus must have been late, because the stand had closed. We had our masks on and Renzo used his technique of full heads when we passed her the first time, only the glims on after we circled and came back. It was almost black when I got down to do the parlay. I asked if she was for Groverhampton and, routine, she said she'd wait for the bus. I told her the bus had broken down, we'd seen it two miles back. I suggested she hop in. She didn't exactly hop, I had to give her a little encouragement. When she was settled between us she saw the masks.

"Who are you?" she asked. She didn't look at all the way she did in class. Being so close to her was different.

"You don't know us," Renzo told her in his kooky mask voice, by which I knew it would be masks to the end.

"And where are you taking me?" They always asked that when Renzo took the cutoff for the marina.

She was true to form, all questions and "Stop! Let me out!" She was a real freeze, you could feel it. "I'm going to get out whether you stop or not." She started wiggling and cutting up.

Renzo opened the glove compartment so she could see the layout. "A joint?" She didn't smoke. "A shot of booze?" She didn't drink. He had other stuff too, including rubbers. She froze even more. She had a little purse with all the junk chicks carry, lipstick, Kleenex, a nail file. Nothing she could use, but I got rid of it. We'd learned to search, like once there was one who had a canopener dingus with mace on the end of it. She started saying please then.

"Please don't. Take me home. Please."

Renzo kept kidding her. She began to cry and went on begging.

"Let me out, please. Anywhere. Oh, please."

Renzo turned into our place by the marina and what happened after that Doc will have to give me something really deep in the vein to get back. Maybe an artery. Because I can't pump that memory back, how it went exactly, play by play. Renzo had her first. It went on too long. It was a mess, and when it was over we drove her to where she lived. We were careful to the end, cutting off the lights as she got out so she wouldn't see the license plates. She could hardly make it. We took off in the dark. Neither of us said anything until we were back on the Pike.

I felt awful, like death. I said why hadn't he stopped, why hadn't we known she'd be cherry.

He was shaking, but trying to play cool. "That's what comes of putting the charge in a hole that hasn't been drilled. Christ. Christ."

I got tired of his saying Christ. I punched him in the arm, hard.

He punched me back, harder. We peeled off our masks and threw them out of the window. It didn't help. When we were back in Groverhampton we had to pass Mama Chiesa. He crossed himself.

"I think we're going to hear about this one," he said.

We did. But not until a lot of other stuff had happened.

I'M calling it as it comes back to me. We'd been stoned, absolutely zonked. It was afternoon of the next day that I began to find my head and remembered it was my day with the Mercedes. Renzo was waiting for me, and we went to an oyster bar near the marina and had bluepoints. We didn't talk about what had happened, but it was there. Then it was a week away, two weeks. We'd started cutting the Lit class right away because we were afraid she'd be there. Then we had to go back or get posted, and she wasn't there. We couldn't figure it.

That first day back Teach was on how life is a potter's wheel and you're the clay, you throw yourself on the wheel and how you shape up is what you are. Well, I was finding out a few things. Like you don't know what you feel about what's happening until it's over and by then it's the past, and if you think about it, it does hawk you. It was paranoia—we were sure somebody was watching us. We were running all the time. I don't think either of us had a heat for a week, no matter how many black olives we washed down with milk to try to get back.

It was winter. Diego had put the snow tires on the Mercedes. Renzo was having problems with the Chevvy, it was always breaking down. We were our own victims, our lives were led for us by our cocks. For ten, maybe fifteen minutes of per se we were left with the rest of the time to kill. And it seemed there's so much more time to kill in winter. It must have been that way with the Smokeys, too, because we saw them all the time. Chasing somebody. Parked in their radar net, waiting. Riding around. One day they gave us the siren and made us pull up. It was a Mercedes day, and I was driving.

"You guys going somewhere?" Little Smokey asked.

"No," I said, which was true. "Just riding around, like you."

He put me through ID and license. Everything was okay.

"So why did you stop us?" Renzo asked him.

"Just checking."

Renzo should have kept his mouth shut, but he said, "Checking what?"

"You should know what we're checking," Little Smokey said. "Okay, fellas, you can go. But watch it."

"Watch what?" Renzo said.

Little Smokey gave him a long look, and we drove on.

"That bastard is the kiss of death," Renzo said. "Christ, that this should be happening to me. Over a cherry."

"If you feel so bad about it, why don't you tell a priest?"

"Button your lip."

Something didn't smell good, though at Lilacs everything seemed to be going great. Our family visit to 25 Wall to be looked over went great. The two O. W. M. who were left in the firm—Mr. Browne had retired—liked what they saw. I'd learned a few things about how to handle it. I always said, "Mr. Homer, Sir," and "Mr. Stanhope, Sir," and they were crazy about it. I'd never lasted at any of my schools as long as Grover Hi, and my grades, all average, pleased them. They had lowered their sights since the days of Merry Hill and St. Andrew's.

"He's looking good."

"—Soon be making adult decisions."

"Not interested in any particular sport?"

"Has a 93 in gym."

"Well. Looks fine. Senior would be pleased."

So everything was fine. We stayed off the scud. Florence's was safer. We were regulars and had tab privileges and didn't have to pay every time. Spiderman and Robin served us before anyone else, and we gave them fives and tens if they'd been in on a deal. But prices had gone up, there was less competition, and now when we needed anything beyond pot or hash we had to score big to pay for it. Like acid had become a hard thing, and if you wanted a coke bag you paid. It seems like once you've had anything, you really never give it up, there are only other things too. Maybe we were doping more than we had, because we felt this thing was happening we couldn't find out about. The whacks came quick when they came.

Whack No. 1 wasn't a real arrest. We always tried to be careful about how fast we drove in Smokey territory, but in the Mercedes it was hard to keep it down. Sixty felt like twenty. But not in the Chevvy, which started to heat up and rattle if you went over thirty. We were depending more and more on the Mercedes. Besides, it was heated, and once we were inside it, cruising along, it was like our private world.

The Smokeys were just waiting for us to make a mistake. One day we were floating along, and I saw the squad car in the rearview mirror coming up fast behind us. I cut down, but it was too late. It was Big Smokey this time. He was alone, and he made us pull over. He gave us a hard time, acting like he didn't know us, putting us through all the checks. He said he'd clocked us at seventy-four in a forty-five-mile zone. This time it would be a ticket.

I noticed though he had his pad out he wasn't writing anything. He was looking across me at Renzo, who had his wallet in his hand. Not flashing it, exactly, but not palming it either. Big Smokey went around to Renzo's side. I didn't look to see what happened then, but something did. When Big Smoke came back to my window he flipped his pad shut.

"Okay for this time," he said. "But keep her down in future." And he took off.

"You bribed him," I said.

"It just didn't happen," Renzo said.

MY BODY went on working, but I couldn't seem to get my head back. I felt unhooked from everything, there was a space between now and what was going to happen, and I couldn't fill the space. I mean, maybe my gut knew what was happening, but it wasn't telling me. Freedom can fuck you up if you don't watch it.

There was this stretch of road outside Groverhampton that led to the bay and the marina. It followed the shoreline and all along were signs warning of soft shoulders that led to the dunes below. I must have driven it hundreds of times, I could have driven it asleep. But the night it happened there was a light film of snow covering everything, not enough for the road people to bother with, the kind that would melt before daylight.

It was after midnight of a Sunday morning, the end of a dead week. We'd been hanging around Florence's. There hadn't been many people there because of the weather, and she'd been a lot of fun, coming out from behind her glass shield to tell her old Hollywood stories and sing songs she'd done in films. Neither Renzo nor I had dates, but there was this woman he'd known somewhere who needed a lift home, and we were driving along the sea road toward Southampton. They were in the back seat, and I was alone in the front. Between the warning signs you couldn't tell where the road was, it was all white.

I saw the headlights of a car coming toward me. There's the space between you and the car, and it's automatic that you have it in mind, and suddenly it's different, and there's

172

no space. I felt the wheel jerk away from me, and my reflexes made me stamp hard on the brakes before I knew what had happened. It was a sudden thing—we bounced off the road into the dunes. I remember Renzo shouting, and then I was out cold. It would be my luck that the next face I looked into was Little Smokey's. He was shaking me, bringing me to. His radio was blasting the news that I was not allowed to drive at night, which he knew anyway. None of us were hurt.

It all went fast after that, but it seemed forever. By the time they'd got Theron out of bed to come down to the police station it was almost three o'clock. And by the time he'd been checked into the situation the woman and Renzo were drinking cokes from a machine they had there. I could see Theron was working on it, throwing his weight. He got the sergeant to send the woman home in a taxi before he went to work on me. He asked first if I was all right.

I was. Only a little shaken up.

He looked at Renzo. "Have you kids been smoking?"

"Only one, before we went to Florence's."

"Florence's," Theron said. "Okay. Now I want you both to walk out with me. Look straight ahead, don't say anything."

I was a little unsteady. Theron took my arm. I know it was a bad moment, but in the middle of it I felt something warm, like the time I had killed the cats. It didn't last. The sergeant at the desk said what a miracle it was that the Mercedes hadn't been damaged, not even a scratch. Theron phoned the garage to pick it up and we all got into the Ferrari and took Renzo home.

He didn't chew me out or anything, only asked a few questions. "How much do you kids smoke?"

"Not much. Now and then."

"You hang out at Florence's?"

"That's where it is."

As we turned into the lane that led to the drive, he switched off the lights. It was bright moonlight. When we were in the garage he said, "I'm not going to give you a hard time about this, it could happen to anybody. We don't want any hassles with Mr. Homer and Mr. Stanhope. Camilla was asleep when they called me, and Diego seems dead to the world. Let it be our secret."

I tried to get back the warm feeling I'd had at the police station, but it had gone. All I could think about was that his turning off the lights was like the way Renzo turned them off for the scud. Everything was more real in the dark.

Then came Whack No. 2. He said, "They've rescinded your license to drive. You can make application for another one in six months. Meantime, Diego can drive you where you want to go."

"Tough shit," I said.

"Shit is tough."

We got upstairs and to bed without waking anybody.

In a funny way it was like love.

It had snowed heavily before daylight. I remember waking to the sound of Diego ploughing the drive down to the lane. He knew something had happened because the garage hadn't brought back the Mercedes.

"What's going on? Boss tell me no more driving for you. Now I take you to school, wherever you want to go."

I kept my promise to Theron, I didn't tell him anything. What I heard under his questions was that I'd been stopped dead and my life put up on jacks. Because it's all wheels, they're the only freedom. With wheels you can be one place one minute and someplace else the next, buzz off and fuck where you've been for the next thing. But no wheels—forget it. You're everybody's prisoner. Especially your own. Try and get away from yourself. Man, that winter my legs were made of lead.

Renzo showed, finally, sounding shave and a haircut at the foot of the drive. He had chains on.

"You were plenty shook up," he said. "You okay now?"

I was okay, until he started going back to the bounce in the dunes, the scene in the station.

"Your old man really has clout," he said.

"Not enough," I said. "They took away my license to drive."

"You shouldn't have been driving. I should have been driving."

I wasn't going to argue it.

"But your old man," he said, "I had no idea he was like that."

"Like what?"

"On it. Big control. I thought he'd be different."

"Like how different?"

"I don't know. I mean, you know—"

I stopped him, reminded him we'd agreed not to talk about Theron.

"Don't worry, you always have me," he said.

We got into a wrangle about it. It had all been great with two cars, but with only the rattlebones we argued a lot about nothing. It wasn't the same when Diego drove me, actually it could fuck things up, and he found out too much. Sometimes I'd even hoof it back to Lilacs rather than call him to come and get me. A few times I even took the Groverhampton taxi, but I don't know, there's something about a taxi that takes the life out of getting places.

That day was like most others. I became part of the house routines again. I spent a lot of time alone, the way I had in the old shrink days. On weekends the same old bridge games went on, with Ummie and Bill and Coo. The talk hadn't changed either. There were Schaafy's great meals all week, then the casseroles she left for Sundays. At Thanksgiving Camilla gave one of her bashes, for people back from where they'd been in summer and the ones who were about to go away for winter. The Haute shit, piled a mile high.

Days when there wasn't Renzo there was only TV. You can go nuts watching it. I'd settle down and try to get with it, but the commercials were just so much more shit. I mean, you get tired of hearing about keeping dry under the arms and bad breath and dandruff and how everybody smells bad and can't shit and hemorrhoids and those maxi and mini pads. I got so browned off I almost kicked in the set. Once I went into the room that had been the old man's library and cranked up all of Theron's big toys at once and let the music rip while they ran down together. Schaafy came running. She didn't think it was funny. "Ach, du armes Kind," she said, which, as I get it, means you poor kid.

The scene then was marking time. Winter was a bitch, as it always is on Long Island. I mean, we'd made it to the moon, but a couple of inches of snow and freezing rain on the expressway could mean there were power failures, no heat, schools closed. Life stopped dead. But I guess the footprints on the moon were still perfect, there's no wind there.

We couldn't get that last scud and the chick out of our minds. All we could do was the next thing. We did a lot of acid, just sailed away on it. We did big doses, a usual dose being one tablet, but we'd take four or five doses and smoke on top of it too. It didn't cut the fear. It's all in your mind, acid, and if your switch is set at fear, that's where it's going to take you. It was easy to keep on it in small doses between the big ones. I never realized how strung out I was, until one day we were coming out of Lit and saw Little Smokey walking down the hall, leaving the Principal's office. He was in a hurry and didn't see us. I wasn't sure that's who it was—acid can do that do you, blur life or sharpen it. But it must have been him.

Renzo said he was getting bad vibes. So was I. There were spaces between. There was another bad sign, too, not anything in itself, but it happened.

One weekend Ummie hadn't come out and Coo had gone somewhere, and they got me to make up the fourth hand at bridge. Camilla was in the kitchen taking out the casserole, and Theron was with her, doing the salad. That left Bill and me alone at the table.

"I saw you down at the parking lot," he said suddenly.

I just looked at him.

"At the supermarket parking lot," he said again.

I asked what he was doing there.

"Well, Diego met me at the station, and there was something Schaafy wanted us to pick up from the market. I stayed in the car while he went in to get it."

He waited for me to say something. I didn't.

"You were parked over by the Pork Chop. With your pal. He's a great looking guy. What's his name?"

"His name is Renzo."

That was as far as it went, because Theron and Camilla came in. It gave me a chill.

I DIDN'T write anything yesterday, and maybe the day before that either, it's hard to remember. Every day's the same. Doc's being away hasn't changed the routine. Tight as ever. Malc for a couple of days, then Whitey or the gorilla. I'm fed like an animal who may swallow the spoon. Followed by my jog and shower and my stint with the ballpoint. Baby Cube's been here and Tweed Suit too, asking the same questions, getting the same answers. They've taken what I write away every day. It must be a pile. Why I'm running dry, maybe.

This has to be a Sunday, it's so quiet here. Quiet enough for me to hear there's a TV set somewhere, I can't tell where because of the baffle of the walls outside the window. Like out in the world there's this heavy news five days a week and then suddenly there's nothing over the weekend but cartoons until the world starts up again on Monday. I bitched about TV commercials, but what wouldn't I give now to see those guys telling chicks how great their hair smells, and the chicks congratulating the guys for not smelling and getting all that dandruff off their collars. Today I could take a few minis and maxis too, I'm so fucking bored, even a little of that female bliss cream chicks squirt up and which I usually hate.

One good thing about everything being the same all the time is that at least days don't get any longer. Even though you can't tell which day it is. Whitey was supervising my shower, I think yesterday. He's such a deadie, such a different deal from Malc I hardly notice him.

He said, "Guess what."

"What?"

"Doc's back."

"Yeah?"

"Yeah. He took all that stuff you write while he's gone to read it at home."

"No shit," I said. To keep the conversation open.

I said to myself, Back to where we were. He'll want to talk about what I wrote, and I won't remember it, and he'll have to remind me, and it'll be the same shit all over again.

For the rest of the day I just stretched out and listened to the TV mumble and did my figure-8 walk. I saw through the grill in the door that there are new magazines on the corner of the table by the elevator. So today when I was fighting Malc off in the shower I decided maybe we could make a deal.

I said, "How about letting me see the new magazines?"

"You know the rules, no nothing for you. Doc would find out."

"I wouldn't tell him."

"But you would," he said. "Shit, you write it all down for him, everything I say, like you're trying to get me. Like you told I tried to peddle you acid."

"How would you know what I write?"

"I can't read much, but some."

"You read me every day?"

"Not every day. But once or twice. Man, you are crazy. Anyway, Doc's back, maybe he straighten you out a little."

I can't say how I felt when he came in. The same. His squint, his hair that sticks up like a Chink's. I've learned not to say anything until he does. He looked at me a full minute.

"Well, Phil, I've read it all."

"I knocked down a few screens for you, right?"

"And for yourself," he said. "We're getting a new dimension."

Okay, I thought, make it We. He's got it all on his side.

"What we want to know now is 'And then what?' "—He puts it in quotes, my kiddie question.

I think he knows by now he can't get certain things out of me, because they're just not there. When I wasn't a gleam in anybody's eye, some membrane didn't synch with another and it was all plastic, and plastic is what he sometimes gets. I mean, I know I've never been able really to give him Camilla, except as a cutout in space, or Theron either. Sometimes even the space they occupied didn't seem to be there. Paper doll mumsy and dadsy.

I said I didn't know And then what? myself. Had never known it. Which is why I asked it. I told him I didn't even remember where I'd left off.

"The night of the accident in the dunes. With your father. At the station."

"I thought I had gotten further than that."

He kept at it—"You said it was like love, Phil."

I'm blank. It goes to show how you can get off one thing and onto something else. He wants me to get on top of it and tell him how it went. Action. Mix it up.

"Keep at it," he said. "Confusion can lead to clarity."

I KNOW Doc doesn't want to hear how the house always smelled of the attar of roses Diego used to wax furniture. But the things I smelled and saw and absorbed through my skin that winter are what help me remember. The rose smell always. The roar of the wind. Water. Sun.

There were a couple of heavy snows when the snow plough didn't get all the way down the lane to our drive and there was no Renzo, not even school. The kind of days you find yourself talking to mirrors. Then the snow melted quickly, and you could smell spring.

I had slept late. Renzo was late coming for me too, and I sat in the garage with Diego. He was taking Schaafy in to shop, and I could go with them, he said. One trip. I decided to wait for Renzo. After they went, I stayed in the garage. Theron had taken to using the Mercedes and the Ferrari stood idle with the keys in it. I was supposed to be on the honor system about not driving. But I've always thought it's a system that works best when you're not alone. Theron's Ferrari was there. A voice was urging me. Why not? Do it. Go. So I settled myself inside, letting it bring back my wheels and freedom. I started the motor, let it warm, then backed out and drove once around the drive. Then I was cutting into the lane and heading toward the expressway.

It was such a great morning for going nowhere. The Island can be like that on late mornings, not crowded, and for a little while you can feel great, even when there's everything the matter with your life.

I was watching my speed, figuring that if the Smokeys were still on the lookout the Ferrari would fool them. And then it happened, this little stretch of time that was a hinge in my life. I saw her. She was new, just made. I'd stopped for a light and saw her across the intersection, sitting in a long car like a tub with no doors, a long-ago sports flyer built high off the wheels. I had time as I crossed the intersection to see the antique license plates. I couldn't wait to cut into the first left turn and go back.

I drew up alongside. She was sitting next to the traffic because it was a right-hand drive, and the wheel seat was empty. She hadn't moved. She was wearing black eyeglasses that covered half her face, so big I could see myself in them.

"You seem to be in trouble," I said. "Can I help?"

She turned the shades on me. Cool as dry ice. "There's no trouble," she answered. "My brother's just gone to telephone, and I'm waiting for him to come back. But thanks anyway," she added, ending it.

I wasn't going to let it end. I pulled up ahead and walked back. She expected it. The armor went up again. Then she lifted the big blacks and looked at me. That look that begins at the feet and moves up to the eyes without missing a thing between.

"I'm Philip Hanway," I said.

She lowered the blinkers, but I still saw her eyes, bright and cornflower blue, like searchlights.

I added that I lived in Groverhampton.

"Oh," she said. "Groverhampton. We drive through there sometimes."

Full crush.

"This is one great car," I said. Because it was.

"It's a Hispano, my brother's. It's always breaking down like this."

I asked if I hadn't seen it at the exhibit of antique cars at Old Westbury.

"My brother doesn't show."

She'd turned me on like a switch. Not like any turnon I'd ever had. I was years ahead of her. I kept staring at her shades, seeing myself in a world already made. She could be the only one. She made me want to get a pad and live in it with her. Marry her. A girl. Not a chick. A girl in a sweater and skirt as blue as her eyes. Soft brown hair drawn back, no makeup, no rings, not even a watch. Big shades cover the eyes, but they make the mouth more of a giveaway. There was no brother in sight.

I said, "Let me take you wherever you're going."

"Um," she said, considering. "Do you know the time?"

I told her.

That decided her. She was terribly late. All right, if I'd be so good. She got onto her feet in the old tub, holding the windscreen for support. She grasped my arms and fell forward against me as I helped her down. I felt her warmth as she settled into the Ferrari beside me.

"Where to?" I asked.

"Um. Oh—Southampton. Keep straight ahead, I'll tell you when to turn."

"I know the turn," I told her.

"This is so comfortable," she said. "That Hispano rides like a dogcart."

Okay, I thought. The dogcart world.

"Are you in the city?"

"No, I told you Groverhampton. Remember?"

"You did." She looked at me sideways through the shades. "And what do you do in your Groverhampton?"

My Groverhampton. Okay to that too. The duchess and the stable boy. Two could play.

"I don't do anything," I said, and then, "Oh, yes, I go to Groverhampton Hi."

She took off the shades. "But you don't look like someone who goes to Groverhampton High. I'm sorry, but couldn't we go faster? I'm so terribly late."

I stepped on it a bit. "I wish you didn't have to be anywhere," I said.

She waited about half a mile, then handed it back. "My mother's giving a lunch for her Rosary Society, and I've got to be there."

"Oh."

"You see, I've just become engaged."

I said something like, "You mean, if you don't show you'll have to confess or light candles?"

It was wrong, I'd gone past Superstar without bending the knee. It was on a platter. A nice Catholic girl. A good girl. Already ascending into the sky away from me. Clouds beneath her feet. Blue robes fluttering down from the drafts of heaven.

"I'm sorry," I said. "I should have smelled the incense."

This was wrong, too, but she was nice about it. She said, "It works for some people. What works for you?"

"Nothing works for me," I said. "Absolutely nothing. When is the wedding?"

"Oh, a long time away. My mother believes in long engagements."

She kept watching me. "Tell me about you," she said.

"Nothing to tell. All you see is what there is."

She laughed. "You mean, you don't know what you want to be when you grow up?"

"I don't want to grow up." It went better after that.

It's a number of miles from Groverhampton to Southampton. We talked about places. Sag Harbor. The Springs. Ox Pasture Road. South Main Street. Like kids upping each other. We started hitting the stretch of big oceanfront estates.

"It's the next turn," she said.

It was a production to end them all, more like a hotel than a house, towering over the walls surrounding it. Beyond it were dunes as far as you could see. Stables. Tennis courts. And a long striped tent on the lawn overlooking the water. Laughter from the party that was already under way. Lined up around the house were strings of Caddies and Rolls-Royces and limousines and there were cops directing traffic. One of them stopped us when we drove up, and when he saw who it was he touched his cap.

"It's all right, Clancy," she said to him. "I'm late, but they can't begin without me."

She started to get out, then hesitated, giving me another of her looks, the longest yet. The blue searchlights dazzled me.

"You don't remember me, do you?" she asked.

"Oh, I'll never forget you," I said.

She shook her head. "But we're old enemies," she said. "And I recognized you the first minute I saw you today."

I drew a blank, but I asked what she meant. "Enemies?"

"The little bits of paper. I remember everything about it." She waited again, but I still wasn't getting it. "Oh, yes," she said. "It couldn't have been anyone else. You were the one."

"If this is some kind of joke, I give up," I told her.

"Child's Garden. You were having trouble keeping your hands to yourself."

It came back to me then, fast, in a flash, like you're supposed to have when you're drowning. The colored cardboards with little round holes, the little round cardboard shapes to be put back into them.

"You touched me," she said, but I'd gotten the cue.

"And you scratched me."

"You scratched back. I bled."

"I bled too. My God!" I said. "You're—Hesper."

The name like a whisper that I'd said to myself, the whisper the shrinks worked so hard to make me forget.

"Yes. I'm Hesper."

Someone opened the car door for her about then, and she

turned and got out. Back to the duchess and the stable boy.

"I'm so grateful to you," she said, "I'd never have made it if it hadn't been for you."

And she was gone.

That was it. It doesn't write out as though there was much time involved, but whenever I remembered it afterward it seemed like a part of a day, hours. We'd talked the whole way, saying things back and forth. The miles were hours in memory. After I'd negotiated the drive, in a fog, I looked back. I've always heard you should never look back, and it's good advice. Because all it did for me was make me feel like getting on the Long Island Railroad and riding to the end of the line and jumping into the sea. You know, like you're trying a new kind of dope and suddenly part of an old trip comes back to you and it's fantastic. Hazy and secret and like a private movie of what your life could have been if things had been different. She'd got off on me, I was sure, and I'd heard that clap of thunder that only comes once. Nothing would ever happen about it, I knew that. That's when I first began to think of it, O.D.-ing out of life, dropping myself out any way I could.

Maybe the curtain should have dropped then, but it got stuck, leaving me stage center with the problem of not knowing the lines. What to do with the world. And myself.

My fog got heavier as I drove back to Groverhampton. I found Renzo at Florence's. The place was after-lunch dead, nobody there but Spiderman behind the bar.

"What's happened to you?" Renzo asked me straight off. "You see a ghost? An old girl friend or something?"

"You didn't come by for me this morning," I said. My reasoning was I guess that if he'd picked me up on time I'd never have taken the Ferrari, and it would never have happened.

He said he had come by, but late. He was sorry, but he'd been on a deal. Spiderman made us a couple of Rusty Nails and sandwiches. For a while it was cool. Renzo told me about the deal, he had two grams of Thailand junk he'd gotten from a guy just back from Nam. He'd expected more and was kind of down about it. I was down myself. I tried to tell him what had happened to me, but he wasn't interested. We got back onto that night and the fuzz. The usual question of was anything going on, and if it was how could we find out. Dead end, and it brought us down even more.

It was one of those days that didn't seem to have any afternoon. We decided to try the Nam junk and take in a meat movie that was playing in Hempstead. We did that sometimes, tripping along with what was going on on the screen, getting onto the moment and staying on it. But the junk worked slow, after the movie we were just where we had been. It was getting dark and I knew I had to be getting back, so after dropping Renzo at Florence's I took the sea road back to Lilacs. All the dune grass leaned one way in the wind. I started really to trip then, my eyes closing on me in the right lane, opening a few seconds later in the left lane and then I'd cut back. I must have zigged all the way.

It's hard to get it back, and it doesn't help much to try to put it in order, the way it happened then, it was such a mixed up thing. But bits and pieces of it are left over in my mind, like the dune grass blowing. It was almost dark when I cut from the lane into the drive, but I could see lights in the big sitting room and a black sedan was in front of the door. Diego was waiting for me in the garage. He didn't say a thing about the Ferrari.

He said, "You better get your ass in there quick. Boss and Boss Lady been in there since four. Police been looking for you."

I could tell right off it was going to be a heavy scene, scary. Theron looked like Chief Thundercloud and Camilla with her two pairs of eyelashes and this nerd in a three-piece suit who was a detective. They were all freaked out from waiting for me to show, and I had that feeling of coming into a room where people have been talking about you. The detective was saying like "You must remember, she's not yet sixteen years old," and "If this comes to court your son will go to prison." They had been on it a long time, but I couldn't get anything in relation to them. I was tripping heavy. It was a feeling it was their party, a game of questions and answers, and I was outside. I was trying to answer their questions, but it was too much. I knew enough when it was like that to clam. And that the best answer is No, or I don't know, or I can't remember. I just gave them the shit as it came. But I was panicked. Clogged. It was hard to get the words, and when I got them they came out wrong. Though I was with them a long time, when it ended, I was light years away from them, I was just by myself.

I think Theron put me to bed. I slept for like forty hours and when I woke up I felt great. But they were still waiting for me, laying for me, as the saying goes.

"What was it you took?" Theron asked.

"I don't know."—I didn't know. Sometimes junk is like that.

"You take a lot of stuff you don't know about, don't you?"

I had to level with him. I was surprised how much he knew. He laid it on the line. He'd given bond or something, and his promise to be responsible for me. I was not to leave the house except to go to school. Diego would take me and bring me back. I was not to go to Florence's. I wasn't to do anything. It was like the index of a long book. He asked me to tell him about the scud and the girl and when I did he stopped me.

"Don't tell me anything more than I already know," he cut in. "It's better for me not to know details. In that way, I figure we can keep it from 25 Wall. Philip—"

He never called me Philip—

—"Philip, if you fuck up on what I'm going to try to do—"

There was lots of that. The bits, the pieces, what was said, what I listened to. It was big trauma, and I could tell right away from the shit being thrown around that there was going to be a deal about it. It was like a net and I was caught in it and there would be a yank and I'd be all fouled up, and then there'd be another yank and I'd get part of the net away from me.

Theron had this lawyer, he was with us every day.

He spouted stuff like, "It's a thing you can do once and once only. Everything is timing. Philip doesn't have to go to prison."

They had me in a box, and it might as well have been prison. I had to learn to live with them all over again and not get uptight or talk about it. I was dead to myself anyway. It didn't take a wizard to know that they were knocking themselves out not for me but keeping things sweet and lovely with the O.W.M. To get settlement and be done with it. And with me.

I'd been told not to speak to Renzo, though of course I tried to. But he wouldn't speak to me, not even the time of day. I could tell Diego had instructions to draw me out, but I wasn't playing. Schaafy pretended there'd just been some schoolboy prank, tried to keep it mellow, but I saw from her eyes she knew it was a heavy rap.

Setting it up took a little over two weeks. The first was taken up with Theron's lawyer talking to me alone, the second finding a hearing date and getting through my head what I was going to say and not say. I was picking cold turkeys, and my head wasn't much of anywhere. It was a real sweat. If anyone had asked me then, I'd have said that on a scale of ten I was batting absolute zero.

THE HEARING was held in chambers on a Saturday morning and took about forty-five minutes. Chambers was the operative word, meaning no jury, and that it was Saturday made it seem more private. It was all bought and paid for, I guess, and the lawyer told Theron and Camilla not to worry, it happened every day. The four of us drove down to the Groverhampton Courthouse together.

We were fifteen minutes early. The judge's chambers were on the top floor, and we had to walk up all these stairs, though there was an elevator. I think the lawyer thought it looked better. We saw the girl and her parents and their lawyer waiting. Nobody looked at anybody else. Then this spade who was the judge's secretary let us in and told us where to sit. We were at the left of the judge's desk and the others across from us, and when Renzo came in at the last minute, he took the only chair left, between us. He was alone, he didn't have a lawyer. The spade asked us over and over if we were comfortable, and everybody said yes.

The spade was named Henry, which we found out when the judge arrived in the next room. "Henry," he kept saying. "Henry, are these the papers? Henry, close the door." Henry closed it, and when it opened again the judge came in. He was dressed to go hunting, just a man too busy to give more than half an hour or so of his time. He sat down behind the desk and started to go through the papers. Henry stood behind him and kept pointing to the papers as the judge read.

"What is the date on this?" the judge asked. "Is this date correct?"

"That's the correct date," Henry said.

"But it doesn't conform," the judge said. "The dates must conform."

They spent about ten minutes on that, then the judge looked at everybody through his glasses. He had eyes like a fish. Then he took his glasses off and started asking questions. Names. Ages. Place of residence. And dates. The date bothered him.

"I can't understand why this wasn't entered correctly in the first place," he said to Henry.

"It's correct now," Henry said.

"Well, I hope so," the judge said. "Now, Miss—?"

Henry told him the girl's name.

The judge said, "Ah, yes. Now, young lady, I want you to tell exactly what happened. I want you to look right into the faces of these boys as you tell it. Take your time."

Everybody until then had avoided looking at anybody but the judge and Henry, so it was a twist. She found it hard to look at us, and she took her time. It was hard looking back at her. I noticed Renzo was looking at the floor. I couldn't help thinking that though the girl had her backups and I had mine, he didn't have anybody. But he had a technique he'd learned from his scrounging life, how to look helpless and afraid and mean at the same time, and it gave him a kind of strength. What the girl was telling the judge didn't sound like anything I remembered, it seemed a story about three other people. The judge nodded his head as she talked, but when she mentioned masks he interrupted.

"Masks?" he said, looking at Henry. "What's this about masks?"

Henry filled him in. "The perpetrators wore masks, Sir."

"Oh, they wore masks, did they?" There was a long silence. "Well," the judge asked then, "what kind of masks were they?"

"I think they were ski masks," the girl said.

The judge thought this over. "Hm. You think they were ski masks."

"They were knitted," the girl said.

"Knitted masks," the judge said. Another silence. He seemed to let it go and turned to her mother. "Madam, is your daughter pregnant?"

"No, your honor, we've had her examined, and she's not pregnant."

Renzo raised his head and gave me a look. The judge saw. He turned to me, then, and asked a lot of questions, very formal, and I answered them, keeping them short, as I'd been told to do. I can't remember them all.

"Now, Philip," he said. "On the night—" He stopped and shuffled through the papers. "Henry, the date. What is the date on that?"

"Here, Sir," Henry said.

The judge looked at the paper Henry gave him. "That's one of the dates," he said, "but here it gives a different date."

"Sir, this is the date," Henry said.

Everybody could see that the old guy was irritated, tired of all the papers. It was all running too long for his hunting. He forgot about me and turned back to the girl.

"Now, the masks, whatever kind they were. Were the, ah, the perpetrators wearing masks when you got into the car?"

"Yes, your honor."

"Did they take them off then or what?"

"They never took them off."

"So you never actually saw their faces."

"No, your honor."

The judge let her think it over. "So," he said then, "what it comes down to is that what you saw was not faces but masks. It's a question of identification."

"I know it was them," the girl said. "You see, I sit between them in my Lit class. The days they come, that is."

The judge wasn't going to get into that. Henry had his hand on the judge's arm. "Sir," he said, handing him a piece of paper, "there's this." He handed him another. "And this, Sir. Both check out, Sir, they check out absolutely."

The judge waited a minute, then stood up. He made a big swoop with his hand, like a cop directing traffic. "Philip," he said, "come with me. And you, too"—he pointed at Renzo. We followed him into the other room. He held the door for us, then closed it.

It was the smallest room I'd ever seen, almost, hardly room for the three of us. The judge put us into two chairs and sat facing us. His face was very close, his fish eyes straight on us.

"Now," he said, "I want you to talk to me. No one is within hearing, and there will be no record of anything you say."

Something had happened to Renzo when the judge closed the door. He suddenly started talking a blue streak, like he'd been wound up. He said that he knew he had done wrong things in his life and was ashamed of them. "My father," he said, but he didn't finish that. It was all that he was sorry for his sins and wanted to atone, wanted to do something to show that this was the way he felt.

The judge listened, and when Renzo had stopped talking, turned to me. "And you, Philip," he said. "You don't say anything."

I couldn't. I was shaking all over, beginning to feel sick. The judge put a hand on my knee. He said, "There, there, my boy. Feelings came before words were invented. Well. Well." He said Well a number of times. I saw Renzo's face—he had found the escape hatch, and his face showed it.

The judge had bought it. All. Renzo's spilling over, my not being able to say anything.

"There is something you can do," he said, "both of you. Our country is at war, it needs young men like you. You can enlist and fight for our country."

"Yes, your honor," Renzo said. "I'd like to do that."

I didn't say anything.

The judge held the door again for us to go back into his chambers. I could see by everyone's faces that they were angry that they had been cut out of it. The judge sat down at his desk, and Renzo and I went back to our chairs.

"Henry," the judge said, gathering up the papers in front of him, "I want these destroyed. I am willing that charges against Philip Hanway and—"

Henry filled him in on Renzo's name.

"Yes. That charges against both be dropped, on the understanding that they enlist at once in the Army of the United States. Conditional upon assurance I receive that they have done so. Dismissed."

That was the end of it. I remember that Camilla and Theron and Renzo and I rode down in the elevator, the lawyer staying on behind, to deliver the baksheesh. The girl and her family and their lawyer walked down the stairs. It was a small elevator.

It was right on from there. Our lawyer told Theron it had been touch and go, it had gone our way because of what had happened in the judge's little room. He called it in ortinis, something like that. But the judge meant business. The shortest distance between Lilacs and the recruiting office was a straight line. No time to be wasted.

Camilla was all freaked out about what could have happened, but Theron told her the O. W. M. would never know a thing about it. The judge had ordered all papers destroyed, and when everybody had tracked out of the judge's chambers, it was an empty room in which nothing had happened. The golden egg was safe and could go on growing. After that she clammed up and refused to communicate, not that that was anything new with her.

I was really stretched. I couldn't even get it together enough to feel sorry for myself. We were all keeping up the automatic process, and maybe it was only natural that in the middle of it all I had shut my ears. I was ready to split, and I could tell they were crazy about letting me escape. My son the soldier. It wasn't like the trip before, we were a new kind of strangers, and it was all zero.

I was making up for the cold turkey, snorting some junk I had stashed away. I couldn't remember what it was, but it worked. It was a groovy way to do it, because it hurried time up a little, it was all such a drag. And I could see some of it clear. I'd believed I could find myself, and had always gotten into trouble trying. It was all connections that hadn't connected, or had connected the wrong way. Like the electric wire was there, and the current to pass through it, which was me, but it didn't go into the wall where the right switch was. My life was a row of wrong switches. The pickup on the expressway shorted me out, too. I'd never felt that way about anyone, ever. I really flipped.

And the lawyer was pressing me the way Camilla and Theron were pressing him. He said to me, "Now we don't want any screwup when you go to enlist." And I asked what he meant. He said, "Well, like taking some kind of pill before your physical. The judge wants you to go." I mean, I was just wrecked from it, I wanted it to be over.

Diego drove me down to the recruiting office. No hassle, they were taking anything with a pulse. I'd wanted to join up with Renzo, but the lawyer thought the less we saw of each other until we'd been processed the better. After I'd been put through, I asked Diego to drive me to Southampton. He knew it was a secret time for me and didn't ask any questions. We parked for about a half hour near the big spread by the sea, and I just sat staring at it, knowing she was there, inside another world, knowing there was nothing I could do. Nobody told me until the day before I was to go that Renzo had been rejected as unfit for the armed forces. Something wrong with his legs or feet, the lawyer said. And I remembered the cookie he wore in one shoe—he'd known all the time he wouldn't be taken because of it. Leaving me to do it alone. I was so pissed off with him I was ready to kill him. I hitched it down to Florence's, where I knew he'd be.

He saw how burned up I was and looked sheepish. It was plenty heavy as I let it all out. I asked him where he got all that shit he threw at the judge about wanting to join the army and make a new man of himself. Had he been on something. He said No, but that as he sat there in the judge's little room, it reminded him that he hadn't been to confession for a long time, it made him feel the judge was like a priest, and he just started mouthing off and couldn't stop.

"Man, you really fucked up," I told him.

"It worked, didn't it?"

"Not for me." I was really hating him then. "My legs are the same length," I said. "You knew that about yourself."

"Well, I should. I've lived with it for years. Hey, you didn't have to go, you could have said you were gay or something."

"That wouldn't have worked. There was this gay who was ahead of me in the line, pulling out all the stops on how he got nervous around beautiful guys and was afraid what he might do if they took him. All they said was, 'That's your problem, sweetheart, just remember to bring your douche bag.' And in he went with the rest."

"When do you go?"

"Tomorrow."

We were sort of apart, then, as far as we ever were, going different directions. I was hating and he was guilty, but keeping it open, letting it burn out. And then we had one last drink and then another and on the third we got it back together.

"Want some dope?" he asked.

"Where is it?"—which was like what I said to him the first time he asked it. Centuries ago, it seemed. We split Florence's and rode around in the Chevvy. It was a real physical trip. He had some blotter acid, the best. We took that and when we began to float lots of stuff came loose.

"Man, am I going to miss you," he said. Like that. It was a lot for him.

I think I said it too. I asked him how about some tail to wind it up big.

He blew up at me. He said, "Never. I'm hooked on it. I want it. I'm a slave to it. I'm trying to fight it. Fuck all cunts."

We ended up doing something else. He knew this dad who'd said to come by anytime, and we did that. The dad had some tabs of mescaline, so we took some of that to keep him company. Soon we were on a trip and a half, almost two trips at once. Renzo and I really got it together then, we just knew it would be forever with us, and it was cool. Some weird stuff went on I can't remember, but I made it down to induction. Stoned. Like real.

IT's been days since I wrote whatever I wrote last, because it's been one interruption after another. Baby Cube's been in and out, and Doc and Tweed Suit together, he's Big Control now. And always Malc, like they're all getting to be really afraid and need protection. But since writing it out, I don't cut up much anymore.

Baby Cube came to ask questions, mostly the usual ones. What did I feel right after I did it, what do I feel now, today, have my feelings changed in any way? Do I ever even begin to be sorry, feel remorse? He did have a couple of new questions, crazy. Had I gone back to get the basting syringe from the tool drawer in the pantry after I did it, or had I taken it with me along with the tools I used? Did I always know the syringe was there, or was that night the first time I ever saw it? As I've said to them a hundred times, I can't see that such details matter. I did it, and so I did it and that's it. I am not going to squeeze my brain about it.

He slipped in a few quick ones, too. Why do I go on refusing to see the aunts? They're dying to see me. After all, aren't they paying for Doc and the defense?

I threw him a question, one I've thrown before. "Why won't you let me see someone I'd like to see?"

"Who?"

"Renzo."

He clammed up. He never will mention Renzo, though I suppose he reads what I write. I really hate him, I always give him the big stare and never look away from him, and after he's looked down at some paper and then looks up, his eyes flicker. Scared to death.

Doc's technique, especially when Tweed Suit's with him, is always to get me on the defensive. He's been picking on what I wrote last time. Or didn't finish, he says. He says there's an invisible row of asterisks. I realize what I put down isn't exactly the way it happened, you can't get life back exactly, or there wouldn't be any time. Writing is the opposite of talking anyway.

"Something's missing at the end, Phil," Doc said. "What was it?"

I went back over what I could remember writing. We're very frank about the dope. So I said, "Yes, we'd taken the acid and then the mesc and that was it."

"That's where the asterisks are. What happened with the, uh, dad?"

Any mention of dads always make him say Uh.

"Some weird stuff went on, you say."

"Did I?" Hearing it back made me feel like an asterisk.

He cued me. "This dad was homosexual, right? Your dropping in on him with Renzo wasn't exactly a social call."

"No. Renzo was really hating cunt, what it had done to us. Besides, it was somewhere to go."

"Was there a sexual encounter?"

I get so browned off at questions like that. I reminded him that from the beginning I've told him Renzo and I never touched. That way.

"Except in the, uh, sandwich. With the girls you picked up. Scudding."

"Yes, well, then," I said.

And he stayed right on it. He said, "But not the night before you left for Vietnam? Not then?" He squinted at me. "You say you and Renzo got it together. You've been very frank about certain things, what went on in the tearoom, for instance. It's odd you can't remember about that last night."

Dirty mans, I thought. I said, "Well, Renzo and I didn't screw each other or anything, if you mean that."

"Then what did happen? Try once more, Phil."

"I really can't get it back. I was stoned, remember? Maybe the dad wanted special effects or something."

"And what might those be?"

"Some of them like leather jazz. What goes with it."

I could see Tweed Suit was goading him on, pointing with his pencil at something on the page Doc held.

Doc didn't let up. "And what goes with that?"

"Listen," I told him, "I may have gotten mixed up in stuff, but I'm anti all that S/M shit. I'm not gay. What I like is girls, not some old dad in leather trying to nail me into a box."

"Interesting," he said. "You said your mother and father had you in a box."

"They did. Lots of them. But don't get any heavier, Doc. It's cunt I like, not some guy's cock or asshole."

That shut him up. I wanted to shut him up. I'm beginning to hate him. Tweed Suit touched his shoulder—signal for We're pushing him too far. Enough for today.

Doc's like a jack in the box, popped right up to his feet. Keeping it positive. "Well, okay, Phil. We've come a long way. Now I hope you're going to write out Vietnam for me. Just as it happened to you. Take it from that night. You were stoned. Like real."

Quoting me back to myself. His We burned me through. I said, "What do you mean, 'we'? It's me. Me. All me. I can't write that—I can't make the Nam trip again. It's dead."

"You can try."

"But not if you hassle me all the time, come in and break me up. I mean, maybe I can write about it, but I can't talk about it."

He gave me his squint. A cheery deal. "All right, Phil, if you want it that way. I'll stay out of it. You write it."

I followed them to the door as Malc let them out, to catch what they said before they got into the elevator. It wasn't much.

"The oral denial," Doc said.

"Yes, and the symbolic realization. . . ."

The elevator clanked shut. Talk about asterisks. Malc came back with my pad and ballpoint. Gave me a wink.

NOTE the blank space. I'll give them asterisks.

VIETNAM. Nam. I don't know how to begin, except to say I think every GI has his own army and his own war. It's a private trip, and if you come back from it, what you bring with you isn't what anybody else does. I mean, every guy has his own wall up, and if it falls down, God.

Just trying to go back and find it, it slips away. Maybe if I could paint pictures I'd do it all over the canvas, everything happening at once.

Doc wants it the way it happened to me. How else does he think he'll get it? The whole stinking fucking mess. America's biggest mistake that hasn't ended yet and maybe will never end.

The first thing I think of is this glass helicopter in the sky, and somebody says it's air conditioned up there inside the bubble, and there I was in the sand pit with rain in my face and my crotch and feet stinking so I could smell them. I hated the copter and the brass inside while I stank and they were so cool. You don't know yourself until it's been like that and getting worse and you can't do anything about it. Except hate.

At least I wasn't my own problem anymore. Three months of basic and I was put into communications and shipped over hardass. Maybe lucky not to be dumped into electronics, the guy who's never been able to find the outlet to plug into. I could walk, I could talk. Walkie-talkie. Corporal Hanway. Assembly required. Batteries not included.

Right away you find it's reality all fucked up. Like when they take your hair and you look in the mirror, you're still there, but what's looking back is somebody else. Behind the glass the quicksilver's already peeling, part of you is gone, and it's this leftover guy who fights the war for you. You learn to leave your head alone, don't think. The bullshit comes from the top, and your dogtag tells you who you are. You get so you live with all the government-issued shit, canteen, field jacket, rifle, your walkie. Most of it recycled stuff from other wars. Like yourself. I mean, we didn't win, and that's what kills most guys who get back. At least I think it killed me.

I just let it happen to me. I thought, If I'm what they're glad to get, I'd hate to see the ones they turned down. It was shoved at me, I hadn't bought it. But maybe it would be the solution for Phil Hanway, syringe child. Maybe I wouldn't have to do it myself. A nice clean land mine. I went on doing the next thing, which wasn't hard. There was never any time that wasn't filled up, no time even to get pissed off about it. I missed Renzo a little, but I couldn't forget he'd gotten me into the whole thing.

Being in means total strangers you become intimate with the first day. All types, like they'd picked one each of everybody and his replacement. Your buddy is what's next to you and you can't help it. Mine was this cube from Mineola who talked all the time. He'd fucked a girl once and never gotten over it. He was in love with the girl because he'd fucked her

198

this one time, and he told me about it every day. He drove the whole platoon nuts. He'd bought the package—we weren't just going to Nam, we were fighting so the U.S. wouldn't be invaded by communists. He said the Russkies surfaced in submarines at night in the East River and swam ashore and in no time were working everywhere, banks, hospitals, filling stations, you name it, getting ready to take it all from inside. At night he forgot the Russkies and groaned how he loved his girl, and how was he going to make it until he got back to her. The other guys got so browned off with him they'd yell, "Knock it off, pull it off, but shut up!" He wouldn't shut up, so one night half a dozen of them pulled it off for him. It didn't help. I figured if we ever got out of where we were and he was in the line of fire, I'd settle it for him. I didn't have to, he was the platoon's first casualty in Nam. The last I saw of buddy boy was when they found his left foot and stuffed it into his plastic bag with the rest of him.

There were Bible boys too. And lots of spades, more of them than anybody. You had to take it all. One of the spades was Candy Boy, he had everything from coke and morph and acid to pinkies, browns, black beauties, Quaalude. A link from the life we'd come from. The needle guys didn't have to do it themselves anymore, the medics did it for them. I was on hash from the start and was getting used to being a fade, and when I was told what I'd be responsible for it gave me a big jolt. I didn't want responsibility. And there were all these voices asking, "Hey, Sarge, what do I do now?"

Two days after we got to Nam, we were all killing people right and left. That was what we were there for, killing. We were supposed to be searching for the Viet Cong and attacking and destroying them. One rule was you were not supposed to shoot an unarmed Vietnamese unless he was running. Or carrying something. Most of them were doing both, so we pretty much shot anything that moved. But nobody knew where the Cong were, or where to attack. It was war, but it didn't have any structure like all those films of battles and bombers dropping it and getting shot down or getting back. Winning or losing. You had to shape it for yourself.

My CO was a guy we called Pappy because he was older than any of the rest of us, twenty-two. He was frantic all the time. He made his own rules, locking into whatever came up next, there were no plans. He had to. We were all green, none of us had ever seen combat. If we had any ideas, it was that it was like football scrimmage, which it wasn't. He'd give the order to raze a whole village if there was suspicion VC were there. And when the smoke cleared, we'd find it had been only women and kids, and we just marched on and left them lying in the rain. If we'd missed somebody they'd throw grenades after us. Some had guns, and when the patrol passed, they'd open up on us. The only reason we went on was because their aim was as bad as ours. We just lived on the ground and in holes and slept or were awake.

There was this white mist hanging over everything, like somebody was doing a movie with dry ice. There were stands of long grass still growing around the sand craters where the napalm hadn't wiped it out. The villages looked like a rash trying to grow on a corpse. The monsoon blew the rains into the foxholes that were filled with dead bodies and blood and urine and the smell of fresh guts.

I'll never forget one that was full of arms and legs and heads, with this one guy lying on top. He was still in one piece because he'd been killed last, maybe with one bullet instead of the dozens the VC usually used. He'd been pissing when they got him, and now he was dead and still pissing. The flies waited until he was through and then went for the whole pile.

They'd been on us first. The flies loved everybody, dead or alive. When they bit you it was like a little injection of death to remind you that you were going to be dead too. By then a kind of flak jacket had grown around our minds, but it still didn't keep the reality out. You had to love the guava, that napalm, the jellied gasoline, the lice, the stench of human flesh burning. Pappy said the thing to remember was to get your body count up, HQ considered any dead Vietnamese Viet Cong. Shoot before you got too close and needed to use your bayonet, because then you saw their eyes.

They were everywhere, these little people, all mixed up with us, yellow like porcelain in the rain and mist. Sometimes the mist would part like a curtain, and we'd see a whole napalm wipeout, families in groups smoldering, the clothes burned off them, hair on fire, arms and legs missing. "They were going to die anyway," Pappy said, killing them was almost a favor. "Fire!" he'd scream, "Fire!" And then "Move!" Sometimes we didn't get them all.

Pappy and I had a little friendship going. I knew he was scared shitless, as I was, but we both pretended and watched out for each other. I gave him my strength, and he gave me his. When the mist came between us, we'd each look for the other and come together again. We'd promised each other that if one of us got it, like in the spine, or all spilled out dying but not dead, the other would finish it. We weren't doing very well, I could see it in his face. Though we were killing everybody, there seemed to be fewer and fewer of us. Now we were six.

I wish I could lay it all out, get it onto someone else, what happened just before I was captured when everything was so fast and then became so slow. But it's still in me, always will be. Suddenly there was this scream above the others. It was someone running toward us, and they were on fire and were half in the mist. The head hair had already gone. Pappy gave me the order to shoot. Then, as the mist cleared a little, we saw that it was a girl, she was pregnant and what she was holding up with both hands as she stumbled was her belly. I'd hit her high, and she fell right in front of us. She was all bloody, lying there with her legs spread out, still screaming. And then her baby popped out, like there was a spring pushing, and we heard the baby's screams along with hers. It happened like that, in seconds.

Pappy threw up all over himself. I knew I was asking for it, but I went over to where the girl and the baby were. She was dead, but the baby was alive, caught between her knees, the cord connecting him to her twisted. I don't know why I did it or how I did it, but I knew you had to cut from the mother and tie the cord, and I did both. The baby looked like a slimy frog, a napalm baby. He slid down along her legs to her feet.

I didn't feel anything, it had happened too quick. I washed my hands in the rain. I was getting a beep on my walkie and out of the corner of my eye I saw Pappy and four other guys crawling toward a stand of tall grass. He was yelling, "Come on, Phil, for Jesus Christ sake come on."

I crawled after them, trying to hold the walkie out of the mud, but it had gone dead. There was a last order from Pappy and then the gunfire, round after round of it. It was VC rifle fire, then silence. I could hear the feet mushing through the grass. We were surrounded.

I COULD SEE what was left of Pappy and the others lying in a pile. Pappy's face had been shot away and blood was spurting up everywhere from the mud. Around me on all sides were VC feet and rifle butts. I was lying with my nose in the grass, hoping they hadn't seen me and would go on. But they'd evidently counted and knew I was the one more. I felt a rifle jab my spine and staggered to my feet. I thought then they would kill me, but they started making signs. They took my rifle and walkie-talkie. I could see by their faces how glad they were to take one alive and leave five dead. I started to cry, the flak had worn away with the girl and the baby and seeing Pappy and the others sinking into the mud. The signs went on, telling me what to do. Hands above my head, then down, they tied my wrists together. More jabs in the back. March. I took one last look at the blood and guts and shit and urine in the mud. The flies were already on Pappy. And the stink, the Nam stink that stayed in your nose and stuck to your skin and grew into your beard followed me.

There were other prisoners behind me. We were marched for weeks, I think it was four, maybe five. We were poked and kicked and beaten, herded like cattle. Some of the way we had leg irons. The food we were given was almost impossible to swallow, but we got it down because hunger was worse. There were vans that took us across the deeper valleys, then the march again. Nobody knew where we were, but the word passed down the line was that it was Laos and we were headed for Hanoi. North. Nobody cared. When we were dumped at the P.O.W. camp it was hard to believe that's what it was. It had high gates and a long drive through gardens to a house covered with vines. It might have been Long Island, until you saw the row of barracks that had been built back of the house, the high walls beyond and the gun towers rising above the trees.

The first night we all slept in one big room and were given medical attention. My feet were like gourds, I could hardly walk with the bandages. The next day came the interrogation—age, serial number, unit, and the first lecture. We were first class criminals, we had no right to be there. Though there was war, it was illegal according to the Geneva Convention, and we were not to expect to be treated according to its rules. Blah blah, on and on, like that. I'd never heard of the Geneva Convention.

We were stripped down to our dogtags then, and we were each given sandals made of old inner tubes, shorts, a toothbrush, two rough blankets, two pairs of pajamas made of stiff black cloth, a cake of brown soap, and a towel. They lined us up and told us not to look at each other or speak. The Camp Commander, who had given the lecture, came out to look us over. He was so proud of his English that he repeated everything, giving us parts of the lecture again along with the camp rules. Strict obedience would be required and enforced. Any breach of rules would lead to solitary. He kept moving us around so the tallest would be at one end and the shortest at the other. Charlies were hung up on size, maybe because they were small, five feet three was tall for them. We were marched in line to the barracks farthest from the main house.

Since I was tallest, I was the first to be dumped into the cell at the beginning of a long corridor. It was so dim I could hardly see. There was a window at one end and after a minute I could make out two beds, a washstand and basin, a slop pail with a board that didn't quite cover it. The walls and floor were cement, and everything smelled of mildew. Patches of damp covered the walls and dripped down onto the floor. Then I saw him.

He got up from one of the beds, and the first thing I noticed was how thin he was. He put out his hand. "From the land of the living to the land of the dead, welcome. Steve Carlen."

His hand was like a gloveful of bones. "I'm Phil Hanway."

He looked at my bandaged feet. "You've just got here," he said.

"Yesterday."

"I've been here since Tet. Put your gear down on whichever bed you like, it doesn't matter. It'll give us something to fight about later."

I guess I stared at him. His mane of uncut hair and his beard made him look wild. His back and ribs were covered with welts. His sternum stuck out over the same kind of shorts I'd been given, and his stomach was swollen and puffed up.

"I've had solitary for a month," he said. "Bread and water. And the cat too."

I took the bed opposite the one he'd gotten up from. It had slats and a sprinkling of straw.

"You should see some of the ones who've been here six years," he said. "You'll see them during exercise. Have they fed you yet?"

"Breakfast. Where do we eat?"

"Here. They bring it." He pointed upward to the ceiling. "See that? That's what we call a forty-watt in America. It'll come on soon, and then they feed us." He'd hardly said this before the bulb came on. It hung from a ceiling so high you couldn't see the end of the cord. It wasn't enough light for a cat. Right away there was the sound of keys in the door and two plates and a pitcher were set down by a guard.

"That's One Hung Low," Steve said. "No speakie Engliss.

You see? It's shit. You'll get so you're crazy about it. If you don't eat it, they take it away and bring it back until you do."

It was warmed over Chinese cabbage, bread and luke-warm tea. I ate it, glad to get it. I was starving.

"Even if the tea's hot, you let it cool," Steve said. "So it all won't go through you before you can digest. But sometimes it goes through anyway."

I'd been looking around as I ate. "Where do we go to crap?"

He pointed to the slop bucket. "That's it for both of us. Every day you ask pretty please for permission from them to let you empty it. They've got plenty of toilet paper, more of that than anything else. You're going to need it."

I was glad I'd eaten. Steve went on filling me in. He'd been in solitary so much he hadn't talked to anyone in months, he said, except the Camp Commander. The guards had been trained not to respond to anything you might say, because the CC considered silence was the best way to wash your brains and indoctrinate you.

I was wrecked from the long march and the interrogation. Steve helped me untie the knot of mosquito netting that hung over my bed and spread out the thin straw. But he went on talking, I could half hear him through my sleep. Sometimes I'd wake and stare up through the netting at the flies on the cord that stretched above the bulb to nowhere, and he'd still be going strong.

The last thing I remember before the cat bulb went off at daylight was his telling me how he'd fallen in love with a spider that lived up beyond the cord, and how the spider had grown to love him. This was because he would catch flies and throw them up into the spider's web, and the spider would come down to eat them. It had been a little spider at the beginning, but now he had grown and was fat because he was in love with Steve.

It was scary. I could tell he still had his marbles, but he had been alone too long. As I lay there watching the daylight coming through the window, Steve fell asleep. But the spider story was true. I could see him moving down his web, stitching back and forth as he waited for his flies. That first long night was one of hundreds like it, and believing in the spider and what Steve said was my first adjustment to my life as a P.O.W.

DAYLIGHT showed me how small the room really was, how near I was to Steve. I could reach out across the space between the beds and touch him. There was another little space where you could stand by the window, and another by the door, barely allowing room for it to open. That was all.

The routines of the camp didn't vary by more than a few minutes. For the first week I would still make the movements of freedom, like raising my left wrist to check the time. But time had dropped away, they had taken my watch along with everything else. For some reason, I'd always wake before the bulb went off, which must have been five o'clock, though the gong for getting up didn't sound until hours later, I guessed it was seven. I'd get up and pee into the slop bucket, careful to aim at the sides rather than what was already in it, so I wouldn't wake Steve. Even the stink of it couldn't turn off my hunger. I'd go back to my bed and wait for One Hung Low to bring our pitcher of cold washing water around eight. There'd be another hour before he brought the first of our two meals.

This was a hard time to bear. Sometimes when the wind blew a certain way, I could smell the food being prepared for the Camp Commander and his staff in the big house. Roast duck. Delicious pork with a sweet herb of some kind. And the bread baking, the most maddening and delicious of all, reminding me of Schaafy. But none of this food was ever given to us. When One Hung rattled the keys and unlocked, what he set on the beds was the same soup made of vegetables that tasted like sweat, often with bean curds in it that looked like something else, the tea, lukewarm or very occasionally hot. Bread like a stone.

Sometimes I'd be unable to eat it and would try to get rid

of it in the slop pail, but One Hung watched for that. Steve would get it down by holding his nose. If my plate went back full, it came back the next time, just as he'd said, and I'd eat it then.

Eating times there'd be a rattlesnake sound outside our door and the radio loudspeaker would blast on, loud enough for the whole corridor. The Voice of Vietnam. News was preceded by a list of prisoners who had broken under the brainwashing lectures and solitary and the cat and signed confessions that they were imperialist war criminals. There were also tapes of these breakdowns, to give you an idea how easy it was to apologize to Ho Chi Minh. The news was always bad for Americans and great for the Cong. We were losing the war mile by mile and battle by battle. Then came the entertainment, a half hour of scratchy old records—Lucienne Boyer singing Nuits Blanches and Dans le petit Café du Coin, Bing's White Christmas. There were ten records, and they were always played in the same order. I hated them all.

The paramedic came every day around noon. For the first weeks I had to soak my feet in purple water and have them rebandaged. They slowly got better. The medic spoke English and wasn't silent like the guards and One Hung, but he wouldn't talk about anything but his duties. Every time he looked at Steve he shook his head.

After that there was nothing until mid-afternoon, when the guards took us out for our exercise and showers. They began with Steve and me and brought us back first, then moved on down the corridor, taking the others two at a time and bringing them back in order. By watching through the grate in the door I got a look at some of them. I saw the ones who'd been there five or six years, like dead people, shuffling, looking straight ahead. Steve was no longer interested in watching. As soon as he'd been out and back, he flopped onto his bed and closed his eyes.

The big decision of our day was which one would ask permission to empty the slop pail. It was their way of telling us we were shit. We carried it on a pole between us to the latrine trench. Often it was so foul we'd gag or throw up and the pail would slip and spill. This made the guards furious, and we'd get the gun butt. Showers and laundry followed, we soaped up with our clothes on and rinsed them along with ourselves. There was an old Gillette safety razor for shaving, but nobody bothered to use it, having long since settled for beards when its blades wore out. I did too. For that little time each day we got away from the smell of the pail and ourselves and each other. When we went back to the cell the stink was waiting, in the straw of the beds, on the floor. It had been there for years.

STEVE was twenty-six, regular army, about six feet tall and with black hair and eyes. His beard had begun to go white, which made his eyes seem more intense. You could see he'd once been great looking, but now he was slumped and his muscles were stringy. His skin hung in folds.

He'd been almost due for thirty days' leave in the States when he was shot down in a helicopter maneuver south of Hanoi. He'd managed to parachute out but had landed in a tree. It had taken him days to untangle himself, and when he did and was climbing down he fell and injured his knee. He couldn't walk, and a VC reconnaissance party captured him. For the first year after Tet he'd been quartered in general barracks with thirty others. The paramed hadn't been able to do much for his knee, it needed surgery, and there was no real hospital, only a clinic ward. Sometimes after exercise period I'd see him lying on his straw, tears squeezing out of his eyes from the pain of having stumped to the showers and back. He'd been beaten so often across the soles of his feet with the cat that he limped even in the cell.

But he could talk and so could I. For the first months all we did was talk. We told the stories of our lives and then told them over, looping back to parts we had forgotten, finding the memory again, picking up from there, getting it all in.

All—Nana. Camilla and Theron, Ummie and Bill and

Coo. The O. W. M. and the deal, the golden egg. Schaafy and Diego. Even the syringe. Steve was a great listener, but now and then he'd interrupt to say something in his soft voice, wasted like the rest of him.

"When does the golden egg hatch?"

"When I get back, I guess."

"I get it. The hero bit. Go on."

I'd for some reason always come back to Pappy's face all shot away with the flies crawling over it. And the girl on fire with her hair burned off and the baby and going over to her to cut the cord away from her and tie it. I couldn't shake it, no matter how often I told it.

"That baby was really you," Steve said one day.

He said things like that. He'd only say them once.

I'd told him about getting a hard on at Child's Garden and touching Hesper, how we'd scratched each other, and the day so many years later when I picked her up on the expressway. Finally I'd told it so often there were no parts I'd forgotten.

Steve waited. Then he said, "It stops there."

"What stops?"

"What started with the scratching. We all scratch the thing we love," he said and laughed.

Even I knew where that came from. Two-bit philosophy. Deep. So I reminded him that I'd only seen her and talked to her that one day.

"It can happen like that. Remember, Dante only saw Beatrice once. It begins there."

"But which is it, stop or begin?"

"Both."

I let it go. He was sick of hearing about it. God only knew how sick I was of some of the stuff he told about his own life. Steve had his marbles, but they were scrambled. I figured he'd been talking to the spider too long.

Or maybe it was because of the echoes he'd been listening to all the years he'd been there.

———

I'D only begun to be aware of them. The whole place was echoes. It was crazy. The cells being built as they were, for isolation, were staggered, none of the doors facing, to discourage communication. The ceiling of the corridor was vaulted and served as a kind of baffle, and our cell, being at the beginning of the corridor, was an acoustic pocket. Sometimes we could hear sounds made by other prisoners and their voices almost as clearly as our own—water pouring from pitchers, slops being poured into pails, crapping and the cursing that went with it. It was all to do with where you were in the cell and where the others were in theirs. Lying on the beds we'd hear one group of guys, but standing by the door or window we could listen to others. Other people's lives. Than which, as Theron used to say.

It was like having a tape system that sometimes worked and other times didn't. But it helps, thinking of it, to get some of it back. Clear or under recorded. Lots of hums and blank stretches. Breaks.

There was always the damp. The damp and the heat. The damp and the cold. The blankets were too much in summer, never enough in winter. The pajamas seemed to hold the damp in, maybe because they never really dried after we washed them.

And the food. Some meals the tea was body temperature, which was like drinking urine. The limp Chinky cabbage lying in the soups. The soups that were cold—pumpkin, squash, pumpkin again. The turdy bean curd. About once a week they'd get our hopes up with a slice of pork belly. And then would come days in a row with nothing but rice. At least the rice stopped the dysentery for a while.

Dysentery was the first fact of life, the whole barracks had it. It went along with the low grade anger and hatred everybody felt for the men who'd put us there. You took your anger with you to the pail. And the baffle pretty much told you what was going on in the cells farther down the corridor. The plain runs were called Kennedys. Anyone managing something solid yelled out for the whole corridor to hear, "WOW I've made a Nixon!" Real shit. Everybody had the

Kissinger Medal for sore asshole. What we all wanted was the L.B.J. Award for the guy who could keep off the pot as long as a day. Steve said he no longer had an asshole, only a mouth, because he vomited up so much of what he forced down. Shit when it went in, shit when it came out.

There were constipation weeks, when the medic would feed us little round black pills. They helped a little, we'd be solid for a day or two, but then the rice would give out and we'd be back on soup, and the squirts would begin all over. It really was Shit Alley.

So much of it was doors being unlocked and opened and slammed shut and locked again. Every hour the guard on duty walked up and down the corridor. There'd be a wipe in the conversation we might be listening to coming from one of the other cells, then after the guard had passed the talk would begin again. I got so I could tell time by the guards' footsteps, they all had different walks. And when the footsteps changed, you knew that eight hours had gone by, and you could start counting the next eight hours. I could even tell which guard was which. The one on at night farted a lot, his replacement snored, and the relief who came on at daylight laughed to himself when the Voice of Vietnam came on.

Steve had his own way of tracking time. I noticed one day that his toothbrush, which he would lay on the windowsill to dry, was worn down at the handle. When I asked him about this, he showed me a place behind the door where he'd marked off weeks and months. The place was secret, so far One Hung, who did the weekly cell inspection, hadn't noticed it because the door opened against it. There were thousands of tiny marks and scrawls. They weren't absolutely accurate, Steve said, because he'd been in solitary so often, and when he was brought back he couldn't always remember how long he'd been away. It was pretty sad.

"So you've had other guys here before me," I said.

"Yeah, lots of them."

I could tell he didn't want to talk about them. There was a scrawl above his markings for the past year—"STEVE

CARLEN DIED HERE." You could see there'd been a date above it, rubbed out.

"That's you," I said. "But you're not dead."

"Yet," he said. "Actually, I die a little all the time, so I don't put in the date." He laughed. "You see, I'm afraid the handle of the toothbrush will wear out before I do."

It was his kind of humor. A toothbrush was forever, like all equipment we'd been issued. If it wore out, there wouldn't be another.

There could be big trauma about something like that. Like when I came I hadn't been issued a comb, and for the first months my hair and beard were a mess. I'd had to beg One Hung to put in a requisition for one, and getting it had been a big struggle. When the comb came it was aluminum and worn down, filthy with the crud of whoever had had it before me. "The comb of somebody dead," Steve said, and maybe he knew. I remember cleaning it with the nail of my right forefinger, which, along with my right thumb I kept sharp for picking my feet. Because by then I'd learned to chew my nails like everyone else.

It wasn't much of a comb, and my head hair was as matted and tangled as my beard. Steve helped me comb out.

"I feel like a fucking hairdresser," he said. He laid his hand on my shoulder for a second before giving me back the comb. I could feel a shiver run through him. "You are one beautiful guy."

Here it comes, I thought. "Look," I told him, "I'm no lady, and get that straight."

"I got it straight the minute you came in the door," he said. "And I'm no lady either. Which leaves us where?"

"The whack," I said.

"Yes, I've heard you jacking off mornings."

"Don't you?"

"Hardly ever anymore," he said. "That goes too after a while. But all of me wants it. Man, it's the only part of me that's never lost weight. It just hangs there, but I can't do anything with it. I think it's the pumpkin soup."

"Ech!" I almost woofed just thinking about it.
We rested it there. Not that it went away.

Twice a week everybody in our barracks marched single file to the main house for indoctrination lectures and further questioning. Sling Shit High, the Camp Commander, delivered the lecture. That was Steve's name for him, and his name did sound like that when he gave it, which he always did before starting. Steve had these names for almost everybody, from One Hung to a fat little Buddha character, Up Yours, who every week came to the cell with the forms we were supposed to sign, admitting our capitalist guilt and making the kowtow to Ho Chi Minh. Ho had a name too, but I forget what it was.

Everything was very formal, like a classroom. Sling would read out our names, and we would answer, and he'd check to make sure the name went with the face. He knew us all. His voice was a cross between a falsetto squeak and a couple of piepans beating together. If anybody laughed when he gave his name, they got the gun butt in the back and never laughed again.

Sling always began by reminding us what he'd covered in his previous lecture, telling us again we were capitalist criminals but that this could be forgiven if we would sign a confession of guilt and read it onto tape that could be played at the beginning of the news. Sling worked from cards and sometimes showed slides, using a long stick to make his points. Now and then there were films, May Day parades in Moscow, really weird propaganda supposed to show capitalist decay that were like old Laurel and Hardy comedies. We really had to hold in on those.

Though Steve and I were allowed to sit together, the guards made sure we didn't talk to other prisoners. He knew the lectures by heart, his lips would move as he listened, or maybe he was just napping. But when we got back to the cell, we'd discuss the session. Steve couldn't get over it that the wash was working on some prisoners, that each week Up Yours would get confessions and signatures from our corridor that would then be read over the air. The ones who gave in and signed then disappeared, maybe to eat the roast pork and wonderful bread we smelled cooking every day.

"He was really slinging the shit today," Steve said one day after Sling had been working unusually hard on us.

"And it was high," I agreed.

I'd noticed that Sling seemed to be watching me as he talked, giving me more than his usual attention. Steve had noticed it too. That day, as was usual on lecture days, we had been given our half-week's ration of cigarettes, six stubby, miserable bitter cylinders that we made last and rationed by sharing them one at a time between us. They were terrible, but they were something to smoke and we always lit up right away.

"Sling's got his eye on you," Steve said as he took a puff and handed the cigarette to me.

"What makes you think so?"

"Look in your pocket," he said.

I did, and there in the back of my shorts was a full pack. The guard must have slipped them in while handing me the others.

"But this is great," I said, right away thinking how I'd spread them out to last, a real treat.

"Don't be too happy about it," Steve said. "It's only the beginning."

"Of what?"

"The softening up."

"Well, I'm not signing any confession," I said to this. "Not for Sling or Up Yours or anybody else. You didn't."

"No, and look at me," Steve said.

We lay there on our beds, underneath the bulb. The spider had had his flies and was quiet. We had an extra cigarette. I could tell Steve had something on his mind.

"Look," he said, "there's something I've been putting off telling you. Now I think I'd better."

"I thought we'd both told each other everything by now."

"Not quite," he said. "You don't think being put in here with me was an accident, do you?"

I hadn't thought about it. What came into my mind as he said this was, Watch those marbles, paranoia. It sure as hell sounded like it.

"You're not the first one," he said. "There've been others. You see, Sling is convinced I know something they haven't been able to get out of me with all the questioning and solitary. And the cat."

"And do you—know something?"

"Christ, no! I'm really the biggest chicken ever hatched. I told them every single thing I had to tell the first week. They broke me right away, but they don't know it."

He told me, then, about how they'd put him in solitary for months at a time and then beaten him with the cat, to get it out of him that way. There wasn't anything to get. But he'd been so desperate sometimes that he'd make up stuff, to make them lay off the cat, and this had been his mistake. Now Sling was convinced he was still withholding information of importance. There'd been two other guys before me, who had been supposed to listen and remember and tell Sling what the secret was. Both had been softened up, and since there wasn't anything to tell, had gotten both solitary and the cat. Steve knew what had happened to the last guy, who'd signed for Up Yours and been blind transferred, but what had become of the first was a mystery.

"I think he died of fever," he said. "They call it that. You hear them screaming and hollering down the corridor and then one day you don't hear them and they're gone."

I didn't know whether to believe him or not. Though he'd given me pretty plain descriptions of what it was like to be given solitary and the cat, I tried not to think about either. I was too terrified to think. I just made it from day to day.

215

I TRIED to think of the days as numbered, as Steve did, but I couldn't. Still, no matter how I tried to cope with it, the hunger, the dysentery, all of it, it did all happen one day at a time. I knew weeks and months were going by, but somehow they were just one godawful heavy blur of time, daylight running into night, nothing changing.

If only I'd had a pencil—there was all that toilet paper, and I could have tried to make something out of it, the way I did in the attic at Lilacs, and the schools. But there was nothing, just talk. Not a book or magazine. It was part of the brain-wash, Steve said, Sling's way of pitting us against each other, getting rid of the personality so Uncle Karl Marx could take over and make you feel nothing.

I felt at first I had an edge, in a way, I'd stood up to Daddy Freud, he hadn't been able to get near me.

The hunger was murder. Slow murder. You'd be sur-prised what you can put in your mouth and get used to, even look forward to. Days when the pork rind showed up in the soup. Days I guess were supposed to be Sundays, when each of us got a tin of sardines. Russian ones.

No, no pencil in that black stinking hole on the other side of the world, nothing but the shit and sweat and shivering and chewed fingers and toenails that scratched you at night when you moved. And talk. Steve and I made it without killing each other because we talked. We talked ourselves hoarse.

Our lives. He'd talk to me and I'd listen, then I'd talk and he'd listen. When we finished one version of our life stories, we'd start all over. It had pretty much got down to our sex histories, past and future.

The first one.

The next one.

The ones after you could stop counting. And after that. Working back and forth as we remembered, like the spider shuttling, running after his flies. Shootoffs, we called them, when we really rubbed it in the nitty gritty and told all.

He'd been a farm boy. The jerking off behind the barn.

One day he and a couple of other kids had tied up a mare and fucked her, getting a shit hemorrhage for their pains.

You didn't have to worry about a guy like that understanding the per se Renzo and I had worked out for ourselves. He listened to my story of the standup at the bar at Florence's with all the gays pushing us together over and over. It really sent him. It even sent me.

I think we talked about sex so much because for a little while it took away the hunger. When we'd stop, the hunger came back like a hook, real pain in the gut, sometimes worse than before we'd started. These times when we forgot our shrunken stomachs were like dreamy banana splits piled high with all the goodies.

Steve knew the damndest stuff.

Like, Women for procreation
　　　 Boys for pleasure
　　　 But melons for delight.

"Man," I told him, "If I had a melon I wouldn't fuck it, I'd gobble it up, rind and all."

"I used to spend my life worrying about procreation," he said. "Any rubber can slip, and pills can miss." Then he laughed—"The only safe way is yourself."

"And the boys?" I'd leveled with him about the Pork Chop, the dads, what could happen in a threesome you couldn't really know about and remember. I'd told him everything, right down to the last night with Renzo and the dad, which ended in a dead spot. We agreed that kink was great if you didn't overdo it, but the real thing was a chick, cunt. The real life fit that would solve everything.

It had been years since he'd had a woman. Looking back, talking it up, was all there was now. It was all going back, you couldn't talk about anything ahead.

The time he'd spent with other prisoners in the general barracks had taught him what can happen when thirty guys are jammed together in hardly any space. The food had been better then but sex always a problem. There was this guy in the next bunk, and another guy beyond it. One of them found a little guy, sort of a pal type, who'd take it up the ass.

217

That had been the start of it. Then others saw what was happening and started buggering him too, trying to make a regular thing of it. The little guy wasn't a fag, just a good looking kid, but once it had started there was no stopping it. Everybody screwed him. He didn't know what to do. He'd been fucked till his ass was ragged.

The more macho guys would fight to get at him first. It was all very tense because it wasn't ever really talked about, and it had to be at night, when the guard might be taking a break or sleeping. The whole barracks would wait for this time when the guard went off or snored, then go for the kid. Sometimes there were three or four on him at once, taking turns, getting off any way they could, making him blow them, anything to get rid of it. It was always with the lights on, so there was no way any guy could close his eyes to what he was doing, what was going on with the others.

One ass wasn't enough for thirty guys, there started to be combos, guys who'd never thought of touching one another in that way, pulling each other off, holding some other guy down to make him do it. Pretty much anything went. And then after it had ended, there would be this silence. But in the daytime all kinds of upmanship and jealousies and hatreds developed about it. Everybody'd stopped speaking to the asshole, and some of them when they remembered what they'd done started knocking him around.

But it didn't end there. Other fights broke out, and like one stud would accuse another of having crabs or dingle-berries, stuff like that. Finally the morale in the barracks got so bad that the Camp Commander got into the act. It wasn't Sling then but some other VC captain who prided himself on keeping a quiet camp with no problems. When he found out what was going on he broke it all up, sending the guys to other barracks and the poor asshole to solitary. Nobody knew how the asshole managed to do what he did—hang himself from the grill in his bunker, using his belt and yanking and straining until his neck broke or he strangled, or both. It was called fever.

I listened as Steve told me this, sort of fast and as though he needed to get rid of it. Like Renzo mouthing off to the judge back in Groverhampton.

"And then what?" I asked.

"I don't know about the others," he said. "I never saw most of them again. But it got to me. This okay kid, the thing just starting and ending like that, being fucked to death. And when you think that a couple of those Vietnamese lovelies on a Saturday night would have changed everything."

"Did you bugger the kid?"

"Everybody did."

"What's it like?"

"Haven't you ever had it that way?"

"No," I said, "only what I told you. Not that."

I saw he had his eyes on a fly. He reached out, caught it, and tossed it up into the spider's web. The spider moved down to get it.

"Well?" I asked.

"Well what?"

"What's buggering a guy like?"

For a long time he didn't answer. Then he said, "Nothing like that really happens, man. Or it's like a lie happening."

His marbles were rolling around that day.

BUT what he'd told me of the poor asshole hanging himself in the bunker made me remember Leake who'd done the same thing at St. Andrew's. It was funny, the way Steve would say things brought back all kinds of stuff I could never get at, to tell Doc. Like looking into the wrong end of a telescope, smaller, clearer, far far away as they say. I told Steve how I'd hitched back from St. Andrew's to Lilacs, broke. Sleeping on the edge of the ledge, waking up starving hungry. Walking across the Queensborough Bridge, hardly making it because I was so dizzy. Going into a burger stand and sitting down at the counter, wondering what I'd say or do next.

Wide open.

There was a little man at the other end of the counter.

He had those eyeglasses that pinch onto the nose. He moved to the stool next to me and started talking to me. Like, "Hi, kid, where you from? Where you going? I saw you when you came in, you look beat."

"I'm hungry," I said.

He snapped his fingers. "Fix him up," he said to the man behind the counter.

"What'll it be, sonny?"

"What you're having. And coffee."

Bluepoints. I washed them down with the hot coffee.

I kept noticing how small he was. He was pitching all this uncle talk. Name. Where did I live. Who were my people?

I'd learned how to answer or not as I pleased.

"You don't look as though you belong here," he said. "Look. Why don't you finish your bluepoints and I'll take you where you're going. That's my car out there," he said, pointing to a Continental Mark IV, as if that would clinch it. It had an M.D. license.

The man behind the counter was reading a paper, but he was listening too. He cleared his throat.

"Kid, how old are you?" the Doc asked.

I told him and right away he cooled. He asked which way I was headed, and when I told him Groverhampton he cooled still more.

"Sorry, I'm for Manhattan," he said, and bolted.

I went back to the expressway and caught a ride almost right away with a blue hair mom type who was going to Groverhampton. When I told her where I lived, she insisted on taking me right to the gates.

"I know who you are," she said. "Your mother's What's-her-Name, something on that magazine, right?"

"Right," I said.

I saw her afterward one day in Groverhampton. She smiled, as though she had something on me, so I kept going.

—That's the kind of anticlimax stuff that would squeeze itself out of my memory in Nam.

"Was that all?" Steve asked, when I told him.

"Yes, that was it."

"You were looking for your old man," he said. "What did he say?"

"He wasn't home."

"And your old lady?"

"I think she was in Europe." I couldn't remember that.

"So who was there?"

"Schaafy and Diego."

"Yeah," he said. "And your grandmother. Nana."

It was my line, I couldn't believe he'd taken it from me, that he'd said it the way he did, spitting it out, as though he hated me and everything I'd told him.

He said, "Mister, you need some new stories to tell. Don't tell me all that shit again. I can't stand it. Not one more word."

What killed me was that he'd said Nana. Always before he'd said grandmother, when we'd been on the same story twice or repeating a name and there'd be pauses. I'd cued him too during his repetitions about his dreary family and his life. But this made me hate him. I called him everything dirty I could think of. I told him how I'd loathed it every time he gave me those capsules of wise guy wisdom—You were looking for your old man. We all scratch the thing we love. I told him I'd never tell him another thing. Not ever.

"Ever is tomorrow," he said. More of his shit.

I didn't answer.

It didn't bother him. He went right on.

"This is perfectly normal, Phil. The honeymoon's coming to its end. We'll bore each other shitless before we're through. But we're in this together. And Sling's got us both by the fucking balls. Let me know when you come out of the icebox."

I didn't stay in the icebox long. That night as we both lay under the cat light trying to sleep, I saw his hand hanging off his bed. I couldn't say anything, but I reached out and touched his fingers. We made a kind of awkward handshake.

STEVE was right about being in it together. We were, and Sling was taking his time. He had a breakdown technique that worked on others, and sooner or later it would work on us. There'd be a tray of great food for one of us, and we'd share it, eating too fast for our shrunken stomachs, sometimes throwing it up afterward. Then there'd be the same shit diet and we'd remember the great food we hadn't been able to keep down. There'd be the packs of cigarettes, then no cigarette ration at all. One interrogation a week after the lectures, then weeks when we seemed to be forgotten, followed by weeks of three, even four sessions with Sling alone for me.

Sling made no secret of what he wanted. If I'd come through with what Steve was continuing to conceal, I'd be given the privilege of signing the confession and the apology to Ho Chi Minh. I'd be transferred to another barracks, I'd never have to see Steve again.

He listened patiently as I told him over and over that I knew nothing, and that Steve knew nothing. I got kind of punchy listening to him, the same questions over and over. Sling's techniques were straight sado—he had a box of some kind of candy made of dates on his desk, and there were always cigarettes, and you had to resist them. They were offered, but if you took them, he'd make you pay. Like throwing up the great food that appeared and then disappeared. Like ordering a sudden cell inspection as though something was wrong, sending One Hung back and forth with Up Yours with their prepared confession papers and telling us there wouldn't be much more time in which to sign. Whatever that meant.

I couldn't tell time the way Steve could, making his marks behind the door, but I could count the days between Sling's questioning. I'd tell Steve what Sling had asked me to confirm about him. He'd say, "Yes, yes, that's the way it goes, and next time it'll be"—whatever it turned out to be. Steve was always right, he'd been through it with the other guys. "Tell him anything you like if it'll keep you out of the hole or away from the cat," he said.

There wasn't anything mysterious about the way Sling was trying to break us. As we'd lie there, mornings and evenings, listening to the Voice on the loudspeaker, there'd be insertion of our names—Corporal Philip Hanway was a candidate for confession—Captain Stephen Carlen, who had been under investigation for some time, was about to receive the punishment due him—Blah Blah Somebody Else had already confessed and signed and was to be congratulated. They'd play his voice, reading his apologies to Ho on tape. You couldn't tell the news from the propaganda.

During any newscast there were always four names worked in—J.F.K., Johnson, Nixon, Kissinger. The whole corridor had built up a hatred for them, and there'd be Bronx cheers and wolf howls whenever they were mentioned. It must have been what Sling wanted, because like the ten scratchy records played afterward that were driving us crazy, the order never changed.

Only the seasons changed. It had been warm and then cold, then warm again. Spring—sometimes the whole corridor smelled of semen, like the broad beans in Diego's garden that used to turn me on. Our hunger was terrible, but was its own kind of turnon. While the switch was on, there was no hunger, I'd be horny just for myself. Pumpkin soup or not, I woke every morning with a hard making a point under my blanket. I'd check to see if Steve was sleeping, then pull off, using my hunger dreams to make it last. Before the dreams went, as dreams do. Like for weeks I dreamed of nothing but chicks and their hair, good old American TV hair in clouds, waving, tossing, always moving but coming to rest as a pillow beneath moist lips and eyelashes and kisses as liquid as the lips.

One morning I was making the most of my hard, this chestnut hair was wrapped around it, and I was going to come into it, a fantasy I'd always had, that never left me. My eyes must have been closed. I slowly became aware that Steve was awake. I opened my eyes and saw that he'd thrown back his blanket and was pulling along with me.

"I thought that had left you," I said.

"But it's back," he said. "Watching you has hyped me up. Go on with your story, kid, help me make it."

"What story?"

"The one you tell yourself before you wake up."

"Do I talk in my sleep?"

"Does he talk in his sleep!"—During these morning times, it was crazy, he always talked to me as though I was somebody else. "Go on," he said, "tell it."

So I told it. It was great, a little like when Rudi Schaaf and I would pull off in the attic at Lilacs. We'd start with, Picture a naked woman, and we'd go on to name all the female parts we knew and describe what we supposed they looked like.

Steve watched me. "I'm going to make it," he said. "Let's make it together."

I was turned on full. "I can't hold off much longer," I said.

So we fined it down and let it go away and come back. And then we came in the same second, shooting up into the air together.

"My God," he said, "I can't stop. It's a three in one. A Casanova."

"You'd better let up," I told him. "One like that can kill you."

"But it was worth it," he said. "It was the greatest of all." He got up and went to the washstand. He threw me my towel and I mopped up. He said, "Hey, kid, know what?"

"What?"

"Now it's come back, I know that Sling will never break me. I was beginning to have doubts."

I don't know why, but our morning jackoffs became a great thing between us. We never touched. I ran all the scales —old Leonardo came in handy, I added what he'd left out— and it brought him back. We were never going to be an item, like a couple down the corridor we could hear but never see, just jackoff buddies. He'd tell me his own hunger dreams, and I'd sometimes do double headers. It was a bond we never talked about.

AFTER about a month of this, we were talking less. Life was longer than the dick. Then one day we could feel a change, nothing we could figure out. Maybe it was that on the loudspeaker there was talk of a peace treaty being signed, or that Sling had heard something from One Hung and Up Yours that made him decide to move on us both.

It happened fast, and we could tell it had all been planned. We heard the keys jangle, and the door opened, and One Hung started shouting. He'd come to do a special inspection, throwing the straw from the beds onto the floor, poking into corners. For the first time he closed the door from the inside and saw Steve's markings on the wall. He let out a cry, then turned to Steve. I flashed a look at Up Yours and decided I had the strength to jump him, but Steve gave me a sign that it would be useless, make things worse, whatever they were. He let them cuff him without resisting, he was almost limp as they marched him off, leaving me to wonder what was next.

About an hour went by, and then they came back for me. They made a point of taking me to the main house the long way, past the six solitary bunkers built back to back behind the latrine and the showers. Steve was being pushed into the bunker nearest me, and I could see One Hung giving him an extra whack with his gun butt.

That wasn't all. There was a flogging going on at the end of the exercise yard, nothing I could see, I could only hear the inhuman screams of the guy getting the cat. As Steve had said, Sling was an artist at what he did. He could really set a stage.

He was sitting behind his desk, smoking. The date candy was there, and he pushed it and a freshly opened pack of cigarettes toward me. For about twenty minutes he kept me standing, one of his techniques, making you wait while he took care of something else. He signed papers and gave them to the aide who always stood by him. He listened to a loudspeaker giving the news in Vietnamese.

I was ready to drop, having had no breakfast. I was seeing him 3D, like I had on somebody else's eyeglasses. It was like that with my ears too. Hunger does that, there's a blank between what's being said and its getting to you. And I was shaking with fear. It got to me that this was special blackmail of some kind and I wasn't up to any cool like Steve's. I was a coward. There was no hero in me. If I'd known anything, if Steve had told me anything, I'd have let it all out after the bunker scene and the screams of the guy getting the cat. When Sling finally got around to me, I was already so soft no more softening was necessary.

But it didn't go that way. He went over our last conversation. He asked all the old questions, and I gave my usual answers, No, No, I didn't know, Steve had never told me anything. He'd had everything from me there was, from life in boot camp in the States to Pappy and the burning girl, but whenever I'd gotten onto them, he stopped me and said it was irrelevant. He was winding up now, I could tell.

"So—you still say you do not know?"

"Yes, I say it."

"And you say that Captain Carlen has never told you anything?"

"Nothing."

"Very well," he said, and gave the guard the signal to take me out. Then, as though it was an afterthought, he opened a drawer in his desk. "One moment, Hanway. There's mail for you. I'm afraid it's been delayed, but then the mail for prisoners often is."

I looked at what he laid on the desk in front of him. They were not envelopes, but reduced photocopies, and even from where I stood I could see they'd been censored and heavily blacked out.

I almost blew up, but I knew I wouldn't do anything, my anger with Up Yours in the cell had been my last strength. He had me.

"And so, Hanway, you'll think further about it. You will read your letters and perhaps decide you have something to tell me."

I took the letters from him and the guard marched me out. The usual route back, this time. It was raining and my bones were cold. Back in the cell I dried off. The only dry things were Steve's pajamas, and I put them on. For maybe an hour I sat, putting the letters in order. There were five letters, three from Camilla and Theron, two from Mr. Homer, and a postcard from Renzo. All the letters had dates six months old, Renzo's card was not dated.

Maybe that's what made me hate the letters—the time in them. And I've often wondered since whether I'd have felt different if I'd had my first meal that day. Instead of listening to my gut cutting up, being so empty, so light in the skull. I read them then, one by one, the ink blackouts made them come through like telegrams. From nowhere. To nobody. Chopped up questionnaires.

Did I know how much they loved me?

Did I know how worried they were that I hadn't written?

Why hadn't I written? They were worried sick.

Mr. Homer was writing separately, to tell me how fine he thought it was that I'd joined up to fight for my country. Which was to tell me the golden egg was well and breathing, he didn't know about the scud.

Would I please let them know if I needed anything?

Had I received the parcels they'd sent? The cigarettes?

That may have been the one that killed me. Parcels.

If only Steve had been there, to show the letters to. He'd always told me letters and parcels were sidetracked. I remembered once the guard slipped me Camels, my brand, probably ones sent to me.

I began to burn. Theron and Camilla had written on the same sheets, signed "Love" at the end. "Much love, Mother." I wondered what much love was. Theron added "Best Love," I didn't know what that was either. They hadn't missed a trick. Bill and Coo and Ummie couldn't wait for me to come back, neither could Schaafy and Diego. I think what killed me was a P.S. of Camilla's—"Very, very dry here." Dry syringe Mom to the life.

Mr. Homer's letters were typewritten on his office paper.

They were hardly blacked out at all—"What a fine young man you have turned out to be—Your grandfather would have been proud."

All loud and clear, in fact deafening. It all seemed written by computers talking to each other. I read it all over and over, and at sometime during that starving afternoon I put the letters into the slop pail. But I kept Renzo's card.

It was one of the kind old Florence had on the cashier's counter for customers to take as souvenirs. It showed her in the restaurant surrounded by her Hollywood mementos, lighting a candle. I read it so often that by the time I'd stuck it in the window I knew it by heart. I still know it.

"Hello, hello. Here I am sitting at the bar with Spider-man and Robin. I think of you a lot. How are you? Are things good for you? Is your head in a healthy happy spot? Please write back, ok? I am heaving stones for old Ruggiero so you can guess the rest. Ren."

That day I had to empty my slop pail in the rain. No showers were permitted. I could hardly make it in and out for the hunger. But Sling knew his business—when One Hung brought my meal I could smell it coming. Roast pork. The wonderful bread I'd smelled baking. Real butter. Some kind of sweet made with mangoes. This time I didn't have to share it. I ate it all, sucked the blood and chewed the bones as they say, licked the plate.

I didn't have any trouble sleeping that night, I didn't even notice the spider or the bulb overhead. It was a little stretch of sweet death, the kind I wanted. I was glad it blacked me out, because it stopped me from thinking about Steve, soaking wet in his cold bunker, gagging on rock cruds and water.

The last thing I noticed was that, while I'd been away from the cell, the log he'd scratched on the wall behind the door had been scrubbed clean. It was a lousy omen.

———

For once I slept through the bulb switchoff and was wakened by the guard bringing breakfast. Sling wanted to make sure I'd gotten the idea. There was a big puffy omelet, bread fresh from the oven, butter, the tea was hot, and there was sugar. I was on the slop pail crapping when I heard the keys jangle, and the guard showed in Sling and Up Yours. They both had Buddha smiles, like they'd come to ask was there anyone for tennis, but when they saw me both turned sour. Poor timing. The whole place stank as it always did, but mornings were the worst. Sling never came to the cells. I sensed it had something to do with the news, which had been good for the Americans, which meant bad for prisoners, because on those days all the Vietnamese were in a poor mood.

Sling was wasting no time. I could tell there'd be no more questions. He even said he was not unreasonable, he understood that some people had poor memory. Up Yours had brought the standard form for me to sign, which would simplify things for everybody, and had it all ready, pen in hand. I read it—the crimes I had committed against the people of Vietnam, Blah Blah, I apologized humbly to Ho Chi Minh and asked for his pardon.

Maybe it was because they'd interrupted my crap. I said, "Shit."

"You will sign now," Sling said.

I thought of Steve in the bunker. "I can't sign," I said.

"What you mean is that you will not."

"Can't and won't."

I could tell Sling was through. He called in the guards who chained my wrists together and clamped leg irons around my ankles, then dragged me out.

They took me the long way again. As we passed the solitary bunkers where Steve was, I saw one door open as before. I guessed it was for me, and I was right, but not yet. We were in the exercise yard then, and I knew I was to get the cat first. I think Sling figured he'd given it to Steve the wrong way, one at a time, but with me he'd do both and get what he wanted.

The cat was a short whip covered with snakeskin. It had eight extensions that made it a real cat-o'-nine-tails. They stripped me and hung me over a hook by my wrist chains, just high enough so my toes touched the ground. The guard with the whip kept walking around me, flipping it, giving me samples of what I was to get. I memorized his face, his slit eyes and flat yellow nose, his smile full of teeth. I started screaming and begging, telling him I'd sign anything if he'd cut me down, but it was too late. The more I begged the better he loved it. Words came out of me I never knew I knew, and he liked that even better. I heard Sling's voice as he began counting.

You don't believe the first lash, or the second. Your ribs move inside you, and on about the fourth you begin counting too. I felt the blood running down my back, a hot stream of it between my buttocks. I felt one of the cat tails cut across my cock.

I fainted then. There is a God.

There was something between the cat and the bunker, maybe the clinic ward. I remember the medic bandaging me, it felt like salt being rubbed in. I asked if my cock had been cut off and he said no, and he showed me—my foreskin had been broken but what it covered was all right. It was swollen hard, my balls were hard too, bursting.

The first thing I remember in the bunker was trying to stretch out. Impossible, it was too small. Not possible to stand, either, or take any position except like a half-open jackknife. The only light came through the grill of the ceiling. There was the stink of others who'd been there before, but soon it was all me. Me and time and death beginning—I thought. No such luck. Death without dying, time without minutes or hours, but still horrible old life going on.

Solitary. All the cement damp of the cell I'd occupied with Steve was squeezed into this cube. I died 100,000 deaths the first day. I'd already lived my life over with Steve, there wasn't anywhere to think back to. I died and was born again every minute. Then I learned to make it two minutes. Finally an hour, then a day. But never more than a day. Every night had to be death so it could all start over at daylight. On the bread and water it wasn't hard to hold in, but soon the ground became damp with what ran out of me. There was no pail, I had to dig with my hands the hole in the corner where I crapped. I thought I had heard silence before, but I was wrong—I missed the loudspeaker with its Voice of Vietnam, the records played over and over. After a while, I could play them in my mind and in the order I'd hated so—and loved it.

I fell in love with myself. I divorced myself. I killed all my enemies, pasting them together with memory. Old Nix. Kiss. J.F.K. Johnson. I pulled Sling's balls from him with tongs, I cut Up Yours into pieces. I sang. I cursed. I remembered. I played over and over with Theron's big toys, ate Schaafy's food, felt the warmth of the seats of the Mercedes where love had been. I thought day after day about the burning girl and the baby I'd birthed, how I should have died along with Pappy and the others. A month of keeping company with your own shit doesn't do much for you, except to kill everything, make you stop feeling.

It was the body that saved me. I'd begun to turn into a gimp from crouching, tensing, never standing, never lying down. As soon as I could take the bandages off my balls I found I could take the lotus position. Then when I did I remembered Quittax, my secret mantra, and I learned to kill time that way. Time that won't split up or go, time the drag, time when the door would open. Somedays it was almost as merciful as my fainting under the cat. That had been God.

God came and went, like Steve's spider.

"Thank you, God, for here I am which means You must exist."

"Fuck you, God, for letting me wake up another morning sitting in my own shit."

"Why can't you do something to time, God, take some of it away?"

"Oh God, God, send me a roast of pork so I can eat it and throw it up and eat it again."

God didn't send me the roast pork.

231

But He sent me hash.

For a few minutes every day when the ceiling grill was unlocked and lifted and my pitcher of water and bread came down, I'd see a flash of daylight. Then there'd be a hand and the face the hand belonged to. Not the last yellow face I'd seen and memorized that went with the cat, another that sometimes smiled and lingered a minute to look down at me. I'd already fallen in love with the hand. I'd have to touch it when I took the pitcher and bread and gave back the pitcher from the day before. One day I held the hand and pressed it and it pressed back, and the day after that the hand came down to me a second time and was holding something. I took it, and the hand went away. What it had given me felt oblong and had a smell of nutmeg and pepper, which told me what it was. Hash.

I licked it. I'd been frozen stiff with the cold, but slowly a wonderful warmth went through me. I went on licking it, the candy of Paradise, and as I warmed the blackness of the bunker changed and I could see myself driving along the expressway with Hesper. We were laughing, and I didn't leave her at the big turnaway house by the sea but went on wherever I wanted. A secret, magic world, all mine, and as it grew around me my mantra changed from Quittax to Hesper. Hes-per. We soared. When my mantra would change back, I'd know it was beginning to be over, the cold would creep through me, the blackness of the bunker would return.

I lived for the hand, and whenever I pressed it, it would come down again with the oblong of hash. It was hash got me through, it was hash that made time run like quicksilver the night the B-52's let it all out on the camp, made me believe that the door of the bunker would open and the blackness and cold would end.

WHEN the door to my bunker opened, my eyes squeezed shut from the daylight, but in the first instant I'd seen that the two men who came for me weren't Vietnamese. They weren't Americans either. When they tried to stand me up I fell, I had solitary legs. They carried me back to the cell, no chains or irons this time, and stretched me out.

"You almost didn't make it, Buddy," one said. "We had to dig you out. It was guess work. We're still digging."

"Steve," was all I could say. "Steve. He was there too."

They told me then that they were Canadian, part of a relief-inspection team, they'd been caught in the bombing along with the VC.

I must have been out of it for a while. The next thing I knew they were carrying in Steve, laying him out on the other bed, covering him with blankets, though the day was warm. We looked like each other, hair and beards matted, filthy beyond belief, and we stank.

"You made it," he said. "First time you always make it."

"You made it too."

"That's what you think. Fifth time you don't make it."

We lay there most of the day, getting out the kinks. When I could get up and walk a little, I put both my blankets on him, because he was shaking. He had a deep cough, and his beard was covered with phlegm he'd tried to wipe away. His arms were like matchsticks, and his hands were all bones, like a skeleton. He was burning up with fever, and his shaking, which came in spasms, almost threw him off the bed.

I wondered where the Canadians were. I beat on the door to get the attention of the guard, but there didn't seem to be one, though we were locked in. Steve's eyes were wide open, and he started talking.

"Hey, it's over—did you know that?"

"I guessed it. We'll get out of here soon."

"You will, but not me. Man, I have had it this time. Is there a wind somewhere?"

"There's no wind," I said.

"Well, what day is it?"

"I don't know."

"Shit," he said, "I thought maybe you'd kept track and I could get my calendar going again."

I decided not to tell him the calendar scratches had been wiped away, he wouldn't have been able to move off the bed anyway.

Suddenly he called out—"Hey, Maggie? Are you here, Maggie?"

It was a name he'd never mentioned in all our long talks together. That was the minute it got to me that he was crazy, that he'd gone somewhere and wasn't going to make it back. He seemed to fall asleep then, but his cough would wake him and all the brown bloody stuff that was matted in his beard started coming up again. His breath came hard, and his chest sounded like a cage of birds. I kept beating on the door and yelling for someone to come, but all I got back was a single voice far down the corridor telling me to cool it.

I turned Steve onto his side, and for a while it helped, at least he wasn't choking on the stuff he was bringing up. He slept, and I slept a little too. It was when the bulb went off in the morning that he turned onto his back and started talking again. He was turned on to death, his voice was almost gone.

"Maggie," he whispered. "Come here."

I got up and sat beside him, telling him there was no Maggie, that he was stuck with me. That soon the medic would come and he'd be getting better.

"Maggie. I wanted to come back, Maggie. I almost did."

"You'll be going back," I said.

He was holding on to me. "Kiss me," he said." Maggie, kiss me."

I couldn't. I think what I thought was, any guy dying wanting to be kissed wouldn't know the difference anyway. I lifted his blanket and folded the top edge of it and pressed it to his mouth—and that did it. Better than me.

"Maggie," he said once more, and then nothing.

This time he was really deeply asleep. He snored. The snore became a rattle. And then I remembered the little firecrackers that had gone off in Nana's chest. Death.

The medic came right after the first meal was brought, not by One Hung but a young Canadian guy who turned white and set down both trays and ran. The medic didn't say anything, just laid the blanket over Steve's face. Though I was more hungry than I'd ever been in all my months at the camp, I couldn't face the food until they took Steve away. The food was cold by then, but I ate it all, everything on both trays.

I NEVER knew why it was Canadians. It's not a gripe, they were okay, but they'd been flown into a situation for one reason and had to cope with another. The bombing had screwed everything up. Some of the rules and routines Sling had insisted on were still operating. Like if the cell door hadn't been locked, if the guard who'd locked it had been on duty, when I called for help maybe Steve would have made it. I tormented myself with this as I tried to make it back from the bunker death. My whole body sometimes shuddered, and I'd wake up screaming. Screams were nothing new on the corridor, which was probably why nobody came.

The door was never locked again. A lot of the prisoners had gone, and those who were left moved around as they pleased, mixing it up and trading stories of the last days of Sling. Some flaky stuff had gone on, one of the six-year men had chewed up a light bulb and bled to death, another had jumped One Hung and found he could talk—he had been the listener for Sling. There were new echoes, but it wasn't the same hearing them without Steve. The loudspeaker blasted at the usual hours, and the news that a peace treaty was being signed repeated over and over. And Westmoreland, the big brass, dished out the Great American Truth at last. The badly battered communist troops failed to engage the allied forces.

No shit! That was what happened?

Great to know.

When I was taken to the showers, I saw there was a big crater from the explosion that had almost buried the bunkers, and almost half of the main house was gone. The bunkers had their doors open and were being aired. I remember how long it took to get the crud off me and how I looked after a haircut and shave. I was about forty pounds light, but at that I had done better than Steve, who must have lost eighty. The greatest thrill was a new toothbrush and American toothpaste and Listerine. I almost drank it. All the time I was half looking for the face that went with the hand that gave me the hash, but no luck.

The men who were left on the corridor had organized a basketball team, and there were movies in the evening. Old copies of Time mag were everywhere, and there were even a few books. But every time I went back to the cell was like being hit over the head, I was knocked out by the bad joke of Steve, the guy who didn't know anything and got it for not knowing.

The Canadians were great on briefing us about what was going to happen. They were sending us Stateside more or less on a time schedule based on the length of time we had been prisoners, which put me somewhere halfway. Time was harder to bear now there was a date and name to every day, without Steve I couldn't shake it, it was all dead time. What's the point telling how down I was? I just made the motions. The Canadian medic loaded us all with vitamins. My shit appointments dropped from six to one a day. The food was plentiful and okay.

My turn came. Six of us were lined up in the exercise yard and given our uniforms back. We all looked thin, like picked birds. We were to be shipped home. We were moved from the camp to Hanoi by copters. Looking down was like seeing the moon. Nothing, not a house, a tree, a bird. Somewhere below maybe was the frog baby. At one point we flew near the sea, and there was one pagoda, leaning. When we got to the Gia Lam airport it turned out that the 141 that was to fly us to Clark in the Philippines was a day late, so we all spent that day in Hanoi getting squashed. There wasn't a guy whose mind wasn't on tail, except me—I was so out of it I couldn't have gotten it up if they'd put a gun to my back.

When we landed at Clark, there was a lot of handshaking and back slapping, as though there'd been no war. At the Clark Field Hospital we were all examined by the medics there, and each man was put in the charge of a sort of social work medic, who would stick with him until the transition back to real life.

Mine was called Brian. I was lucky to get him, because he'd been around. He had a tiger tattooed on one forearm and a lion on the other, and he got my number right away. I got his too. After we'd jawed a while, he got down to it.

"How's the market?" he asked.

I asked him back what market.

"Well, you've been on something, what was it?"

"Hash. It got me through the worst." I told him about Sling and Steve and the corridor and how Steve had died, about Sling and what we called him.

He liked that. "We all know that shit," he said, "he's famous for his paranoia from one end of Nam to the other." He said, "You've got great veins, Phil. I can tell you our flight to Frisco isn't going to be anything you'll want to remember. I can fix you up."

My kind of guy. He gave me a ball. I never knew what the stuff was, but it was great. Even on it the flight was rough. There were two medics flying with us and a couple of nurses. They talked all the way about the war with two officers who'd been squeezed into the plane at the last minute. About Napalm and Napalm B, canister bomb units, free fire zones. It's lucky I was bombed myself or I couldn't have stood it. Brian sat next to me the whole way to Travis, the Air Force Base outside Frisco.

He stayed with me through the whole rehabilitation trip. After the debriefing at Travis we were quartered at Betterman, a hospital in the center of S.F.

It wasn't exactly a gas. I had nightmares regularly and couldn't get used to the ward where my bed was. Brian wasn't an asshole like so many of the other medic/sponsors, he understood what I needed was trips now and then to get me back to wherever I was supposed to get back to. The wards, all of them, were full of paras and quads, already married to their wheels. The guy in the bed next to mine looked like a movie star and mostly stayed where he was, except when they lifted him out and made him move. He didn't want to communicate at first, lots of the cases just lay like frozen corpses, staring, but after a while he thawed. He threw back the sheet and showed me—he'd had everything shot away, cock and balls, there wasn't even any hair around where they had been. He had a plastic tube that drained into a bag strapped to his leg. The worst of it was that at night he'd feel he had a hard and would reach down to take care of it, and there would be nothing. He even dreamed he had wet dreams, but of course he couldn't feel anything. Anybody could tell that no matter what they were doing to compensate him, as it was called, he was slowly going nuts. I was so depressed about him that I asked Brian if I could be moved to another ward.

He said No, it was probably the most effective part of my therapy, to discover how lucky I'd been. Besides, he said, there were cases in the other wards that were worse, did I care to hear about them? I didn't. But there was a problem. I was getting my nuts back with all the shots and steaks and wanted to pull off mornings. Lots of the other guys did, and it was awful to see what this did to the guy without anything to pull, the groans he made, and sometimes he cried. I solved it by whacking off during my shower. I sometimes took several showers a day, and I still felt dirty from all the Nam shit, the bunker.

I'd have never made it back without Brian. He had a real head shop in the dispensary, everything from rolling papers— he even had E-Z Widers—to tiny needles that would go into, say, a thumb vein, if it had to be. He doped a little himself, but was a careful one, he knew where the door to crazy was.

We'd sit around on the veranda and talk. I just laid back and let it all out. I was still blown out. I'd have flipped all over again if it hadn't been for him. Some days I walked away and sat by myself. Times with him it was just making conversation, nothing heavy. He understood that the big thing for me would have been to be with Hesper and spend all the time of my life with her, grow together, be one. But as the weeks piled up he'd always ask if I didn't want to talk to her, there was the chaplain who did nothing but make connections with families and wives.

"Phil," he said one day, "you're going to have to begin to communicate. The padre will set it all up. There are special lines for it, always open."

"I don't want to talk to anybody," I said. I could tell he was trying to say they'd done all they could for me there, that it was up to outside now to finish it, bring me back.

Back—I was terrified of going back because it would be that same spook world of Camilla and Theron and Haute, the same. But at the same time I felt like some sea animal that had been on land and had to go back. The padre, when I told him this, said lots of guys felt like that, but wouldn't I at least talk to home base?

I'd said no about a hundred times. The padre was the kind of chaplain who looked as though a couple of aspirins would do him good. I mean, he had no idea where I was in my head. He never let up, and one day he said he had Camilla and Theron on the phone and they were dying to hear my voice. They were at the other end, and I heard their voices and they heard mine, like they said, as though I was in the next room. They played it very mellow, but it didn't work. I simply didn't know them, I couldn't even remember what they were going to look like when they got me back. But the padre enjoyed it.

Later that week Brian was due to fly back to be like a shepherd to his next guy. He left me cold, holding the bag. No goodby. I'd been his problem, and he'd given it the three months and now it was over, and all the getting together of Phil Hanway had been just a professional gig. Plastic.

Plastic—Hey, Doc. Doc! That's the key word.
That was that trip, Doc.
Color me orange.
Roger and over and out.

———

239

IT's got to be today, not the tomorrow we worried about yesterday, as they say. Anyway, I wrote it like it came out. And did I make sounds of being glad I'd finished it? I can't remember, except that Malc hotfooted it in and took away what I'd written. Doc came in and made with his approval smile, and a blond nurse who almost made me come in my pants took a blood test.

My Nam thinkback must be proof that you can't just give yourself orders to remember and get it all back. Though I wrote my ass off trying, I didn't begin to get it all in. Like when Nana and the nannies were training me for the pot and the first time I did it by myself I gave them a big holler, I did it, I did it.

So I've done my Nixon, solid. My Kiss and L.B.J. and J.F.K. and a little extra for Westmoreland. But shitting them out didn't get rid of them. It all still stinks on ice—like coming back to Camilla and Theron, who'd thrown me at them in the first place. Because what it was, it was like a heavy stone in my throat I had to swallow. Too far down to spit out now, and if I didn't swallow it down I'd choke and couldn't tell the rest. Now instead of the relief you feel from feeling it go down, I feel it in me, something I'll never digest, that will be there always. Hate.

So now the ballpoint's back and a blank page staring at me. I ground it out, and now we're sitting back to engine again, ready to wind up. Baby Cube and the other lawyers have read it as well as Doc, and I heard Tweed Suit crack that if I hadn't turned into a murderer I'd have made it as a writer. Anyhow, now they look as though they believe how I got the welts on my back and butt, I wasn't shitting them on the early tapes.

Doc didn't exactly give me 10/4 to my Roger and out.

The very first thing he asked was, "What were you on and where did you get it?"

I don't have these big baby blue eyes for nothing, so I gave him Innocent & Hurt No. 2. And no answer. There isn't going to be one.

"Was it Malc gave it to you?" he asked.

"I don't know where you're at, Doc," I said. "If you mean once there was a guy with nuts in his head and he saw a pill on the floor and picked it up, maybe he thought it was an aspirin."

I was willing to tease that far. After a while he got tired of asking, the blood test would tell him anyway, he said.

"So why did you ask?" I threw it right back.

"Your recall is extraordinary," he said. "But now I want you to forget all that Nixon hate, the war in Vietnam's over, and the President himself says we should put it behind us."

"Just give me a pot," I said, "I'll fill it full."

"No-no-no," Doc said, impatient. "What we want now is—what you call the next thing."

"But I put down the last thing. Plastic. That's the key word."

"Yes, yes, the allusion didn't escape me."

I told him how Baby Cube keeps asking me whether I took it upstairs with the tools or went back for it.

"Don't you remember?"

"All I remember was what I did with it and that it was the last thing."

"Well," Doc said, flipping through his stuff, "it's listed here, Exhibit twelve, one plastic basting syringe of a type used in kitchens. Let's not get off on that. What we have to do now is finish up. Take it from when you came back."

"Not 'we,' " I reminded him, "it's my story, Doc."

"Merely a manner of speaking. So—okay. You'll go on? And don't pull punches, write exactly what you felt, repeat, felt."

IN the bunker I'd lost days and got hooked into that block of time that was thick, and I couldn't separate it into any meaning. But the flight back from Frisco to New York narrowed time down for me. I could feel it all beginning again, days that had hours, drinks at Florence's, cruising for tail, getting high in the old way, crashing, waking up. The same thing, and man was I ready for it.

Theron was waiting for me beyond the barrier, alone. I was glad of that.

"Phil," he said, "Phil—you look okay!"

There was a second with the past between us, and then he threw his arms around me. His smooth cheeks, the clean smell of him—it made me remember what Ummie had once said, "A really clean man, you could eat off any part of him."

Crazy what you remember. And when you remember it. We said all the stuff you say at such times. Great flight. No, no, no baggage, my kit was all of it. No lag.

"Your mother wanted to be here, but she's stuck at Heathrow. Fog."

I felt even gladder to know she was stuck. It somehow got me in the tear glands, I was misty. As we walked toward the Ferrari, right away I could feel the space there always was around him, people giving him room, letting him through first. But I really felt I was back when I sank into the seat beside him. The flight had been hardass, but now there was an almost magical quiet within the car with the air conditioning and Theron handing me a cigarette and lighting it. Like a marriage between father and son. It didn't last, soon came the separation that would always be between us, the quarrels, the quarrel.

But for that afternoon it was one of our rare twosomes—like at breakfasts long ago. After Schaafy and Diego had got it all over about missing me, Theron and I settled down to drinks before the lunch Schaafy had made and Diego would serve. I had to pee monstrously, as happens to me on planes. In the powder room, off his room with the big toys.

"How's about a killing martini?"

"Great," I said. I hadn't expected this one to one, I was feeling really weird stuff, even a little kinky, some of it. I mean as I watched him chill glasses and mix drinks, I could see that for guys who dug guys he'd be just about it. His great forearms, the way his nipples grooved against his shirt, even the Roman coins around his neck were okay, right. But then

I found I was looking at myself, what I'd be back to when my weight came back to me. I hadn't had martinis—since when? It was a great lunch. I kind of got sleepy, jag hitting me, and he went with me up to my room.

Exactly as it was. It all went like velvet as I stripped for bed, and then he saw the welts the cat had left.

It took several seconds before he could say anything. Then all he said was, "Christ. Christ, Phil. Oh, Christ."

"Cover up," he said.

I was dreamy from the drinks. He covered me.

He said, "I want to do something for you. Today. Tell me what I can do when you wake up."

"I want to get laid," I said. "But I want to crash first."

I remember he pulled up the blanket to my chin. It touched my mouth. Like the kiss I didn't give Steve. Fifteen, twelve, Christ, centuries too late. If he'd kissed me, I'd have kissed him back.

But he didn't.

Doc wants instant replay—what was my 10/20 then? All I can get back of it now is scrambled, tangled, you know the way tape can be stopped too fast and has to be cut and patched? This will be like that.

I knew it had been one of those little daddy honeymoons with Theron, like the night the snow had covered everything and we'd gone into the dunes, those breakfasts when I'd found he wasn't dumb. And I knew it would be over suddenly, and it was.

When I came downstairs, he was stretched out watching TV, a drink beside him. As though I'd never been away. There were still people in the world like him, showered and fit inside his turtleneck, looking younger than he was, laid back, easy. Me—I was shredded.

"Schaafy's kept dinner warm for you," he said.

I didn't want any dinner.

"Okay." He rang to tell her. I wouldn't get arguments

anymore, the boy who was on his way back from where he'd been. Dealing with the shock of returning to real life that the shrinks at Betterman had warned about. From shitbox to perfect small oval room with daddy and his shit elegance. Even the smell of Diego's rose wax was there.

I asked what day it was.

"What day? Why, Friday."

Friday. Okay. A day you could tear away from tomorrow's Saturday like a cobweb.

There were cobwebs all right—I had come back into his life but he hadn't come back into mine. But we were talking easy, mostly he was talking, briefing me on Bill and Coo and Ummie, who'd been asked for the weekend after this. And I was being polite. I even asked if David was still at the shop, and he said No, David was gone, there was Teddy instead.

Teddy Bear, I thought. Teddywegs.

"I'm picking Camilla up at Kennedy tomorrow afternoon," he said, which translated Be here, for Our Talk.

"You got our letters?"

I said I had.

"And Mr. Homer's?"

I knew it by heart.

"They're ready to settle," he said, and waited for me to say something, but I didn't.

I think my silences began then.

"Well," he said, "I imagine you'll have a lot to tell us when we're all back together."

Together? Tell—them? I could never tell them anything.

"I'll still have to drive you," he said, reminding me that I still had no wheels. "Monday you can apply for your license. Now I must take you where you want to go. Florence's?"

"Where it's at for me." I'd said it before.

It was all the same, the white gravel of the drive kept raked by Diego, spattering. A windstorm had taken a willow down by the gates, it had fallen across the lane and had been cut up for firewood and stacked. A home cue—it should have brought me back, but it didn't. There was a moon, and that was the first flash I had of not seeing and hearing what was in

244

front of me, but what I'd left behind—the pagoda leaning toward the sea, the clatter of copters. Theron was saying something, repeating it.

"I think it's going to be smooth sailing from here on in, Phil, but remember—no mistakes now."

Now? It was all mistakes.

Florence's was jammed. She was sitting behind her glass screen, shouting orders. After a double take she asked why I wasn't in uniform. I told her I wanted to forget it, I'd flushed my dogtag down the john, got rid of everything.

"I suppose you're looking for your sidekick," she said—I didn't like sidekick.

"Has Renzo been here?"

"That one," she answered, not too nicely. "Still peddling whatever it is he's peddling. He's in and out."

Spiderman and Robin made such a scene over seeing me again that I carried my drink to a booth, where I could watch the bar. I needed to catch my breath. What I was feeling was like a carbon copy. I wasn't making it back. I knew that—my months at the Nam Tourist Camp had done wonders for cueing me into myself. It wasn't that anything was different. I mean, here I was sitting on a hard, needing to get my cock out of my pants so I could get rid of Jack the Jerk and my fantasies about Hesper. And no wheels and no Renzo. I was still able to keep things separate, she could be any girl who would jump out of a cake, as long as she didn't have corn-flower blue eyes and silky brown hair. I'd squeeze my eyes shut and supply those.

She came in alone, blond hair parted in the middle and hanging down her back. She stood at the bar. I could see that Spiderman and Robin knew her. She looked like maybe a Lib girl, looking for another Lib so they could talk about male chauvinist pigs—it was that year. Or a Nice Girl—Allow 4 to 6 weeks for delivery, return guaranteed. She kept giving me the eye. There was something familiar about her, but you know how they all are, always changing hair color, makeup, mood dressing, whatever. Then we crossed glances, and she walked over.

"How've you been?" she asked, easing in beside me. Well, I wasn't going to fight it.

I said a little of this and that.

"I heard on the grapevine you've been to the wars," she said.

Well, all right—Uncle always has more than one war going. So I said Yes, I'd been in Nam.

"And you've come back all in one piece."

"Not quite. I've got the map of North Nam all over my back."

"You mean—scars? But that's all right, I'm queer for scars."

If she hadn't been dressed I'd have gotten it then, who she was. My backthink was working backasswards—the big white studio with the beams, the pot, the popper, the couple who'd wanted the 3-decker. The guy blowing me.

"But you've changed yourself," I remember saying. "What happened to your guy? You had a guy."

"Harry," she said. "He's gone over to the boys. We split months ago. I'm keeping bachelor hall now."

"Loning it?"—I helped her out, she needed it.

"Don't worry about Harry," she said.

If there was one thing I wasn't worrying about it was Harry. I needed more help than she did.

"Let's fuck," I said.

"Okay, let's."

We went past Florence, who gave us a wink. It was hardly any time before we were at her place.

"I remember it," I said.

"Well, the house was always mine. It was mine, luckily, because Harry didn't leave me much."

What he did leave her that I'd not had time for that first time was a string of Chinky porno hanging on the walls. They all had poems explaining what was going on. She wanted to talk, though, wanted to know what it had been like in Nam.

"Were you a mortar squad leader or what? I had a friend who was whatever that is."

"We're not going to talk about that," I told her. It came back to me then that what she'd liked before was shock, so to hurry things up, I flashed, and she was crazy about it, went to work right away. Harry had taught her a lot, but all it did was wake me up. I stopped her, told her I wanted to begin straight and let the kook work itself out. And we did just about everything the Chinks hanging on the walls did— Double Lotus, Jade Lute, Call Soul Back. We'd have done Chin Chin if there'd been a horse handy. It was great. I mean, I'd looked at the damn thing standing up every morning for so long I didn't pull out till the very end. By the time we fell asleep I'd had all I wanted.

It was daylight when I woke, without a hard, which must have been the first time in my life. She was moving around between the bath and kitchen, being the little woman, while I made the trip back with the Chink porno. Like all night rooms, the day made it smaller. I worked back, went over Theron's meeting me and my nap and Florence's, but I couldn't seem to be where I was. I mean, I couldn't get back.

She brought me coffee. We shared a joint, which helped a little.

"That was something," she said. She would talk about it, which I didn't like, so I was giving her no answers. I got it back that I hadn't even tried to turn her eyes blue. "If Harry had been here—"

"Stop talking about Harry," I said.

I was all stuck together and needed a shower. I asked where it was, and she showed me. I was still sleeping, really, and in the back of my mind was the thought that she had the wheels and I didn't. As I thought this, I felt her step in beside me. I had to open my eyes to believe it and got soap in them.

"Once more, for me. Please?"

"Feel it," I said. "You've had it."

She felt me, and I couldn't believe it, I was getting hard. Then I was hard, hard as I'd been anytime in the night, giving it to her, having to jackknife a little because she wasn't tall. Whether or not it was the joint, I don't know, but I came again and too fast. It split my guts, half orgasm and half pain, and the soap burned my cock as I withdrew. She took off then and let me finish my shower.

I was shot and put on my clothes any old whichway, and she drove me back to Groverhampton. I remember it seemed hundreds of miles. But Florence's was opening, I could see Robin washing the front windows, and I asked her to drop me there.

It was a real drop. I stood a minute, holding onto the car door, hating her, feeling sorry for her, feeling sorrier for myself.

"Call me," she said, just because she had to say something.

"I'll never call you. Why don't you go back to Harry?"

That burned her up. "You shit," she said, "why don't you go back to whoever she is? If you know who she is."

"Oh, I know who she is," I said, and slammed the door.

ROBIN wiped his squeegee with his sponge and gave me a wink that said what there was to say, then told me someone was waiting for me inside. I knew it had to be Renzo, and there he was, holding the bar down alone, drinking the Rusty Nail that Robin always fixed for him on bad mornings. We stared at one another. He had grown a beard that cut off half his expression and was wearing a three-piece suit and a shirt and tie. But his eyes hadn't changed, whatever I couldn't remember about the dead spot with the dad the night before I left for Nam, it was still like blood brothers, the time between wiped out.

He rushed to me and grabbed my hands. "Are you still wearing that cookie in your shoe?" I asked—it just slipped out.

He made a face. "Man, don't beat me about that," he said. "Every time I take a step I think of you. How you took it for me. You look great." It was a goddamn lie, I was fucked out and looked it, what was worse, I felt like it.

"I saw who brought you," he said. "Chinese paintings, right?"

"Right," I said.

"And got the last drop out of you in the shower?"

"Right again."

Robin asked what I'd have and Renzo said it with me— "Six of your best hen fruit lightly scrambled, plenty of bacon." And the rest of the joke, "Doesn't put it back, only time and rest can do that."

I should have noticed the wedding ring before I did, one of those old-fashioned heavy ones.

"So what color is the icebox?" I asked him.

"Funny you should ask," he answered, cool. "It's yellow because the kitchen's yellow. Ellie wanted it that way." Then he stopped, waited. "You mean you didn't know? You didn't get my letter? The invitation, all that jazz?"

"Only a postcard—You were heaving stones for old Ruggiero."

"Yeah, I was heaving then," he said. I noticed he had two cigarettes burning in his tray. He asked Robin for another Rusty Nail as I wolfed my eggs.

"It began that way," he said. "You want the long or short version?"

I didn't care.

"Well," he said, "that was about as close a thing as you could get, that morning we had with the old judge." I agreed. He asked me to believe he'd had his own Nam, sitting in it—did I remember that last night, what he'd said about cunt? How it had him by both balls, was driving him crazy wanting it every night, making him a cunt slave? He was determined to win out over it, before he had another scud. He'd tried to pick up on what was going on around him, get his lifestyle together, find a base to work from. His old man and old lady gave him no rest about the job Ruggiero was offering him. He'd taken it, finally, and the deal was clear from the start. He'd moved bricks one by one, laid stones one at a time, mixed cement in cold weather. And sat around evenings with Ellie. The more he sat, the easier old Ruggiero made it for him, moving him up to supervising the contracts he had for housing developments all over the Island. Now he had it soft, selling to couples who bought even before the units were finished. That explained the suit and tie—he was showing one at noon. He looked at his watch, no longer a Timex, but about a thousand in gold. Matching the ring. All that was missing was the slave bracelet on his other wrist.

I guess I showed what I was thinking because he said, "Hey, here I am running off about me when it's you I want to know about."

I started something—can't remember what—but it didn't matter because in a minute he was off again about himself. He'd bought the whole package, the icebox wasn't a joke to him now. He said he didn't have any more money now than when he'd been dealing. Whenever he did anything it had to be around the edges, the drug scene wasn't what it used to be, and besides, he had to worry now what old Ruggiero would find out.

The old guy had it all his own way, and why not? He'd done the handsome. When Renzo and Ellie left Mama Chiesa after the wedding, there'd been a new Caddy DeVille waiting to take them to the boat, they'd spent their honeymoon in Bermuda. The old man was so hung on Ellie's happiness he'd deeded over one of his houses in his Groverhampton development, practically complete with crib and baby buggy.

It had been great the first months, Renzo'd been sure he'd found the solution, but then Ellie got pregnant and after that it was all different. She'd had a hard time from the beginning and her doctors told her to do nothing strenuous, they were still worried she might not carry to term. Whenever he went home after work the house was full of women—her mother, his mother, one of Ellie's sisters who was pregnant too. He was expected to have one beer and get through dinner and then watch TV. He was up to here from it, he said, between hand jobs in the bathroom and a couple of visits to the Pork Chop tearoom, he hadn't really got his nuts off in three months. But the worst was the way old Ruggiero watched him. He'd sort of set up a date mechanism at the Pork Chop with a fruit who'd do him twice a week when the old guy looked at him funny and asked why he'd seen the DeVille parked in the shopping center lot. He hadn't really said anything, except that in a good Italian family it was the women who took care of the food, and he'd learned when he was young that in a wife's last months a husband's best friend was his fist.

So that was why Renzo was here, pulling himself together to show a house in Ruggiero's Groverhampton complex— which meant he'd have to go home for lunch and face it, explain why he'd hauled ass last night and gotten laid by one of the Florence regulars.

He kept looking at his watch. "That's it about me," he said, and sort of looked at me the old buddy way. "You still haven't any wheels, have you?"

I told him No, I was going to apply for a regular license as soon as I could get down to the courthouse.

"But it's on my way," he said. "I've just got time to take you down and home."

It was a solution for me, I didn't want to hear any more about Ellie and old Ruggiero, and by now I knew I'd never be able to tell him much about Nam, even if he'd listen. Or about Hesper. Or the girl on fire and the frog baby. I thought, Forget it.

All the way down to the courthouse in the DeVille he kept on.

Like, "I know what I'm doing, I'm plugging into the computer. It's all sick, man, all bullshit. Suicide, no matter how you do it. . . ."

I thought, You're telling me, good buddy.

At the courthouse they brought out a folder with HANWAY, PHILIP on it. They kind of held it away from me like a doctor does when he's writing something down about you, so I couldn't guess what was in it. It didn't exactly make me feel Welcome Back from Doing My Duty for My Country, but I filled out the application, and they said it would be the routine number of days.

When Renzo dropped me at Lilacs, he didn't do it the old

251

way, leaving me at the gates to walk up, but made a big V in the gravel that Diego would have to rake back. I figured that showed he'd made it, not that I gave a shit by then. I was a little spaced out anyway, and what I thought as I crashed for the afternoon was what Steve would have said about it back in the damp two-by-four hole on the corridor—Friendship dies.

It sure as hell does. Did. Well, he had his Ellie, and I had my Hesper. Hes-per. Kind of.

THERE's a day between what I wrote last and Malc took away, or maybe it's two days. Anyway, forget as you go is my rule now. But I do recall that after I'd finished the part about the Lib girl in the shower and Renzo, I felt fucked out in the same way I did at the time it happened. I think in some ways writing is like sex, you reach down for the last one you know you should let wait for next time, and you have it, and then you pay for it.

So there's been a little intermission while Doc and Tweed Suit and Baby Cube lawyer try to paste it all together. They don't care what I hear, they're like Camilla and Theron used to be at 25 Wall, just yakking about me in the third person. As if I'm not here. Or soon not to be. Doc sort of paid me a compliment, I mean he left me these pills to take if I get tired. Not aspirins, I don't know what they are. Truth pills? A little like truth serum, maybe, but not that Pentothal, which anybody who's ever doped can tell you is for amateurs.

Tweed Suit is impatient. He says to Doc, "But we already have this part on the early tapes, don't we?"

"No, no," Doc tells him. "This is new material we're getting here, he's never talked about—this. Not on tape."

Tweed Suit: "So we absolutely need it?"

Doc: "Defense insists we get it exactly."

Defense, I think, what defense? If anybody ever tried to tell it as it mounted up, it's P.T.H. Anyhow, Malc's brought the pad back. They seem to like what they're getting.

I'M not going to tell it by days, because I don't know exactly how many there were. Maybe enough days to make up a week, a little more.

It came, the family reunion, the clutch. I'd had some kind of weird nightmare during my nap, the kind without any people in it, not much of anything else either. But scary, like that dead landscape under the copter as we flew over—not the kind of dream that leaves you or you can shake off. Maybe it was still in my mind when I went downstairs so Camilla could do the mother part. She did it, the way Theron had. Nothing you could believe. It was like we were actors who'd never met reading a script for the first time and looking at each other, Did I get that right? No? Well, it'll all come right during rehearsals. And it wasn't tension, because it was very controlled at first, like stick with it and it'll work out.

But it didn't. All through the dinner Schaafy had made with all the things I liked and Diego handing and serving they filled me in on what had gone on while I was away. Bill and Coo, Ummie. Bill had had his gall bladder out. Ummie had had another lift, and this time she'd gone to that plastic surgeon in Brazil who does the presidents and their wives. Camilla was thinking of having it. She was very full of herself and excited because Haute was going to do a big issue commemorating—I forget what. And Theron and the new Teddy were going to Houston next month to do a big house there. They saved Mr. Homer and Mr. Stanhope to the end, but they played it too fast, like an encore—how wonderful it was that we could expect the big decision about old Gramps's money very soon, as soon as I felt really back and comfortable we'd go. . . .

Well, I listened, but with what's maybe that third ear you hear about, and I answered and talked along like that soldier hero back for the laurel wreath. Only what they were laying on me all over again felt like a crown of thorns. There was a voice under my real voice that kept laughing at them and

253

answering their throwaway lines. Like, You just think there's going to be a commemoration number of your fucking mag, You just think you and Teddywegs are going to Houston. . . . We talked and we talked, and it was all this performance because I was so completely somewhere else. Maybe getting echoes of the scud days and the time in the judge's chambers, I don't know.

So then there was the rest of the weekend with nobody there but as Camilla said, "Just us," and if there were a few rough patches pretending it would take a little time to catch up. They were in their world, and I was in mine, but I was beginning like they say to have a premonition. One night some people came into the empty landscape I went on dreaming about. I couldn't see their faces, all I could get back into daylight was that I'd been ordering a couple of coffins, identical ones. A perfect pair, as Theron would have said. They were really just exactly alike, right down to the bronze trimmings and handles.

But behind my eyes as I slept there always seemed to be some daylight, like they say when a dog sleeps one eye is always a little bit open. I guess it was insomnia. The real daylight left me feeling squashed and flattened out, I felt sort of sick, as if I had to throw up that stone I'd swallowed. And the big golden egg had gone on growing, and they wanted me to be there when it broke. I just clammed when they talked about that and the O. W. M.

My new silences bothered them. They kept asking me "Is everything okay? Do you want me to drive you anywhere before I go? Or Diego can take you. Do you have walking around money?" Underneath they were really giving me orders, not reasons, the way they always had. Boy, did I know them and their techniques. I knew them as well as I knew how my ass looks in a mirror. That was a scene that really sucked. I felt suffocated and full of rage I'd never known in Nam, even in solitary. Maybe I was just one more pathetic mess. Though I did what I did every day, I knew I couldn't go on doing it much longer.

I wasn't the only guy back from Nam having troubles

finding something to do. One morning I met this strung out mess who'd been back for a year. He'd never been able to get a job, not even the one he had left to go. He'd worked a few weeks at a filling station on the Million Dollar Mile, but that pooped out. He had wheels, though, and a pad over his old man's garage, and a couple of times I'd crashed there. But he'd get very heavy about a new kind of clap he'd brought home with him that no doctor had been able to get rid of so he couldn't screw. The whole shitting mess had made him hate everybody. Like Renzo hated it, but in a different way.

My way of hating was this rage I felt about everything, myself included. It was like something I'd been dipped in and was hardening, like a glass suit you couldn't see. When I'd touch something, there'd seem to be this invisible distance between me and the thing. Or it could be a person. I mean I wasn't sure I'd really touched the thing or seen the person. And it could chip or crack, I'd get mad as anything about stuff I once never paid any attention to. It had something to do with memory too, as if the remembered things had been put in a jar and fermented, grown stronger. One day this guy with the wheels drove me to Southampton, so I could look at Hesper's house, be really sure it was there. It was, and there were all these cars around it, like before, a party going on, and I could remember everything about her and that day. And under that memory was a secret memory of things that hadn't happened really, lots of memory layers beneath that.

I could see that Camilla and Theron were waiting for me to feel better—they called it that. They didn't see that I had my own private revolution going on in me, that every day I set out to wipe out that part of me they had made. Their orderly lives were disorder to me, the only order I could make for myself was breaking their rules. I think during those days I at last became myself. I had read about Zen, and it had one thing right—you couldn't help reacting, hating, whatever, but whatever you did was already wrong. The answer I came up with was that I had to cut myself off not only from them but from myself too. There was a third world in me and among the buried memories I'd catch glimpses of it sometimes. Another thing I was sure of too—communication with them was impossible. If their world was full of shit, so was mine, and I had to do something to get rid of it all. I mean all. Them. And then me.

It's getting to be hell trying to keep this straight, I mean like in any kind of order. Because I did all this dreaming. Nightmares. I tried not to, but there's no stopping what goes on when you're asleep. During the day I was conscious of trying to get myself so tired I'd just black out during the hours I used to sleep. But no go on that, the stuff I'd brought back with me couldn't be kicked that way. I was always waking up thinking I'd screamed, though I guess I didn't, because nobody came to ask if I'd had a nightmare. And I'd sweat, my bed when I got out of it—you'd have thought it was summer camp and somebody in the bunk over me had wet his bed.

Every one of those days I went down to the mailbox before Diego, to see if my license had come. There was never anything for me. This might be a different story if it had come through, it wouldn't have been all feet feet feet. I got over my draining by the Lib girl, and there it was again in the mornings. Omar under the tent, raring to go. I didn't touch it. Being back had given me one decision, No Hands, if I got it off it would be some other way. The real way, I mean you don't do the work yourself.

So I just hung out with Schaafy and Diego catching up on things until it was time for Florence's to open, and when I got there, I got a lot of attention. Robin had sort of taken Renzo's spot as the one who could get you dope if you needed it, you just told him in the morning, and by afternoon he'd have it. Anything, including a thing new to me, angel dust.

I saw Renzo a couple of times, lunching his customers for old Ruggiero's houses. He'd come up to the bar to speak to me, but it wasn't the same, what there had been was gone. What the shit did I care that he'd sold two houses in one day?

That Ellie's doctor was encouraged about her and was letting him take her to a movie to get her out of the house? We were down to dialogue like, "Hey, man, you making it in the head? Do you need to go anywhere? If you do, just give me the orders."

Orders, shit. I needed to be somewhere, but not places he went. And he was nobody to tell about a girl on fire throwing a green frog baby. He acted like he thought I was ready for the rubber room, and I thought, Shit in your own pants, man, not in mine.

So what it came down to was I'd stand around and rap with what Florence called her Blue Collar Set, and by the time she made her big lunch entrance at noon, I'd already had it for then. I was finding out how much time there is in the world and how hard it was going to be to kill it. And don't think Hesper was giving me any rest either. She was always just under what I was thinking. The guy with the clap who'd driven me over to Southampton thought I was out of my mind. He said she was Old Tammany stuff, they'd made their money long before there were taxes. He said they owned us, even if there would be revolution they'd come out the people on top. "Forget it," he said.

I couldn't forget her. Every single thing about that day was fresh in my mind, perfect. The way she'd lifted the shades and the cornflower blue eyes. Her voice. Even things she'd said, her Groverhampton putdown—"We go through Groverhampton sometimes." Child's Garden—the scratching.

So this day that it happened I was just hanging out on a street corner where the expressway goes through Grover-hampton and becomes Main Street. And suddenly there was all this noise like a parade coming from Southampton way, lots of car horns blowing and people cheering. I thought at first it was an Italian wedding. It was a wedding party, only I could see from the first car it was no Eyetye couple but some classy bunch driving through in a hurry to get somewhere else. There were two motorcycle cops clearing the way. The cars had chauffeurs. The first hint I got of who it was who'd gotten married was when I saw this big old sports flyer rolling along right in the middle of all the Rolls and Caddies. It was the Hispano I'd first seen Hesper stranded in, and the whole thing was covered with flowers. The guys in it were in morning clothes and throwing streamers right and left, and the guy driving must have been her brother. The guys with him were yelling, not giving a shit about what anybody thought, they had the motorcycle cops, and there were sirens, and it was a really wild thing. Then a light changed somewhere ahead, and the whole production came to a stop.

I stood where I was, like they say with my hair on my head and my teeth in my mouth, watching. All the world loves a wedding, and it was the kind of day lucky for brides, the sun was shining and hot. The whole thing made me feel like a nothing, a nerd.

And then I saw her. Sitting in the back of the biggest Rolls and looking the part, a rich, Catholic bride who was still a virgin and had a right to wear all the white stuff and orange blossoms. Next to her was what she married, this cube with a Wall Street haircut and a big stock with a stickpin up to his chin. They were behaving like royalty for the benefit of all the nobodies lining the sidewalk, smiling and waving.

Her Rolls slowed so close to the curb where I was standing that I could have reached out and touched it. I could see her almost as close as she'd been to me as we drove along the roads to her house that morning long ago. She was looking the other way at first, but then she turned her head and saw me. The cornflower blue eyes, and she was smiling. The smile turned off as she recognized me and became a stare. But she raised her hand and made a little sign, just for me. It was only seconds before the Rolls started up again, and then there were more sirens and the last cars speeded up until they were out of sight.

I stood there a while. Frozen. I had nowhere to move to anyway. I remember the bank on the corner was closing, so it must have been after three. What I did then was the nearest thing—I crossed the street to the Groverhampton movie house and bought a ticket and went in so I could flop. The film had started, I couldn't get what it was about, except there was this space chick who floated around upside down and there were great tit shots when they fell out of her silver space suit. Every guy in the place let out a big sigh. One at the end of the row I was sitting in had his fly open and was giving himself a hand job.

I had a hard on myself, one big enough to show through my pants. But I'd made a promise to myself No More Jerk, and there I was in the movie house beginning to groove. Except for the tit and ass shots the thing was a drag, so after an hour and a half of it I got up and left.

Groverhampton's not a big place, everything is pretty close to everything else, and as I walked away I found myself passing the Pork Chop with its stand of sumac. Always before I'd come to it from the supermarket side, you'd never have guessed what was between where I was and the place I'd always parked with Renzo.

I STILL had my hard. You don't reason with a hard. I was thinking that if I could get off before going back to Lilacs maybe I could crash for that night and not have those dreams. Because they were getting wilder, my mental tapes were just waiting for sleep to start up and play all kinds of under the lid stuff—those plastic needles they shot into those little people that went to their lungs and livers—M-16's firing and shaking your hips loose—and always it was stone age and some crazy counting thing I'd begun to do before waking up wet, 2,4,5-T, the stuff that made the babies come out slimy frogs. . . .

I stretched my eyes open and went through the sumac to the old door which hadn't changed, still had the curtain of woodbine hanging over it, and went in.

The bulb that used to be over the three urinals had gone out and the place was dark, though I could feel it was packed and there were too many there for what they had come for. It was like an old painting in the dark, there were faces but I couldn't see them, just shadows. After a second I could just

259

make out the watchqueen at the window and could tell from the sucking sounds coming from the toilet stalls that there was action there.

There was this minute when I went over to the end urinal to whiz out and they could tell I'd come to play. I didn't zip up, I was so hot for it I couldn't have gotten it back in my pants anyway, even if they'd let me. But straight off I felt hands groping me, playing with my balls, and other hands behind pulled my pants down to my knees and the game was on. Other hands began to feel my ass, but I yanked back my elbows to show I didn't play that game. The door opened and a big guy in a sweatshirt squeezed through. One of the others braced himself against the door so no one else could get in. After that the door didn't open except for the ones who were through and went out.

Up to then it was general action. The sweatshirt was down on his knees sucking, and over by the watchqueen there was just enough dim light to see a guy getting it up the ass and sucking everybody around him he could reach. The place was so crowded it was hard to move. When somebody lit a cigarette, it made a little light for a second to see by, and it was a real orgy.

There was a guy in the first toilet booth, the one with the glory hole, and he was working the whole place. When he'd sucked off one, the next would move up and stick his cock through. Not everybody left after they'd been done but stood against the wall watching what they could and getting a charge out of it. I thought how weird that all this was going on a stone's throw from all the moms in the supermarket with their kids riding ahead of them in carts.

The guys who were handling and stroking me seemed to be playing some game with whoever was behind the glory hole, and when he had finished a trick he had been doing I felt myself being pushed into place to be next. I was right up against the side of the stall and my cock went through the hole while these guys held me. I was ready.

From the start I knew the glory man was a quick tongue artist and was going to give me a great time. I mean he must have been wild in there, he'd suck like a maniac and then suddenly stop. He could tell when I was about to go off and he'd hold me still while I cooled down, then started all over.

I was getting wild myself. My chest was flat against the side of the stall and trembling and I had to reach up to the top to hold myself steady. Because the guys behind me were going as far as they could with my ass tight like it is when you're on the point of coming, doing a dry fuck between my legs. It went on a long time but it couldn't go on forever, and finally I came way down in his throat and he swallowed me without a gulp. No chick or guy had ever given me a job like that and its being secret like it was made it somehow even greater.

But anybody can tell you what you feel like after one like that. I felt sick, and all the anger came back, and all I wanted to do was pull up my pants and get the hell out, which I did. There were two black lines across my palms from where I'd clutched the top of the stall.

I was still breathing hard, and I went over to a ledge there was just beyond the path to the parking lot and sat down. The sun had set and the ledge was cold and there wasn't much light, but enough for me to see the guys coming out. One at a time, checking their zippers and putting on their square faces before getting into their cars and driving away. I could tell they'd been the ones holding me against the stall, but none of them looked my way or saw me. One last guy went in, I figured the one behind the glory hole must have given him a quickie or he was straight, because he came out fast.

It was getting dark, and I was about to get up when—I think it was the shoes that gave it to me. I saw the shoes on the very last one who came out, and then I looked up and saw his pants and top and the rest of him. If there'd been any doubt it would have vanished when I saw him whip out a comb and run it through his hair.

It was Theron. Theron had been the one inside the stall.

—Doc wants me to tell how I felt. For a minute I didn't feel anything, because I couldn't believe it. And then I believed it and felt cold, because I'd slumped back onto the stone as he made the turn in the path to the parking lot. I remember having this crazy thought that here was my ride home—I even recognized the motor of the Ferrari starting up, thinking that its tappets don't sound like any other engine in the world. I think now I was hoping for doubt to set in, if there'd been any doubt. There wasn't.

What I did then was like one of my dreams beginning. I must have gone into the market and called the taxi, because I remember getting out and paying the driver who didn't have change so I gave him a five.

The lights were on all over the house. Camilla was sitting with her martini in the room next to the dining room, and she said something about not taking too long because Schaafy had made a soufflé. I showered and changed, and Theron must have had the same idea because I met him at the top of the stairs on his way down, and he said, "When did you come in? You should have called me to come and get you."

I think I didn't answer, I was numb, so numb I knew I'd get through cocktails smooth as anything before my reaction came. And I did, keeping it up in front of Diego and Schaafy, who came in, and Theron and Camilla told her how they'd liked the dinner.

THAT was the night before the last night, as Doc calls it.

I had my glass suit on, tight. It was lucky I had some stuff Robin had given me, not Q, but a little like it, enough to keep the distance I needed between me and them, otherwise I couldn't have handled it. It turned into the knockdown drag-out we should have had years ago, and when it came, it was like a wind that tore away everything right down to the bones.

Camilla was being Mother Control, trying to get it back to where it had been, when they were telling me and I was doing it. Schaafy had made all kinds of things I like. I was hungry, and I ate everything. But I couldn't seem to look at Theron or say much while the two of them were keeping it up for the servants. Both talking shop, Camilla on the special issue of Haute that had gone to press, Theron on his trip to Texas. They were keeping it all down, easy, throwing me a question now and then.

They'd had it from Diego that my driver's license hadn't come, they said they were sure it was a matter of days, I'd find it in the mailbox and then wouldn't have to be dependent on them. Theron asked if I'd seen my friend Renzo, and I gave him a yes on that. He'd heard he'd married and settled down and was doing great in real estate. A hint, like they say plainer than print, of a lecture to come, which as things turned out I'd never have to listen to. And Camilla asked what I'd done with my day and I told her I'd been to the movies. There weren't going to be any lies from me, if she'd asked what I did after that, I'd have told her that too. Underneath it all they were waiting for Schaafy and Diego to go, so they could lay it on me about doing the trip to 25 Wall. Before the image of the returning hero faded.

A little thing triggered it. They reminded me Bill and Coo and Ummie were coming for the weekend, and there'd be the London editor of Haute too, Lady Alice Somebody and a few more. It sounded like twenty.

That was when I said "Shit."

Camilla always said it was a word she couldn't bear, though Theron used it all the time, everybody did, but she played Miss Dainty when she heard it. The way I said it must have splattered. They looked at each other as if to say we've been told he may be difficult during this period, we must be patient.

She tried, "Darling," she said, "no need to be unpleasant—"

"Why not?" I asked them both.

Theron didn't say anything, just stared at me. I wanted to call him cocksucker and maybe would have, except they'd only have thought it part of my busting out. But in that second I found out that I was going to call him that, later.

Camilla moved to her usual place on the sofa. She said, "I think it's time we had our talk, Philip. Theron—a brandy."

He always did as she asked, brought brandies.

"All right," I said, "let's talk. Mother. Mommy. Mumsy. Daddy. Daddums—but brandy isn't going to do it."

It wasn't. It couldn't. And it didn't, but they gave me some anyway. And they gave me the looks that said He's been through terrible things, we must be patient.

I was patient too. The stuff Robin had given me was holding me up. They did most of the talking. Yards and yards of the same old stuff, if it had been tape there'd have been like a two-hour reel. Most of it I wiped as it came. I can still hear their voices, not together, but two tapes running at once. I watched them. They were like a virus I'd catch all over again every time I came back to the house. They were my bad luck, and I was theirs.

They tried it several ways. Wasn't it wonderful that we were almost through having to be checked and approved by the O. W. M.? The blind Trust would end and distribution would be made the way old Grampa had intended. There were lots of things they couldn't finish, and they interrupted each other a lot. There was my silence too as I let them tangle themselves up. But I answered sometimes when the old chestnuts got too near the fire—"You're young, you can't understand certain things—At your age it's different—You've got to learn...."

I let them really sweat it, all through how they'd done everything for me, but I'd been stubborn and perverse—that was what one of the shrinks had said, perverse—and how they'd known about the kind of things I did and what they'd gone through to keep the O. W. M. from finding out about the scud. And what a miracle it was that now it was all working out. There was a lot about now I was old enough to do the signing, after which it would be on the belt.

"But I'm not signing anything," I said.

They pretended they didn't hear. After all, I'd been through such terrible things, I couldn't know what I was saying.

"You don't understand," Theron said. "This will be it. And you only have to sign once."

I remember saying over and over that I'd never sign anything, but they weren't getting it that I was through. I kept thinking of things they'd said and I'd said and Nana had said and Ummie had said, and I was going round and round but just the same in a straight line.

"It'll only be this one more time, Philip."

"It'll be for us all, Philip."

They were Philipping me to death. I've forgotten whatever it was I said that stopped them, but suddenly I thought, I've got to tell them now, I won't have to write any more notes to myself and stash them in the attic. And I started throwing the shit back at them, right in the face, telling them about what I remembered of Nana's talks with Ummie, what had come up the dumb-waiter shaft, the lunch when I was hiding on the sofa. Ummie telling Bill and Coo how they'd done it with a basting syringe from the kitchen. I left out the part about the vomit.

Silence fell like a lead pipe.

I really had got to them, and now I had the knife in, I was going to turn it. I said, "If you were going to make a baby to get the gold, why did you stop with me? I might have died on you, you should have had a spare. Did you lose the syringe or what?"

It had gutted me to finally say it, and I could see it was a big deal for them too, getting it all at once like that. If they'd said anything back to me. I don't know what I expected them to say, maybe deny it, but they didn't—some last crazy hope I had that it might not be true wasn't there. Their silence stung me. They were so serious not saying anything.

That minute when they admitted it is as bright in my mind as now, the three of us in that oval room off the dining room. I can pick the highlights off all the gold leaf and shit elegance, if shit had highlights, and hate myself for going to pieces the way I did. Blubbering stuff about how I'd needed to be touched, how I'd waited for them to love me. That was a mess, but it didn't touch them.

When Camilla started talking again it was something about how nobody's able to know about any marriage, except the ones inside it. And Theron said if I didn't believe I was their child I should look in a mirror, I was the spitting image. I gave them more than shit on that stuff, I told them it was finished before it started, if there'd been no fuck it wasn't a marriage, it was all plastic, like me. The syringe baby.

It got even wilder. It must have been the top of my trip. I said stuff like if he'd been a cuntlapper there might at least have been spit to make the spitting image, but since he didn't even do that I understood why he stuck to doing what he did.

That was where he made his mistake. "Meaning what?" he said.

"That you're a great man at the glory hole," I answered.

As I said this to him he froze—I'd seen the same expression on the faces of guys in Nam who'd been shot in the stomach and who knew even before blood came that it was death. It was the bottom of the well, and I knew it as I said it.

We were all standing by then. Though Camilla looked as though she hadn't understood, she was shaking.

She said, "You filthy, dreadful, horrible boy. You bastard. Get out."

"Oh, I'll get out," I said, "and I'll remember the bastard part. I'll go tomorrow."

"Go now," she said.

I was so bombed I couldn't go anywhere, and Theron saw that. There was more of the same, and finally it came down to why didn't I go to bed—they said it to me like I was a kid.

I made a lousy exit, slow. There wouldn't be any hurry about anything now. By the time I'd stumbled in the dark upstairs there was nothing but the noises of the world and silence, going from one place to the next, crashing to try to die a little while until the noises began again. But I could still hear the two of them downstairs, fighting it out tooth and nail, yelling and screaming. They must have come out into the hall then, because their voices came up the stairwell, clear as if they were in the room. They had finished with me, doing their regular goodnight thing, making sure the burglar alarms were on, turning off switches.

"Don't forget—tomorrow's Thursday," Camilla said. Which was code for Schaafy and Diego and the black girl would all have the day off. The warmup casserole in the refrigerator.

"I won't," Theron answered. "I've got a full day. Teddy and I have to go over everything for Texas. Don't count on me, I'll be late."

"I'll be late myself," Camilla said. "Bill's giving a cocktail thing for Lady Alice, and you know how his parties run on."

It flashed through my mind that at least Lady Alice would be one spook I wouldn't have to meet. They were hanging around down there. I heard Theron let out a breath.

He said, "Don't worry about Philip signing. I know how to do it. But I can't do it tomorrow. Day after tomorrow."

I thought, That's what you think. It was the only time I ever felt really sorry for them—they didn't know there wouldn't be a day after tomorrow. The switches they were turning off were so loud in my head I got up and closed my door.

I WAS surprised when Malc brought back the pad and ball-point today. I thought I was through. I think I got the quarrel right, that night before the very last. Put it down pretty much the way it was. The end. Over. Finished. They've got everything else, fingerprints, the blood tests, sperm and hair samples, the syringe in its own box numbered Exhibit whatever it is. Probably even some fly that watched as I did it. There was a fly, I remember now, after I'd ripped her open.

But trust Doc. Now he wants what he calls the doing of it, as though it was something separate, when it was all part of one thing.

I told him I'd about had it with the writing, what more was there to tell?

"Tell what you were thinking that last day," he said.

267

"Your feelings as you went along. The thoughts you can remember."

I don't think I felt or thought as much as he thinks. A lot of stuff must have gone past me, though. Like the fly on the ceiling.

When I finally woke up that day, it was almost half over. I'd been knocked out by what Robin gave me and the brandy and slept hard. No insomnia that night, and only dreams that faded with waking up. Maybe what Doc calls my deep unconscious made sure I wouldn't have to see them before they left for work. Because that's the way I thought of them. They. Them. Glued together with hatred. Me, separate, glued to nothing, hating them. My splitting away from them had been lousy, after all that hassle just going up to bed like their little boy who'd been naughty. Their locking up bit showed they still thought they had the power trip on me.

The sunshine told me how late it was, and I put it together the way you do, Who am I? Where am I? What day? It wasn't my fault it was Thursday.

I listened for Thursday sounds, which usually meant no sounds at all. Schaafy was always gone from Wednesday night till she came back Friday morning. Diego, though he usually slept over into Thursday, took the black girl to her train early. Spanish Harlem was his gig, and sometimes he had trouble making it back for Friday breakfast. But I heard sounds that had to be him, his footsteps on the drive, going to the mailbox and back. Next thing I knew he was opening my door.

He was a great guy, Diego. He'd worried about me and had brought me coffee. "Yes, sir, Marse Philip. Piping hot. I brought you a Bromo too, in case you need it."

I needed it. I asked if my driver's license had come. It hadn't.

"Now, you just stay right there," he said, "I make you a nice little breakfast before I go. How about a pair of eggs?"

Ech. His act. I couldn't play it back.

"What happen last night?" he asked. "Boss, he leave late, Boss Lady even later than him. They looked wrecked. I seen from the ashtrays and glasses it must have been a wild one."

I wasn't going to fill him in. He decided to go then.

"Have a good day, okay?"

"You too," I said.

I was alone in the house then. Thursday alone. It hadn't happened in a long time. I think you're more yourself when you're in an empty house, my mind was never clearer than on that day.

It was a waiting day, and even though it was half over, I was having my trouble with time. It was dragging its ass. The clocks in the house ticked slow, and this slowness made a kind of fear that crept inside my glass suit and stayed there. The worst kind of fear there is, because I didn't know what I was afraid of.

I did all the things you do, showered and shaved, got dressed. There were only the noises I made, the doors I opened and closed. I made a last tour of the house, looked at everything. Schaafy's kitchen was dead without her TV. I switched it on and there it all still was—the same great chicks tossing their hair, the worst breath of the day, brushing to avoid cavities, everybody worried about smelling bad, the maxis and the minis. The room with Theron's big toys was deadest. All dead for me. Dead life.

Last night had been the kissoff. Thoughts kept running through my head. It was a great time to die. It came to me then what the fear was—that nothing must happen to me until I'd done them and after them myself. However it would happen, however I'd do it would be the right way, and doing myself wouldn't be hard because they'd killed me long ago. And long ago I'd known I'd kill them. It was like hunting. They'd been the ones stalking me, but as things were turning out there was a switch—they'd made me the way I was so I could stalk them, hunt them down, finish it.

It's a hell of a long way from noon to the end of any day. I knew I'd have to be tripping to do it, be at the top of the trip. Which meant I'd have to climb up the day instead of down. Robin would help me with that. And did. And I did everything right as I left the house, like making sure the light winkers were on, the burglar alarms set, all doors locked.

Part of the day's a blank, but I stayed the way I was. I was hungry, and I ate after I'd hitched it into Groverhampton. I saw the hundreds of faces anybody sees every day, on the streets, in the cubicles you go in and out of. And I did it right, because when I settled at the end of the bar at Florence's, it was night.

I'd better tell the kind of trip it was. Angel dust. PCP, psylo—can't spell it. Everybody says dust anyway. Robin didn't just hand you anything, he was like a doctor, what worked was the right thing, and he always knew how much. He didn't fuck around with Busy Bees or Shermans, joints with dust shaken in, he gave me plain dust from a plastic bag, fresh from the wings of the angel it had come from. He said take it straight and stand up to the bar and keep the drinks down and let it take. He warned me how crazy dust is, how you could take several doses and nothing would happen, and then the next one would send you flying where you wanted to go. Name your place and you'll get there.

It was a new thing. At first I was just mellow, you know, hugging my beers, floating, then I felt a big jump. Nobody could tell I was turning on. There were the regulars who were always there, the gays jamming the end of the bar. A couple near me were dusting too. I think I talked with them, but they were way ahead of me, having trouble organizing their thoughts or something. They went away. There was something a little gagging in the first taste, but after that it was all okay.

I didn't mind anything because reality was exactly like itself, and the time thing that usually bugged me was totally fucked. Time could be a long thing or just nothing, I could take a whole day for my next breath or a minute. It was now, not before, not after, not slowed up or anything. So I was grooving through the evening. And the people I knew said "Hi, Phil." Florence was doing her perf at a table of people who'd once been big in Hollywood, or were big now. How do you tell? There were funny little side things, like I went to the john a lot because of the beer, and the gays wanted to do me, but I said I was saving it. I wrote something on the wall and then I'd go back to the bar and Robin.

I was over the edge where I needed to be. I mean it was the beginning of a high better than I'd had with anything else. It was a whole new way of feeling what was coming up and going past. I heard the voices I wanted to hear, theirs, loud and clear and slowed so I got every word, and I'd pick certain words and hang on to them. I felt my head and body were making it together, everything else could fall down but I was indestructible. I mean like I could have thrown a brick through the bar mirror and it wouldn't have happened. I could have heard the way a knife would sound going in and coming out. Fabulous.

That was what I felt when I left the bar and started walking back to Lilacs. I knew there was a first step to doing it, and I was in fine shape for it. I could have jogged to Canada and never noticed it, it was that kind of super high. I talked to myself a little as I went along. There was a moon. This was the trip I'd bought a ticket for. It wasn't at all like being out of your mind. I was all mind and tuned up, looking around corners and there wasn't anything but what I was going to do. I finally knew what the old guy meant when he said space and time are the same. So I could do it, and I did it.

MAYBE it was like a separate thing, the way Doc thinks of it, the time when I went to the house and did them, to where I crashed in the Ferrari. Dust isn't like acid or the mushroom or other junk, if you can think slow and careful it comes back, like a cassette, press the memory button, and it runs itself.

No trouble seeing the house in the moonlight. I walked to it across the lawn instead of the drive. Quiet. Lights were on in Camilla's bedroom so I knew she was there. I couldn't tell about Theron because his rooms were in the back. She'd set the burglar alarm, the whistle sounded the second I opened the door. I rushed to cut it off before the wowser

271

would begin, and right away she came out of her bedroom at the top of the stairs and called out.

"Theron? Is that you?"

This told me there would be two acts, Theron wasn't home. I switched the hall lights on.

"Oh, you," she said when she saw me. "I thought I told you to get out. You said you'd go."

"I need some of my things," I said.

"Well, get them and get out." She went back into her room and slammed the door. She could hold on to anger, she was still as hot as the night before.

I went through the dining room, through the green baize door to the serving pantry, found the drawer beneath the sink where Diego kept the house tools, just taking them as they came to hand. The big wooden mallet he used for crushing ice, a chisel, one of those dinguses with a razor blade for scraping paint. I must have taken the syringe then too, it must have been in the drawer, because later I had it to do with it what I did—what the lawyers harp on. I was careful to turn out lights as I went back, Theron would come in that way, and I took my time going up the stairs.

Through the door I could hear that Camilla was running a bath, but when she heard me come in she cut it off. It dripped. I couldn't help noticing how the drip alternated with the tick of her clock on the mantel. The clock was some old forest god holding a nymph in his lap and the face of the clock was in her belly. Everything going in twos, you might say. The tick and the drip. Her, me.

"Don't think I don't hear you," she said from the bath. "This damned faucet!"

The drip only made the clock sound louder. She came out into the room, she'd thrown her terry cloth robe over her shoulders and held it in front of her. She hadn't put her arms in the sleeves—I was noticing every little thing like that— because what she had to say wouldn't take half a minute.

She said, "Philip, I don't know what this is, but if you think we're going to stand here and talk about last night you're mistaken. That was it, the last time."

"You're right about the last time," I told her. I was standing with my back against the door, holding the tools behind me. I'd always had my back against something, fighting her, because she was my mother.

"Well, then take whatever it is you came to get and go," she said. She looked past me at the clock, then her eyes came back to me.

"Twenty minutes to two," I said. "Right?"

I could feel time stretching itself.

"Your father will be home any minute," she answered. "He'll be tired and in no mood to talk to you."

"Oh, I think he'll talk to me."

"I've just told you, Philip, we're not going to go over all that again."

I was trying to hang loose, but she was really fucking me up. Saying things twice was wrecking me. I mean, I was tied to this scene, and the script was a drag, I wanted to say words over the words she was saying. I noticed she was wearing the kind of mules she did, the kind with four-inch steel heels.

She moved it for me. "What's that you're holding behind you?"

I held the tools out for her to see. It was a slow take, like she was trying to tell herself I was the plumber who'd come to fix the drip.

She said, "Philip, what on earth—?" Still thinking words would do it.

"Don't ask me what," I said. "I won't know what I'm going to do until I do it."

"My God!" she said. "You're on something—you're insane!" And then she screamed.

I let her scream it out, it couldn't have mattered less, no one could hear. I began to notice that when I winked my eyes what I saw with them closed was different from when I had them open. The clock said one time, but the drip of the faucet said another. She'd gotten the idea. During one of my blinks she made a dash for the phone, but stopping her was nothing. That was when time stopped stretching and snapped together. I remember she had cold cream on her face

273

and neck, and it got on my hands. She fell to the floor when I hit her and her robe fell off too.

"How dare you!" She was yelling. She tried a lot of others. Like "Don't touch me! Philip—you're hurting me." And, "Your father—"

I let it build, took my time answering.

I told her not to worry about him, she never had before. I told her she'd be first and he'd be second, the way she'd always liked it. I noticed my words came out slow but even, like something I'd learned long ago. I was kind of seeing myself and her from above, as though the roof of the house was off, and we were two other people. But it was when I lifted her onto the bed and stretched her out flat that she got it through her head how it was going to be.

Once her robe was off she wasn't anybody, just any broad. My head began to pound, like the clock ticking and the tap dripping. Everything was too loud, deafening. My zipper when I pulled it down was like a roar. The dust was holding me up great, doing it for me. I was hard without thinking and going into where I had come out of was the most natural thing in the world. I was having no more problem keeping it in the family than any of those old Egyptians who never let anybody else get in edgewise. She opened her eyes wide, then squeezed them shut. I'd never been primed like that, it was going to be a shortie, which can be the greatest if you start slow and keep going slow straight to the end, not stopping. She waited until I was right on it before she started fighting, fingernails, teeth, all she had, kicking the heels of her mules into my ass. It was that four inches of steel that did it, she'd found the cleft in my butt and jabbed until I howled and jackknifed back. I was at the top of my charge and came all over her belly. Nothing knocks you out like coming before you're ready, and for a minute she had me. If she hadn't kept it up with the heel of the slipper, maybe I'd have slunk away then and done myself in somehow and that would have been the end.

But the slipper was killing me. I was flat on her and she couldn't move, but I could reach back and wrench off the slipper and I did. I heard her other leg drop and the other slipper fall. I was knocked out for a minute, thinking how she'd bitched me to the end, cutting off what I was, my life, and in that minute I knew we were even. Almost. The rest would be easy. I was heavy on top of her and she couldn't move. When my strength came back I really went to work, doing a knee job on her chest, to get the wind out of her, stop the screaming.

But she still had breath to call out "Help! Help me!" It was the crack of her ribs that made me hear the clock and the faucet drip again, check the time—it struck once, ping, only two thirty. Too long. I still had one mule in my hand, and I started beating her with the heel. Her eyes were open and she was watching, like she was counting, but it was only "Stop! Oh, Philip!" It was because I was Philip that I couldn't stop, went on beating her in the belly with the heel. It was that heel that turned the trick, I didn't have to use the mallet or chisel or razor thing. Not that she was dead, even near dying, but there was this stink from one place I'd gone deeper than the others and a piece of gut came through. It was the stink of that made me decide to hurry and finish her. I remembered the cats. I went down the hall to Theron's bedroom and yanked a light cord from one of his lamps and came back. It was a lot like the wire and the cats, I'd tighten the cord around her neck and she'd seem to be gone, but when I loosened up there'd be this breath like a golf ball was in her throat and she'd still be breathing. She didn't have nine lives, and the third time did it. It was over, there was no pulse, and her face sagged to one side. Her eyes were open.

I wasn't going to close them, do anything else to her. I wanted her the way she was, naked on the bed, waiting. I moved as far from her as I could get, to the window, open with the night air coming in fresh. I was gagging from the stink, but there was nothing to throw up. I wanted to keep everything down anyway, so my high would hold and it did. I think the air helped, because when I saw the headlamps of the Ferrari turn into the gates and come up the drive, I was as ready as I'd been when I came in.

275

It was like always, the way he slowed while the automatic doors to the garage opened, and he drove in and the doors went back down. The little silence then while he came in through the kitchen, and I could guess he was checking all the locks before coming up the stairs to his rooms. I could tell from his step on the stairs he was tired, holding the banisters. Then came the second he stopped. He called out for Camilla, the way she'd called for him when I came in, and when there was no answer he called again.

I stayed as still as Camilla, then moved from my window to behind the door. I had the tools in my hand, ready, because I knew his strength, and I was going to need all mine and the tools too. One more "Camilla" and he came up fast, and I could hear him gag as he came through the door. The first second I could get the right leverage I let him have it square across the back of the neck with the mallet. He'd been carrying his jacket, and he dropped it as he fell to his knees, his hands ahead of him on the floor.

It was going to be a hard job. He had shoulders like a rock, but I could tell I'd hit the spine in the right place. He made a noise, Uh, breathing in—I'd got his wind out of him first whack—and then he turned his head a little and saw me. He couldn't really get up yet, and I wasn't in any hurry now, I was going to make this one last until I'd told him everything that had been going around in my brain since that afternoon I'd seen him leave the tearoom.

"What," he said. No question, a word to float on breath, to find out if he had any. He didn't have much, but he was getting up, gasping. Then he saw her, on the bed, eyes looking at him dead straight. And dead.

He looked at me. Either I was bleary or he was. No words from him. The words were going to be mine, I'd ask the questions, he'd give the answers. Though he tried, he couldn't talk.

"How's everything at the glory hole?" I asked him.

He closed his eyes as I asked it. He was on his feet, but just.

"You—" He started but couldn't go on. I knew it was now

276

or never. If he got even half pulled together I knew it wouldn't be him but me. He was sweating and through his shirt I could see his chest raising and falling back, trying to get breath. This time I let him have the mallet on the side of the head, the temple, and he turned a little and then fell full length on his side onto the floor.

The one thing for me was that he should answer what I said, it was all just words, what he was, what he'd done to me by being what he was. But all he kept repeating was that What, he couldn't get out more, only kept shaking his head and looking over at the bed and up at me and then at the bed again and the syringe where I'd laid it.

There was only one way it could go now. The tap was still dripping, and the clock was striking. Three. The stink in the room was getting worse, something had happened on the bed and blood was spreading. And with him it wasn't the way it had been with her, that she was nobody, he was Theron himself to the end. I told him I'd got her ready for him, all he had to do was go ahead, but he couldn't get it. He reached for my knees for support to get up, and that was when I dug the chisel between his collarbones. If I'd thought I'd seen blood with her, I was learning from him, it spouted out of him, was everywhere.

I still had to move him to the bed. It was the hardest work of my life, but I did it, stripping him, hoisting him on top of her. The dead must be heavier, balancing him was no problem, but I was starting to shake and was just able to do the last thing, stick the syringe up him where it belonged and run.

There was air on the stairs, but the blood on my hands slipped on the banisters as I went down. It went on to everything, the doors I went through, the green baize door, the swinging pantry door to the kitchen. I had to keep going—the keys to the Ferrari were where they always were, hanging in the key cabinet next to the door to the garages. But when I took them down, they were bloody too.

Blood from me. I don't know how I slowed enough to do the cleanup on myself I had to do, get rid of the stink and blood and scrub up, but I did it. Clean clothes—I even washed the keys to the Ferrari, even got the Twistems right on the plastic garbage bag I stuffed the bloody clothes into and threw into a ditch when I was under way.

THE FERRARI was still warm, not only the engine but the seat too, where he'd sat, warm as he probably still was—I thought of things like that. The way I smelled the butts he'd smoked driving out from town in the ashtray. I knew from the minute I turned out of the drive into the lane what I was going to do and how I was going to do it. The straightest way, the shortest I could make it to the marina stretch of road that flared toward the abutment where I'd crash and end it. I knew to the second how the Ferrari picked up speed, how fast it would be going when we hit the wall of stone together—100 would be nothing. I thought a lot of other stuff too, nothing deep, only that at last I'd gotten away from them, the way I'd always come back to them. I'd done something right at last, the end had grown out of the beginning, the bars of my playpen, my bed. After Nana. It wasn't quite the end yet but soon would be when I made the marina.

The windows were open, and the air was great, but the wind didn't seem to move, though the moon was there, moving left and right as I moved. There were tides in the ocean. And I'd only done what had to be, it came from the core, they were the murderers who'd made me so I could kill them. I'd been where he'd never been and now was. A circle almost, but with a gap—

—The gap was that it wasn't all back roads, to make the turn for the marina I'd have to get onto the expressway. The dust seemed to be hitting me in drifts now, and I wanted to hurry. But I knew better, I was watching my speed up to the turn, after which I'd open full up. I mean, I was the most careful thing on the road, because the dust was putting what had happened behind what was going to happen and did.

I braked for the stop, all wheels dead, and had just turned

for the marina when I saw the squad car ease up beside me. It would be the Smokeys, Big and Little, behind the flash they turned in my eyes.

"Hanway, draw over."—I knew both voices.

"Pull over, Hanway."

Nothing was going to stop me now. I had the advantage, I accelerated, a little sooner than I'd intended, and there were two curves I had to brake for before the long stretch. They were tailing me close, siren wailing, lights flashing, beginning to play chicken. They played harder after the second curve. I was doing about sixty by then, but so were they, steering hard right and I heard the zing of fenders just brushing. Every time they chickened me I got nearer to the road shoulder. I felt a road marker go down, but whether I'd hit it or not I couldn't tell because I was watching the mirror. I passed seventy, but they were up to that, and playing rougher. It was more than that, I don't know how much more, when they drove me over the road edge and I remembered that the marker had read Soft Shoulders. I saw the pines ahead and felt the first flip as I went over and I knew I went over once again but there was nothing else until I tasted gasoline and they pried me out.

That's when you came in, Doc. Over and out.

I GUESS Doc and the lawyers got what they wanted at last. I couldn't write much more anyway, I'm so wasted from putting down as much as I did. Because there were things I did to them before I stuck the syringe up that I keep secret, even from myself. And don't remember all I did tell, only that when I started looking back over the pages I wanted to tear them up. That was when Malc and I think it was Sidney and some nurse came in and held me down—they'd been monitoring me all the time on the TV. It was my biggest cutup yet, a dilly, because Doc came in to do the injection. In a deep vein—"Hold perfectly still, Philip, that's the boy"—and in it went, and I went out. What I thought as they held me was that this would be the way it would be in prison like Malc tells me it'll be, the six guys on me, and up my ass they'll go until I get so I'm crazy about it.

You're in another world while you're under, like dead, but flashes of life come through sometimes, and you can tell what's going on. Life on a slant but true. People coming in and out. Doc, mostly. But Malc too and Tweed Suit and Baby Cube and one of the other lawyers. And Mr. Stanhope, who'd never come before, shaking his head as he looked at me and saying, "A terrible thing, terrible, what a shame it was it had to happen." And Doc saying, "Tell the ladies we did all we could, but I'll be seeing them privately anyway." Lots and lots of that stuff but what came through strongest was "Out, we've got to get this one out."

It was Malc got me on my feet the next morning and showered and shaved me. We skipped the jog. The needle shower woke me up as it always did, and if he'd tried to blow me I'd have let him. But he wasn't interested and was in a hurry and looked away from me instead of at me the way he once did. Back in the room the clothes they'd taken from me when they brought me in were on the bed, and there were my shoes with laces and my belt, even a sport jacket I hadn't been wearing.

"The ladies bring that," Malc said. "They want you to look nice in court."

I don't know why they cared how I looked in court because they weren't even there. Wherever court was, I was taken there in a closed van, it might have been anywhere. There were only the lawyers and Doc and Tweed Suit. And me. We all had to stand. I was the star, but I didn't have many lines. As Nana might have put it, I hardly had a chance to say I, Yes or No.

The judge looked like all judges, except from the neck up. I couldn't remember him, though in the forty minutes or however long it was I memorized his face. Big double chins, a deep voice that sounded tired, he coughed a lot into his handkerchief. When he came in he brought with him what they called the manuscript, everything I'd written, but not on the pad sheets, it had all been typed up. I couldn't believe how much of it there was. The judge put it to the left of him and sometimes touched it as he talked. Everybody talked, back and forth, and it started with the same old questions.

"Philip Tenys Hanway."

I answered that one. And the ones "Where was I the night of—" "At Florence's, Chez Florence—Yes—And after that I walked it to Lilacs and did them—"

Baby Cube and Doc were going to earn their money. Doc read out a summary from one sheet of paper. There was a lot of explanation for the judge, I'd heard many of those words like obscene, revolting, disgusting. "Psychopathy, your honor, is not a mental illness. Though he suffers from a severe personality disorder, a plea of insanity cannot be entered.

"He is sane."

Nothing more about diminished responsibility.

And the judge keeping his oar in, earning his money too— "I have read the manuscript, Doctor, every word of it."

"The delay, your honor, has been made necessary by the complexity of—"

The judge blew his nose. "Yes, yes, yes. The original indictment on two charges of murder has been changed to two charges of first degree manslaughter. Very well." He blew his nose again. "Philip Tenys Hanway, do you willfully and truly plead guilty on all counts?"

Baby Cube answered for me. "He pleads guilty on all counts, your honor."

The judge nodded, then turned to me. Did I wish to make a statement before he pronounced sentence.

I let them all wait a good minute before I said "No." If I'd said anything, it would have been that the dice had been loaded against me from the very start. It had all been suicide and would be suicide to the very end. I was wrecked from standing, from all the listening, though I got it that there were two sentences. One was 8⅓ to 25 years, the other 8⅓ to

30 years. I wondered which was for Camilla, which for Theron. I wondered what I'd do with ⅓ of a year. I still do wonder.

I CAN tell this is the last day because they've almost forgotten me. They even left the pad and ballpoint behind. I've gotten so in the habit of scribbling that I'm doing it now.

Last night I stretched out on this rock mattress for what has to be the last time. They didn't give me anything to sleep, so I just stayed awake, trying to put together all the pieces they've hacked off me and a few I've hacked off myself by writing it out. I didn't get much of anywhere.

What I thought over and over again was what I knew anyway before I came here. That you lose them all, things that happen, and people, one by one. If you don't dump them first, they dump you. There is no love in America. Like Renzo could have come to see me, just once. And Schaafy and Diego and Bill and Coo and Ummie. But nobody except the aunts I didn't want to see came. They must have everything they wanted by now. If like they said to me through the glass they were saving my heritage for me until I get out, it's a laugh. Because they'll be dead by then, and I'll be somebody else. And old Mr. Stanhope's visit was like leaving cards on people you don't want to see, or like viewing the dead.

It all changed after they brought me back from the court. The forgetting of P. T. H., as though we haven't spent the last weeks and months together. Doc and Tweed Suit and Baby Cube winding it up. They looked at each other as they talked but never at me, as though I'm the first motherfucker in history. Like Malc in the shower yesterday, no longer interested.

I'm a number now. There's a red card thumbtacked outside my door I can see through the grill. Across the top in big letters is TRANSPORT, and written below is HANWAY, P. T. 8808.

I heard the early shift come on, and it was Whitey who

shoved my breakfast at me, which told me it was Saturday. Didn't wait while I ate to make sure I wouldn't swallow the spoon. There wasn't any toothbrush afterward either.

Malc knew I'd be going, and no matter all the makes he'd tried on me I thought he was a friend. But he went the same as Doc and the others. Not even shake hands. I guess you don't say goodby to numbers in the world of numbers where I'll be just one more.

I can tell there's not going to be a jog and shower either, like the no toothbrush. The beginning I guess of how Malc told me it would be, a bath once a week if you're lucky. You learn to smell yourself so you won't smell the others. I had a few sample whiffs at the jail in Groverhampton. Armpits, crotches, ball gas, feet. And I've imagined being the victim, like that old cat burglar said, Sweetass. What I'm going to get for letting life happen.

Lots of people walking up and down the hall now. A spade in a clerical collar looked in at me, then changed his mind and went on. The desk nurse is raising her voice now, then shouting.

"You want 8808?"

And a voice coming nearer. "Yeh, 8808. Hanway."

The keys in the door.

8808. That's me.

ABOUT THE AUTHOR

Edmund Schiddel, a Chicagoan by birth and a Pennsylvanian by adoption, is the author of A BUCKS COUNTY TRILOGY: *The Devil in Bucks County, Scandal's Child,* and *The Good and Bad Weather* and other novels. The TRILOGY has been widely translated and in numerous impressions has sold millions of copies. His most recent work of fiction, *The Swing,* was published in 1975. *Bad Boy* is his twelfth novel.